THE
GRASS
PEOPLE

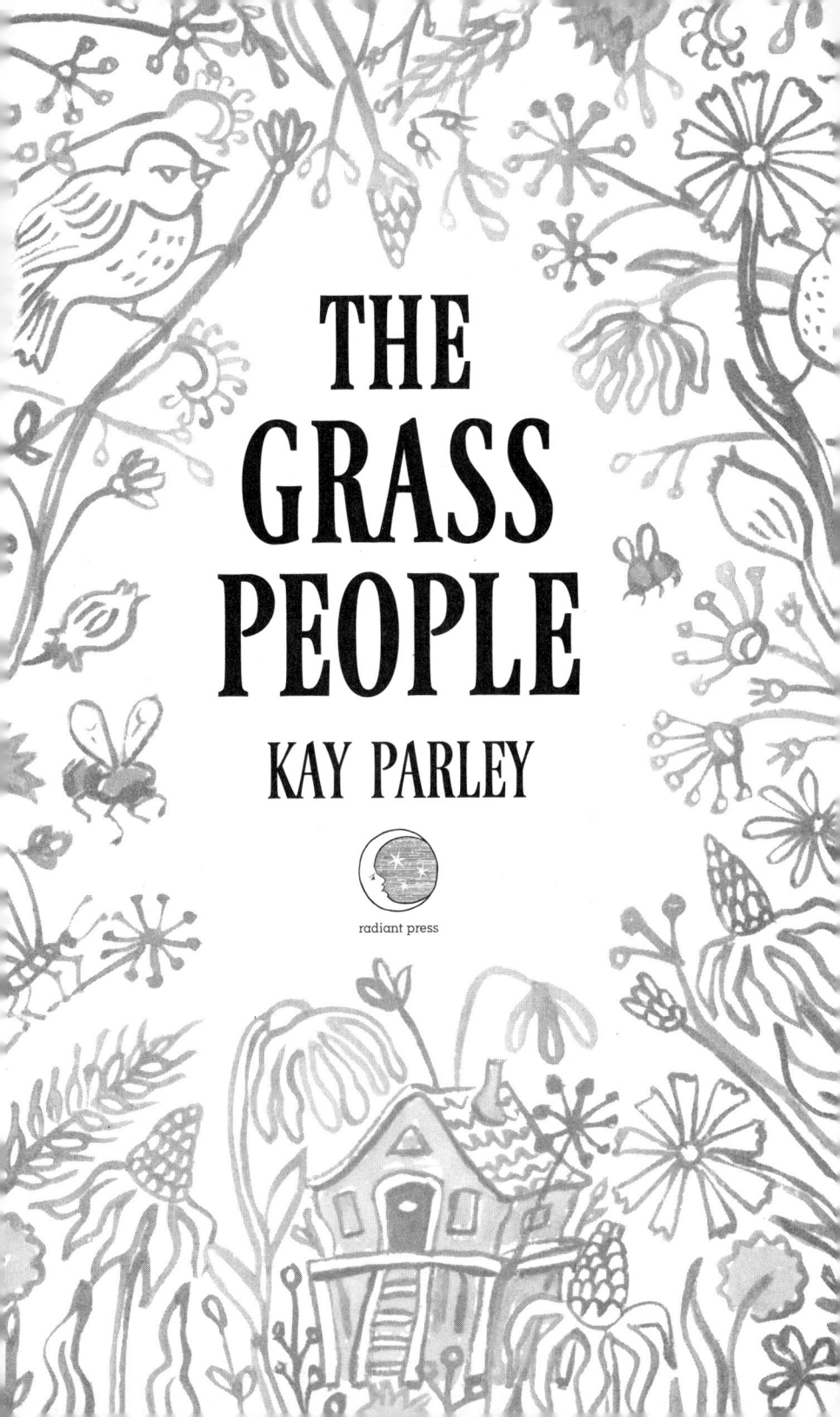

THE GRASS PEOPLE

KAY PARLEY

radiant press

Copyright @ 2018 Kay Parley

All rights reserved. No part of this publication may be reproduced, stored in a retrieval system or transmitted, in any form or by any means without the prior written permission of the publisher or by licensed agreement with Access: The Canadian Copyright Licensing Agency (contact accesscopyright.ca).

Editor: Alison Lohans
Copy editor: Scott Boyes
Cover art: Gerri Ann Siwek
Illustrations: Kay Parley
Book and cover design: Tania Wolk, Third Wolf Studio
Proofreader: Della Mac Neil
Printed and bound in Canada at Friesens, Altona, MB

The publisher gratefully acknowledges the support
of Creative Saskatchewan and the Saskatchewan Arts Board.

Library and Archives Canada Cataloguing in Publication

Parley, Kay, author
The grass people / Kay Parley.

ISBN 978-1-77518-390-7 (softcover)

I. Title.

PS8631.A764G73 2018   C813'.6   C2018-904748-8

Radiant Press
Box 33128 Cathedral PO
Regina, SK S4T 7X2
info@radiantpress.ca
www.radiantpress.ca

I dedicate this fairy tale for adults
to #27 and the loved ones I knew in those days.

🐇 🐇 🐇

In memory of Mum and Dad
and the aunts and uncles
who filled my life with storybooks
and stimulating ideas.

ACKNOWLEDGEMENTS

First, I thank my publisher, who remembered the manuscript. I wish to express my appreciation to all those who boosted my confidence as I worked on *The Grass People*. So much encouragement came from Lillian Gray, Norma Hawkins, Lorna Bell, Will Ferguson, Sean Ferguson, Dr. Anne Saddlemeyer and Dr. Gwyn Gilliland. Judith Silverthorne not only offered encouragement, but put some concrete foundation under this effort. The book could not have gone ahead without Judith's help. I also want to thank Kelsey Gottfried for typing the story into a computer, and I am extremely grateful to Linda Van Havere for the many hours she spent proofreading. Nor will I forget the little group of residents at The Bentley who had the patience to listen to the entire story read aloud and never seemed to lose interest. You have all shared.
Thank you.

– Kay Parley

Little Folks in the Grass

In the grass
A thousand little people pass,
And all about a myriad little eyes look out,
For there are houses every side
Where the little folks abide,
Where the little folks take tea
On a grass blade near a tree;
Where they hold their Sabbath meetings,
Pass each other, giving greetings,
So remember when you pass
Through the grass;
Little folks are everywhere;
Walk quite softly, take great care
Lest you hurt them unaware,
Lest the giant that is YOU
Pull a house down with his shoe,
Pull a house down roof and all,
Killing children, great and small;
So the wee eyes look at you
As you walk the meadows through;
So remember when you pass
Through the grass.

–Annette Wynne

PART 1 1
THE MOWER

PART 2 69
HOYIM'S TRADE

PART 3 185
THE SEED

PART 4 335
THE PROGRESS

PART 5 419
THE BOOK OF NANTA

GLOSSARY 455
ILLUSTRATIONS 462
AUTHOR'S NOTE 468

Our survival depends on community, like bees or ants.
–The Dalai Lama

PART 1

THE MOWER

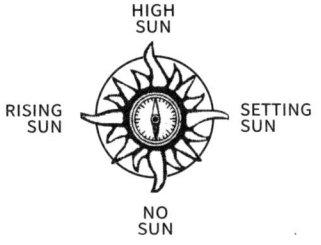

I

KOALEE HAD BEEN OUT to the pea trees and was on her way home with four ripe green balls in a bag over her arm. Her knife, safe in its sheath, hung from her belt. She planned the green soup she would make for dinner from one pea and tried to visualize how much meal could be ground from the other three if they were halved and put to dry.

The healthy baby boy on her back was asleep, warm and limp. Koalee's heart danced at the wonder of him, for he was perfect, with his thoughtful eyes and his busy little hands. A sudden stirring in the grass woods by the trail made her nervous. Koalee froze with her hand on her knife.

A field mouse ran across the path and she relaxed. Field mice were friendly and never hurt the grass people. She tried to hurry home but her short legs slowed her a little. When she walked beside others, she frequently found herself trotting to keep up. She was plump, with wakeful blue eyes and a tiny nose with a dignified tilt. As always, her hair was wound through a flat comb and coiled on top of her head to add to her height.

The peas were growing heavy. Koalee set them down and rested. How pleasant the day was. The grass woods kept the trail cool and shaded, but sunlight still filtered through in bright patches. She breathed in deeply and checked the sky. There was no sign of clouds. She felt behind her to make sure the coil of rope was securely fastened below the baby's carrier. Grass people never went up trail without a rope.

Koalee picked up her bag and started out again. At an edible seed tree, she added several seeds to her bag, although that made it even heavier. On the trail behind her, she heard footsteps and wheels. Soon Lenk the builder came toward her at an easy run, pulling his trail runner behind him. He drew up beside her.

"Your bag looks heavy," he said. "Put it in the runner. I'll take it as far as my place."

Koalee thanked him and gratefully added her peas to his load. Lenk had a load of grain heads, seven at least.

"Your wife will have meal for a hundred loaves out of this," Koalee exaggerated.

"It's good grain, too," Lenk replied. "Not a soft spot or mark on it. What's Dyra doing today?"

"Putting tar on the house." Koalee stretched her back. The baby continued to sleep.

"Koalee! He's tarred it twice since we built it two years ago. If a flood comes, your house will float, believe me."

"It's the baby," Koalee explained. "Dyra wants everything safe for the baby."

"Of course."

Koalee adjusted the baby carrier to prepare for the walk home.

"Look over there, can you see the yellow petals? I think it's a sunflower tree." Lenk pointed to a spot much further away in the grass woods. Sunflowers were highly prized for the nourishment the seeds provided, as well as the strong but light wood in their stems. Grass people often made a half-day trip up trail to cut down a flower and celebrated afterward with a picnic in the woods. It would take at least six of them to cut it down and haul the pieces back to the village. It wouldn't be difficult to find a group willing to make a day of it.

"Let's remember the spot and we'll come back later to cut it down."

Lenk nodded and then looked startled. "Did you hear that?"

Koalee had heard it. There was the sound of a heavy thud and another and another. The earth beneath her feet trembled.

A dark, ominous shape blotted out the sun.

The four-legged shadow...

Koalee and Lenk hid in the shelter of the woods and watched the trail. Would it go toward the village where their family and friends lived? The earth shook again as the shadow approached. The baby woke and whimpered.

The darkness was all encompassing.

"It's going toward my house!" Lenk yelled as he raced up the trail and around the bend.

Koalee heard him scream, the shadow had already disappeared. She ran after him and found him stumbling up the trail, in anguish, uttering moans and prayers to Life to undo what was done. His house, the best-built house in the settlement, was only half-standing. The wing where the kitchen had been was a heap of splintered wood. Koalee knew Lenk was not agonizing over the house.

"Maybe they weren't there," she said hopefully. But even as she said it, Lenk's oldest son Rels ran toward them screaming, *"Mother!"*

The three ran together, Koalee pressing her hands against her ribs, she could barely breathe. The baby bounced on her back, wailing.

"Mother was in the kitchen!" Rels gasped, "And the twins! Balink stayed late at school."

"Then I have two," Lenk said in a hollow voice.

But he had three. The twins had been playing under the porch in the float space, Atje in the spot where the four-legged shadow had tramped. The other twin, Tuje, was at the opposite end. He'd been struck by a falling log and was unconscious, but he was alive.

Wishing she knew more about injuries, Koalee removed the debris around the boy and checked him for broken bones, then covered him with a blanket found amid the timbers.

Lenk found his wife's body and Rels moved aside broken sections of roof. The whole fireplace wall had caved in on her. Koalee watched as he cradled her body, praying to Life to bring her back to him. The child Atje's body was crushed. She turned away from the tragic sight, thankful that her own baby was alive in his carrier on her back.

"I'll send the doctor, and tell the dolenter," she said. "You will stay with us tonight. I'll take your trail runner home."

She knew neither of them heard her. I must not break down, she told herself, this must be faced.

Dazed, she stroked Tuje's unconscious brow, murmuring encouragement to him. Looking past the ruined kitchen, she saw where the four-legged shadow had stepped, enormous prints, as wide as the house itself. Lenk had built his house beneath a low rise in the grass woods, for shelter. A giant foot had stepped on the rise and crashed onto the porch. She went over to where Lenk sat, near the body of his wife, and touched his shoulder, he was sobbing and didn't look up.

Koalee then hurried back to Tuje but the child was still unresponsive. Rels was a dependable boy, she took his hand to lead him to Tuje.

"Your little brother lives," she said, "but he may be badly hurt. Watch over him closely until the doctor comes. Don't move him, keep him warm. I'll go to the village now as fast as I can."

With tears spilling down his cheeks, Rels nodded that he understood and sat down beside his brother.

Squirming in his backpack, her own baby was crying to be fed but he would have to wait. Koalee made haste to the village. After summoning the doctor, she paused to feed the baby. The doctor's wife had gone immediately to find Balink at the school to tell her the tragic news. By the time Koalee had passed through the street of shops and arrived at the dolenter's house, she'd regained some of her composure.

"Koalee, did you see the four-legged shadow?" asked a villager, "Thank Life it passed by!"

"It didn't pass by." Koalee murmured. "It took Lenk's wife and one of the twins."

When she told the dolenter, he replied with his usual dour expression, "Life is angry. We will hold a special prayer meeting after the burial rites. Everyone must come."

Koalee felt her cheeks burning. Dyra often stayed away from meetings. He said they depressed him. The dolenter must have read her mind because he said, "Dyra will not miss the next morning meeting, your baby will be accepted into Life."

※ ※ ※

In spite of the fact that their baby was to be accepted, Dyra had to be reminded twice to put on his best clothes for the meeting. He was sitting in his favorite nook in the float space under the raft, reading his *History of the Settlement*. At Koalee's second call, he shut the book reluctantly.

"There is not a word in there about fear," he said, "Or the mower, or the four-legged shadow. They speak of death by flood or by accident, by cats, by sickness or old age, but not once do they blame Life for death. There's been a change in people's thinking, Koalee. Our ancestors loved Life, they had more hope and courage. When they built the meeting house it was to praise and celebrate Life."

Koalee was in the kitchen. "You know the dolenter explained that," she said, clearing up after the morning meal. "When the ancestors came here, there was no mower and no four-legged shadow. But they didn't live right and disappointed Life, so these things were sent to punish them."

"How could there have been a place with no mower and no four-legged shadow? They had to come from somewhere Koalee. And what did they do wrong? Maybe there's a place where they don't exist."

"Dyra, let's talk about this later."

"I was just thinking," he said. "If there is a place like that, I want to take you and the baby there. When I think of Lenk's wife and little Atje, I'd give anything to find a safe place."

Dyra went to change and when he stepped back into the kitchen in his best clothes, Koalee stopped to admire him. As far as she was concerned, Dyra was one of the best looking men in the village. He stood all of eight steps tall. Though he had the sturdy muscles common to grassmen, his legs were long and slender. Now that summer was wearing on, his skin was sun-baked almost to the colour of a seed. His eyes, blue-grey and curious as a child's, were startling in their clarity. Above them, a wide forehead suggested his high intelligence. Koalee had made Dyra's coat, embroidered with vines and flowers down the front. The bottom was stiffened to curve out at the sides, just enough to be in fashion.

Beside him, Koalee felt diminutive. Her hair was soft, as light in colour as the brush grass, but it lacked the lustre of Dyra's, whose hair glinted with red-gold lights in the sun.

As she helped him put the carrier on his back and placed the baby in it, she noticed that when Dyra looked at the baby, he seemed worried.

"The mower never comes here," she said.

"No, but you know what happened in the next settlement high sun. The mower appeared and half the settlement was killed before they got away. And do you know what they said? 'Life is angry.' That's what Lenk said. The first thing he said to me that night— 'Life is angry.' Koalee, I want a god that doesn't get angry."

They paused at the bottom of the steps.

"Please don't talk like that." Koalee begged as they started toward the village. "If the dolenter heard you he might not accept our baby into Life. You're not in good favour with the dolenter, Dyra."

He was smart, Koalee thought, smarter than anyone in the village, unless it was the doctor. They were both so young, maybe that's what was wrong. He could do anything: build, or grow trees, even make inventions, yet he was little more than a boy. Dyra knew his father's trade and ground reading glasses and magnifiers. Now he'd ground his own telescope lenses so he could study the skies and he questioned everything. Koalee was extremely proud of him.

Where the trail divided, they were joined by Lenk, with his daughter Balink and his two sons. Tuje still limped. Not many days had passed since their great loss and all were downcast. The burial rites still fresh in their memories.

"I am lucky," Lenk said mechanically, "that Life spared these three."

"You will eat with us tonight," said Koalee.

She felt bad for Lenk as they went through the village. This was such a happy day for her and Dyra, having the baby accepted into Life. Friends beamed delightedly when they saw them, knowing why Dyra looked so handsome and why Koalee was wearing a dress as pretty as a yellow buttercup. Then they would speak to Lenk and

7

his family and their faces would fall.

No one could enter the meeting house before the baby. They gathered near the doors while the dolenter watched closely to see that everyone was there. When it was time, he beckoned to Dyra and Koalee, who joined him at the door. The dolenter lifted the baby from his carrier and held him in view of the villagers.

"I accept this child in the name of Life," he said. "His name, I am told, is Hoyim."

The dolenter handed the baby to Koalee, and stood behind them as they waited at the door. Family and friends came then, led by Koalee's parents, her brothers and sisters, then Dyra's parents, his siblings and their families. Each one stopped to greet the baby and said, "Welcome to Life, Hoyim," before entering the meeting house.

Dyra and Koalee sat in the place reserved for them. The dolenter spoke of the miracle of Life and reminded them that the newly accepted were a sign the settlement would survive and flourish. They sang the acceptance song:

> *A seed in a seed in a seed*
> *Forever and ever,*
> *I understand now*
> *Why Life calls to Life*
> *To pass it on.*

The young girls showered petals of grass daisies over Koalee and the baby. The Chief Councillor made his speech of gratitude for all Dyra's kin had done for the village and handed Dyra the script of acceptance. All around them friends and relatives smiled.

When the ceremony was over and the dolenter had cautioned them all to be faithful to Life and to keep the Way of the grass people, the Chief Councillor took charge of the meeting. The sunflower tree was ripe for harvest and he asked for volunteers to help with the felling. He announced the date of the next celebration, when two apprentices, recently made craftsmen, would mark their new status.

The joy in Koalee's heart kept time as she bounced Hoyim on her knee to amuse him. Despite the tragic losses to Lenk's family, the life of the village was going on in its familiar predictable way. She loved being part of this group of friends and relations. She loved the rituals; she appreciated the continuity of it all. As the dolenter prepared to lead a prayer of dismissal, he said in surprise, "It's certainly unusual for an elf to come to our meetings. Their religion is not ours, and I don't know what prompted him to come here, but I want to say that he is welcome."

People turned to stare. The elf looked unaffected by the dolenter's words. He was fair and slight, somewhat smaller than a grassman. His clothing was leaf green, he had peculiar slanted eyes and antennae rose from his head. There was something commanding in his manner, as if he held himself the natural superior of grassmen and had no need to prove it. People near the door said later that the elf had appeared suddenly on the ledge of an open window. Few had seen an elf so close, and they were awed.

The unexpected turn of events seemed to confuse the dolenter. He forgot that he'd been about to give a prayer of dismissal, and instead began to read from the sacred book about the time when grass people lived in harmony with nature, when there was no mower. He spoke about the Dokrimalitzla, a grass person and spiritual leader, who must be discovered rather than appointed. A leader who could hear the elves and give the grass people guidance and warn them of danger. They had been without one for over forty years. He ended by reminding them that grass people had fallen out of favour with Life, and that only by being diligent in their labour and faithful in their prayers, could they hope to return to favour.

The elf appeared to be concentrating very hard, but not on the dolenter. He was focusing on the back of Dyra's head. His thoughts were transmitted so clearly that Dyra heard them.

The mower is coming; the elf was saying. The mower is coming *here*. It may be less than ten days. You must leave this settlement. You must leave tonight, and you must take your family with you.

Our parents? Our...

They will be safe.

Why are you telling me? Dyra thought, feeling confused.

The elf was quick to answer. I'm trying to warn them all, but you're the only one listening.

The baby Hoyim was restless. Koalee tried unsuccessfully to calm him.

Leave, was the elf's message. Take only what you can carry and go. Take the trail to the tall woods. I will find you there and tell you more.

The baby was whimpering, so Koalee carried him out. In the midst of this distraction, no one saw the elf disappear.

II

KOALEE PREPARED THE EVENING meal early. When it was over, Lenk's three children went out to sit on the steps and watch the seed birds. The day was still bright, and Dyra brought out his telescope to show Lenk how close it brought the woods or a cloud in the sky.

"Does the dolenter know you made this?" Lenk asked.

"I suppose someone's told him," Dyra said.

"It's strange he hasn't made you give it to the settlement. It would be useful for spotting danger."

"I have an idea," Dyra said cautiously. "You'll think it's impossible, Lenk, but if I could get to a high place that was out of the grass woods..."

Koalee joined them, with baby Hoyim in her arms.

"If you got to a high place, out of the grass woods, a big bird would pick you off," Lenk said bluntly.

"But if I could, and a bird didn't get me, I could set up my telescope!" Dyra dared not speak directly about the elf's astonishing warning. "The next time the four-legged shadow went by, I could see all of it."

Lenk was visibly upset.

"I know you don't want to talk about it, Lenk," he said, "but that's the whole point. It has to be stopped. But we can't stop it unless we know what it is."

"We can't stop it, Dyra. It's like a flood or a grass fire, only worse. The dolenter says it's sent by Life to punish us. You can't see it because it's just a shadow—a dark shadow over everything. Koalee can tell you. She was with me when it happened."

Koalee nodded.

"I've been under it too," Dyra argued, "and that's why I know. The people are too scared to look up and see it. All they see is the shadow."

For a moment Lenk made no reply. He ran his strong builder's hands through his dark hair and gave an involuntary shudder. Dyra and Koalee watched him and waited. Koalee thought he was heroic, considering the pain and loss he had suffered. Her heart went out to him in sympathy.

Dyra waited respectfully. Lenk was eleven years older and the younger man knew him as a man of caution. He also trusted Lenk's responses because they came from the woodworker's unique blend of intuition and feeling.

After a moment Lenk raised his head. "Nobody wants to see such death and destruction," he said. "It's evil—a great evil thing. It will destroy you if you challenge it."

Dyra felt the fear, it made him hesitate. But his friend was mistaken.

"It's not just a shadow," he said. "It has weight, as you know. We've seen the prints of its feet. Don't you want to learn the Truth?"

"The dolenter has the Truth. It's in the sacred book."

"Not the mower. And *not* the four-legged shadow."

The baby began to fuss, so Koalee took him inside to put him to bed.

"I don't want to talk about this any more," Lenk said. "My children mustn't overhear."

"I'm sorry, Lenk." Dyra put his hand on his friend's shoulder. "I know it is hard for you. I had reason. I'm going to that high place to see. I believed you were the one man with reason and courage enough to come too. I want you with me, Lenk."

Lenk shook his head. "Even if I had the courage, I can't go," he said. He gestured toward his children, playing a subdued game close by.

Dyra spoke with confidence. "We can take our families. With two of us we could survive in the tall woods."

"It's not the tall woods I'm afraid of," Lenk muttered.

"Promise me then," Dyra pressed. "If I go, I may go suddenly. Tell no one where I've gone, especially not the dolenter, he would try to stop us. If I find a safe place and send a message back to you, promise me you'll come at once. A new settlement will need a good builder."

"Dyra, I can't promise! This isn't the time to talk of a new start. Not yet."

"I've heard you say you'd like to see a different land," Dyra countered.

"I've talked of the red valley. You haven't thought of that? Going to end of settlement? Don't you remember that dolenter who went setting sun years ago and came back the following summer with a wife? He was raised in Nanta's village, and he said it was a wonderful place of truth and freedom. He even knew Nanta!"

"Nanta's village?"

"He's begun to admit craftsmen."

"It would be worth it to see the look on the dolenter's face. He doesn't believe Nanta's village exists."

"Of course it exists."

For a moment Dyra was caught up in that dream. The legend of Nanta had thrilled young grassmen for as long as Dyra could remember. What if...? No, the elf had made it clear they were to meet in the tall woods, it would not be the red valley.

Dyra resumed the conversation. "One more thing, Lenk. Is my trail runner as good as yours?"

"Of course. I made them both."

"Well, I lent mine to the miller's wife yesterday. I need one early in the morning. Could I walk home with you and borrow yours?"

Lenk considered for a moment. "I guess I don't need it. I'm cementing in pyles for the new float space, so I won't be doing errands for a day or two."

"Then if I get lost you can tell the miller's wife you own my trail runner."

"You better not get lost."

Dyra called to Koalee that he would walk home with Lenk. She came out to say goodnight to Lenk and the children. As Dyra left, he asked her to wrap up his telescope so well it could withstand a fall, and promised to come right back. Not having heard the entire conversation with Lenk, Koalee didn't understand her husband's plans, but she double-wrapped the telescope and laid it on the table. Then she began cooking the flatbread batter she'd mixed. She was still at it and had a stack of bread beside her when Dyra returned.

"I don't know why I did this," she laughed. "It will last a week."

"It's a good thing you did, because we're going up trail," he replied. "We may be gone a week. We'll take it."

"Up trail?" Koalee asked, flustered. "Where to? Why didn't you say something?"

"I wasn't sure until I spoke with Lenk tonight. Now I know. We have to go, Koalee. I have to go, and I won't go without you and Hoyim."

"But who are we to visit? What settlement?" Koalee set more batter to cook.

"We're not going to a settlement. We may start our own."

Koalee stared. "You can't! You don't have the dolenter's permission."

Then, at Koalee's indignant look, Dyra added, "It's for the baby and for us. There's great danger coming."

"You feel danger? But my family won't believe that. They wouldn't come."

"It's not likely anyone would come."

"It's what you were talking to Lenk about. The high place?"

"Yes."

"We can't tell anybody because someone would tell the dolenter and he'd stop us?"

"And confiscate my telescope."

"I can't even say goodbye to my family? Do we have to go *tonight?*"

Dyra nodded. "It will be dark in an hour. You've had a busy day. Can you walk a long distance without sleep?"

Koalee drew in a sharp breath. "I'll have to, but I can't stop worrying about our families. If the mower comes…"

"Lenk knows we're going. We can trust him. He'll make sure our families are safe. We'll leave a note for your father saying that we've gone to visit a few settlements and they'll hear from us. Let's go take a last look at the house while it's still light."

They went down the steps, crossed the road to the clearing and stood hand-in-hand looking at their house—the house Dyra had helped Lenk build when he and Koalee were married, the house where Hoyim was born.

Like the houses of all grass people, theirs was on a raft set high on pyles to keep it safe from deep water. In the cold season, the float space beneath the raft was walled with canvas and used for storage, but in summer it was a pleasant shelter, safely out of reach of birds of prey. Dyra had spent many a day reading in a shady corner, and Koalee often sat there to sew or prepare roots and seeds. They had watched over the burning of the lime to make the cement that held the pyles in place, they had stained the pyles and the staircase with dye from berries and flowers.

The house itself hugged low against the raft, smoke still curling out of the squat chimney. It was tough and enduring, woven and interlaced from woody trees in such a way that no animal or storm could harm it. The windows, glazed by Koalee's father, glinted as if they were flashing a message of farewell.

Tears ran down Koalee's cheeks. "I haven't picked my seed tree and it's ripe. I was going to pick it tomorrow. We might never see it again."

"We might. If we can find out what the four-legged shadow is. Maybe it can be conquered. Maybe it can be killed."

"Not alone. You can't do that alone. Oh, Dyra, all the work you did! It was all for nothing. If we have to build a new house where there is no settlement, how can we possibly do that?"

"It's for the baby," Dyra insisted. "If he stays here, they'll teach him to fear Life and to pray, and question nothing. I want him to love Life and to question everything." If the mower came, as the elf had warned, and if they survived... He wondered if he should tell Koalee what the elf had spoken into his mind.

"Not to pray?" Koalee was puzzled.

"To pray, certainly, but not out of fear. We may not find it, Koalee, the place that's safe, but we must try."

For the next hour and more they worked feverishly, gathering what they would take, packing and re-packing the trail runner. Into the covered box went the well-wrapped telescope, their wax, oil and medicines, juice for the baby, and all the utensils the box would hold. Koalee's needles and thread took little space. Into the canvas went the rest of Dyra's tools, pots and pans, a bag of food containing their ground meal, the flatbread, and fresh roots. There wasn't room for much clothing, but they loaded the canvas with blankets and their warmest clothes.

"We can't take your grindstones, Dyra. How will you make lenses?" Koalee asked.

"There may not be anyone to buy lenses. If there are, I'll have to make new grindstones, as my ancestors did." Dyra was squeezing his most valuable books into available spaces: *Housebuilding*, *Foods*, and *The History of the Settlement*.

"And the sacred book," Koalee reminded him. "Our family portraits are in it. We can't leave those."

"We're going to have to leave your grandmother's mirror. It's very heavy."

"When my parents get the note, they'll save all the valuable things. We'll see them again. I know we will." Koalee took a deep breath.

Dyra stuffed the pebble gun and knives into the side of the canvas, where he could easily reach them.

"How can you pull all of that, Dyra? It's too heavy," Koalee warned.

"I'll do it."

"What if the trail gives out?"

"It won't. The elf told me it goes at least as far as the tall woods."

"The elf?" Koalee cried.

"He told me," Dyra said grimly. "The mower is coming."

"The elf said this? Then we should go."

At last the trail runner was ready. In Dyra's backpack were his books on lens making and his most valuable tools. They dressed in light, warm clothing and pulled their cover clothes over all. Their pockets were stuffed with seeds, and from their belts hung ropes and knives and trail torches.

"We mustn't use them," Dyra warned, fastening the torch to Koalee's belt. "Not until we're clear of the settlement."

"It's good that it's late. Everyone will be asleep. Dyra, will we regret this when we're lost in the do-lan in the middle of the night?"

"We might. Let's get the baby."

Hoyim's necessities had been packed in his own light bag. Koalee would backpack the baby. They kissed; Dyra put out the lamp and they went down the steps for the last time.

Neither spoke for some time, then Dyra asked quietly, "Can you see well enough to keep on the trail?"

"Yes. I can't get off the trail without bumping against the grass woods." Koalee walked cautiously ahead, Dyra followed pulling the heavy trail runner. A rope from Koalee's belt was tied to his own so they wouldn't be separated in the darkness. The baby slept.

III

Their progress was slower than expected, but at last Dyra smelled the green lake.

"There's no grass woods along the trail here," Dyra warned, but he'd spoken too late. Koalee skidded over an embankment. It was a gentle slope and she fell on her side, so the baby was unharmed, but the shock woke him and he whimpered.

"At least you didn't fall in the water," said Dyra, helping her up. "Trail torches until we hit the woods again."

Koalee was shaken, but otherwise she was fine. She fed the baby and he fell asleep. Koalee longed for sleep herself but they had to be past the green lake by daybreak, too many birds and animals came there to drink. Beyond the lake was a place of stones where they might find safe shelter.

"Owls are out," she remarked as she lit her torch.

"They can see us with or without a light," Dyra reminded her.

They were both exhausted when they came to the place of stones and finally found a hiding place—two huge boulders against an embankment, forming a cave. Dyra piled small stones at the entrance to block them safely inside with the trail runner. After tending to the baby, they ate fruit and flatbread, spread their blankets and slept.

When Koalee awoke, it was late afternoon, Dyra sat watching her.

"We'll stay here tonight," he said. "There's not enough time to reach the tall woods by dark, we can build a fire here."

He removed some entrance stones and brought in a few armloads of grass and sticks.

They had water to drink and cook gruel, but none to wash the baby's clothes. Dyra climbed the embankment and looked about, but there was no sign of water. He returned with an armload of moss. "From now on we stuff his pants with moss, like the ancients," he announced.

The fire warmed the cave; they ate well and felt comfortable. Koalee sang to the baby.

They fell asleep again before dark.

They awoke rested, filled their flasks with dew and washed the baby's clothing in dripping leaves. As they packed the trail runner, ready to leave, Dyra reached into his pocket for a seed and turned pale. In his pocket was the note he had written to Koalee's father, the note he'd intended to leave in the kitchen. Perhaps he had better not tell Koalee. She'd worry too much.

But Koalee saw the note. Her reaction was straightforward. "We have to go back."

"We can't go back."

"Our families will worry!"

"They'll see everything we left; they'll think we've gone for a few days. We'll get word to them, I promise. There's a village up trail and traders will call there."

"No. We have to go back. My mother..."

"Koalee, we can't risk it. We left because it isn't safe there, remember? The elf said the mower is coming *soon*. And Lenk knows my plan. I don't think he'll tell, but he might, if pressed. We didn't have the dolenter's permission. I'd be questioned if we went back now. People wouldn't even buy my lenses."

"Dyra, what will happen to our families?"

"They won't be blamed. I'm more worried about their safety. We just have to trust the elf. And Lenk knows. We can trust Lenk."

"But the mower..."

"The elf assured me they'd be safe."

"Oh Dyra, we should have stayed."

"I never dared say this when we were in the village, but I hated it there."

"Dyra!"

"I've hated it ever since I read *The History of the Settlement* and learned that Life should be love and joy. I hate them for telling me Life brings the four-legged shadow because I break my pact with Nature. I'm true to Nature. The dolenter would confiscate my telescope just because I wanted to learn the truth. I really hated the village."

"Dyra, you can't hate your parents. And your brothers and sisters. You can't hate Lenk."

"You're right. I don't hate them. I want to save them. It's the dolenter who angers me. If there's an enemy destroying us, we should learn what it is and conquer it. Not just kneel down and say, 'It's Life's will,' and die. The farther we get, the more freedom we'll find. Don't forget we've got an elf for an ally. Come! Up trail!"

The way was smooth and the pulling easy. When they passed a place where they could see for a long distance, Dyra walked to where he could see above the growth.

Koalee ran after him. "Dyra! You're forgetting what the elders say. Never go where the tops of the woods are cut off."

"I know. It means the mower. But if one were coming, we'd hear it. And there's no shadow."

"No, Dyra!" Koalee was so frightened she could hardly speak. "It's not the mower I meant. It's cats."

"Any cat in the area would find us on the trail as easily as here."

Still, Dyra returned to the trail, but as long as they were passing the place where the woods were cut off, he kept his pebble gun in his hand.

The grass trail went on and on. When they needed to eat, they didn't dare build a fire because the dry grass might ignite and start a grass fire. They had no idea where water could be found.

"Sometimes it rains a free-floater after a hot day like this. If it does, where would we climb? Dyra, we don't have a chance, do we?" Koalee asked.

"Don't think like that. We'll be in the tall woods by nightfall. It will be moist and cool."

A sudden commotion rose on the trail ahead. A dozen grass people ran toward them screaming, "The mower! The mower! Look out!"

In the midst of the shouts, a great noisy shadow fell over everything. Some of the grass people fell to their knees, covering their eyes and ears.

"Don't go! Don't go that way," a young man begged of Dyra, who remained on the trail.

There were prayers shouted of 'Life help us!'

A woman faced the shadow stonily. "My husband," she gasped. "He stopped to help a child. They're all...half of our village..."

Dyra and Koalee had never experienced the mower. They were almost paralysed by the sound of it. Then it came into view, crossing the trail where they would have been, had the grass people not halted their progress. Its size and power were horrifying beyond anything they could have imagined, and it moved fast as a spinning wheel, shearing off thousands of grass woods as if with a giant knife.

Lenk had said, "It's evil—a great evil thing. It will destroy you if you challenge it." For a moment Dyra faltered, wanting to fall to his knees as well. But he stood firm with his arm around Koalee, trying to keep their baby from seeing this monstrous thing. All around them a great wind roared, with pieces of debris and dust flying everywhere.

As the shadow lifted and the sound grew less deafening, the grass people scattered in panic, running in the direction they'd already been going. They had suffered the shock of seeing their village destroyed and their families killed—but Dyra's head was clear, so he took charge.

"Don't go that way!" he shouted. "Go back!" He grabbed the man who seemed to be their leader by the arm. "The mower doesn't cut the same woods twice in the same day," he said, remembering everything he'd been told about the mower. "Get your people back! They must get to where the woods are already cut, before the mower returns."

The man understood. Dyra ran with him, turning the grass people around. He waved to Koalee to go ahead. She ran with the children and four of the adults and disappeared from sight. The woman who'd lost her husband seemed too senseless to comprehend. One young couple insisted stubbornly they must run on. As they stood arguing, the dark shadow fell again and its deafening roar increased. Dyra knew instinctively that it would cross the trail right where they stood. His eyes fell upon an animal hole that he and Koalee had passed only moments before. He dived for it shouting, "Down here!"

They slipped and tumbled down a long passage and came to rest in a roomy space. The leader was there along with the bereaved woman and three more. The stubborn young couple had run on. The roaring mower went directly over their heads, and the earth shook with its weight. Earth fell down the passage, plunging them into complete darkness. People screamed.

Dyra drew in a deep breath, praying to Life that Koalee and their baby were unharmed.

"Be quiet!" a voice said. "Don't attract attention."

"I hope there are no animals down here," someone whispered.

"This is a grass animal's route, they won't harm us."

"Our only hope is to dig our way out."

Even though Dyra could see nothing in the blackness, he squeezed his eyes shut. A scrabbling sound told him there was indeed an animal nearby. Dyra felt a warm, furry being brush against him and sniff. His heart almost stopped.

Satisfied that they were grass people, the animal did them no harm. Perhaps it sensed their plight for it began digging rapidly and they soon saw daylight. As soon as it had broken through, the animal peered back at them and they saw that it was a mole.

The new way was narrow and steep, but Dyra managed to scramble out. At the top he uncoiled his rope and secured it to a shorn tree, lowering the end so the others would have an easier ascent. Where were Koalee and Hoyim?

"Find your friends," he said, "and then come back where it's safe. I'm going to find my wife."

He found Koalee in tears near some shorn grass, clutching the baby in her arms. "Dyra," she sobbed, "I want to go home!"

Dyra pulled his wife and child close to him. "So do I. But the important thing now is to escape the mower."

At the terrifying word, Koalee's eyes grew wide. "We thought you were all killed!"

"We were down an animal hole."

"Oh, Dyra!" Koalee hugged him, with the baby in between.

Dyra noticed the children, seated on a blanket in the shade of the trail runner. They all looked bereft; what could be done about them?

The mower came yet again, but further up the trail. This time no one panicked. Some of the grassmen had found the bodies of the stubborn, young couple, and they returned quietly.

"They were...severed," said the leader. "You wouldn't have known what they were." He held the young woman's comb in his hand.

"Will you go back to your village?" Dyra asked the leader.

The man sighed. "We have to go and look. We may be the only people left. I'm sure half our buildings were destroyed."

"Is this the first time the mower has come?" Dyra asked.

"No, but it always stopped short of the village. We lost a country house and one or two pea trees. Never any villagers."

"You can't stay there," Dyra insisted. "Where the mower comes, it will come again."

The leader was clearly making an effort to think. "Where is your settlement?" he asked.

"Don't go there!" Dyra said sharply. "The mower is going to come there. I know."

"Why not come with us through the tall woods? All the villages setting sun of the tall woods are filled. They are close to Karep. I would like to keep what's left of our village together," the man replied.

"We may found a new settlement. Your chances would be better."

The leader hesitated for a moment, but then shook his head. "Where is your settlement?"

Dyra sighed. "Two days up trail is a green lake. Our settlement is one day's march rising sun, then no sun beyond. There are many settlements nearby, but I warn you again. They are all in danger."

The warning was to no avail; the grass people planned to return to their village to gather whatever they could carry of what remained. Koalee gave the strangers the last of the fruit, knowing there would be an abundance in the tall woods, and most of their flatbread, since they could make fire in the woods as well. She thought again of the destruction of Lenk's house. This was far worse.

"We'll bury our dead," the leader announced, "and pack food and blankets, weapons— but no more than you can carry. You must all find flasks for dew. Rest until dawn, then we'll leave for the settlements beyond the green lake."

Dyra told them of the cave at the place of stones, warned them of the large birds at the green lake, and wished them good fortune. The leader stood and formally introduced himself.

"I am Gozer," he said, giving the two-handed bow. "We have shared misfortune and you were a good friend to strangers. Life preserve you."

Dyra returned the bow. "I am Dyra. I won't forget you. Will you do one favour for us?"

"You have only to ask," replied the other.

Dyra took the note from his pocket. "When you come to our settlement, give this to the glass blower. My wife, Koalee, is his daughter. Our families will be worried."

"Gladly," said Gozer and he called, "Everybody witness. If I die up trail, see that this note is delivered to the glass blower in the settlement beyond the green lake."

The afternoon was wearing on and Dyra doubted they could reach the tall woods by nightfall, so in the end they spent the night in Gozer's village. It had been a village much like the one they called home. Dyra could see the traces of where the street of shops and neat houses on rafts had been, in some places only the pyles remained. Everywhere the walls, chimneys and furniture lay in heaps concealing the crushed bodies of the villagers. Dyra helped bury them and Koalee gathered food to prepare a supper for the survivors. Nineteen grass people had been found alive and, despite the tragedy, there were some happy reunions. A child found his mother. A man had found his wife. There were shouts of joy and happy tears when brothers and sisters believed dead were reunited.

When they gathered for the meal, the connection to and fondness for their home overwhelmed some of Gozer's villagers. Not surprisingly, a few voices were raised to protest the idea of moving.

Gozer didn't argue the point at all. He simply said, "Where the mower comes, it comes again. We go up trail rising sun at dawn."

One tall young man sat over his meal in silence and never touched it. After the others had eaten, he found a quidda and began to pluck at its strings.

"Sing it out, smith," said the man beside him. "Sing it for all of us." So the young man sang a sad song of farewell to their village, and to his family:

>*When I was a boy*
>*Flying feathers in trials*
>*I thought that my roots*
>*Were as deep as the pyles.*
>*I thought that my home*
>*Was my refuge for life*
>*I thought that my village*
>*Was sheltered from strife.*
>
>*An apprentice at forge*
>*I would make the blades ring,*
>*For I knew that by evening*
>*I'd dance and I'd sing.*
>*My lady, my beauty,*
>*Her hair and her smiles*
>*Had me rafting a house*
>*On our very own pyles.*
>
>*My babe in his backpack,*
>*My parents at home,*
>*'Twas all that I wanted,*
>*'Twas all that I've known.*

The mower took all,
My lady, my home,
My babe in his backpack—I'm left all alone.

Oh, Life, keep my village
In store through the years,
And let me return
When I've shed all my tears.
Then nothing will vanish, nothing will die,
And we'll walk with my lady,
My baby and I.

The villagers dispersed quietly after the song to find shelter. Dyra and Koalee slept that night in a house that had been spared. In the morning it took all of Koalee's willpower to watch the twenty-eight grass people and their children set off in the direction of the green lake, then turn and set her own steps toward the tall woods.

IV

THEY MADE AN EARLY START. By the time the sun was high in the sky, they were close to the tall woods. The baby had slept well and was happy in his carrier.

A moment later Dyra froze, a shadow hovered above Koalee and the baby, a shadow with terrible reaching claws. Koalee looked up and screamed, then used her body to shield the baby. Dyra's heart raced and he felt a cold terror. He raised his gun and fired. His stone must have stunned the wheeler, for it veered in its flight. The bird circled, its circles carrying it farther away. Finally Dyra lowered the gun. He laid a comforting hand on Koalee's shoulder as she stood up. "Steady," he said. "It's gone." The shadow and Koalee's fear had startled the baby, so Dyra took him from his carrier.

"We're all going to be killed!" Koalee gasped, still shaking. "Soon all the grass people will be gone."

"Of course not," Dyra reassured her. "We escaped the mower. And think of all the other birds we've seen on the trail—birds far bigger than this. They never hurt us." He bounced the baby, whose cries became laughter.

"Seed eaters," Koalee scoffed. "Of course they didn't hurt us. Your gun can't kill wheelers like that one."

"No, but it stings them badly. The dangers were the same at home. It's being alone in a strange place that makes them worse."

"And there's no guard tower."

"Look, let's put the books and the baby bag in the trail runner. I'll take Hoyim and you carry the gun. You're a better shot, and you can keep watch."

So they went on. The only time Koalee relaxed her vigil was when the trail went up a slope so steep Dyra needed help, so she put the gun in the canvas and pushed. No birds appeared.

The tall woods gave them a sense of safety. It was moist and cool there, as Dyra had predicted. There was scarcely any grass, but many kinds of trees weren't much taller than grass and had great spreading leaves. Some were like the berry trees at home, with huge juicy red fruits, and some had sweet-smelling flowers. Songbirds kept up a merry chatter and flashed brightly coloured feathers as they flew from tree to tree. There were many more insects, but insects never hurt the grass people.

Koalee wrinkled her nose. The smell of dry dust so common in the do-lan was missing here. Instead there was a steamy smell of growth and decay and... fungus! "There are edible kloros here," she announced. "I smell them. But we can't live on fruit and mushrooms. I don't see any grain or peas."

"It's too bad we can't settle here," Dyra agreed. "It's such a beautiful place. Life seems to have given it something special."

"There are so many dangers up trail. Admit it, Dyra. We are lucky to have come this far."

"Life *is* with us, and the elf will meet us here. He promised. Meantime we've got all day to build a temporary shelter."

There was one great disadvantage to the tall woods. The floor was a thick mat of leaves which often hid broken branches or deep holes. After a few stumbles they learned to tread carefully and soon got into the habit of testing the leaves with a stick before taking a step. The trail runner was useless except on the trail, and the trail was obscured in places and had to be cleared. Moving the trail runner was hard work.

At last they found a little clearing at the base of a massive tree. The soil was soft, there was a dead tree on the ground they could easily sink pyles into, and logs were plentiful and simple to fashion into a small raft. When that was done they were hungry and ate nut meat and berries and the last piece of flatbread.

They wondered how they would manage to raise the raft, but Dyra's ingenuity didn't fail. Using logs propped against the fallen tree for a ramp, he rigged pulleys. The raft inched up the ramp, and finally fell onto the pyles. The fallen tree made an easy ladder, and they ran up and down carrying blankets and tools. Koalee gathered armloads of moss and made a soft bed. Dyra roofed the shelter and walled it on three sides with branches.

Koalee put the baby down to sleep, then dug a firepit while Dyra searched for stones to build a stove. In no time Koalee had mixed a batter and was making a fresh stack of flatbread. While Dyra went hunting, she prepared a pot of soup to simmer until their evening meal. A few insects buzzed around and one or two woods creatures came to investigate, but nothing harmed her. She felt safe for the first time since leaving home.

Dyra came back dragging the carcass of a fat grasshopper. They dismembered it, and into the soup it went. There would be good meat for the family tonight. On an excursion to pick more fruit, Koalee found a seed tree. Suddenly all was going well. After their best evening meal since leaving home, they built the fire high and lingered over their tea.

Koalee fed and changed baby Hoyim and tucked him in the shelter to sleep. But he whimpered and was restless, so she brought him down again and sat on a stump trying to amuse him. Darkness had fallen and it was cool. Dyra fetched Koalee's cloak and wrapped it around his wife and child then stirred the fire.

"We should read from the sacred book," Koalee suggested. "About how it was before the mower."

Dyra was tired. "I'd rather not. Not tonight."

Then a strange feeling came over Koalee. In her arms, the baby stiffened. Nervously she looked around. Far up trail, faint lights spun in little circles.

"Dyra. Those lights..."

"I see them. They'll be fireflies."

"Fireflies don't talk."

"Shh. I hear it too." Dyra's hand went to his knife.

Hoyim gave a delighted laugh.

"It must be all right," Koalee said. "Hoyim knows." Taking the baby, she went to stand beside Dyra.

A short march up trail two small lights appeared. They watched as someone walked toward them, merrily rotating both wrists as she watched what looked like lighted bracelets. Dyra and Koalee viewed her in amazement.

A few moments later an elf came striding confidently along the trail behind her. His fair hair and skin shone, so that his whole being seemed to glow. He was scattering something that looked like gold dust. Where it fell, a soft luminescence lit his path and then fell into darkness when he'd passed. He stepped into the circle of the campfire. Dyra and Koalee saw that, save for his bow and quiver of arrows, the only baggage he carried was a small shoulder pack.

"I am Radd," he said and, stepping aside, he added, "The fairy's name is Violet."

Never in their lives had Dyra or Koalee seen anyone so beautiful. Slim as a twig and smaller than Koalee, Violet stood before them like a lovely creature of the night—an exotic moth. Her hair was black against her pale skin; her sloping eyes glinted under long, thin brows like the eyes of a wild thing. A wisp of dress floated around her in cobweb-fine layers of misty grey and blue. Around her neck was a woven necklace fine as lace, and on each wrist she wore a crystal bangle that looked as if it were made of light. A pair of thin, green straps indicated that she was wearing sandals. On one toe an enormous, purple amethyst glinted in the firelight.

Stunned, it took Koalee a moment to remember her manners. When she found her voice, she invited Violet to sit on the stump. Violet ignored her. Instead, her eyes made a rapid survey of the fire and its surroundings.

"I am Dyra," Dyra announced, "and this is Koalee."

Radd acknowledged them both, but Violet simply made a quick step toward the baby and spun one of her lighted bracelets for him. Hoyim watched with fascination, but Violet soon moved to the stump as if it were her own discovery, and sat down.

Radd had settled himself on the moss. "Don't mind her," he said. "She often doesn't talk."

Violet's silence made her seem even more mysterious.

"It took you longer to get here than I expected," said Radd.

Koalee told him of the day at the place of stones where they'd rested, and Dyra explained about the mower and the night in the village. While they were talking, each of them snuck quick glances at Violet. She watched the firelight play on Radd's face and on her toe ring, as it touched a leaf here, a branch there. She listened to a night bird call in the tree above. Sometimes her attention lingered for a time, and sometimes it flitted as fast as her flickering eyes could move. Short or long, it was a concentration as pure as her crystals. For one so finely tuned to her environment, Violet seemed to have an astonishing capacity for shutting grass people—and elves—out of her world.

It was as if a butterfly had alighted nearby, Dyra thought. She was oblivious to the others around her, yet Dyra and Koalee felt as if she was carrying their minds to some place where only the winged could go.

"You didn't need to build that," Radd said, indicating the raft. "It takes a lot of rain to cause a flood in the tall woods."

"Grass people have to be careful," said Dyra.

Violet gave a little smile that indicated she'd heard the remark. The fire was getting low, and a moment later she gave a slight shiver and spoke for the first time. "I'm cold," she said, reaching her hand toward Radd without looking at him. "Hand me my bag."

Radd gave her the bag he'd worn on his shoulder, and she drew out a gossamer shawl even finer than her dress. When she wrapped it around her, tiny stars in its folds reflected the fire. She picked up a delicate twig and stirred the fire, concentrating on the sparks. Then, as suddenly as a sparrow taking flight, she ran to a hollow in the moss at the foot of the tree, folded her wings, wrapped her cloak about her, and lay down to sleep.

"You should sleep too," said Radd. "You're tired and we have a lot to do tomorrow."

As he followed Koalee and the sleeping Hoyim up to the raft, Dyra heard Radd say quietly to Violet, "You behaved abominably, of course," but he said it more as a fact than a criticism.

Morning came to the tall woods with such noise and activity that Dyra and Koalee felt their ears might shatter. In the grass, morning came softly. A ground animal might chatter, a seed bird peep, an early insect give a faint hum. Sometimes the sound of Lenk's hammer could be heard up trail. How they missed Lenk's hammering. Here, the humming of insects was magnified, as if the sound was unable to escape through the green canopy above, and the din of the birds was beyond belief.

Dyra began to laugh. "Are they making us welcome, or telling us to leave?" he asked.

The baby seemed to enjoy the sounds. He submitted happily to being washed and fed, while his father went off to collect dew. Dyra returned to camp bearing two flasks and a bundle of firewood. Koalee had started a fire and was making pancakes. A large juicy red fruit was waiting to be seeded. Everything about the camp smelled fresh.

Dyra laid a blanket on the moss, where he set Hoyim, and wove a cage of branches so he couldn't crawl away. Lately the baby had become very active.

There was no sign of elf or fairy, and Koalee and Dyra began to wonder if they'd dreamed them—but in a short while Radd appeared. He'd fashioned a bag from vines and was carrying an egg.

Koalee was overwhelmed. "These are worth gold in our village," she said. "A grassman risks his life a dozen times to get up to where the nests are, and often the bird won't let him take the eggs."

"This one is fresh laid," said Radd. "The bird will lay another to fill her nest."

Koalee studied him for a moment. "How did you ever manage to get this?" she asked. "You don't have wings either."

"I have other means of moving from place to place." The elf offered no further explanation.

Koalee pierced the shell and dribbled some of the egg into boiling water to cook. The rest she spilled on a clean flat stone for drying, it would be saved to use later.

Dyra wanted to ask if Violet was coming back, but didn't want to appear too curious. "You arrived last night," he said. "But you've said nothing about why you told me to come here, or how long we'll stay, or where we will go. Why did we have to leave that same night? Why couldn't we have waited to say goodbye to our families?"

Radd's face was stern. "The dolenter might have learned of it, and you wouldn't have been able to leave. Second, had you not left when you did, you could not have saved Gozer and his villagers, and he could not have taken your message to your village. Third, the timer is set. It must be done precisely. It was not an accident that you forgot to leave the note."

Dyra and Koalee realized for the first time that there was something cold and mechanical about the elf. He had nice manners and he could be kind, but he was not like the grass people. He accepted their invitation to join them for breakfast and talked of the grass woods beyond the tall woods where the mower had never been and might never come. Not even a four-legged shadow was likely to come there. He advised them not to eat all their seeds because if they did settle there, they would have to start their own trees.

Koalee asked if there were trees which produced fibres for spinning and weaving and was told they were plentiful. Dyra asked about wood for buildings and about the type of stones he needed for grinding. The elf assured him there would be no shortage.

Dyra went to the fire to pour more tea and get another pancake. As he did so, he saw Violet coming along the trail. His heart almost jumped out of his chest. Violet was extremely different from the grasswomen in the village. She looked fresh, as if she had just bathed in dew and indeed her hair was wet. She was wearing a different dress made of green leaves, woven through were golden threads that glinted like arrows of sunshine. In the daylight, her crystal bracelets sparkled with rainbows. In place of the amethyst, she wore a ruby on her toe. Its red glow nearly hypnotized him.

Violet paid no attention to the grassman. There were butterflies to watch and chase, berries to inspect, woods scents to smell. She danced for the pure joy of the morning without self-consciousness, then flew and lighted on a tree branch where she gave close scrutiny to a cocoon attached there.

"You will open," Dyra heard her murmuring to the cocoon, "and you'll have wings almost as pretty as mine."

"Dyra?"

Suddenly he realized that Koalee was speaking to him. He apologized for not listening.

"Dyra, I want to find those kloros. Can you watch Hoyim?"

Feeling a little ashamed, Dyra agreed to look after the baby, and sat down beside him. When he next glanced up at the tree, Violet was lying full length along the branch, holding up her foot to trap a sunbeam in her ruby toe ring. Dyra heard her give a soft giggle, and it struck him that the pleasure she took in distractions was very like the pleasure Hoyim was taking in the moss flower he was showing to him.

What was her secret? Dyra wondered. How could one be so free of responsibilities?

A giant caterpillar crawled toward her foot. It neither startled nor frightened her, but she flew away as if conceding territory. She flew down to the tree where Koalee had been picking red fruit and hovered there, she took a big bite from one fruit and left it. From there she went straight down to the moss, where she squatted in front of the baby, touching her bracelets together to amuse him. The crystal rang like tiny bells, and Hoyim was delighted, but Violet tired of the game and flitted away. After a moment she looked back at the baby. There was a peculiar glint in her eyes.

Radd had just entered the clearing and saw the look. It made him frown.

Koalee returned dragging a morel almost as tall as herself, enough food for several meals.

Dyra smiled in appreciation, then turned to Radd, who was staring up at the sky. "Won't you tell us more?"

The elf hushed him. "Not now. I'm listening." He saw that Dyra was puzzled, for there were no unusual sounds in the woods. He tapped his head.

Dyra realized Radd was listening to a voice in his mind, as he himself had heard in the meeting house. The thought was, grass people can do it. It's just that you've forgotten.

Dyra leaned back on the moss and laughed. The elf smiled. "Just as you have forgotten much of what your ancestors knew."

"Do you read our sacred book?"

"I don't have to read. I listen."

"Our ancestors believed Life was good."

"It is."

"But there was no mower then."

"There is always a mower."

The remark startled Dyra. Koalee, slicing a piece of morel ready for the fire, said, "A brown bird is lying beside the trail. Perhaps he met the mower."

Dyra went over to where she pointed. "No, this is natural death," he protested. "The mower is not natural."

"So you conclude that Life is angry," Radd said. "What would you say if I told you the mower was invented by men like you, except that they are the height of a four-legged shadow?"

"A man can't invent something that hurts other men. And who ever heard of a man as high as the tall trees?"

"They aren't that tall."

"There truly *are* such men?" Koalee asked.

"I observe," said the elf. "What I don't hear, I see."

Deep in thought, Dyra began strolling up the trail. "Is it true," he asked, "that the grass people once had the same religion as the elves?"

Matching Dyra's pace, the elf smiled patiently. "Religion? We elves believe in the timer. It would be better to say we *know* of the timer, because when you hear the thoughts of the world, you know how they are organized into plans, and how the plans work out when the time is right. Men become confused when they don't recognize the plan."

"But don't you believe in Life?"

The elf looked amused. "It is *all* Life," he said, "even that dead bird back there. We understand the oneness of Life."

"What's the oneness of Life?"

"Is Koalee different from the giant squirrel up there, feeding her family?"

"The dolenter taught us that grassmen are superior to other forms of Life. We aren't the same."

"Dyra, Life is Life. It doesn't exist solely for grass people. All the rest of the world mates when the timer says 'mate' and has its young when the timer says 'have your young', and dies when the timer says 'die'. But men think they are far superior. The tall men are even more arrogant than grassmen. You've seen what their invention, the mower, can do to Life."

"If you think so little of grassmen, why did you try to save me?"

Radd didn't give him a direct answer. "My concern is just as much with the birds and those red berries, or our friend the squirrel," he said. "You grassmen speak of Life as if it were a god, Dyra. Life is a child born in the days before form. That child is my concern, the inventions of the tall men will destroy Life unless we elves can get them to listen. They must be brought back to an awareness of the timer. It is the same with grass people."

"Our sacred book has passages like that—warning about taking Life and death into our own hands."

"The answer to your original question is 'yes'," Radd said as they turned back toward camp. "The grass people did share the same beliefs as the elves, long ago."

"Then is it true that you wrote our sacred book?"

The elf glanced at Dyra without a change in his expression. "The elves gave the knowledge of Life to the grass people as a gift, at the time we found your first Dokrimalitzla. We didn't write it; we conferred it and a grassman recorded it on paper. Surely you haven't forgotten that?" Radd sounded impatient. He turned and sipped some nectar from a sunburst flower. Then he collected some of its pollen and rolled it up inside a yellow petal, which he took with him. "I'm surprised you took an elf's advice," he remarked.

"I've been curious for a long time," Dyra admitted.

"Then perhaps it's surprising that your wife was willing to come."

"When I told her an elf advised it, she had no doubts. I think there's more faith in the old religion in the village than they care to say. They'd listen if you talked to them."

"I can't talk to them. They have to think. Your dolenter does not hear at all."

Coming into the camp, they saw Koalee feeding soft gruel to the baby and chatting to him. Violet was perched on the stump, watching with unusual concentration. Radd slipped the yellow charm he'd made out of sight beneath his jerkin. Excusing himself, he called Violet aside.

"I know what you're thinking," he reprimanded her. "If you want to stay with me, you must behave yourself. That is *their* baby, and that's how it stays."

Violet gave no response in words but she sprang up impulsively and clung to Radd, wrapping her arms about his neck and her legs about his body.

Dyra was embarrassed; he hadn't meant to watch. Radd hadn't noticed him, but Dyra was sure Violet had. He turned quickly away, only to note that, right before his eyes, a pair of insects were mating on a branch.

🦋 🦋 🦋

Dyra and Koalee worked together over their noon meal, she prepared greens while he arranged slabs of morel on a stick and hung them to smoke over the fire. Violet joined them, but when she tasted the smoked morel, she promptly spat it out and contented herself with a raw piece. Next moment she was seated cross-legged in front of a seed bird, watching him feed and trying to hold a conversation with him. When the bird flew away, so did Violet.

Radd appeared later, carrying a sprig of green that he said made a very fine brew to give the baby should he ever be sick. Then he took the charm from his neck and handed it to Koalee.

"Wear this," he said. "Don't take it off as long as we're with you. It's made from what you call 'sunburst flower', and it makes a powerful charm against fairy spells."

Koalee glanced questioningly up at the trees but Violet had flown away. Radd nodded. "She can be a selfish fairy, but this will protect you."

Feeling more at ease, Dyra asked Radd about his bow.

Radd explained obligingly how it was made and how it was used, and how arrows were winged. "You could bring down a wheeler with this if you had to," he said. "I'll help you make one—and one for your wife too."

While Radd and Dyra went searching for wood, Koalee washed their clothing and spread it on the raft to dry. She backpacked Hoyim up trail a short distance in search of a seed tree and happened upon the sunburst flower. Smiling, she took a petal and rolled up a bundle in imitation of the one Radd had given her. She found no seed tree, but she found flowers with sweet nectar and siphoned off all she could reach.

"Sweet syrup for pancakes tomorrow morning," she mused, and as soon as she was back in camp she put the nectar on to boil with a whole red fruit mashed into the mixture.

Dyra sniffed happily as he entered the camp. "It even masks the smell of the woods," he said.

When the sun made few shadows in the clearing, Radd left his work on the bows and arrows and announced their first lesson. As with the pebble gun, Koalee soon excelled with Radd's bow.

"She has eyes like a wheeler," Dyra bragged. "I'll never have to make lenses for her."

Violet returned as dusk fell. She was in a particularly lively mood. She raced to the baby and tinkled her bracelets together to amuse him. The two laughed together. Then Violet had another impulse. She went to an open part of the clearing and began to do a fascinating dance step, dancing in a wide circle.

Radd set down the arrow he was working on. "She's honouring you," he said. "Not many men have seen the fairy ring." Then, as if he couldn't resist, he got up and danced with her. It was growing dark enough that Violet's bracelets were lighting up, and the ruby on her foot glowed darkly. She danced and spun, with a hypnotic grace and beauty that Dyra had never witnessed before.

Dyra felt her powerful spell on him again. He felt an urge to enter the ring and seize Violet in his arms and fly with her into the tall trees. Koalee had gone up to the shelter. When she came slowly down the fallen tree, watching the dance, she was wearing her pretty yellow dress. Dyra didn't notice. She hid her disappointment by putting leaves in the boiling water for tea.

Radd stopped dancing and announced, "Now you'll do one of your dances for us."

"We didn't dance much in our village," Dyra apologized, "and we have no musicians. We'd have to sing for ourselves."

Koalee looked quite eager, so Dyra agreed. Then, for the first time, he realized what she was wearing.

"How did you manage to sneak in that dress?" he asked.

"It was in Hoyim's bag. I carried it."

Violet had been standing quite motionless, looking down at the place where she had danced, and she motioned to them to move closer to the fire. Koalee and Dyra sang a folk song and went through the steps as they had often danced at weddings or birthday parties in the village. Radd watched without emotion but with interest, as if he were learning. Violet watched as a bird might watch the ritual dance of another species, having nothing to do with her. The tune amused her, though, for she tapped her foot to it and, once it was familiar, she kept time with her bracelets.

Dyra and Koalee's dance was a married dance, done only by couples among the villagers.

TOGETHER:	Let's be a forest
	Let's be leaves,
	Let's be the sunshine, let's be the breeze,
SHE:	I'll be the cough. Khh!
	And you'll be the sneeze!
HE:	A-choo!
TOGETHER:	It's celebration time!
HE:	You'll be a butterfly,
	I'll be a worm.
SHE:	I'll dance around you and make you squirm.
HE:	Let's both be birds, then, my lovely young lass.
	What are you now, dear?
SHE:	The blue-eyed grass!
HE:	I'll be a leaf that has left the tree.
SHE:	You'll float around hand-in-hand with me.
HE:	Hop like the bunnies,

	Buzz like the bees,
SHE:	Dance like the elves
	In the moonlit trees,
	Together: Or just be ourselves
	On a happy village night,
	tripping up the street
	By the lampman's light.
	Watch out for the centipede! Isn't he a sight?
	It's celebration time!
HE:	Let's be lovers
SHE:	Let's be friends.
HE:	Let's be grateful
	For the joy Life sends.
TOGETHER:	Let's not be married
	'Til the party ends!
	It's celebration time!

Koalee and Dyra ended their song and dance, breathless and flushed. They staggered to the log, laughing, with their arms around each other. When they'd had their tea and gone up to the shelter, Koalee folded her yellow dress carefully and put it back in Hoyim's bag.

"I'm glad you brought that," said Dyra. "You look pretty." He paused, and then could not help himself. "Did you ever see anything like that fairy ring?"

Koalee hesitated slightly, "She's an enchanting creature," she agreed. She felt for Radd's charm and satisfied herself that it was safely around her neck. Then she reached for her sewing bag and took out the charm she'd made for Dyra, wondering how to present it to him.

No, Koalee, something seemed to say to her, Dyra has to do this himself. There are other ways to help him.

Koalee returned the charm to its hiding place. She reached toward him and kissed him. "Dyra, I love you. You do remarkable things. Hoyim loves you too."

Dyra seemed more relaxed. "You were so good with Radd's bow

today. When the baby is old enough, I'm going to send you out to do the hunting."

Koalee smiled. "When the baby is old enough, I'm going to have another."

V

Dyra awoke so early in the morning that the sun had not yet risen. The woods were chill and grey.

"Koalee," he whispered.

She stirred and half-opened her eyes. "Is the baby all right?"

"He's fine. I'm taking my new bow and going hunting. I may come back with nothing, but I've got to try."

Koalee murmured and went back to sleep.

After eating some flatbread, Dyra took a long stick and set off in a new direction. Very few creatures were stirring, and the woods were still peaceful, though once he was sure he saw a little man in a peaked hat hurrying toward a tall tree.

Dyra had no luck with his hunting. The woods were soon a-hum, and the noise distracted him. The only time he saw an insect he and Koalee liked to eat, he missed. This meant he lost his arrow. Determined to find it, he searched under the spreading trees until he became aware of a bright patch of light ahead, and the smell of water. A lake!

Dyra went to investigate. The water was clean and clear. Trees grew in the lake, and their flat leaves lay like saucers on the water. A large winged creature was seated on one of those leaves. Dyra crept nearer to see what it was.

Violet had finished her morning swim and had just crawled up on the lily pad to dry her wings. The sun turned the water to silver around her, her shimmering wings seemed to be fashioned from the water itself. She was wearing only two pieces of transparent fabric patterned in flowers of pink and violet. On her bare foot, the ruby ring flamed.

Dyra was unaware that the fairy's green dress and sandals were lying at his feet. This was the first time he'd had a chance to watch Violet without Radd or Koalee present, and he lingered while he had the opportunity to feast his eyes on her. He ventured out of his hiding place and stood staring in wonderment. Violet sensed his presence; she turned slowly toward the shore and a sly smile played about her features. She was well within earshot and what she said carried to him clearly—

"Shall I claim *you*, grassman?"

Dyra's face reddened, though his heart raced. Thinking of Koalee, he shook his head.

The rejection appeared to have no effect on Violet, for she coolly turned her head and didn't watch as Dyra stumbled away. A frog sat himself on the lily pad opposite hers and opened his mouth, only wanting a good breath of air, but Violet took it as an affront.

"Don't you dare!" she snapped. She slid back into the water for another swim. She was not aware that the ruby ring had slipped off her toe.

Dyra got back to camp with nothing to show for the hunt except a lighter step and a clean conscience. How was it that he'd allowed the fairy to make such a claim on him? A grassman shouldn't have such feelings for anyone other than his wife. Shame burned in him, but with it came relief. For the first time since he'd laid eyes on Violet, he felt free of her.

Koalee read his face and was happy. She poured sweet, red syrup over his pancakes and offered him tea.

"Radd will teach me archery again this afternoon," she said cheerfully. "Oh, by the way, look." She pointed to the place where Radd and Violet had danced. A ring of toadstools had sprung up there overnight.

They had the camp to themselves for some time. "I think I saw a gnome," Dyra remarked as they tidied up the camp. "I'm not sure."

"You didn't speak?" Koalee asked.

"He was too far away. And in a hurry." Dyra drew in a breath. "I saw Violet too," he added. "She was taking a swim."

"She plays," Koalee remarked, rattling a seed for Hoyim. "She senses the world just as Hoyim does. As if her eyes and her nose did her thinking. Do you imagine there are grass people like that, for whom life is all pleasure?"

"If there are they're not mentioned in any of my books. There were no such people in our village."

"Grass people find pleasure their way. Remember how happy the weaver could be fussing with his designs? And the time he made the tiles for his step."

Dyra nodded, "The doctor always seemed happy too. I could never see how tending sick people could make a man happy, but he was never sad."

"And don't forget my little sister Flon. Mother insists that Flon is elfin."

"But there was no one in our village like Violet."

"I'm glad," Koalee said. "Fairies don't help with the work."

If Life was all pleasure for Violet, it didn't look that way when she next arrived. She was neither flying nor dancing, but moving slowly and watching her feet as they scraped toe-first over the leaves. Then she crumpled up beside the largest toadstool and sat there beneath a tall, blue flowering tree.

Koalee and Dyra left her alone, and she paid no attention to them. Twice she sneezed, but that was the only sound she made. When Radd arrived he took in the scene at once and went straight to her. Violet sneezed again.

"What are you doing sitting under a bluebell?" the elf asked. "You know the pollen makes you sneeze."

Violet sat up, clasping her arms around her legs.

Radd squatted down beside her. "What have you done now?" The fairy wiggled her toe.

"You lost a toe ring? Which one?"

Another silent message.

"The ruby? The one you liked best. No wonder you're pouting. How did you lose it? Swimming!"

Radd fetched the shoulder pack and handed it to her. "Look, I'll dive and try to find it. Meanwhile, you've got others."

44

Unenthusiastically, Violet searched in her bag and produced the amethyst. It didn't go with her green dress so she pitched it back in. Out came a peridot, which was instantly thrown onto the floor of the woods. Last came a tawny topaz. She tried it on and stood up to consider it, then changed her mind and retrieved the peridot. She tossed the topaz back in the bag and then walked away, leaving the bag lying among the toadstools.

"Well!" said Dyra, when Violet was out of hearing. "You made far less fuss over leaving home and family and all your treasures than she made over that ring."

"But I don't have such jewellry," Koalee laughed.

"Maybe someday the trader will find such a stone and I'll be rich enough to buy it for you."

Koalee looked fondly at Hoyim. "Here's my jewel," she said. "I only wish we were safe in a house of our own, and we could find out about our families."

"We will," Dyra promised.

Radd eventually returned with Violet's ring. "You're lucky," he told her. "It wedged in a branch. If it had fallen to the bottom, it would've sunk from sight."

Violet snatched it without a word of thanks.

"We'll work hard at your archery today," Radd told the grass people. "Then make what preparations you can for breaking camp. We leave at daybreak tomorrow."

"It's just as well," Dyra said, though he felt a bit apprehensive at the news. "We're growing soft in the tall woods."

After archery practice, Dyra went with Radd to cut some fine bark from a birch tree. Koalee busied herself grinding seeds against a stone. Several times she checked on Hoyim, playing in his cage of branches, and handed him a shiny seed shell to play with. Hoyim was easy to entertain, and his mother noted happily that he seemed content to spend longer studying objects than most babies she'd seen. This meant he was intelligent. What a fine, fine baby! Koalee smiled at the thought.

Dyra returned alone. "Radd heard an angry bird, and went to investigate," he said, and looked around. "Where's Hoyim?"

Koalee gestured toward the cage. What she saw made her heart freeze. The cage was empty.

"He *was* here." The thin, small voice that emerged didn't sound like her own. "I checked on him not a moment ago! He's got to be..." She found it hard to breathe.

Dyra stiffened. "Don't let fear take you!" he ordered. "Go around the big tree that way, and I'll go this way."

They ran in opposite directions, looking everywhere and calling for Hoyim. They checked under spreading trees and under dead leaves. But there was no sight or sound. Koalee was trembling uncontrollably.

"Path next!" Dyra directed. He was pale and breathless as he pointed one direction to Koalee and took the other himself.

They went as far up trail as each could see from the campsite. It was impossible that a creeping baby grassman could have come so far in such a short time. There was only one possible explanation—a bird or an animal— had taken Hoyim.

Back at camp, a sobbing Koalee looked pitifully at Dyra, sure that he would never forgive her. How had she not noticed him escaping? Dyra took her in his arms and held her.

"Be steady," he said. "Remember Violet? Radd warned us about her. Fairies do steal babies. If Violet has taken Hoyim, surely Radd will persuade her to bring him back."

"Dyra, if I've lost Hoyim..." Koalee couldn't even imagine the grief. She mustn't believe he was gone. Not her baby. What would be the use of life without him?

Dyra drew in a shaky breath. "The sensible thing to do is to imagine ourselves being Hoyim. If you crawled away from the branches, which way would you go?"

"I...I'd go to me!" Koalee exclaimed.

"Toward the firepit and his mother. Or you might try your luck crawling away from your mother, just to see how big the world is. You go that way, and I'll go to the firepit. Don't miss a crevice."

Radd appeared suddenly beside the fallen tree. "You have lost Hoyim," he stated.

Dyra was on his hands and knees, looking beneath the edge of every stone and root. He stood up to face the elf. "Radd, if he's to be found, you're the one who can find him."

"I am listening."

"Violet?" asked Koalee.

"No, it is not Violet," he said. "As I told Koalee, the charm will protect her. Hoyim has done this under this own power, and has got himself cornered."

Radd led the way toward a large dead tree. Wails were coming from the trunk—Koalee gasped and pressed her hands to her heart. Radd pushed aside a loose flap of bark and there, healthy but crying his heart out, was Hoyim. He'd crawled into a hollow in the base of the tree, and couldn't get out.

As Dyra carefully lifted the baby out, again Koalee began to cry; she cried harder as Dyra placed their baby in her arms. Hoyim looked bewildered, wondering what was wrong with his mother.

"It's into the backpack with you," she said at last.

"Thank Life," Dyra said.

"And Radd," Koalee added.

"Thank Life for bringing Radd."

It wasn't until evening that Hoyim's parents had recovered enough to discuss the next day's plans with Radd. Using a piece of birch bark, Radd drew a map showing the location of their camp as well as the village they'd left behind. He indicated the trail they would follow.

"Here the earth rises sharply," he said, pointing to a place beyond the tall woods. "If you insist on seeing the world for yourself, you'll have to walk up there—but it's dangerous, and will take time."

"We have to go," Dyra said. "It was one of my reasons for leaving the village."

Radd seemed to sigh. "You can't settle there, you understand. It's windy and rocky, and grains and peas won't grow. Wheelers circle there. If we go, we go at night. They won't harm an elf, but it may be difficult to protect you."

Koalee held Hoyim closer. "*Must* we go, Dyra?"

"If others follow us, I need to give them answers. What if the dolenter came too? I'd have no more arguments than I had before.

We must go."

"Take my word for it," said Radd. "There *are* men like you. But much taller."

"I don't doubt you," Dyra assured him. "But I have to see for myself. I can't write a history of our new settlement and say, 'An elf told me.' I have to say that I investigated."

Fortunately, the creatures of the woods settled down early. Hoyim was either upset by his interlude penned in a tree, or else he sensed that he was to be packed up trail again, for he was restless. Trying to quiet him, and wishing it would grow darker, Koalee became aware of a giant presence right outside the shelter. "What's that?" she asked in alarm.

Dyra peered through the branches. "It's a huge squirrel," he reported. "He's at the trail runner."

"The food! Dyra, what can we do? Shoot him?"

"We can't shoot creatures unless we need them for food—or if they threaten our lives."

Something crashed, startling the squirrel; Koalee heard his hasty retreat. This made Hoyim cry again. Koalee gave a weary sigh. The trail runner had overturned, and the contents of the canvas were scattered. They had to use their torches to find everything. Dyra unwrapped his telescope and was relieved to find it unbroken. To Koalee's surprise, the meal and flatbread were untouched. But the earthenware nutmeat jar was lying near the fire, almost empty. It took a long search to find the wooden lid.

"Do you want to go back to Gozer's village?" Dyra asked. "We might find some there."

Koalee considered, but shook her head. "No. We'll make do with what we have."

Radd, stretched out on the moss, stirred in his sleep. Dyra remembered what the elf had said about the timer and abandoned the idea of returning to Gozer's village. In her hollow, Violet slept with a smile on her lips. The rest of the night was uneventful and they woke before dawn.

"You had some trouble with a squirrel," Radd remarked. "I saw it in my dream. You didn't recover all your belongings. Look over there."

Dyra found his tree chopper where the elf had indicated. "Thanks!" he said. "How could I have managed without my tree chopper?"

It was obvious that the elf felt impatient, having to wait while all the equipment was loaded, but finally they were on their way. The distance through the woods was short compared to the trail they'd already travelled, but it was slow going having to test the ground at every step. Once a leaf gave way beneath Dyra and he sank up to his armpits. Radd, walking lightly over the leaves without a walking stick, never seemed to have any trouble.

Violet flew much of the time and, when she walked, usually brought up the rear. When she did happen to be in view, she was a source of entertainment as she flitted about exploring the woods. Once they caught a glimpse of her teasing a bee: "You're in the wrong flower, bee. Your sisters will sting you for this!" Sometimes she ran up to tall trees and peered into the crevices in the bark. Dyra watched her fly up to a spreading tree and pick one of its dark blue berries. She bit into it joyously, and then suddenly showed the first generous impulse they'd seen her exhibit. She grabbed another berry and ran to Koalee.

"Here, grasswoman," she said. "It is for you."

Koalee smiled and thanked her. Mystified, she looked to Radd. "You gave her morel," said Radd. "Violet doesn't forget."

When they stopped for their noon meal, Dyra felt his heart leap at the sight of a sunny expanse of grassland beyond the woods.

"There is much to do," said Radd. "After we have eaten, I'll take you to the branch in the trail so you'll know the way to the new land in case I must leave you. Your trail runner will be safe in the hollow of this tree, and here's a corner we can line with moss where your wife and baby can rest."

"Hoyim and I are going to the high place with you," Koalee protested.

"It's foolish," said Radd, "but I know you will anyway. I meant you should rest now. It's a steep climb, and you'll have to backpack."

After eating, Dyra removed the book and tools from his backpack, replacing them with his telescope. He then went off with Radd, carrying his bow and arrows on his back and his pebble gun in his hand.

Violet had been plucking the tiniest leaves from a tree that was turning gold and gave a delighted cry when she saw another whose leaves were dark red. Apparently torn between wanting to finish her collecting and wanting to go with Radd and Dyra, at the last minute she stuffed her leaves into her shoulder pack, gave it to Radd to carry and went with them.

It was a delight to set foot on the do-lan trail again, but Dyra saw at once that this trail was not made by grassmen. Animal droppings lay about.

"Ground animals made this trail," Radd explained. "If grassmen were ever here it was not recorded. The tall men were here many years ago. Further ahead you'll see a mountain of stones where a stable for their domestic animals stood. They won't come back because the earth here wouldn't grow enough food for them."

"Then how can we survive?" Suddenly Dyra was more anxious.

"The tall men are such an enormous size and need far more food. This land will grow more than enough for a whole settlement, and it is rich in berry trees and seed trees. About six days up trail, if there was a trail, you'd come to the red valley and end of settlement, but of course there is no trail. This one goes only about one day."

It was not a long journey to the place where the trail divided. Radd pointed out the way to the new land and then led Dyra a short distance up the hill.

"Do you still think you can get up there?" he asked. "If you do, we must go tonight."

"I can't see through my telescope at night."

"That's why you must prepare to survive up there for a full day."

When they arrived back at the tall woods, Koalee came out to meet them. She was in good spirits. While Dyra greeted the baby, she took a large fruit from her bag.

"Thorn apple!" he exclaimed. He halved and quartered the fruit, setting it out rosy side up for all of them to enjoy.

"Wait until you see what else I found," Koalee exulted. She led them to a clump of flowering trees bearing great blooms of purpley pink. "Fell one for me, Dyra, please. This makes the very best tea for winter sickness."

It took only a few strokes with the tree chopper to bring one down, but when he looked to her for thanks, she gave him a teasing grin. "It's the roots I need," she said.

Laughing, Dyra set about digging up the roots and chopping them into short lengths.

When they arrived back at camp and had eaten their last loaf of meal, Radd announced, "Now we sleep until dark. Tonight we must travel."

When Radd woke them later, the sun had set and they needed a fire to see. Dyra's backpack was ready and Hoyim would ride in Koalee's. Radd informed them that Violet was not accompanying them but she had offered her shoulder bag to use for food supplies. They waited at the edge of the woods until moonrise. The moon was not bright, but it gave enough light that they could follow the trail. When the earth became steep, they struggled. Koalee found the climbing especially hard—Hoyim was growing big and heavy. Dyra urged her to go back to the trail runner, but she refused.

They stopped often to rest, sometimes hiding near a sheltering stone. It was disquieting in the shadows and hard to tell if anything else was nearby. Snakes, for example, liked stones. Not that grass snakes would harm them, but to have one slither around you in the dark was unsettling. It was comforting to have the elf along. His mind told him when living things were around, and he kept attuned for owls and wheelers.

Very little grass grew on the slope, and there was nothing to bind the earth. A misstep could cause them to fall; they were in constant danger of landslides. Sometimes a tumbling rock hurtled by, bounding down the hillside.

Once Koalee came close to panic. Hearing loose earth above, she ducked beneath a large rock. A shower of pebbles bounced past, and when she felt it was safe to leave, she realized she'd dropped her staff and bow. It was too dark to see them, so she lit her torch. Radd hurried to help her.

The stir woke Hoyim, and he cried to be fed. The first hint of daylight appeared in the sky.

"We're high enough now," said Radd. "We can find shelter, and you can set your telescope."

They built a barricade against a deeply-set rock, leaving a narrow opening for a door. When Dyra arranged a shelf in the stone wall and set up his telescope, he was so excited he didn't want to stop to eat with the others. It did not take him long, even in the soft light. He could see their village—the street of shops and even their house!

"Come, Koalee!" he called, and helped her locate her parents' home. "It's just as I knew it would be!" he exclaimed. "I knew if I could get to a high place I could see it all." Then he had a second thought. "But how will I see a four-legged shadow unless one actually comes?"

"The timer is set," said Radd.

The shelter was cramped, Hoyim fretted, and they had nothing to entertain him. Dyra stepped outside to break off a twig. He would carve out a whistle or a toy to amuse the baby. Hurrying to find the right twig, he was too intent to notice the shadow. When Koalee screamed his name, he dashed for the shelter. A bird longer than a raft fell to earth and lay kicking and thrashing. Both Radd and Koalee stood outside with their bows bent and new arrows ready. Only then did Dyra notice the small shaft in the bird's neck.

"I told you that you could bring down a wheeler if you had to," said Radd calmly. "I'll get your arrow back when he stops moving."

Shaking, Dyra held Koalee as if he'd never let go. After that he was content to stay in the shelter. The bird was far too large for them to move, and its body was a constant reminder that the hilltop was a place of danger.

"You should have listened to me, grassman, you need to stay alert," the elf said without recrimination.

The sun failed to grow bright and it looked as if it might rain, but instead it began to blow earth. Koalee made a tent with her under blouse to shelter the baby and her own face. They were relieved to hear Radd say, "At the very worst, the wind should fall by sunset."

It didn't take long. It was not yet mid-afternoon when it began to blow cooler and a light shower cleared the dust from the air. In a little while the sun shone and Dyra set up his telescope again.

"I wonder if they had the earth wind at the village," Dyra mused.

The elf had been listening to his inner messages, "They have worse trouble than that," he said.

VI

Dyra trained the telescope on the village. It looked as it had before, except that now the day's activities were beginning. Grasswomen with baskets on their arms were coming and going to the shops. The weaver was sweeping the tiles in front of his door. Dyra called, "Come and see Koalee, I can almost see the sign on your father's shop."

Koalee smiled as she looked through the telescope. "It was worth all to see this! I can see my mother and sisters in the float space! And there goes Syl! I wonder if they know I'm watching them. Oh, Dyra! *No!*"

Koalee froze in wide-eyed horror. Dyra grabbed the telescope. A shadow had fallen across the village. It appeared to be going in the direction of Lenk's house. Not Lenk! Dyra forced himself to look. It was not a shadow, but a tall man, formed like a grassman, just as the elf had said, and he was riding on an animal—an enormous four-legged animal with feet as big as a house. The man's skin was sun-bronzed to a tone very like Dyra's own, and he wore trousers of a dull, grey colour which almost matched his own cover clothes. As he watched, the man got off the animal and bent to pull some grass trees with such ease that Dyra couldn't believe what he was seeing.

"Oh, Life!" Dyra groaned. "He's let the animal go and it's walking straight into the village. He doesn't know, does he? He doesn't *know!*"

"No," said Radd, "And we haven't been able to get him to listen."

Dyra saw the man say something to the animal, and the giant creature turned and went to him, stumbling against the meeting house. Dirt and splinters erupted before Dyra's eyes.

"He has destroyed the village!" he cried.

Koalee seized the telescope and adjusted the lens. "No," she said. "He hasn't destroyed my father's house, or ours. The meeting house is gone and the dolenter's house."

Dyra took the telescope again and noted the direction in which the animal was moving. The man mounted it once more. "I think Lenk was spared," Dyra said. "Pray to Life it missed the school and the children."

"He will come back," said Radd, "and bring the mower. One of my elves went to tell the villagers what to do."

"Is there a temporary camp between my house and the green lake?"

"There is. That's where Gozer and his villagers planned to settle. My friend will bring the survivors there."

"Survivors?"

"Six are killed. Over sixty of your villagers remain."

"Our families?" Koalee gasped, trembling.

"As far as I know, your relatives are safe," the elf assured them. "And Gozer's camp will not be harmed. The mower won't come because there are too many furry trees."

Dyra felt rather like a god, standing in the high place watching the world, but an utterly futile god. He could do nothing but trust the elf and pray. Koalee found the courage to look again and made a methodical count of the houses that remained. The villagers were running back and forth now, inspecting the damage, comforting each other, and—oh, no!—clearing fallen timbers from what must be a body.

Watching, Koalee imagined she could hear the screams.

"Trust Life," said the elf. "Life always wins."

Dyra looked at the dead wheeler, still lying beside the seed tree. "Did you have the right to take that life to save mine?" he asked.

"Strictly speaking, no. But all creatures have the right to fight for survival. Grassmen have superior weapons because grassmen are small and weak."

Drya lifted Hoyim from Koalee's backpack and held him.

55

"Grassmen do not kill other men," he said.

"The tall man doesn't know," Radd repeated. "He doesn't know that you exist."

"Dyra—it's the mower!"

At Koalee's shriek, Dyra looked through the telescope. He could see the tall man again. This time he was seated on an enormous machine that moved by itself. The tops of trees were slashed off in an instant, flying through the air and falling chaotically in a whirlwind of debris. The mower skirted the far side of the green lake, barely missed Lenk's house, took the pea trees and part of the grain, and almost touched the neighbouring village. From there it went straight on to the next settlement and tore right through its centre.

Dyra's breath was knocked from him. It would have taken a grassperson a long day's march to reach the next village. The mower had done it in half a dozen blinks.

"It's coming back rising sun," Radd announced. "My people will tell them not to run that way. If they listen, we can save them."

"I can't stand this," Koalee said, reaching to hold Hoyim. "Dyra, don't watch any more."

Dyra felt himself very close to panic. "Life is like a twisted branch," he moaned, stepping away. "Will the way of the grass people ever be smooth again?"

The elf's answer might as well have been a riddle. "Look to the red valley," he said.

Dyra wondered for a moment what the elf meant, then he sat studying the baby for a while. Eventually, he returned to the telescope and watched until dusk.

"There are dozens of lights on the trail," he announced, "and Gozer's camp is alive with them."

"Good," said Radd. "Sleep now; we'll depart after dark. The descent can be worse than the climb."

When night came, they chose the easiest slope and literally crept down the hill. Koalee was nervous about Hoyim so Dyra carried him. It took all night, but they went without mishap and Hoyim slept peacefully. They arrived back at the place where they'd left the trail runner as the woods were waking and settled down to sleep in their bed of moss.

When Koalee awoke, she saw Violet watching her. The fairy signalled to her to follow and disappeared up the hollow tree.

Koalee obligingly followed.

There was a room above, a cozy space just big enough for two, with a tiny round window. Violet had put down moss for a bed and, in the furthest corner, she had created a nest by padding a curve of bark with thistledown and white cotton-fluff. A pink petal was laid over the nest. Violet motioned to Koalee to come forward. Beneath that rosy quilt lay a newborn baby fairy.

Koalee caught her breath. "Dyra!" she called. "Come up here!"

Dyra came, blinking with sleep. They made a quiet fuss over the baby, secretly thinking it wasn't half as handsome as Hoyim, but awed by how tiny it was and curious about its wings, which were little more than damp stumps on its shoulders.

Violet's pride glowed in her face. "Her name is Golden," she said, gently holding the sleeping baby fairy's tiny hand.

They left her in the nest and went to find Radd. "She'll never tell us where she got it, of course," Radd said. "But now she'll settle down for a while. The baby won't be able to fly for a few weeks."

For a moment Dyra re-lived the magic of those first few days of knowing Violet. How precious it was—the beauty, and the total freedom she epitomized. Yet he was glad to know there was one thing that could make Violet commit herself for a time.

"I'll go to Gozer's camp now," Radd announced. "Your best plan would be to go to the end of the animal trail and build a temporary raft there. Then break trail into the new land beyond. In four days, you should come to a small lake. It's safe and clean and you can walk around it in a day. No mud bottom. No big birds, except a pair of ducks, and they'll never harm grass people. Winds are light there, though from rising sun they can be cold."

"Then, when the wind is no sun it will be bitter," said Koalee.

"You would be wise to cure any field furs you find. Also, dig a drainage ditch under your float space to the crease and you'll be remarkably free of floods. There's a rise in the earth beyond the lake to afford shelter."

"Then the lake rises," Dyra observed.

"Yes, it does. It goes high in the wet season. I wanted to warn you. It will be hard work, breaking trail that far, but it will be worth it. And you *will* have help."

With that, Radd handed Koalee two eggs, picked up his bow, and left them.

Dyra got busy cutting wood for a signpost. If Radd was right—and he usually was—their friends would follow them. When the sign was ready, he burned the message into the wood: *New Land, Dyra*, with an arrow pointing in the direction they would go.

Meanwhile Koalee busied herself making flatbread for their next journey. They gathered all they could of roots and berries, medicine herbs, and moss. Violet spent the time finishing a dress, and Hoyim sat with her, watching the bright golden thread flash up and down. When Violet finished stitching, she stood up, whisked her green dress over her head, and tossed it carelessly under a thorn bush.

Koalee was covetous. Is she going to discard it? she wondered, thinking how fine she would look in it.

"Don't even think about it," Dyra warned, seeing her glance. "Fairies are jealous, especially of green. It would be very bad luck to take her cast-off clothes."

Oblivious to them, Violet fastened her new dress around her. The woods seemed to come alive with colour. The dress had a bandeau at the top of the same deep rich red as the skirt, and the two parts were linked by one tiny brown and yellow leaf. Golden threads twinkled here and there, especially in the top. Violet took a handful of pollen from a flower and rubbed it at random over the dress. It turned to gold dust at her touch, and when she shook the last of it from her hand, it fell like a shower of golden rain.

Violet was so delighted that she spun about on one foot, and when Hoyim laughed, she crouched before him and tinkled her crystal bracelets together to make him crow some more. Then she noted her ruby toe ring, frowned, and decided to change it for the topaz. Soon afterwards, she returned to the hollow tree to check on Golden.

"We'll have to watch Hoyim," Dyra remarked. "Or when he grows up, he may run off with a fairy."

The discarded green dress lay forgotten under the thorn bush.

Dyra and Koalee spent their last night in the hollow tree. Very early in the morning they ate part of an egg, gathered dew, and packed the trail runner. When they saw Violet watching them from the little window in her nest, they smiled and went in to see the baby fairy again. To their amazement her wings had opened, and now she could sit up and take note of her surroundings.

Koalee couldn't imagine a grass baby developing so fast. Golden could already drink nectar from the hollow seed cup Violet held for her.

Violet preceded them when they went back outside. She ran to Hoyim to let him hear her bracelets one more time, and then she kissed the top of his head. She showed no emotion, but to Koalee's amazement, she saw a tear slip from Violet's eye and fall into Hoyim's light hair. Then she ran back to her nest. From inside, they heard her call, "Good trail, grass people."

"Good trail to you, too," they said quietly.

Koalee bent to pick up Hoyim. Something twinkled like a star in his hair where Violet's tear had fallen. She took the object in her fingers. It was a diamond.

"No, don't go to her," said Dyra, reading his wife's mind. "She doesn't want to be thanked. That's why she hurried away."

"But don't you realize what this is?"

Dyra took the stone. "A trader would give me enough for this to let us live in comfort for the rest of our lives."

"Don't sell it!" Koalee cried, aghast.

"I won't," Dyra promised. "If a fairy leaves a farewell present it's very good luck."

They looked up at the little window, but Violet was not to be seen. Koalee deliberately took the flower charm Radd had given her from around her neck and tossed it away. It landed on top of Violet's discarded dress.

Progress was slow until they were out of the tall woods, but once they reached the do-lan they moved rapidly. The trail runner felt suddenly lighter, and they soon reached the place where the trail divided. Dyra dug a posthole and set up his sign.

"I hope someone sees it," said Koalee.

The sun had scarcely reached its height when they came to end of trail.

After a meal, Koalee offered to start digging the holes for the pyles needed for the new raft. "Why are we building a raft here, anyway?" she asked.

Dyra looked up from chopping wood. "Because Radd told us to."

"But why? For only two or three nights?"

"Four. Radd said it might take four days to the lake."

It would cost two days, but now that they had decided to do the job right, they could see the advantage. If in the future any grassman went up trail, the raft would be a wonderful safe place to rest for a night.

As they searched for stones, they found they were building only a short distance from the giant stoneworks Radd had mentioned—the remains of a building made by tall men.

"Can you imagine being big enough to move stones like that?" asked Koalee. "Can you imagine the size of the animals that must have lived in it?"

"I can imagine. It would be the four-legged shadow," Dyra replied. "The one that destroyed the village was taller than the spreading trees."

They spent a few minutes thinking about the village and their families, then they reluctantly left the stoneworks and went back to work. Dyra cut and built four wind guards, and Koalee plaited tough fibers, coiling them into a rope for the anchor chain. Raft poles and flood markers were cut from the tallest, straightest trees.

Their plan was to build a low, one-roomed shelter large enough that six grassmen could sleep in it. Koalee meant to work on a ladder, but suddenly she had an idea. She set about constructing steps of stone. She stood back and admired her work when they were done.

They both felt safe and peaceful. Wheelers were keeping their distance. Grass animals would never bother them unless their burrows were threatened. A harmless golden grass snake streaked by. Insects were numerous and noisy, and occasionally a seed bird stopped for a meal. They didn't feel alone.

The shelter was completed on the third day when the sky clouded over, there was a misty rain that produced enough water to allow them to have baths and wash their clothes. The next morning, they took the tree chopper, ropes and knives, backpacked Hoyim, and set off in earnest to break trail.

The work went faster than Radd had predicted. The rain had softened the earth, and the bladed grass trees pulled loose with just a tug of the rope. They were muddy and tired when they came upon another animal track, which they followed gratefully. Then, to their disappointment, it turned in a wide curve and started toward rising sun. They would have to begin clearing again.

"We won't work on this today," Dyra announced. "By the time we get back to the shelter, we'll be hungry for our evening meal."

"The silver trees are so strong," Koalee remarked back at the shelter, as the heavy perfume filled her senses. "Let's eat the smell, instead of food."

"There may not be any food, the trail runner is out on the trail," Dyra said.

"But we put it in the shelter and shut the door," said Koalee. "Dyra, what happened?"

Suddenly he seemed overjoyed and broke into a run. "Koalee, it's *my* trail runner!"

"Returning your trail runner," said Lenk.

Lenk's three children had been hiding in the shelter and ran out as Koalee and Hoyim arrived. There were excited shouts and hugs and kisses and a few tears. Koalee asked breathlessly about their families and was assured they were all well. Lenk appeared puzzled by her worry, but all he said was, "So this is where you're settling."

"Not exactly. We've got three days' hard trail breaking to get to that place," Dyra replied.

"Radd said we'd have help. But Lenk, how much harm did the mower do? How many were killed? Who was hurt?" asked Koalee.

Lenk looked at his oldest son but got no assistance. "What

mower?" they asked.

"You didn't know?"

It turned out that Lenk and his family had been a full week up trail. They'd set out while Dyra and Koalee were still at their first camp in the tall woods, and had come slowly, for the two youngest were small and each had to carry a pack. At one point they made their way through unbroken trail to avoid a place where the woods were cut off. They'd had no idea that the mower had come to the village.

Dyra was happy to hear that, because it meant Lenk had come because he trusted Dyra, not because he was forced to leave. But now they had no way of knowing if others would follow.

Lenk had prepared an enormous stew of roots and greens and a fat grasshopper. He'd even made dumplings. It was the best meal they'd had in days, and the talk was so fast it was hard to keep up. Lenk's daughter Balink took care of Hoyim, so Dyra and Koalee could turn all their attention to the news. Lenk and Rels spoke of finding the raft in the tall woods and camping several nights, and how they'd been sure they'd taken the wrong trail until they came to the signpost. And they had seen the high place. Had Dyra really climbed it? And Koalee?

Lenk and his family listened in awe and were stunned to learn of tall men who rode on the four-legged shadow.

"For tall men to harm grassmen is wrong," Lenk protested. "It spoils the world for me to think of that."

"Oh, but there is hope!" Dyra said. "They're giants, but they are men who must have families, maybe we can stop fearing them and try to find ways to talk to them, to live in harmony."

"A *man* killed my wife and child? That is too evil to think about."

"No, Lenk, it was the animal that did it. The man didn't know. It was not deliberate. Anyway, if the elf is right, where we plan to settle the four-legged shadow never comes," Dyra said with confidence. "I only hope more villagers will follow."

"I backpacked all Dad's fine tools," said Rels, nodding toward his father. "Whether anyone comes or not, we'll build the best village you ever saw."

"We'll build it so strong," piped Tuje, the youngest, "that the mower can't hurt it."

They needed their optimism, for the next two days of trail breaking were arduous, and the more they broke, the longer was the trip back and forth to the shelter. Koalee stayed with the children, and Lenk and his boy Rels worked with Dyra chopping trees. Once they were down, Rels cleared away the branches and undergrowth, but there was still the problem of the stumps. When they were too close together, the grassmen had to dig down until the roots were loose and then tie rope around them to pull them out.

"We'll have to do daily trail maintenance," said Lenk, "or it will soon grow over. There's a task for you, son."

On the fourth day, just as Radd had predicted, they came to the end of the woody grove and stood in matted blade grass by a lake. Choosing a place above the water mark, they went to work with renewed zeal.

"You were the first grassman to come here," Lenk remarked to his friend. "You should name the lake."

"Yes, I'll think about a name."

It was a long way around the lake, and on the sixth day they rested because they were too exhausted to keep moving. But early the next morning they went back to work, determined to complete the trail and build at least one house-sized raft. Meanwhile, at the shelter, Koalee began the task of making strong rope for new anchors.

"We couldn't have done this alone," she told Dyra that night, "We must have been crazy to attempt it."

The trail was finished, ten strong pyles cemented in, and an extra-large raft, lashed and equipped with wind guards, was ready when they went up trail again with the runners. Rels had already begun his task of maintenance and was diligently pulling new trees the moment a sprout showed.

They stopped to eat lunch by the lake. When Koalee saw the clear, clean water, she decided that they must bathe. She took Hoyim into the water with her. Dyra laughed to see his son splashing happily.

"I was going to call it Glass Lake," he said, "but I will call it Hoyim's Lake. My son was the first grassman in it and he took his first swim here."

Lenk had elected to stand guard for wheelers, and suddenly he called, "Listen!"

There were voices up trail. A great crowd filed out of the woods. Friends and family surrounded Dyra. He greeted his parents, his brothers and sister, nieces and nephew. Over their heads he saw that Koalee was in the arms of her family. Amidst the shouts of greeting, of joy and excitement, Gozer came forward.

"There were days of debate before our departure," he reported. "Your village had no leader. Your dolenter and Chief Councillor were both killed by the mower. Then an elf came and advised us. I said I would lead your villagers to you."

"All these people!" Koalee exclaimed. "Thank Life they are safe."

"Our village will move on," said Gozer. "You have your ways and we have ours, and it will be easier to be neighbours. The elf said there was safe land a day no sun from here."

"You'll have to break trail."

"We can easily do that. I've been admiring the new trail you've broken. May we camp with you until it's done?"

"Of course. But we only have one raft. It won't hold half of us," Dyra said.

"We'll have three more by nightfall!" Gozer exclaimed.

He picked up his load and signalled to the group to follow, and then turned once more to Dyra. "I should have listened to you the day of the mower. I made the wrong decision."

Dyra looked at all the friends and relations Gozer had led safely to the new land. "It was Life's decision," he said.

VII

It was spring and Dyra was enjoying a noon rest, sitting in the sun on the top step of his stairs. All around him were the busy sounds of the village. All winter the grassmen had been building, and it was still going on. Houses were as yet roughly finished inside because everyone had been needed on the rafts and houses, the finishing touches had to wait. He had found time to make a stove, a table, a spinning wheel and loom, because they were essential. They had slept on grass until Koalee wove a tick and stuffed it with cotton she had gathered in the autumn. It had been a hard winter. There had been no time to make jars and preserve food and no traders had come.

They had made Dyra Chief Councillor and he gave first priority to the making of mill stones so the village had a mill. All the children had been put to seed collecting, and one day a group of them was sent to explore the animal trail where they found grain trees. Load after load was brought in, and meal had seen them through the cold season.

Three of Dyra's concerns were more pressing than the rest. One was the need for wax. They had no bee man and, until the traders came, there would be a shortage of wax for cooking. It meant training a crew to handle the sticky combs, and it meant some dangerous climbing. He thought about the active young men in the village and who would be suitable for the crew.

Another concern was the need to mount a big expedition, taking the telescope to the high place. There was talk in the village of building a meeting house and finding a dolenter, and Dyra knew, before that happened, the people had to see the mower and the four-legged shadow themselves. He had talked to Gozer about it. If Dyra went, Gozer and his chief villagers would go. Yes, it had to be done and every man who climbed would have to bring his wife. Koalee had managed the climb and so could others. There would be no dark nameless shadows in this village.

Third among Dyra's major concerns was his trade. Over the cold season he had painstakingly made the tools he had been unable to bring, and he had the fairy's diamond as well. Now that Koalee's father was blowing glass again, he should get settled to work once more. Being Chief Councillor weighed heavily on his mind. When planting was done and the high place conquered, they should do something, with Gozer's cooperation, about improving the trail through the tall woods. Then they must mark the trail out of the tall woods at high sun, to beckon the traders.

He heard Lenk's hammer. Lenk must be finished his noon break then, and Dyra should get busy too. Lenk was building a house for the widow from Gozer's village, the woman who had gone down the animal hole with Dyra. In exchange for the house, she would cook for the family and help raise Tuje and Balink. Grass people never married twice, but sometimes widows arranged things this way. Lenk would see that she was comfortable and well provided for, and his children would want for nothing in comfort and care.

"Dyra, is the gate shut? Is it safe to put Hoyim outside?" Koalee asked.

Dyra stirred and called that the gate was closed. As he turned again, something fluttered past him in front of the spreading trees and he felt his mind transported to another world. Surely it was a fairy!

Koalee came out with Hoyim. "What are you thinking about all this time? The peaman?"

Dyra laughed. "I was wondering who carries Violet's shoulder bag for her when Radd is gone."

Koalee laughed too and, because they did, so did Hoyim. Dyra got up and went down the steps to see who he could find to help the peaman.

Was it a fairy, he wondered, or just a leaf blowing in the wind?

PART 2

HOYIM'S TRADE

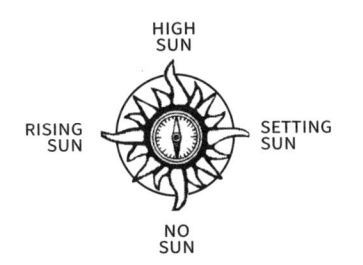

```
        HIGH
         SUN
RISING  ☀  SETTING
  SUN       SUN
         NO
         SUN
```

I

"KOALEE! COME QUICKLY! Doctor wants you."
Koalee was hanging laundry to dry on the line, but at the name "doctor" she dropped the wet clothes into a box and ran to where the young messenger was fidgeting. "Cat!" he told her breathlessly. "It's Ston."

"Where is he?" Koalee asked.

"Doctor's house."

The doctor's wife had died a year previously, and now that Koalee's youngest was in school, she had some free time. The doctor was training her to assist him and was very pleased with her, often referring to her as "his bright assistant."

The doctor's house was on the far side of the village, and in times of emergency it was quite a distance. Running made her short of breath, so she didn't ask any questions, but the child running with her informed her that the cat was dead. There was a brief story about somebody named Kezel pulling the cat's tail just in time to save Ston.

Rels was waiting by the steps of the doctor's house. "Doctor doesn't have much hope for him, Koalee," he said. "He's bad."

"Did you bring him in, Rels?"

"Dad and I. Ston was coming up trail pulling his runner, and the cat pounced out of the grass. Dad shot him three times before he killed him, and Ston would have been gone if it hadn't been for Kezel."

Kezel? Koalee didn't want to waste time asking about this person, so she ran into the infirmary.

Ston lay on the table. The doctor was sewing up a hideous deep gash that seemed to have nearly severed his left shoulder and upper arm. Ston had been given a drowsy herb, and if Koalee hadn't known, she would have taken the patient for dead. He was not a young man, or a very robust one, and now he was so pale he appeared blue. There were deep wounds all over his face.

"Back's worst," said the doctor. "We'll turn him over as soon as we can." He nodded toward the stove where boiled water waited, saying, "Wash him gently and mind you don't start any fresh bleeding. Clean all the wounds. Who else is here?"

"Rels is still here," Koalee said.

The youth came up the stairs three at a time at her call.

"There are three herbs on the top shelf, Rels," the doctor said. "They're marked *heart stimulant*, and on the third shelf down there is one marked *blood*. Bring them and let me check what you find."

Rels did as he was told, and the doctor interrupted his stitching to point to one of the jars. "Take a scant of that and put it in a clean saucepan, and then add exactly three times as much of each of the other herbs. Pour in a cup of boiling water and let it simmer."

As soon as the water had been poured, the doctor said, "Koalee, please get the other jar on the table marked *blood*. Add from that until the mixture is the colour of flaxseed."

Ston was suddenly whiter and bluer, and seemed to be fading away. The doctor bent and began whispering into the man's ear.

Ston breathed, but otherwise showed no improvement.

"It's his back," said the doctor briskly. "Rels..."

Rels helped turn the patient. The absorbent bandages beneath him were soaked through with blood, and the gaping wounds were dark and ugly. The doctor probed them until they bled again, then immediately put on another powder from the shelf. The bleeding stopped, and clean bandages were bound in place. When Koalee had a free hand, she rubbed Ston's arms and legs wherever they were uninjured, and Rels followed her lead. The doctor quickly sewed up the smaller wounds. They noticed with relief that Ston's flesh was beginning to feel warm again, and a hint of colour was returning.

"Not a broken bone," the doctor remarked, as if he could hardly believe it. "One more second and his back would have snapped. He may not walk again though, the way that claw sank into the hip near the spine."

Rels said, "It's easier to put a house together than a body, isn't it?"

The doctor smiled. "Now we turn him again. Easy. I have to finish the shoulder before it's too late."

As he stitched, he told them it was fortunate Ston had become unconscious as soon as the cat grabbed him. Because he was limp, it probably prevented fractures.

"How often have you done something like this?" Koalee asked.

"Not very often. When a grassman meets a cat, there isn't usually anything left for the doctor. Ston was incredibly lucky."

Koalee tied the last bandage, and then replaced the bloody sheet with a clean one, finally covering him with a light, warm blanket. The doctor's wife had made the infirmary blankets out of woven thistledown.

The saucepan had simmered until there was very little moisture left. The doctor cooled it by adding brandy, and Koalee began feeding it to the waking patient in small sips. Ston tried to smile.

"You must lie still," said the doctor. "A grassman doesn't dance on the day of the cat." He sprinkled still another powder into the mixture in the saucepan. "I'm giving you something to ease the pain. You must take every bit of it. Then we'll let you sleep again."

They left the patient long enough to step out on the raft for fresh air. The doctor asked Koalee if she could come back at the supper hour and spend the evening with Ston, so he could visit another patient.

"I can," she replied, "Dyra is very busy making blue lenses for the cornman. The sun has been troubling his eyes."

"Yes. I ordered those lenses."

"I'll leave supper ready and try to persuade Hoyim to help the children with their lessons and see they get to bed on time."

"Doesn't Hoyim enjoy that?"

"I wish I knew *what* Hoyim enjoyed," Koalee sighed. "Nothing pleases him since he left school."

"He must find himself," said the doctor. "Some children take a little time."

"He's thirteen! He should be settled into training for his trade by next year."

"Be patient," advised the doctor. "Every grassman has his place. Certainly there will be a place for a smart boy like Hoyim."

"Dad will be needing me," said Rels. "Thank Life for Kezel."

"Kezel again! Who is Kezel?" asked Koalee, now that she had time to consider it.

Rels laughed. "Apparently he's an eggman," he told her.

"A *what*?"

"I'll tell you another time, when I'm not in a hurry," Rels said. "Anyway, that's something you'd better see for yourself."

As she walked towards home, Koalee checked the shadow and saw that it was time for the noon meal. It was market day too, and she'd meant to go shopping as soon as the washing was hung. Well, there wouldn't be much left now. She would send Hoyim to collect roots and berries instead. He was on trail maintenance with another boy his age, but the trail was in good condition, so the boys usually spent two or three days at home between trips.

Her thoughts wandered to Ston but quickly returned to Hoyim. Be patient, the doctor had said. It was just that Hoyim had always been such a bright and beautiful child, and they had high hopes for him. But ever since he finished his last school year, Hoyim had been moody and lazy. Yes, *lazy* was the word for it. Of course Dyra could have moods too, and he liked to spend time reading and thinking, but Dyra's thoughts were original and purposeful. As for Koalee, she took pride in the fact that she'd always been a practical and busy person. If Hoyim had taken after her, he would have no difficulty deciding what had to be done and then going ahead and doing it.

The children would be coming from school at any minute. Another man, realizing his wife was late, might go ahead and make the noon meal, but she knew better than to count on Dyra. His mind would be on the blue lenses, or possibly on the blue lenses *and* some plan for the village at the same time—but he would not likely focus upon the immediate needs of the family.

As she neared her home, the miller's wife greeted her. She was out delivering meal, once again struggling with a load that was too heavy.

"The trouble is the trail runner, not the meal," she explained. "You know how I was constantly breaking my old one? I asked Lenk to build me one with wood twice as thick. He did, and now I can hardly pull the thing."

Koalee considered the problem. "You'll have to take fewer sacks at a time," she said.

"I'd have to make more trips," the other woman replied.

"Well, is that better than this?"

"I suppose so. I should stop anyway. I'm getting too old for it. If my son hadn't taken guard duty for a whole season..."

"It's ridiculous. Brond's the strongest man in the village. Make him do the deliveries."

"He's the only one who can move the heavy machinery. My husband isn't young himself any more."

Koalee was quite certain the miller's wife would do as she pleased. No one had ever known her to back down easily. She was a hard woman to convince, but Koalee tried.

"You will cut your loads in half," she said. "That's an order from the doctor's assistant. You'll put your shoulders out if you keep this up."

Feeling proud of herself, Koalee waved goodbye and hurried home.

To her surprise, her son Hoyim was in the kitchen cooking. She thought perhaps there was hope for her teenage boy after all. He had grown to be almost the same height as his father.

"Syl and I got these in the lake," he said, indicating three silvery fish that were bubbling merrily away in a pan of oil.

"What a relief! I was worried about what we'd eat."

The fish were Dyra's idea, of course. He'd ordered an expedition to the tall woods and they'd gathered fish and snails at the lake where Violet used to swim. They brought them back and put them into Hoyim's Lake. Here they thrived, so now there were fish to eat, if they were lucky enough to catch them when they were tiny.

"You were at the doctor's?" Hoyim asked.

"I suppose you heard about Ston?" Koalee said.

"I did. I just wish I'd been there to see it!"

"You would have been sick if you'd seen it, believe me."

"Oh, I don't mean Ston. I mean Kezel. The whole village is talking about him."

"Hoyim, just what and who is Kezel?"

The two youngest burst into the house at that moment, home from school and hungry. "Kezel! Kezel!" chorused Nila and Belm together. "Kezel saved Ston, Mother! He pulled the cat's tail. Really he did."

All through the noon meal, the children talked about their new hero, and Dyra and Koalee were able to piece together a story that certainly stretched the imagination. According to what Rels had said at the doctor's, the cat pounced on Ston and had him right under his paws, and Lenk picked up his pebble gun and fired and hit the cat in the face. But the cat didn't let Ston go. Just then Kezel had come out of nowhere and grabbed the tip of the cat's tail. He pulled with all his might, and the cat dropped Ston and turned around so fast they thought he'd have Kezel in an instant. But Kezel grabbed a rope that was hanging from a tree and began to swing back and forth in front of the cat. When the cat came near to getting him, he swung up to a high branch. Meanwhile Lenk had two more good shots at the cat and hit him on a spot in the throat that killed him.

"Where did this Kezel come from?" Dyra wanted to know.

"I think he came swinging in on the end of his rope," said five-year-old Belm. His nine-year-old sister Nila shook her head. "Dad means where does he live?"

"I guess he doesn't live anywhere," Hoyim explained.

Dyra and Koalee exchanged looks. Neither of them could imagine a grassman who didn't live anywhere. "That's impossible."

"That's true," Hoyim insisted. "He travels from village to village. He lives alone, I think—in the tall woods." Hoyim seemed to be very informed.

"*Our* tall woods?" Dyra asked.

"No. Tall woods far away."

"He lives in a tree," said Belm.

"That's true too," said Hoyim. "He told Rels. He builds a house in a tall tree, and he doesn't need a raft."

Koalee tried to imagine a house in a tall tree.

"What kind of stair would he need?" she asked, awed.

The children laughed.

"He doesn't use a stair," Nila told her. "He swings up on ropes. It's fact, Mother. Don't look so unbelieving."

"Doesn't he have a trade?"

"Of course he does! He's an eggman."

"I never heard of such a thing. I mean, I've heard of a foolish young man climbing into a spreading tree once in his lifetime to impress a young lady..." Koalee glanced at Dyra as she spoke "...but no grassman earns a living as an eggman. He'd be dead. Or else he'd be a fool. Only an elf can gather eggs safely."

"Who said anything about 'safely'?" Hoyim asked. "Kezel lives dangerously, Mother."

Dyra had been thoughtful. "I imagine he'll pass on through now," he said hopefully.

"Not if I have anything to do with it," said Hoyim. "We want him to stay. All the boys want him to stay."

"And the girls," added Nila.

"Is Kezel married?" asked Dyra.

"I don't think so. He could live in our tall woods."

Hoyim sensed that his father was unenthusiastic about the idea, so he turned to his mother. "We'd have fresh eggs in the village every week. Just think, Mother. Eggs!"

"Eggs would be very nice," she said, "but they are only for a short part of the year." She knew from Dyra's expression that he was worried.

Dyra seemed to have reached a decision.

"Look, I don't want you children seeing anything of this Kezel or asking him to stay in the village until the council has a chance to meet him and find out the kind of person he is," he said. "He's been a hero and he's saved Ston. We owe him a welcome for that, and we'll certainly give him a banquet and a formal thank you, but when it comes to having someone settle with us, we have to think about that."

"But he wouldn't be with us," said Nila. "He'd be in the tall woods."

"Your father is Chief Councillor," Koalee reminded her. "He must think first of the good of the village."

II

Hoyim was sulky again after his father's dictum, but when Koalee told him she had missed the market and needed his help to collect roots and berries to see them through the next few days, he took a gathering bag and left. Koalee at last completed her laundry and her other household tasks. She knew Hoyim was unhappy that he would be left to look after the children in the evening, but the doctor couldn't leave just anybody to watch over Ston.

Koalee wanted badly to have a talk with Dyra without the children around, but she didn't want to interfere with his work. Lens making was an exacting and painstaking process, and Dyra needed his full concentration. It wouldn't do to keep the cornman waiting too long because the doctor had mentioned the possibility of his going blind unless something was done to protect his eyes from the sun.

Koalee contented herself by studying a book the doctor had lent her on how to apply heat and cold. She must also review the circulation of the blood, and be familiar with the necessary herbs, because the next time the doctor saw her he would ask the ingredients of Ston's medicine, and what each herb was for. She hoped he would teach her the power of suggestion—she had seen him whisper into a patient's ear on other occasions and was curious.

There was so much to be learned! All her life, Koalee had known when to keep a sick person warm, and what herbs to give for fever, for vomiting, or to stop the food from running too quickly through the body. She had known of roots and leaves that stopped bleeding and healed wounds, and she knew of the more dangerous drugs that stopped pain, but she was only beginning to understand how complicated a grassperson's body was. She knew how to immobilize a broken limb, though she wasn't sure whether she would be able to set a broken bone. She knew how to lance boils. She was learning about herbs she'd never heard of, that put patients to sleep or into dream-like states to help them relax or endure pain. The doctor taught her as the cases came in. There were skin rashes caused by heat, and by microscopic insects, and by poisonous leaves, and she not only had to learn to tell the difference between them by their appearance and location, but also which ointments should be used.

"When you are not as busy, I'll teach you to mix herbs and ointments," the doctor had said. "But there is a great deal to it, and what I need most now is for you to tend the sick."

Her neighbour came puffing up the stairs and entered at the open kitchen door, shooing away a leggy mosquito that had alighted there. "Pesky things!" she said. "They're everywhere these days. You weren't at market, Koalee. The doctor needed you?"

"Yes, he did."

"Are you expecting too much of yourself? You have no time for your neighbours any more."

Koalee managed to control a sigh. "Of course I do. I was just about to make a cup of tea."

Her neighbour sat down on the kitchen bench and prepared to stay.

Dyra's voice called from the workroom, "Do I hear teacups? Will you bring me some tea, Koalee?"

Koalee did so, and Dyra looked up from his work with a grin. "You wanted to study, didn't you?" he whispered.

"I am Chief Councillor's wife," she whispered back. "I am hospitable."

They exchanged smiles and Koalee returned to her guest feeling better. All the sweet-shopkeeper's wife wanted, of course, was to hear the details about Ston. Koalee tried to be tactful without revealing too much.

When the neighbour left, Koalee stood for a moment on the raft and looked across the village. She could see at least nine houses from where she stood. Right before her were the rafts belonging to Dyra's father, and to his brother Doba. To the right was the home of the cobbler's assistant, and beyond that the leatherman's house. The leatherman was Lenk's cousin, and his wife was Dyra's sister Creu. At the moment Creu was seated on a bench, shelling seeds. Her brown head was bent over her work, but she sensed Koalee watching and looked up to smile and wave. Creu was a great favourite of Dyra's.

Koalee's own family lived too far away to be visible, but they would be at the shop at this time of day. Her brother Hent was preparing to take over the role of chief glass-blower from her father. Her brother Syl was the cutter and her sister Flon managed the shop. Her mother was probably at home, as usual, doing her housework, neighbouring with Pora and the rootman's widow. From where Koalee stood, she could see the weaver in his garden, fussing with his trees. He had grown so interested in his garden that he seldom did any weaving any more—it was a good thing his son Doen was industrious.

It went through Koalee's mind that if their house were in the country, as it was in the old village, where there were fewer distractions, perhaps Hoyim wouldn't be taking such a long time to make up his mind about a trade. Here in the village he saw the other children and young people every day. Perhaps they talked too much among themselves and that was why they didn't listen to their parents as they should.

The basketmaker's wife was coming along the market street. She made no move to turn down Dyra's Road, so Koalee concluded that she was on an errand.

Koalee called to her, "A pleasant day!"

The basketmaker's wife called back and stopped, encouraging the tiny one who ran by her side to wave to Koalee. Koalee laughed. The basketmaker's wife had three tiny ones too young for school—the one trotting at her side, the one in the trail runner, and the new baby in the backpack. She had a load, but Koalee envied her.

There was no doubt, Koalee decided as she turned back into the house, that she was happy when her mind was focused upon children, meals, and preparing the clothing. Now that she was working for the doctor, they bought their ground meal from the miller, and she was even buying cloth from the weaver while her own spinning wheel and loom sat idle. She wondered if she was really spending enough time teaching Nila to spin and weave.

But the doctor needs me, she told herself, and what I am doing is important. Just think of the knowledge I can pass on to others.

With that thought, Koalee returned to her studies with renewed spirit, and did not break her concentration until Hoyim's return.

Hoyim was in a mood again; his whole manner was petty and impatient. He came in wordlessly and helped himself to a pastry before he spoke.

"When's Father going to call the council together and meet Kezel?" he asked.

"I don't know, and we won't bother him about it until the blue lenses are finished."

"But Kezel may go away."

Koalee felt herself growing irritable. "If he goes, he goes," she snapped. "If he doesn't have the patience to understand how things are done in this village, he doesn't belong here, does he?"

Hoyim looked as if he might have answered her back, but instead he turned in silence and walked out of the kitchen.

"Oh dear," sighed Koalee. The doctor told me to be patient with him and look at me. Where have we failed him? Have we let him think for himself too much? His father is also a person who questions everything.

Koalee was almost afraid to leave the children in Hoyim's charge when he was in a mood like this, but Dyra assured her that he wouldn't put the final touches on the lenses until the morning light, and he could supervise the children for the evening. They agreed that she would stop on her way to the doctor's and ask both of the other councillors to come to a meeting about the eggman.

Koalee ate hurriedly and took a bundle of flatbread. She would prepare soup at the doctor's to feed to Ston, and she could have some too. Then she zig-zagged across the village to deliver the message to the councillors.

Lenk said, "I was going over to see him anyway," adding that he'd heard Ston was still holding steady.

Yansa the potter, who had become paunchy and heavy of jaw, said "Not the meeting house?" and Koalee had to explain to him about the children. She could feel him thinking, What's wrong with Hoyim that he can't be trusted with his own family?

I'm growing much too sensitive about Hoyim, she told herself.

The doctor was packing his trail runner with medicines he might need that evening, but he came back inside to give Koalee instructions. It was so complicated that Koalee felt her mind snap to attention and forget her problems—as if a switch had been flipped in her brain.

Ston was in a half sleep, but if he woke and complained of pain, she had to know exactly how much powder to give him. If the smaller cuts began to burn and itch, as they might, there was an ointment to apply. On no account was she to re-open the serious wounds. If his fever climbed, there was another herb to be brewed, and if it reached the critical level she was to administer a cold sponge bath.

"I hope I won't be long," the doctor told her. "If the cobbler wasn't near death, I wouldn't leave Ston at all. Over-excitement is his greatest risk. If he gets restless, give him another calming brew; it's best to keep him sleepy. If he becomes too restless, use this."

He indicated two straps that passed under the bed where Ston lay, both equipped with buckles. Koalee had often wondered what they were for.

The doctor saw her expression. "That's right. Tie him down. And don't wait too long. If he starts to look dazed and confused, and sits up, get these on him right away, or we may have a sick man running up trail for the tall woods."

Koalee felt very ill at ease. She hadn't expected tending the sick to include a warning like this. She busied herself making a thin broth, in case Ston could take nourishment. Every few minutes she managed to persuade him to take a sip of water, because this was the most important thing of all. Checking his forehead for fever, she found him warm as to be expected, with such wounds. He groaned once. Because he was obviously in pain, she carefully measured a speck of powder into water, and spooned it into his mouth. Koalee smoothed the bed beneath her patient and cooled his brow with a damp cloth.

The doctor was gone longer than she'd expected. The cobbler must be gasping for air again, in one of the attacks which could bring the end of Life. Feeling apprehensive, Koalee wished Dyra would arrive. The meeting must be taking a long time.

Then it happened. Under her hand, Ston's fever began to spike so sharply that Koalee could almost feel his forehead and cheeks bursting into fire. She ran for the basin to start the sponge bath, but even as she did so, Ston began to toss and moan and tried to sit up. Without hesitating, Koalee placed the straps over his chest and thighs and buckled them tight.

I can't believe I'm doing this, she thought. Tying down a friend of mine.

But the doctor never gave orders unless they were important. Ston's hands began to paw wildly. He clawed at the straps, trying to free himself. His eyes looked panicked and unseeing. He clearly didn't know her, or even where he was.

"So this is over-excitement." Koalee made a mental note of every detail so she would recognize its warning signs another time. Nila had been like this once with a fever, but she was small and Dyra had held her, comforting her while controlling her at the same time. Koalee couldn't get Ston to drink water now, because his hands were free and he swung at her with his good arm. To her horror, he found the bandage on his shoulder and began tearing it off.

Desperate, Koalee snatched extra bandages and wrapped Ston's hand into an awkward, useless appendage. Thank Life that she was strong and healthy, for Ston fought like a man totally unaware that he was injured or in pain.

Exhausted, she still had to force more of the sleeping powder into her patient. Beginning this new battle of trying to get him to swallow, she still had to find ways of putting a cold cloth to his face and brow.

"Ston, *please* cool off!" she begged.

The doctor walked in. With an apology for being so long, he added,

"I was afraid of this. What have you been up to?" He smiled at the sight of Ston's now-useless wrapped hand.

"He began to tear off his bandages." Koalee brushed a hand across her own weary face.

The doctor wasted not a moment, sprinkling fresh healing powder on the shoulder wound and re-bandaged it.

"That's good thinking," he said. "But it's my fault. I should have told you to put the strap across his arms, too."

When Dyra finally arrived, Koalee was brewing up the fever tea. "Take this young woman home," the doctor said to Dyra. "She has proved her worth here, tonight." Turning to Koalee, he added, "I hope you can come back again in the morning, Koalee. If he's over the worst there will be no need to stay—but just in case I need you."

"Dyra," she said, as they reached the bottom of the steps and started toward home, "I'm not sure I can keep this up. It isn't fair to you and the children. I'm here all the time."

"He'll recover, and everything will return to the way it was. You helped save Ston's life, Koalee. Do you know anyone else in the village who has the brains, and the interest, to do what you're doing?"

"I wish I could start teaching Nila. But she's too young."

"You'll teach her yet. And someday people will say, 'It was a good thing Koalee learned to assist him, because the doctor's wife died, and now look at all the villagers who know these skills.' Perhaps others in your family will learn."

"I thought I was good at what I do every day, gathering and preserving and making cloth."

"You are. You're a capable grasswoman, Koalee. I know what you mean, though, about wishing you could teach Nila. I wish I could teach Hoyim to make lenses."

"The doctor said to give him time."

"I don't think so. Hoyim is not a lens maker. Belm is already far more interested in the workroom than Hoyim ever was. It looks as if I'll have to wait a few years to pass on my skills."

"You won't force him?"

"Hoyim forced would not be a good lens maker. My father didn't force me. It was expected, of course, because Doba can't do it. Anything else I wanted to do was impossible, anyway."

"What else did you want to do, Dyra?"

Dyra smiled. "I wanted adventure. I wanted to visit fairyland. I wanted to go exploring new territory and found a new settlement."

"But now you've done all that!"

"I used to dream of seeing the red valley, and meeting Nanta."

"The dolenter at Gozer's village is from Nanta's village. If you would be friendlier with him, he might take you there."

"It's too late, Koalee. Nanta left Life many years ago, long before the dolenter Tokra came to Gozer's village."

"I don't suppose Life ever grants anyone the chance to do everything he wants to do," Koalee mused.

After a moment Dyra laughed. "I also wanted to write a history of our new settlement. I haven't done that yet, but I do have the paper and I've made the pens and ink. When the blue lenses are finished, I am going down to the float space to write the first chapter."

"You will! You really will. Dyra, what happened at the meeting tonight?" Koalee asked as they approached their home.

"There's to be a gathering of the entire village tomorrow for the evening meal. All are to bring food. At least, there will be a meeting if we can get word to Kezel. There will be a formal thank you, and a picnic on the grass, and some dancing. The Chief Councillor has decreed that his wife will wear the dress she dyed with red berries, and a fairy diamond in her ear."

Koalee laughed as they came close to their raft, but then she clutched Dyra's arm. "What's that? Dangling there, under the float space? Dyra, be careful! It might be a worm."

The sky was dark, and their only light was faint moonlight. Dyra picked up a stick and touched the thing; it didn't seem to be alive. He took it in his hands. "It's a rope."

"Oh, no! Someone is trying to swing up into the seed tree. What will come of this?"

Dyra tugged at the rope. "It's well fastened. It's Hoyim's doing I'm sure, but there's not enough space for Hoyim in the float space. He must've done this for Nila and Belm."

"Do you suppose Hoyim is doing any sensible thinking? Do you suppose he has a dream he's keeping from us?"

"Perhaps. I don't know what it might be, Koalee. Maybe he wants to get to a high place where he can see everything. A man needs a lot of courage for that."

Koalee put her hand on the rope and spoke softly, for fear Hoyim would overhear. "As long as his high place isn't simply a bird's nest in a tall tree," she said.

III

DYRA HAD BEEN JOKING about the diamond in her ear, of course, but Koalee found that he was serious enough about her wearing it. Years ago he'd mounted the fairy's diamond in the end of a rod, so he could use it for glass cutting. Now he'd figured out an ingenious way to fasten the rod to her dress so she could wear the diamond as a piece of jewellry.

"Violet gave the diamond to all of us," he explained, "and I've been using it exclusively for work all these years. I thought it was time we let people see it."

Koalee felt wonderful. The diamond sparkled on her berry-red dress, her cheeks glowed with excitement, and she laced the bodice of her dress tightly so it would show her plumpness to advantage. She pinned her long wavy hair up on top of her head and went to check on the children.

The boys were scrubbed and combed and dressed in their best. Nila had a new dress of blue linen and a ribbon for her hair. As Koalee tied the ribbon, she had a vague premonition. She thought about how often her daughter had peculiar insights about the village and the people in it. It had never occurred to Koalee that Nila was very different from the boys. She was delicate, that was true. If there was illness in the family, it was Nila who was most likely to have it, but she was mostly a very ordinary little girl. She liked to talk a lot, and laugh and play. She was friendly, seldom alone, and she had a thoughtful side. She could be outspoken, but that was not an unusual trait in this family.

Suddenly Koalee asked, "Nila, have you ever been in the sleeping room in the weaver's house?"

No, Nila had never been there.

"Then how did you know that the weaver and his wife slept in a bed made of the wild cherry tree and that they had a red mat on the floor?"

"I don't know. I just knew."

"Did you ever see the door to the sleeping room open?"

"I don't think so." Her daughter squirmed because Koalee was taking too long with her hair.

"How did you know that Brond spilled a whole basket of meal the other day, before anyone else in the village knew?"

"I saw it."

"But you were in school."

"I see things sometimes."

"In your mind? Like an elf?"

Nila gave her sunniest smile. "Just like an elf, Mother."

Koalee shook her head. "Nila," she said, "are you going to be another fuelman?"

"The fuelman doesn't see things. He just has hunches."

"How do you know that?"

"He told me."

That was something else about Nila, Koalee thought. She seemed to be on familiar terms with every single person in the village. As for "seeing things", there were grass people who could talk to the elves in their minds – Dyra's experience was not unique --and it was known among some children. Yet Dyra had been the only link to Radd. Koalee wondered why she'd had that strange feeling about Nila. She must talk to Dyra about it.

Dyra was wearing his new coat. He looked wonderful in his meeting clothes. Now that he was older, Koalee had made him a coat that was a little longer. He looked very much the Chief Councillor.

Three baskets of food sat ready on the table, fresh fruit, various breads, and fried grasshoppers. No one would accuse Dyra's family of not bringing their share to the picnic supper.

Everyone in the village had caught the excitement. People waved to them from windows as they passed, calling. "We'll be there in a minute."

Many of the villagers were gathered on the grass beside the meeting house when they arrived. They greeted Dyra's brother Hryn and his wife Neev, who were shepherding their three children. The sweet-shop keeper's wife, who usually wore the sourest face in the village, was laying out her pastries with a broad smile. Koalee's brother Syl, the glass cutter in their family business, was at the centre of a small knot of people. Syl liked to spend every spare minute out on Hoyim's Lake in his bark boat, fishing. The grassmen made much of it.

"Did the wind blow you in, Syl?"

"Fish weren't catching, eh?"

"I don't see you at the end of the lineup when I put my fish in the market!" Syl teased.

Creu and Romo arrived holding hands and beaming with pride over twelve-year-old Pettis, who was bright and talented. The weaver's wife chased away a grasshopper that had landed on her picnic basket, squashing the contents badly. A fussy woman, she was looking enviously at Lenk's widow (it was their custom to call those adopted by a family that person's widow), whose dress of soft brown had tiny, almost unnoticeable puffs of creamy lace at her wrists and a wonderful new style of petals. Tall and slender, with a touch of grey in her hair, the widow was beautiful and graceful, educated and well-mannered too. Then the weaver's wife regained her composure. The miller's wife had arrived.

"Will you look at what the miller's wife is wearing tonight!" the weaver's wife whispered to Yansa's wife, and they shook their heads in mutual glee.

The miller's wife provided a great deal of amusement with her outlandish clothes. Tonight she was in a black jacket with stand-up shoulders, appliqued all over with enormous white flowers, worn over a puff of bright orange skirt that made her look like a roly-poly ball.

Syl's wife, Deeka, murmured to Koalee, "The colours that woman wears! It's a wonder a big bird doesn't pick her off."

"They think she's a flower," was the answer.

Seeing that Nila was staring with open delight, Koalee reminded her daughter to be polite—but she had to turn away to hide her laughter.

When Lenk's son Rels arrived with the eggman, the children's exuberance was matched only by the momentary surprise of the adults. The eggman was not properly dressed for the occasion. His skin was bronze and glistened as though he had bathed in gold. But he wore no coat, though the evening chill was coming and the occasion was formal.

Koalee whispered to Dyra, "If he has no permanent house, he probably has no extra clothing."

"Possibly so." Dyra frowned, but he led the other councillors forward to greet Kezel formally and thank him for saving the life of Ston.

Kezel didn't bow or make a fine speech. He just said, "I'm glad to know you," and held out his hand in the grassman's informal greeting.

"This is a strange man, Nila," Koalee remarked to her daughter. "I don't understand his ways."

Nor could she understand his appearance. His shirt had a wide collar that bared his shoulders. His trousers were gathered below the knees and tucked into leggings made of strips of cloth wound around his leg until they disappeared into tightly laced boots. His hair was curly, and cropped so that it fuzzed all over his head like a seeded dandelion. In his left earlobe he wore a hoop of gold. Besides the rope on his belt, he carried another long rope looped about his left arm. Only his dagger in its sheath looked like standard grassman equipment.

The eggman sensed the disapproving stares of the adults, and he apologized with ease. "Please forgive the way I'm dressed. I don't get invited to banquets every day." His voice had a richness and candour about it such as no one in the village had ever heard, and his smile seemed to light up the entire assembly.

It was then that Koalee realized to her consternation that the eggman was incredibly handsome. Tall and lithe, he carried himself with such confidence. His eyes were clear and piercing. Lenk had always been considered the best looking man in the village, and Dyra was handsome, as was Doen the weaver's son—but nobody had ever seen a grassman with the dashing air of Kezel.

Because he was the Chief Councillor, Dyra invited Kezel to sit with his family for the supper. Koalee found herself blushing and embarrassed when she met him. The other councillors and their families sitting with them seemed quieter and shyer than usual.

To break the tension, Dyra asked the eggman about his origins. Kezel revealed only that he came from setting sun, and had travelled far, over many years. He seemed more willing to talk about his work, confirming that he made his living gathering eggs and selling them at village markets. Even in the largest villages nobody could compete with him.

"When you have a lot of eggs for sale you can sell cheaper than anyone else," he said.

The youngest children were watching him open-mouthed.

"Aren't you afraid?" Hoyim asked.

"Afraid? Wouldn't you be afraid, swinging from branch to branch in a high tree, with a mother bird swooping at you from one side and a father bird attacking from the other? Fear is exciting! Fear is thrilling. That's why I do it."

"Not for the money?" asked Koalee's brother Hent.

"I don't need money. I have no wife and family. All I need is a house in a tree and what I can carry."

The grassmen were puzzled. It was impossible for them to think in terms of fear as thrilling. Grassmen focused on safety.

"I can't understand a man not having a wife," said Yansa.

"There are other ways of getting satisfaction," said Kezel, and the villagers exchanged looks of dismay. Did he mean that his "thrilling" fears were enough for him? Or did he perhaps mean that he might go so far as to interfere with another grassman's wife or daughter? Surely not.

Dyra knew that he should find out about that, but he didn't dare ask in the presence of so many others, so he let it go. He also wanted to ask if the eggman planned to stay for long, but he was afraid their guest might take it as an invitation, so instead he asked, "How did you ever get started at such a dangerous trade?"

The eggman's ready laughter showed that he enjoyed the question.

"I went up the first time on a dare," he explained. "I told the other boys I could climb to the top of the tallest tree, and they all came to watch. I took a hatchet and ropes—we'd been studying knotting at school—and it took me a long time, but branch by branch I got to the top. If the boys hadn't been watching, I'd have quit halfway or sooner. But after doing it once it got easier. I invented a basket sling that could carry an egg or two, and I started raiding nests. That's when it got really dangerous. Studying birds, I learned how they attack if the nest is threatened, so I knew what to expect. My best chance is to wait for one of their enemies to come along. Sometimes both parents will set off to chase a predator, and that's when I can swing in and out before they know what's happened."

The children were awestruck, and the more impressed they became, the more anxious their parents felt. Kezel's quick senses were aware of that, but he did not slow down at all. "There's nothing like swinging in a sling in the top of a tall tree!" Kezel said directly to the children. "The speed. The wind in your hair. Just think of it! I go up there and fly with the birds! It's no wonder that I choose to stay in this trade."

Dyra opened his mouth to suggest that the dancing begin, but Kezel reached for another slab of red fruit. It would be rude to interrupt while the guest of honour was still eating. Kezel took advantage of this extra time to add unwelcome news.

"I've built myself a house in the tall woods high sun," he announced. "I was collecting, and scouting around for villages, when I saw the cat. Had you not invited me tonight, I would have been to see you today in any case. I would like permission to sell eggs in your market as long as I'm in the tall woods."

Dyra was caught unprepared, and instinctively turned to Koalee. Koalee was thinking fast. Obviously it was too late to stop Kezel from settling in their tall woods, and it would be nice to have eggs. Although she felt apprehensive, she nodded to Dyra, who then turned to Lenk. Lenk raised a questioning eyebrow to the widow, who had been his helper for many years, and she too nodded. Yansa's wife had been nudging her husband to follow their lead, and soon it was unanimous.

"Our village is large," said Dyra. "You can't possibly supply enough eggs for every table. There will be fighting over them."

"Send the trail boys with trail runners," challenged Kezel, "and I guarantee you we'll come in with eggs for every table in town."

Dyra still looked skeptical.

"All right then, a wager. I'll wager you all the money I make in the entire year against your wife's diamond that I can put an egg on every village table next market day. At one quarter the usual price."

Dyra's face darkened. "We don't make wagers in this village," he said.

Kezel apologized, but his apology seemed more light-hearted than serious.

Dyra turned to the musicians and suggested that the dancing begin.

Dancing was clearly one of Kezel's favourite pastimes, and they couldn't have found a better way of entertaining him. He maintained formality well enough not to dance until the Chief Councillor had first danced with his wife, and then he immediately asked to dance with Koalee. Koalee was quite breathless by the time it was over. To everyone's amazement Kezel made the rounds of every grasswoman in the village and kept up his energy as long as the musicians played. He danced several times with Koalee's sister Flon, whose mood seemed to match his own. Unlike Koalee and their sister Pora, Flon resembled their father. She was tall and slender, with eyes of very bright blue, and she walked as if she might suddenly sprout wings and become airborne with the birds. Dancing, she was light as a leaf.

"Kezel will be too tired to swing on any ropes tomorrow," Dyra remarked. "Maybe I should have made the wager."

It was a wonderful party, except for an exciting moment when a spark from the campfire caught in grass nearby. The men rushed to get the fire beaters, while women climbed to the neighbouring houses and brought back all the dew water they could find to throw on the fire.

Dyra watched Kezel in the thick of it, wielding a fire beater along with the villagers, and felt a twinge of admiration for the young man. He was wild all right, and a dangerous influence for the children. But his mind and body appeared to function with absolute perfection.

No, he thought, It's a good thing I didn't make that wager.

And it was, because on market day Hoyim and the peaman's son and the other trail boys pulled trail runners into the village, following a triumphant eggman who was pulling the fifth load. As promised, there was an egg on every table in the village that day.

IV

Koalee spent the night at the infirmary watching Ston while the doctor stayed with the cobbler because his breathing was laboured. Ston was a good patient, eating well, submitting without complaint to the painful changing of his dressings, and speaking quite normally when he was not in a drugged sleep. He still needed powders for pain, and he could not sit up. Koalee had little to do but feed him, administer his medicines, and keep him clean, but he couldn't be left alone because he was unable to help himself. His back and shoulder were terribly swollen and discoloured—but his body, stronger than they had expected, was gradually winning the fight.

It was not so with the cobbler. The doctor returned just before sunrise and told Koalee the sad news. "We kept him in the fresh air all night, but he got worse. If I ever have another case like this, I'm not sure I'll put them outside. There's so much we don't know."

Ston had been dozing, but he muttered, "Did you say the cobbler died?"

"Yes, Ston. I'm afraid so."

"Just think," Ston mused. "I've come through all this, and he's the one who had to go from Life."

"You're a lucky man, Ston," said the doctor. "But while we're on unhappy topics, I think it's time to tell you—that left arm won't be much good to you again. The muscles were too badly torn."

"I know that, doctor. I've been lying here thinking what's to become of me. I've no wife and family any more to care for me."

The doctor knew that Ston was worried about far more than his left arm. "You haven't a worry in Life," he assured Ston. "You know our village cares for its own. The cobbler's wife is a widow now. Give her time and she might decide to be adopted."

Ston gave a wry smile. "This time I'd be the adopted one, I'm afraid," he said.

Koalee hurried home to give the news to Dyra. After thirteen years, there still was no permanent dolenter in the village, and Dyra was in no hurry to find one. The dolenter from Gozer's village came whenever he was needed, and Dyra respected him, but treated him formally and kept his distance. It irked Koalee, and she and Dyra had words about it more than once. She thought the dolenter Tokra was a very fine man. But Dyra couldn't rid himself of his resentment of the dolenter in their old village. In any event, Dyra would send for Tokra now, to hold rites for the cobbler.

The first step was to send Hoyim to find out if Gozer's trail maintenance boys were at the raft no sun of town. If they weren't, then a messenger would be dispatched to Gozer's village at once.

Hoyim complained about being roused, but he went, and came back with the news that Gozer's boys hadn't been seen for two days.

"Send girls," said Nila, sleepily entering the kitchen and sniffing around to see if breakfast had started.

"Trail is grassman's work," Dyra said.

"You say you want to try new things, and then you don't."

"All right. When you can shoot the bow as well as your mother, when you can pull the trail runner, when you spend the night alone on a temporary raft, then I'll send you with messages to Gozer's village. Does that satisfy you?"

Nila grinned and set out dishes for their gruel.

Koalee stayed up until the family had eaten and the children were at school, and then fell asleep. She drifted off, wondering foggily if Hoyim had remembered to take a flint. Neither he nor the peaman's son was any use with a fire stick.

Koalee dreamed of water—water everywhere, rising so high she thought it would come right over the edge of the raft. When she awoke, it was raining so heavily she knew the teacher would send the children home from school. Surely Hoyim would have the sense to turn back from trail?

She tried to check to see if the children were coming, but the wind was too strong. Buckling the heavy storm-cord to her belt, she fought her way to the wind guards to make sure they were securely fastened. Her neighbour was doing the same thing and trying to call to Koalee, but the wind carried away the sound of her voice. It was several moments before Koalee understood. The teacher wouldn't send the children home in this storm; they would be safe in the school.

Koalee's ankles were awash as rain flooded the raft. Soaked through and through, she checked the last two wind guards, clinging to the fence to keep from being blown over the edge.

She turned to fight her way back to the gate and was startled to see something standing inside the fence. The day had grown dark as evening and she thought for an instant it might be a giant insect. Then the figure spoke, saying, "Koalee, let me help you."

"Radd?"

It really was Radd. He helped her into the house, where he stood smiling with water dripping from his face and clothing. There was no sparkle of gold dust in his hair now, and he was a bedraggled-looking elf, but he hadn't aged a single day.

"I don't usually get caught in storms," he said. "Koalee, you and the villagers must stop buying eggs."

"Is that what you came to tell me? In the midst of *this*?" Koalee grabbed a cloth to dry herself. Shivering, she began building up the fire.

"That's what I started out to do. Kezel gathers too many eggs. He takes eggs that won't be re-laid and doesn't even remember to thank Life. The birds are unhappy about it, and so am I. If the village stops buying, he'll stop gathering."

"He'll move on to other tall woods," Koalee pointed out, still shivering.

"If he does, I'll follow him," the elf replied. "Koalee, get into dry clothing. You'll become ill."

Koalee went to her sleeping room and changed from the skin out.

She put on her old cover clothes and came back wrapped in her heavy cloak.

"You look just as you did the first time I saw you in the tall woods," said Radd.

"You have a good memory."

"Yes, I have total memory," he said factually, then looked up at the way the wind was bending the spreading tree. "At the moment there are more pressing problems than birds, at least for you."

"My own family will be at the shop. I'm sure Dyra's father is home, but I'm worried about Dyra and the children. Dyra said something about going to the tannery to find Lenk."

Radd read her mind. "I can't move any farther in this, Koalee. I was very lucky to reach my destination the first time. The power in a storm disrupts our thought connections. When it abates, I'll check the school for you. The lake is rising very fast."

"You told us the lake never came above the water line," Koalee reminded him. "We've been here thirteen years and it never has."

"There hasn't been a storm like this in longer than that," said the elf. "And you know the houses on this street are the lowest in the village."

"The doctor's house is high. I hope Ston is in no danger."

"Oh, yes. Ston, and Kezel's grand entrance. Sometimes I suspect him of staging these things. There's usually some excitement wherever that grassman goes."

Koalee asked, "How is Violet?"

Radd laughed. "Violet will always be the same. She's a day or two older and a day or two smarter, but no wiser. You could see her if you tried. She still spends a lot of time in your tall woods."

"And Golden?"

"Golden," he said, with a frown on his face, "has been travelling with the eggman. The friendship will be useful, but I can't explain it yet."

The news embarrassed Koalee a little. Grassmen should travel with grasswomen, not with fairies. And then only when they were properly married. She turned to the stove to see if the water was boiling for tea. Through the sail-shaped window she could see that the deluge continued unabated.

"Oh Life," she prayed silently. "If the boys went up trail before this started, let them be on a raft or else in a very tall tree." But she knew there was only one tall tree between the village and the tall woods, and how could they climb it anyway? Hoyim was not an eggman; he was only a thirteen-year-old boy.

"You will have some loaf?" Koalee asked. "Nut meat? Some pancakes with peameal in the center?"

Radd nodded and added, "Your village is thriving."

Koalee was desperate to keep her mind off the flood. "I have melon juice," she added. "We just siphoned off a melon yesterday. You'd like that."

"Settle and eat, Koalee. Please don't worry about me."

Koalee went to stand at the window. "It's come, Radd. The water is lapping under the float space next door, so it's reached ours, too. I haven't been in a free-floater in nearly twenty years."

"This is going to be one."

"My neighbour has tethered herself in the doorway to watch, in case she has to open the wind guards. I should do the same."

"You daren't open them too soon. A gust could hurl us into the flood, house and all."

Koalee buckled the tether to her belt once more, while Radd buckled another. They fought their way out to the raft and looked down the stairs. The water had already covered seven or eight steps.

"It's coming fast," said Koalee, fighting a tremor in her voice. "We can let the center guards go on all but the wind side."

Dyra had built the wind guards so they were safe, but at the same time easy to handle. When they were undone, the big bolts slid back fairly easily. There were still three guards to go when the water was at the top step—and then Radd noticed that the sweet-shop keeper's wife next door was having trouble. Within minutes, unless her raft floated free, the water could enter her house and she might drown. Despite the wild wind and pelting rain, Radd didn't hesitate. He disappeared and, an instant later, reappeared in his elfin form on the neighbour's raft. With his help, a stubborn bolt came undone. Then he was back, helping Koalee as she struggled to reach the last wind guard. By now the water was lapping over the edge of the raft. They breathed with relief as the raft tilted and took to the water, tugging at the anchor rope but riding safe.

Koalee watched with unblinking eyes. "Since the lake is up, it will take a long time to go down."

"It depends on how soon everything dries up," said Radd.

"There won't be any food in the school, or if someone is up a tree. I hope the doctor is home with Ston."

※ ※ ※

"It can't storm like this forever. I'll investigate as soon as I can; I promise you."

Koalee had to content herself with that. She busied herself making up a couch where the elf could sleep that night.

"I'm not used to such a luxury," he said, almost in jest. "I sleep on the floor of the woods, as you well know." He was listening intently again. "I have bad news," he said suddenly.

"Someone has drowned?"

"I'm afraid so but it isn't clear. I think... There's another emergency! Your neighbours are cutting their anchor cords."

They dashed to the door. Koalee grabbed the tether in passing and fumbled in her haste to put it on. The raft was already tilting as the anchor reached the limit of the rope.

In a moment, raft and house would be tugged into the flood. Koalee slid downward toward the fence, thankful that it was there, and wrapped her legs around a post for safety. She seized her knife and began to hack at the anchor cord. Radd was behind her, holding Koalee tightly by her belt. With his other hand, he unfastened the hatchet. "Stay back," he said, "I've got it."

Through the hammering rain, the hatchet severed what was left of the rope. Now they were up to their waists in water, which had reached beyond the doorsill and was entering the house. The rope snapped; the raft titled crazily for a minute and then began to spin in dizzying circles. It hit one of the flood markers with such an impact that Koalee thought it had broken. Life carry us into the center of the village, she prayed.

But it was not to be. The raft was being swept away from the village instead. Koalee looked to the elf for reassurance, but Radd was listening to his inner voice. "I have to leave you, Koalee," he said after a moment. "I'm needed in the village. Keep calm, and you'll be all right." And then he was gone.

Koalee watched him materialize at the nearest house. She checked the raft poles and her supplies. There was food and fuel enough to last a few days, if she was careful. All she could do now was wait and hope. It occurred to Koalee that if she wasn't so worried about her family and friends, she might even enjoy the excitement.

❋ ❋ ❋

As soon as they heard that all the houses in the lower street had to cut anchor, the children had visions of their parents being lost forever. The teacher reassured them that their houses were built to keep them safe and they would be unharmed.

When finally the rain slowed, the men went out in the bark boats to distribute food where it was needed, or to bring people to higher ground. It was slow work, and they could only find three of the four boats. The children were all in the school, and as the school raft was high, it was decided to leave them there. Two women were rowed over to help prepare meals for all of the children and the teacher. Blankets and food were brought in.

The doctor had been shopping when the storm began. While the shopkeepers urged him to stay on one of their rafts until it was over, a premonition told him it would be a bad one, and he insisted upon going home because of Ston. He was nearly drowned fighting his way up the slope to his house, and by the time he reached the stair to the infirmary, the muddy water was swirling to his knees. He was chilled and exhausted.

"You shouldn't have come through this," Ston told him from his bed. "I'd have been all right."

"That's just it," said the doctor, getting out of his wet clothes. "I was afraid you'd take a notion to go out and unlock the wind guards if a free-floater came."

Ston knew he was joking. The doctor sneezed loudly, and Ston frowned. "I might undo wind guards," he said, "but I can't look after you if you get sick, doctor."

"I won't get sick," the doctor assured him, taking an herb from his shelves to brew a tea for himself. "The only trouble is, you and I will live on meal and roots for a few days, unless this goes down fast. My trail runner is floating in the lake by now, with all the nice fresh fruit and morels I bought."

When Radd appeared on the raft, the doctor assured him that they did not need food. "Ston and I aren't going to starve. Is anyone drowned, or hurt?"

"Balink."

"Oh no, not Balink! Drowned?"

"Yes. At least I've made no contact."

"The baby?"

"The baby is fine. Balink left him for a minute to see her foster mother next door, and when they realized the rain was really bad, she went back. The water had covered two or three steps by the time Balink reached her house. Her foster mother saw her slip and go under, and she did not come back up. She couldn't reach her, of course. I took the baby to his grandmother. Balink's husband is there now."

"She...You haven't found her?"

"No."

The doctor recalled the day of the four-legged shadow, when Lenk's wife and one of the twins were killed. "Does Lenk know?" he asked.

"Not yet. Lenk is still building at the tannery. I have information that the builders are safe on the tannery raft."

"We're going to be picking people up all over the countryside after this goes down."

The doctor stood in the open doorway surveying the flood, but his mind was on Balink and what a dreadful loss she would be to the village. Then something in the distance caught his eyes. "What's that?" he asked. "That's not one of our boats."

The elf laughed. "No, that's a fairy boat. A fairy has been sailing it on a lake in the tall woods."

"Have the fairies come to help us, then?"

"I doubt it. But it looks as if they have lent their boat."

Grass people stood at windows and on their rafts and watched in awe as the fairy boat glided up the river that had recently been the street of shops. It was long and narrow as a pea pod, with a curved prow that cut effortlessly through the water, and it was winged with a sail of violet silk that blended exquisitely into water and sky. The other side of the sail was a glittering gold that shone so brightly it looked as if the sun had broken through the dark sky and the misty curtain of rain.

The boat came at a speed much faster than the simple bark boats of the grass people. The eggman was on board, handling the sail as deftly as he handled his tree ropes. He tossed a rope to the potter, who anchored it securely, and then Kezel jumped out and climbed up beside the potter.

"I've come to offer my services. A fairy I know has lent me this boat," Kezel announced hurriedly. "Where is your Chief Councillor?"

"Life knows," said Yansa. "We're worried about Dyra. He left early with his son and the peaman's son, in the direction of the tannery. He wanted to see Lenk about the cobbler's funeral."

"The boys would have gone up trail for the tall woods."

"It's a long day to the tall woods. They wouldn't have had time to get to the temporary shelter," said Koalee's father, who was particularly upset.

"I passed the temporary shelter," said Kezel. "All you could see was the peak of the roof. If the boys had been there, they'd have cut anchor. Our only hope is that they were near spreading trees when the lake came up."

"There aren't any spreading trees up trail," said Yansa pessimistically.

"There are silver trees," said a new voice, and they looked around to see Radd. "If the boys had sense to realize how bad the storm would be, and went to the silver trees, they might be all right."

"Get in the boat and save your strength," Kezel said. "We'll check the tannery first, for Dyra, and then we'll go to the silver trees. At the speed this boat goes it won't take us long."

Radd saw the logic in the plan, so the two boarded the fairy boat.

"I swear to Life," said Yansa, watching them glide away, "that eggman is half elf."

But Kezel was only a grassman and, had Radd not been with him, he would have passed Dyra by, because Dyra was not far from the village. He had been to the tannery and back again, and when the water reached his ankles, he looked around in vain for anything to climb except some seed trees. His survival instincts told him to go to the right of trail where the land was higher, and he fought his way into a thicket of seed trees where he climbed one that was taller and sturdier than the rest. There he settled on a comfortable branch about halfway up, to wait until the storm was over.

Dyra had a long wait. The storm beat him almost senseless, and he anchored himself with his rope in case he should lose consciousness. He hoped Koalee would unfasten the wind guards. After a time the water rose halfway up to his feet, and was still coming fast. Trying not to panic, Dyra cut notches higher in the tree and edged his way up. He clung to the tree with his own strength, praying to Life that it was strong enough to both hold his weight and stand against a flood.

Later, Dyra saw one of his neighbours' houses rafting by. He called to them, but his voice was lost in the storm. All he could do now was worry. Had the children been at home?

Dyra edged his way to the very top of the tree and roped himself as tightly as he could, trying to come to grips with the realization that this might be his last day in Life.

Time went on. When Dyra felt strong enough, he prayed for Koalee and the children, and for Hoyim and his friend up trail, for all his loved ones in the village. At last the seed tree gave under the pressure of the water, and Dyra felt himself falling with it. He was too weak to undo the rope. With a forceful bounce, the tree came to rest against its neighbour, settling itself against a strong upper branch. Exhausted beyond belief, Dyra threw himself upon the goodness of Life and rested his head against the saving branch and slept.

A voice spoke in his mind, awakening him. I am picking up your thoughts, Dyra.

Where are you?

Dyra was ill. His body shook with cold and hunger, and yet his face felt hot as fire. His stomach was rolling. His head pained. His sight was blurred, but his mind said automatically, right of trail.

Dyra realized the cold flood waters were up to his knees. He was hearing voices in his mind. He must be close to death.

"Koalee?" he mumbled.

Now he was seeing visions. A boat such as one could see only in dreams wove its way among the tops of the seed trees, flying a sail of violet and gold. He imagined he saw Radd on board. He hadn't seen Radd for many years.

It is paradise, he thought. It is very beautiful. And then it seemed the eggman was unfastening his rope and helping Radd to get him into the boat. They edged out of the seed trees and flew over the water.

"I live in Truth!" said Dyra, and thought he'd shouted it.

When Dyra woke, he was lying in a bed next to Ston's, swathed in warm blankets. The doctor said, "You threw up everything in your stomach and it wants filling again. Open your mouth and take this soup. It will bring your strength back."

Dyra sat up weakly. "Koalee? The children?"

"We don't know about Hoyim, Dyra, but the children are safe on the school raft. Koalee decided to cut anchor and go for a voyage. Don't worry about her. The elf is here. When the flood goes down he'll locate all our drifters. He's searching for Hoyim now."

Dyra lay back gratefully on the pillow. "Did I come here in a boat?"

"Yes, you did."

"Did it have a sail of purple and gold?"

"Yes, it did. It was a fairy boat."

"Thank goodness," said Dyra. "I thought I was seeing things."

Meanwhile, the fairy boat was out in the centre of the flooded Hoyim's Lake, heading for the opposite shore. There it picked up the trail and raced with the wind until it was abreast of the silver trees. Their odour was clean and strong after the rain, and the boat turned toward them as if drawn by their scent. When Radd found the boys, his first thought was that they would no doubt have survived for a week. They'd quickly gathered and chopped enough branches to lash together a rough raft that was fastened securely, ready for use in case they needed to float. They were up there now, trail runner and all, well fed, wrapped in blankets, simply waiting for the flood waters to recede.

As he reached to help load the refugees onto their boat, Radd joked, "I think I'll leave you here. You can start a settlement."

But Kezel brought the fairy boat to the base of the tree and the refugees were loaded on board.

"Do you know if anyone else was up trail?" Radd asked.

"I don't think so," said Hoyim. "Dad was going to send a message to Gozer, but we couldn't find anyone free, so he was going to go and talk to Lenk about whether they should postpone the rites. We didn't see anyone else up trail."

When Radd told him what had befallen his parents, Hoyim met the news of Dyra's rescue with vast relief, but about Koalee he laughed. He had no doubt in the world that the raft would carry her safely to a landing place.

Radd went off to see if he could find anyone else who needed help, and the eggman took the boys to the village before sailing to the tannery. A search led Kezel to a clump of spreading trees.

"We blew in here," said the tanner, "A branch damaged my roof, but it's good shelter, so we won't pole out until the water goes down."

Kezel asked if they had enough food, and was told that Tuje, Lenk's younger son, had taken the tanner's bark boat and gone into the village for supplies.

"Well, I guess you don't need me," said Kezel. "Good luck!" He sailed away to search for more survivors. He passed two of the floating houses, but no one wanted to abandon his house to return to the village. The rafts were drifting gently, now that the wind had died, and they all hoped to be able to pole back to their pyles.

Only when Kezel returned to the village did he learn that Balink was drowned and her younger brother was in a state of shock over the news. And so he turned the prow of the fairy boat and sailed back to the tannery to bring Lenk and Rels back to their grieving household. The eggman was glad to take his leave.

"We owe you another debt," said Yansa.

"I'm good in an emergency," said the eggman simply. "I'll be on my way now."

The villagers watched until the gold and violet sail disappeared across the lake, still weaving the same dreamlike spell.

"I can't believe this happened," said Yansa. With Dyra in infirmary and Lenk in mourning, the entire burden of government lay on his shoulders.

One mournful toll of the bell on the guard tower told them that the boatmen had a job to do. No one had remembered, in the midst of the crisis, that Duff the hunter was alone on the tower, still standing watch.

V

KOALEE WAS CHILLY. The wide expanse of water frightened her and intensified her loneliness, but she didn't dare stay inside the house. For one thing, she tended to seasickness, and she had to be in the fresh air. For another thing, she might run into an obstacle or floating debris unless she was on the alert with the raft poles.

As a result, she ate cold food, though she did go inside often enough to keep the fire smouldering and the water warm. She had to have a spot of heat somewhere, to compensate for this dismal voyage. She longed for the sun to shine and considered that, if it grew warm on the raft, she might be able to do a little studying, but the day continued dark as evening. She wanted badly to get some sleep, but it was more important not to be sick, so she brought their most comfortable chair out and prepared to sleep sitting up. It would be dangerous not to be watching, but it would soon be too dark to see anyway. She would just have to trust to luck. She made sure that the gate was firmly locked, so she wouldn't slide off the raft, and double checked the raft poles to see that they were securely fastened. Then she wrapped herself into a cocoon of three blankets and let herself drift.

If the raft bumped into any obstacles in the night, Koalee never knew. She woke violently ill and threw up over the fence railing. Then she crawled back to her blankets and curled up on the raft beside the chair. She was still there when daylight came, and someone was shaking her, saying, "Koalee. Please wake up!"

Koalee screamed. She was ill and dizzy. The figure was fluctuating before her eyes, but she had never seen anything so terrifying. It appeared to be human, and yet its skin was a hideous texture and black as tar.

It said, "Koalee, don't be frightened. It's me. Balink."

It took a moment for Koalee to see this was true, and that Balink's skin was not rotten, but instead covered with tar. In her weak condition, Koalee just smiled.

Balink was a much better sailor than Koalee, and instead of being sick she was ravenously hungry. She brought Koalee hot water to drink, and Koalee managed to keep it down. But she had to ask Balink not to sit there in front of her guzzling nut meat and loaf as if she'd never seen food before. When she had eaten enough, Balink brought out a large pot of hot water and some soap and tried to scrub the tar from her body.

"It was in the boat," she explained, scraping at the goo. "Syl had been working on the boat, I think. Anyway, it's oily, and I knew that oil would protect me from the rain and cold, so I coated myself with it. I think it saved my life. I was soaked to the skin and it's been a long, cold ride." She paused, and frowned anxiously.

"Koalee, I have to get back. They'll think I'm drowned. And my baby. He'll need milk. What if he can't live on gruel?"

"Please don't worry," said Koalee, far too out of spirit to follow much of what Balink saying. "What boat?"

"The bark boat. There."

Koalee saw vaguely that a bark boat was tied to the gate post.

"I have to get back, Koalee. Have you anything I can use for an oar? I almost caught hold of a branch once, but it floated out of reach."

Koalee was beginning to feel better. The hot water was settling nicely in her stomach and the dizziness was going away.

"No," she said. "Anyway, we'd be better to stay with the raft. I want to pole the house back home as soon as I can reach bottom."

"I don't think you can reach bottom. I think we're in the middle of Hoyim's Lake, and it's deep enough without a flood. Koalee, how will I get this stuff off? Is it on me forever and ever?"

Koalee managed a smile. "Look on the shelf under my washing table. Dyra has some cleaner he uses on his hands when he's tarring the house. And a scrub brush."

After a few minutes of energetic scrubbing, Balink began to look slightly like herself, and when the worst was off her face and hands, she stripped to the waist.

"I don't want to be immodest," she said. "But I don't want to clean it off inside and dirty up your house."

"I'm so glad you're here, Balink."

"*You're* glad I'm here! These clothes may as well go right in the fire next time it needs building up. Have you got anything I can wear?"

"Everything. Just help yourself. Balink, what are you doing out here? You didn't put that tar on just to come hunting for me."

"I'll fall down exhausted yet," Balink went on, ignoring Koalee's question. "It's just the way I am. I don't give up with the roof half-on, as Dad says. I need to get home to Doen and my baby, and I'll keep going until I do."

Koalee looked at her sternly. "I know enough about sickness to know that you should drink herb tea and sleep for a day. You're over-excited, Balink. What happened?"

"I was next door at the widow's—I left the baby at home sleeping, so when the rain started coming down as if the sky had burst, I went back in case he woke up, or a free-floater came. But the water was already over my ankles, and it was rising fast."

"I never saw water rise so fast," Koalee agreed.

"Well, by the time I got to my stairs it was over my knees and I could hardly move through the current. I got hold of the stair rail, but my foot slipped on the first step and caught between the boards. I had to go underwater to get free."

"Balink! It's a good thing you swim well."

"Once my foot was out, the current swung me around. When I managed to get back on my feet, I was up to my neck in water under the float space."

Koalee shuddered. "Couldn't you swim back to the stair?"

"The current was terrible. I swam for Doen's work table and climbed up on it. But when I tried to get to the wind guards, my hands were so cold, I couldn't hold on to anything. That's when the bark boat floated under the float space, just as if it knew I needed it."

Life was with me, Koalee. I'll say a prayer of thanks every day for the rest of my life. I just jumped in, and it's been my home ever since. The only things in it were the jar of tar, and a trowel. All I could do was let the flood take me, same as you did."

Koalee was alert now. "But why will they think you drowned? They'll think you're safe at home."

"No, they won't. The widow came out to see I got home safely. She'd never have seen me come up under the float space."

"Oh, Balink! But what an escape! All I had to do was cut anchor, and I had an elf to help me."

"I couldn't stop crying, the whole time I was putting on the tar, and then half the night, too. I was afraid nobody would come to let down the wind guards, and the baby would drown."

"The elf was going to check everything," Koalee said. "Your baby will be safe, Balink. I'm sure of it."

"Worst of it, I went to the widow's without my belt. I don't even have my rope and knife. Do you have fish hooks?"

"Yes. We have three, right beside the tethers. I never thought of that."

Balink tethered herself and settled on the edge of the raft to go fishing. Now that Koalee was over the worst of her sickness, she was beginning to feel hungry. She decided to make tea and open a jar of preserved fruit to celebrate.

"I feel too exposed out here," Balink called. "Are you well enough to shoot if a wheeler shows up?"

Koalee was happy to report that she could keep a steady hand on her bow now.

No wheeler came, but the sky darkened again. Thunder sounded, and they feared another torrent. It did rain, but softly. Balink had to abandon her fishing. As desperately as Koalee wanted company, she knew that Balink needed to rest. She made a cup of tea and led her to Nila's bed, persuading her to lie down for just a little while. Balink slept for the rest of the day. Koalee had slipped one of the doctor's drowsy herbs into her tea.

"That sleep has relaxed me," Balink confessed on awakening, joining Koalee for the evening meal. "It feels good not to have to be doing something every minute. But now I'm sad again, and I don't like that."

"Better be sad for a day now," said Koalee, "than to run yourself sick and not be able to enjoy your baby when you get back to him."

Balink accepted that without argument and offered to sit watch outside while Koalee slept. Gratefully, Koalee climbed into her own bed and had her first good rest in thirty-six hours. Once she awoke and felt the raft drifting. She smiled. A breeze must be stirring the water. There was hope that they might be moving to a shallower place.

What she didn't know was that Balink had started to pole. The air was warmer, the rain had ceased, and the sky was clearing. A few stars peeped out. Balink poled slowly and easily, hoping that when dawn arrived, she might recognize a familiar landmark.

When the dawn light came, there were no familiar landmarks. But Balink was sure, by the way the tops of the seed trees were peeking out of the flood, that they were no longer adrift on Hoyim's Lake.

When Koalee awoke, her heart felt light and happy. She cooked a hot meal of mush and made a strong seccar drink to start them on their day. Then she took up the other pole and went to work.

They poled for hours before they came to a landmark that showed they'd been going in the wrong direction. The giant stoneworks that had once belonged to the tall men were sticking up out of the water. The two women groaned.

"The stoneworks are setting sun of trail." Koalee remembered. "If we'd been going the right way, we'd have been home long ago. And now we'll never be able to go all the way back today. First thing we know, the water will go down, and my house will be gone to ground."

"Look, Koalee!"

Koalee looked where Balink was pointing and was dumbfounded. Surely that was a grassperson's house! Curious, they moved closer. It looked like the miller's house, and in fact the figure waving to them looked like the miller's wife.

"I've gone to ground," the miller's wife greeted them, when they got within hearing distance. "In the silliest place. The raft caught on this rock and never came off. The water's gone down today. I guess this means a new house."

"I was afraid you might have been caught out making deliveries."

"No, I was home. Good thing too, or maybe not. If I hadn't been there to cut anchor, the house would have drowned. But it would have dried out again, eh? And at least it would be there. Now it's here—and a tall man saw it! He saw me, too."

"WHAT?"

"A tall man. I thought if I ever saw a tall man I'd be scared to death, but I wasn't at all. It was so interesting. But I was sure scared when he picked up my house."

"He picked up...?" Both Koalee and Balink were wondering whether the miller's wife had taken leave of her senses—but then again, the miller's wife *never* took leave of her senses. They poled closer.

"Don't come too close," the miller's wife warned. "You might go aground too. Can't Balink come over in that bark boat?"

"She can if you'll throw us a rope. Bring everything you want to save. We'll have to make more than one trip."

"How much can your raft hold?"

"It can hold your house! Dyra made this raft to hold a hundred people when the village was being settled. The problem is, the bark boat can't take much weight."

"Can it take a mattress? I don't like to lose my mattress."

"I think so. Maybe chairs and tables."

"I don't like to put you to too many trips."

"We have nothing else to do."

"Fine. You help me and my stores aboard, and I'll pole you home. If you'd heaved sacks of meal forty-five years like me, you'd have stronger arms."

Balink ran ferry service for more than an hour before they had all of the treasures from the miller's house in Dyra's house.

"Now sit down and give me the pole," the miller's wife commanded. "And let me tell you about the tall man."

The other two exchanged glances and settled down to enjoy the tale.

"When I looked out my window this morning, he was coming right through the water," the miller's wife began. "It didn't even reach up to his knees. He was coming and shaking his head, as if the water worried him. Then he tripped on one of the rocks and nearly fell in, but he got upright and rubbed his leg, saying something loud. I couldn't understand him, but you could tell he was mad about that. I never thought to get scared. Then I saw him look straight at my home. He stopped and shook his head again, and then reached out his hand. I knew he was going to pick up the house. I was sure scared then! I believed he might break it in those big hands, or turn it upside down with me in it, or even throw it into the flood. So I started waving my arms to attract his attention, and he saw me. That's when he picked up the house. He picked it up real gentle so he wouldn't jiggle me, and lifted it up until it was even with his eyes, and we stared at each other. His eyes were nice, but they looked as startled as mine. I couldn't understand anything he said, but he said something to me, and I got the feeling he didn't believe in me any more than I believed in him."

Koalee and Balink weren't sure what to think. If this was all in her imagination, the miller's wife was producing a great deal of detail.

"You don't believe I respect the Truth, do you?" she challenged. "I'm telling the truth. And something else. It went through my mind this could be the tall man who destroyed our old village, and Gozer's village, and killed our dolenter. I thought I should frown at him, but then I remembered how Dyra tells us if we ever get a chance to talk to the tall men we should do that, and try to make friends with them. So I gave him a big smile through the window, and he gave me a smile back, and then he looked funny and put the house down again, real gentle, and walked away as fast as he could. I'll tell you something—I don't think he's going to tell any of the other tall men about this."

The miller's wife poled in silence for a few minutes, her ample bosom heaving a little with the effort of using up so much wind to tell her tale. Then she said, "Koalee, you're the Chief Councillor's wife. Do you think you could keep from telling Dyra? I maybe shouldn't have told you."

"If your story is true—if the tall men are coming here—Dyra *has* to know, and soon."

"Yes, but if Dyra knows, and the other men, there'll be a state of war!"

"No! No! Dyra has constantly said he wanted to make friends of the tall men," Koalee protested. "Not war."

"You know how the grass people get when you say you saw the tall men through the telescope? Gozer said he'd 'get the better of them.' That's exactly what he said. Well, I've seen a tall man close up, and it would take a lot of Gozers to get the better of just one of them, believe me."

"Then all the more reason for Dyra and his council to find out about this man. Before Gozer does anything foolish."

"Koalee, I don't know if I can make you see this, but it's just something I know. I don't think the tall men are coming here. I don't think that man will be back at all."

"What makes you so sure?"

"Well, it was partly the way he shook his head about the flood. If he was thinking of moving back here, I think maybe the flood changed his mind. And..."

The miller's wife glanced at her friends coyly, as if she wasn't sure whether she should give her next reason.

"Yes?"

"Well, I think I scared him. I don't know why, because I was nice to him, and I think he liked me too, but I scared him just the same. He kept shaking his head like he meant no. I don't think he'll be back, because I saw the way he went." She paused for another breath. "I'm not going to be able to pole as well as I thought I could," she added.

"Never mind," said Koalee. "I'll take a turn now. We'll get there when we get there."

Balink was looking very thoughtful; then she said, "If we don't say anything to anyone else in the village about your experience, you'll miss the chance to be a very famous person."

"I know. I thought of that," said the miller's wife a trifle wistfully. "But I guess I could give up being famous if it meant keeping people from getting themselves into trouble with the tall men."

The last remark gave Koalee an idea. "I have it! We won't tell a single grassperson, but I will tell Radd. He'll read the tall man's mind and tell me if there's any danger of the mower."

She wouldn't have long to consider that decision, because suddenly Radd materialised at the door.

"I've had trouble finding you," he said. "My distance sense hasn't entirely corrected itself since the storm. You are all well?"

They assured him that they were fine, and when Koalee introduced him to her companions, Radd confirmed Balink's fear. The village did indeed believe her to be drowned, and her family were in mourning.

"I apologize," said Radd. "I might have reached your mind, but it didn't occur to me to search beyond the village."

The news of people mourning her loss made Balink more impatient to get back home.

"I saw you yesterday, becalmed out in the middle of the lake," Radd told them, "But I didn't stop because the lampman was unaccounted for. I searched most of the day. No one is where you expect him to be."

"Did you find him? Is he all right?"

"He's fine. His raft was wedged between the trunks of a spreading tree. He has his neighbour the singer with him."

"Thank goodness!" said Koalee.

"Yes. The lampman said the singer just stood on the raft looking at the flood as if he didn't know what to do. The lampman threw him a rope, and he had the sense to catch it—so the lampman hauled him over to his raft just before he cut anchor."

"The dear lampman. That was a risk. Did they get the raft out of the tree?"

"Oh yes. The village men brought ropes and tree choppers. The raft came down with a great splash."

"It's a very small raft," remarked the miller's wife, as if that explained everything.

"How did you leave your raft?" Radd asked, then read her mind. "Oh, you went to ground."

The miller's wife reddened. "My house is gone forever," she said sadly. "It has no wind guards. It will blow away in the first gale."

Radd asked for its location. Before he could leave, Koalee quickly explained about the tall man. Then the elf went off to check on the house, informing them that if it was still safe, he'd go straight to the village and ask the men to try to get the miller's house afloat once more.

The women ate an enormous meal. Now that they were sure they'd soon be home, they weren't afraid to use the combined supplies of Koalee and the miller's wife. It gave them renewed strength, and they took relays on the two poles, gliding steadily ahead. When darkness fell, the stars were a bright map overhead. It was not yet dawn when they saw the village.

The water level had fallen greatly, but was still deep enough in the low street to return the house to its pyles. In the soft, grey light they slid silently toward the flood markers.

Balink threw off her heavy clothes and leaped into the water. "Balink! Have you taken leave of your senses?"

There was no answer, of course. Both Koalee and the miller's wife felt a moment of dread. Wasn't it enough that Balink was believed drowned, without making it a reality?

Then a triumphant Balink broke the surface, waving the end of the anchor rope. She pulled herself back onto the raft. "Give me a rope," she said. "I'll knot your anchor cord back in place. Now you won't have to worry about anything."

VI

THE SILENT HOMECOMING had not gone unwitnessed. Dyra's brother Doba had been watching anxiously, often getting up in the night to see if he could see a sign of Koalee's raft, and finally he was rewarded.

"Thank Life," he muttered.

Doba the berryman was not bright like Dyra, but he was a kindly person. He awakened his wife and told her the good news, and then he roused his son and daughter. Brond, the miller's assistant, was big and friendly and a little slow, like his father, but Bekra the herb seller was small and dark and quick, looking much more mature than her twenty years. It was typical of Doba's family that they stood on the raft quietly discussing whether it would be kinder to call across to Doba's father, or let him sleep a little longer.

"Well, I think we ought to tell somebody," said Bekra, who often grew impatient with her parents' tedious discussions. "It's time Dyra knew. If you'd just call grandfather, he can shout over to the leatherman."

"That's a good plan," said her father.

It had occurred to Doba that it would have been sensible for Dyra to stay on *his* raft now that he was out of infirmary. After all, he was the older brother, and his raft was right next to Dyra's own. The fact was that Dyra found Doba and his family singularly unstimulating. It spoke well for Dyra's diplomacy that his older brother hadn't an inkling of how he felt. After all, Dyra loved Doba, and so it was easy to make Doba feel warmly accepted, even if he did choose to stay with his younger brother Hryn, instead.

As it happened, Doba and his little clan had no need to come to a decision, for while they debated, Koalee herself came outside. It was growing light enough that she saw them at once. The children were still at the school, and safe. Hoyim had been found in the silver trees. Yes, Koalee had heard that from the elf. Where was he now? Last heard, he was with his grandparents at the glass-blower's house.

At the sound of voices, Balink and the miller's wife rushed outside. The village had heard the news that they were all right. The baby was at the widow's. Doen was at home. He hadn't gone with the boats because he wanted to be in the village if Balink got back. But when Balink took an eager step to the edge of the deck ... NO! SHE MUST NOT SWIM There was sickness in the water!

Bekra the herb woman had some knowledge of sickness, and she managed to get the attention away from her parents and give an explanation to the women on Dyra's raft. The elf had gone from house-to-house, delivering a message from the doctor: that villagers usually got fevers when there was a flood. It was not good water because of the many things that floated in it, some of them dead. When it went down, any water storage vats were to be emptied and cleaned, and no one was to use the water for any purpose at all, not even washing.

"I'll take a chance," said Balink. "To get to my baby."

"Please, Balink," Koalee begged. "The doctor is a wise man. And it's true about the dead things. We've seen dozens; remember the longbeast we saw yesterday, and how bad it smelled?"

"I've spent days in the flood, and I was just in it minutes ago," said Balink. "And I'm not sick yet. I'm not going to let a few more strokes in flood water keep me from my baby."

"The baby is well," Kyb assured her. Doba's wife had a great love of babies and had been receiving regular bulletins about Balink's infant.

The shouting awakened Dyra's parents, who rushed outside and joined in the welcome. As the sun rose, there were people on all the nearby rafts joining in the celebration. The miller's wife was giving Balink firm resistance to her proposed swim. "Your baby wants you five or six hours late and *alive*, not right this minute and dead tomorrow," she said.

"But Koalee has herbs that will keep me from getting a fever. She gave me some on the raft."

"And how do you expect to carry them with you through the water?"

Balink saw the logic of that, and finally agreed reluctantly to wait for the boats.

Dyra, meanwhile, could not see Koalee for his sister's house was in the way, and Koalee could not see Dyra, so his sister Creu ran back and forth relaying their messages. How was she? How did he look? Yes, her family knew that her raft had been seen, and that the other women were with her.

"Did you know you were the last raft to come back?" called Dyra's father. "Except for the miller's?"

"I'm not surprised. How did my neighbour make out?"

"Lenk went out in the boats and poled her in."

Regrets were voiced that there was no way of relaying a message to the widow.

Lenk and his sons were all out with the boats, and so was the fuelman. Perhaps when the message got as far as the back road, it would reach the guard tower, and if they rang the bell, the widow and Doen might realize what it meant.

"Is my baby to hear the bell ringing and know it says 'Mother is back'?" Balink wondered.

"We must stop shouting," Koalee called to her neighbours. "We'll lose our voices. I'll go in now. I must tidy the house before Dyra and the children come home." To Balink she said, "Come and get busy. The time will pass faster if you have something to do."

They set about putting the miller's wife's hastily boarded possessions in order.

"I guess we can't wash anything," said Koalee with regret.

"I will sew a dress," announced the miller's wife.

Koalee suspected that the miller's wife handled every problem by sewing a dress, because she could be counted on to appear in an eye-catching new garment every few weeks. At the moment she was wearing one of her favourite daytime dresses, a blousy jacket of light green, with a skirt of darker green petals over an underskirt of rose.

Balink watched in awe as lengths of cloth emerged from her friend's stores. Bright sky. Rosy purple. Twilight blue. Light green.

"Are you going to put all those colours together?" she asked. "I wish you'd tell me the secret of your dyes."

"Oh no. When my grandmother told me these secrets, she made me promise never to tell anyone but family. I will pass them to my son's daughter, and nobody else." The miller's wife gave a smug grin. "The weaver has offered to pay me for the secrets, more than once."

"I know a secret myself," Koalee bragged. "I can dye a very pretty yellow."

"Yellows aren't hard," countered the miller's wife. "It's just a matter of knowing which flowers give the right pollen."

"You should open a dye shop," Balink suggested. "You wouldn't have to tell anybody the secrets. You could buy white cloth from the weaver and dye it. Every grasswoman in the village would buy from you, and the traders..."

The miller's wife glanced at her cloth of green and rose and yellow and blue. "My clothes would lose their effect," she said. "I'd be invisible. Here, tear me strips from the purple and dark blue—sixteen purple and twelve blues, I think."

She set to work with high abandon. Neither of her friends could imagine what she planned to do with all the colourful pieces, and they watched with delight as the strips were painstakingly fitted together to form a striped skirt and bodice and two big striped puffs for the sleeves.

"I've seen you wear brighter dresses," said Koalee.

"I won't disappoint you, then," said the miller's wife, and hastily added a strip of orange to the green. "I do like orange," she said joyfully. "My, wouldn't the tall man jump if he saw me in this?"

Both Koalee and Balink knew the miller's wife had gone to the trouble of making a dress to cheer them and take their minds off the flood, and they loved her for it. But the mention of the tall man made them uneasy. When Koalee told the story to Radd during the brief time he was on the raft, the elf had promised to let her know if he learned anything of the tall man's plans. It puzzled Koalee that the miller's wife, who claimed actual close contact with the tall man, was the least concerned of all. Could it be that the tall men were less frightening the closer one came to them?

By the time Koalee mixed pancakes for their noon meal, the dress was almost complete. They were roused by shouts and rushed outside to find out what was happening. The boats were back. Lenk was alongside, waving jubilantly.

"We got the miller's house off! We got it off and moving!"

Balink didn't hesitate. She was into her father's boat, and Lenk took her hands, then let them go. He placed his hands on her shoulders, and just looked at her for a moment, as everyone looked at them. When he finally spoke, all he said was, "Doen and the baby are at the widow's." It was all there, unsaid, the great fear and anguish his family experienced, and now the wondrous relief at having her back.

Eventually the miller's wife interrupted. "Is that old fool going to bring the house back himself?"

"He's got help," Lenk told her. "We'll get that house back up on the pyles for you. Sure glad you're back, Koalee," he added.

"So are we!" said Koalee.

"I'll go get Dyra now, and then your children, if you like."

"If I like! But first take Balink to her baby."

"We'll bring what food and water can be shared," said Lenk. "We need to supply every house, because we may be in for a week of mud once this goes down."

"Lenk, wait!" Koalee cried, "Nobody seems to know where Hoyim is, only that he's safe."

"Hoyim's out in the boats. He's been doing a grassman's work in the flood, Koalee. He'll be back with the papermaker."

"Thank Life!" exclaimed Koalee.

Lenk brought Dyra home as soon as he'd delivered Balink to her baby, and then taken the miller's wife to her son's house.

Koalee threw her arms about her husband and clung tightly.

"I felt so useless," he said. "You were out there somewhere where I couldn't help you. Yansa was running the village in the midst of this crisis, and I couldn't even go out with the boats last night. The doctor was very definite about it. But I see you've still got Syl's boat tied to the gate. I'm going to make rounds of the village."

"Dyra, should you?" Koalee said anxiously.

"I'm fine, now, the people should know their Chief Councillor is concerned."

"There aren't any oars."

"There's a paddle in my workroom. I'll have a cup of your good hot tea before I go."

Koalee produced the tea and some food, and Dyra began to nibble thoughtfully.

"Koalee," he said finally, "I believed my day in Life was over."

"Don't talk about that," she advised.

"I have to. Had Radd and the eggman not come when they did, I doubt if I would have lived. I must have been in the cold water for hours. I guess everyone has their limits."

"Life saved you. That's all that matters."

"I did a lot of thinking when I was in the infirmary, about what would happen to you and the children if Life ended for me. I spoke to the doctor about it."

"And he said you were young and tough and you would live for fifty years?"

"He said if it happened, he would adopt you if you were willing."

"You shouldn't have said that without consulting me."

"How could I consult you? You were floating somewhere in the middle of Hoyim's Lake. I'm sorry, Koalee, I was worried and ill. It seemed the right time. Naturally, we didn't make any agreement. Not without your consent."

"It's a good thing you're getting back into action. It doesn't pay to have you lying around ill."

"Face this just for a moment, Koalee. Would you agree to it? I'd feel easier if I knew."

Koalee agreed. "I can be of use to him. He could teach a great deal to the children. Now, don't talk about it any more, because it will not happen."

Dyra looked down at his cup of tea and smiled. "Neev is the

sweetest person and a fine hostess, but she can't make tea. I've missed this the past few days."

"Don't be too greedy. Water is more precious than eggs today."

"I know. Koalee, I think we should move."

"Why? There hasn't been a flood in the thirteen years we've been here. We could simply equip all the houses in the low street with longer anchors."

"I don't think so. The whole middle street floated, and on Market Street they were this close to having to cut anchor."

"You don't mean you want to move the village?"

"No. I meant our own raft. There's room for a raft high ground beside the doctor. The flood didn't even cover the stairs up that way. Look how handy you'd be to your work. And my shop would be on the street of shops, where it really belongs."

Koalee admitted that it was an excellent plan. "Will you close the lower street? Will everybody have to move?"

"Council can't say to a man, 'You have to move'. If they want to, we'll see they have help. There's room along the major drainage ditch, and it's nice out on the back road by the burials. It will be like starting to build the village again."

Children's voices preceded the arrival of Nila and Belm, and highly excited. Koalee rushed over and took her children into her arms.

They squirmed away but stayed close to hear about their mother's voyage. They wanted to know all about the coming of Balink, and the discovery of the miller's wife, and Radd. They took it all in with their rapid young minds, and Koalee was sorely tempted to tell them the tale of the miller's wife and the tall man. But she kept silent about that.

"You went *everywhere*," Nila commented wistfully, "And we were stuck in one place. And now we'll be stuck here until the mud dries."

"I have an idea," said Belm excitedly.

"Not now," said Dyra. "It's time I took back the reins of government. I'll be home for the evening meal, unless Syl steals back his boat."

"That's what I want to tell you," Belm insisted. "My idea."

"Very well, what's your idea?" asked Dyra patiently.

"Why doesn't every house in the village have a bridge to the house next door, like the bridges between the shops? Then when we're in the mud we can still walk all over."

Dyra looked at his son in amazement, and then shook his head. "Nobody wants the entire village walking on their rafts, passing by their windows any time of the day or night," he said.

"Then take up the bridges unless there's a flood, and then we can pass them over and bolt them down the way the shop bridges are bolted down."

"Where would we keep the bridges between floods? They'd have to awfully big bridges."

Nila answered, "Fasten them behind the house with the raft poles?"

"I'm living with a whole family of inventors," Koalee remarked proudly.

But Dyra seemed less impressed. "I don't think it would work, son," he told Belm kindly. "The bridges would have to be so long and strong they'd be too much for one or two people to handle."

Belm looked crestfallen. Dyra stooped to kiss him before he left. "Don't stop thinking, Belm," he said. "It was a wonderful idea. I'll speak to council about it, and maybe it will lead us to find something that will work."

I wish Hoyim would invent something, Koalee was thinking, as she kissed Dyra goodbye and turned back to the children. "Spellers and numbers," she announced. "We can't neglect your schoolwork for a flood."

Nila thought she had the better of her mother. "We left our books at the school."

"Oh. Then, in that case it will be reading. You will go and get your father's *History of the Settlement* and read the first chapter to Belm and me. I have been curious to know what was in that book, and so should you."

Nila loved to read, so there was no protest. Koalee settled with her mending and gave Belm some drawing markers, so he could amuse himself if he lost interest. But Belm didn't lose interest in the story. Instead, he cut in with a dozen questions about the old settlement, and where it was, and when it all happened, and had Koalee and Dyra been there then? The interruptions annoyed Nila—but Koalee found them gratifying.

VII

Two days of hot sun caused the flood waters to go down rapidly. The drainage ditches carried much of the mud down the slope. The hot weather lasted, and it wasn't long before the remaining mud dried and was cleaned from the streets. The village returned to a normal routine.

Now the grass people became concerned about the rites for the cobbler. He had been buried, as was the custom, on the day of his death, but his rites had never been held. A messenger from Gozer's village came with the news that they had experienced a free-floater and wanted to know if all was well with Dyra. He returned with a message for the dolenter, and the rites were held in the meeting house, followed by a special meeting of thanks to Life for bringing them all through the flood safely.

Koalee seized upon the opportunity, as she often did. "We should have a dolenter here," she told Dyra. "We shouldn't have to send to Gozer whenever we have need of one. It's not fair to Tokra, either, risking trail for us."

Dyra shook his head. "Our village is a happy place. No fear. No dark shadows. I may admit a dolenter, if I hear of one who has no anger and knows how to love. Not otherwise."

"Tokra is like that."

"Tokra pleases me very well, but he is dolenter for Gozer's village, so we can't ask Tokra. Anyway, having a dolenter in Gozer's village is close enough. Yansa feels the same way. The dolenter in the old village interfered too much with council."

Koalee felt guilty over Dyra's attitude to dolenters, but she knew that at the moment it was more important for him to concentrate on the replacement of water storage vats, which had been carried away in the flood, not to mention the dilemma over whether or not the entire mill street should be moved to higher ground.

The question of who would move, and where, was causing feverish excitement. The sweet-shopkeeper had already hired Rels to construct a small raft behind his shop. Lenk was helping the metalsmith build a new house on the back road, and when those were finished, they would begin work on Dyra's new house beyond the infirmary. The basketmaker had selected a site on the major drainage ditch, next door to the portrait painter, and he was building a house himself, with the help of his wife and friends and neighbours. The singer who played in the marketplace, and never seemed to know whether his house was wet or dry, would stay in the low street. The miller and his wife would stay as long as the mill was there.

The grasswomen organized a bee to help the cornman's wife clean the dirt out of the house that had drowned, but the cornman wouldn't consider moving. What was one flood in thirteen years? The lampman also refused to think of moving. He loved his little raft across from the miller, right where the trail from the tall woods entered the village, and he wouldn't feel at home anywhere else. It was important that he be there all night to keep the first lamp burning. What if a wanderer should come up trail in the darkness, and not be able to see the village lights? No, the lampman would stay.

In the midst of the building flurry, the news came around that Koalee's sister Flon had hired Tuje to construct a raft for her next door to Rels. Koalee didn't know whether to be horrified or to cry. Grasswomen only lived alone if they were adopted widows. Whoever heard of a grasswoman building a house? She and Hoyim had one more cause for disagreement.

"I think it's wonderful," said Hoyim. "Aunt Flon does what she wants to do, and she doesn't care what people think."

"It's not wonderful," Koalee retorted. "It's glar. It's inconsiderate and irresponsible. And what grassman will want to marry a woman who already owns a house?"

"You're jealous because Aunt Flon has the money to build it."

"She only has money because my father pays her to keep the glass shop. He never paid me when I kept it, before I was married."

"But Syl helped you in those days."

"Syl was no help! Syl was seven and in school."

"I bet the eggman would marry Aunt Flon."

"Hoyim that will do."

"Well, he sure paid a lot of attention to her at the dancing."

"Hoyim, don't you ever speak lightly of the Truth. Dancing is one thing. Getting married is far more serious, like a trade."

Hoyim had grown more confident and much more willing to talk since the flood. "I know," he said. "I have to make my mind up about a trade. I'm trying."

Koalee felt encouraged, and she decided that the time was right to mention the ideas that had been going about in her head.

"The cobbler's apprentice is now cobbler and will need an apprentice," she said. "There would be a future for you there, Hoyim, if it interests you."

"I thought of that. I'm not a shoemaker."

"How do you know?"

"I went to the shop and watched, lots of times."

Koalee had another of the uneasy pangs that she experienced whenever she realized that much went on with Hoyim of which she had no knowledge.

"Have you considered becoming a doctor?"

"*What?*"

"A doctor. The doctor is over fifty, Hoyim. I'm sure if I asked him he'd take you to apprentice. If you show promise, he'd send you to the master doctor in Karep—the big village, high sun-setting sun, where none of us has ever been. You'd have to go with the traders and spend two years, but just think of all that you would learn."

Hoyim was looking at his mother in such amazement that she assumed for a moment she had given him a welcome idea. But she soon found she was mistaken.

"How did you even think of such a thing?" he asked incredulously.

"I don't like looking after sick people. Don't get me mixed up with what *you* like, Mother."

Koalee felt her impatience rising. "Well, if you will not do the traditional thing and follow your father's trade, there is one other opportunity," she said sharply. "My father wants to retire. His breath is growing short. That means Hent will have more work than he can handle. If you want to become a glass-blower, all you have to do is say so."

Hoyim looked for a moment as if he would turn on his heel and stamp out in a temper, but he controlled it. "Mother, I don't want to be a glass-blower," he said firmly. "I never did want to be a glass-blower. But I don't know what I want to be. I think I want to invent some trade that never was. Do you understand? In the meantime, if it will make you happy, I'll go to Grandfather and tell him I'd like to try blowing glass. No commitment. Just try it for a little while, if only to say I didn't like it."

"Your father will never agree to such a thing."

"Yes, he will. Father knows that when a mind is thinking it has to move freely. He won't make me agree and say 'This is to be my life' before I know what my life is to be. I can go to my own grandfather's shop and practice blowing glass without being called an apprentice, so that is what I will do."

Koalee felt more desperate than ever. But she knew there was nothing to do except pray that Hoyim would find glass to be what he really wanted after all.

Hoyim continued to maintain trail, spending three days in the village between trips, and whenever he was at home he dutifully spent the three days in the glass-blower's shop. On his third journey up trail, Koalee went to the shop to inspect his work.

"It won't do," said Hent, showing her Hoyim's attempts. "It's not that he couldn't. He just doesn't want to. This is his only success."

He reached into a drawer and produced something that made Koalee's head spin.

Hent was holding a matching pair of glass bracelets.

Koalee ran from the shop, leaving her brother wondering what had happened. She rushed along the middle street so blindly that when the wife of the smith's son called, "A pleasant day, Koalee. Market tomorrow," Koalee had to remind herself to answer. She hurried down the second path and into Dyra's Road, arriving at her home, she drew up breathlessly in front of Dyra. He was at his table in the float space, working on his history of the new settlement. Koalee knew that he would hate to be interrupted, just as she knew that the doctor would be disappointed if she came late to infirmary, but she blurted out the story.

"I often wondered if it would affect him," Dyra said thoughtfully. "He may have been old enough to remember a lot. Not many grass babies make friends with a fairy in their first year of life."

"You don't think she put him under a spell?" Koalee demanded. "You don't think that's what's wrong with Hoyim?"

Dyra looked at her steadily. "Koalee, go to work. An afternoon at infirmary will calm you. No, I don't think Violet cast a spell on him. I'll think about this. I promise."

Koalee had to be satisfied with that. She took a shortcut up the weaver's street and was not terribly late for infirmary. They only had two patients. The shopkeepers' lungs had been bad ever since the flood and he came for more medicine. The gunmaker had a painful swollen thumb.

As soon as the doctor had seen to them, he showed Koalee how to exercise Ston's legs. Ston could wiggle his toes, bend his knees, and feel pressure or pain all up his legs. The doctor entertained high hopes that he might walk again. The shoulder was not yet in condition to move, but there were hand and finger exercises for him to do. Koalee was to help him through all the exercises from now on. Dyra had been right. Once her mind was on her work she settled down, and Hoyim and the glass bracelets receded to the back of her mind.

But they hadn't left Dyra's mind. It occurred to him that it was time he led a personal expedition to the tall woods to check on the state of the trail, and to bring back some resources such as birch bark, which could be found there. He would take Hoyim with him. Perhaps the experience would unlock old memories in the boy's mind. Old memories, Dyra believed, could contain clues about the significance of fantasies or one's plans and ambitions. What secret desires had been simmering in the depths of his son's mind since those idyllic days spent with Radd and Violet in the tall woods? If they were there, then the boy should be faced with reality. Fairyland, Dyra had learned, didn't hold much substance compared to a solid day-to-day existence in the village. It was a lesson Hoyim had had no opportunity to learn, so learn it he must.

It was also troubling Dyra that he'd had no opportunity to formally thank Radd for all the invaluable assistance he'd given the villagers at the time of the flood. He would organize the trip as soon as market day was over.

Dyra's active mind went to work on the plans, even as part of it returned to the task of writing his history. He had got to the place where they went down the animal hole to escape the mower—the day he first met Lenk's widow. He'd intended to leave out much of the story of Violet, since it was really only Radd who was directly concerned with their search for the site of the new settlement. Now Dyra changed his mind. Violet had also influenced their lives, and perhaps this influence was still being felt. Violet would therefore be mentioned in his history—not only mentioned but fully described.

Market days were exciting, but there was something special in the air this morning.

The sun gave promise of being warm and bright, and everyone was out at dawn collecting the dew before it had a chance to dry.

Dyra met the fuelman at the edge of the spreading trees, hoisting a bundle of branches to his back.

"I don't know why I'm collecting," the fuelman said. "I rafted enough driftwood during the flood to do the village through two cold seasons. Habit, I guess."

"Pays to be prepared," said Dyra.

"Traders will be here today." The fuelman winked. He prided himself on his extra sight. The strange thing was, he was usually right. "It will be a good market," he added.

Dyra re-crossed the road. Turning toward home, he heard Bekra calling to him, "A pleasant day!"

Bekra had done her hair in some new way. Goodness! His niece looked about as fancy as the weaver's wife, and she was wearing a dress as red as the hips of the pink thorn tree.

With her almost constant frown and dark eyes much too small to be attractive, Bekra was not the prettiest of grasswomen, but there was something different about her today. Dyra had never seen a red like that in the village, except on the miller's wife, and then only rarely.

He stood staring at her and forgot to answer, until Bekra's laughter brought him back to reality. Then he wished her a pleasant day and waved.

His father had just emerged from his door, so Dyra called to him. "A pleasant day, Father. Can I get your dew water for you?"

"No thanks," called the old lens maker. "It's a fine morning. I want fresh air."

Dyra took a last look at Bekra's red dress as she trotted up the market street then wondered about the future of his niece. Such a strange girl, far too bright to have been born into Doba's family. Her skin had already begun to age and sometimes her eyes had a sly, crafty look. She didn't seem to have any real friends. She was fond of money, too, and that was not a quality much admired among the grass people. Money went to houses, cloth, treats, and necessities, but grass people prided themselves on their craftsmanship, knowing they could do without money if need be. Yet Bekra was suspected of hoarding it. She must be getting rich, for her tiny shop, though the smallest on the street of shops, was continually busy. Grass people used herbs constantly, if they were too busy to go collecting for themselves, they stopped in to buy from Bekra. If they collected more herbs than needed, they had only to go to Bekra, who bought their surplus. Whenever a youngster was seen coming out of the sweet-shop after school, munching on a pastry, parents would say, "So you've been selling herbs to Bekra?"

"Well," Dyra shrugged, starting up his stair, "she must have parted with some of her money to get that red dress. If there's any chance of the traders coming today, I'd better see the musician. People will want dancing tonight."

The musician was a man who had a wife and two children and

lived out on the back road near the guard tower. He was the man who organized all the local music makers to play for the dancing and special celebrations. He was the man who sang at meetings, and who taught the children to play instruments. He was very much a part of village tradition, whereas 'the other musician,' usually designated as 'the singer behind the market,' was considered an outsider. He had come from nowhere, told no one of his origins, and without even asking permission, settled on a small raft that had been vacated by one of the hunters. He had never married and seldom spoke to anyone. He accepted the lampman as his neighbour with a kind of nonchalance, and the lampman reported that he ate very little and spent most of his time staring into space. Whenever he heard that there was to be dancing or some special event, his eyes would light up and he would smile, and then he'd brush his clothes and comb his hair and appear on time, carrying his quidda. He could play all evening without tiring. It was as if he suddenly came to life. Music was everything to him. Very often, in the early morning or on a warm summer evening, the villagers would listen to him playing and singing to please himself. If the musician joined in the song, throwing his fine voice across the street of shops, the singer behind the market might pace up his music and sing louder, or he might fall silent. It depended upon his mood.

The singer behind the market was the self-appointed entertainer on market day. He had been coming to market since his first week in the village. He took up a station in the shelter of the market stalls, set a basket beside him, and played and sang all day. His music was not as refined or as predictable as what the musician played, but people liked it and shoppers often tossed a coin into his basket.

Dyra thought he heard him now, singing a soft morning song to entertain the sellers as they set up their stalls. He went inside smiling, and found Koalee up and busy, in a happy mood.

"I hear the singer behind the market," Dyra announced. "And I saw Bekra off to work. It's going to be a wonderful market day."

"Has the cornman paid you for the blue lenses yet?" Koalee wanted to know.

"He has indeed."

"If Bilik is selling lace, I want to buy some of that nice, creamy kind like the widow wore to the eggman's party."

"I thought the doctor paid you for helping him?"

"I spent my money on cloth to make Belm a suit. Children grow, Dyra."

"All right, we still need to replace the jar the flood carried away. Hryn will make it for us cheap, and you can pay for it next time the doctor pays you. So you can be as frivolous as you like at market today."

"I'm never frivolous."

"You can afford to be. I've just had an order from Gozer's village for four fire-starting magnifiers, and lenses for an old man."

"We're rich!"

"We're in Life. That's all that counts."

Long before school would have started on a normal day, Dyra's whole family were headed toward the marketplace.

There were eight stalls in the marketplace and, with the addition of tables in the street, there were as many as twenty displays. The whole village would be there. Usually they bought foodstuffs early, and then spent several hours visiting. Koalee never got tired of the excitement of the market, but this morning it was particularly lively.

"The traders are in!" called Belm, running ahead.

"I might have known," said Dyra. "The fuelman knew it. That man is uncanny." He hurried his steps, because if there were any disputes with the strangers, the Chief Councillor would have to be there. Koalee and Nila brought up the rear, for Koalee's short legs could never travel very fast. Hoyim had already darted ahead of the family group.

There were four traders, each with a trail runner loaded with rarities the villagers would never see at any other time. They had taken over the centre stall and the one beside it, across from Bekra's shop. Their trail runners were behind their counters, and they were hanging items where they would be easy to see. They had also set up a target, offering prizes for archery. There were kites for sale, with feathers so bright no bird could possibly have worn them. On display were rings and necklaces set with jewels, pieces of cloth of a colour and weave no woman in the village could duplicate. There were items of silver and gold and pans their local metalsmith could never make.

Koalee noticed Hoyim staring at a cold weather coat lined in fine grey mouse fur and embroidered all over in glorious silks. She knew Hoyim needed a new coat for the next cold season, but this wouldn't do. She moved over to him and said, "Your father can't afford a coat like this for you, Hoyim."

"I know," he said. "Anyway, Uncle should have the business."

"Not that he needs it," said his mother. Romo's skill as a leatherman must be known to the ends of the grassman's world.

The lampman was negotiating with the traders, asking them to buy some of his lamps to sell in other villages. They weren't offering enough for such lovely lamps, and Yansa stepped up and made the deal, getting twice as much for the lampman. Yansa always watched over him, he was a gentle and kind grassman, but no businessman.

Koalee waved to Doba to let him know that soon she would be over to buy fruit at his berry stall. She greeted neighbours and was jostled by children, and calculated how long it would be before she had time to treat herself to a nibble from the tempting table set up by the sweet-shopkeeper and the baker's wife.

The bell on the guard tower rang three. The grass people, tuned to the sound as if it were an extension of the nervous system, didn't wait. By the time the second ring of three sounded, adults and children alike were sheltering in the float spaces beneath the shops, anxiously counting heads. The wheeler circled the village and, seeing no movement in the streets, disappeared rising sun. Confident that the bell would warn them, should the wheeler return, the villagers went back to the market stalls as if nothing had happened.

It was then Koalee noted that the rootman's widow had brought lace. She hoped some of that fine, creamy lace would be found among it.

The rootman had had a busy week. His counter was heaped. He had dug one of the giant, white roots, twice as tall as himself, that grew near the stoneworks, and sawed it into pieces. One piece would be a burden to carry, but Koalee made up her mind to buy one anyway. They made wonderful puddings. The gunmaker had a stall today. The wood of one of his guns was polished like glass. The hunters had a well laden table. And what was *this*?

Koalee came face-to-face with the weaver and Balink, shopping with her baby in its backpack. Balink laughed at her surprised expression.

"Trees, Koalee," said the weaver, as if she didn't recognize the big, green plants with their roots wrapped in cloth, sitting in tubs of water.

"But what are they doing here? Last I saw of these trees, they were growing in your garden."

The weaver beamed. "I grew them so other people can enjoy them. They're too big now for one man's garden. I've brought them to sell."

"But..." Koalee was dumbfounded. "I'll have to speak to Dyra before I decide."

Yansa had already seen the trees, and fetched Dyra. All three councillors walked toward the weaver.

"This should have been discussed in council," Dyra told him firmly but kindly. After all, the old man was growing rather strange, as everyone knew, and he must be shown understanding.

"Ah, but I've done it," the weaver insisted. "I've really invented a dwarf tree this time. Think how beautiful the village will be with these trees beside every raft."

Dyra resisted the temptation to smile and let him get away with it. "Last time you invented a dwarf tree, it grew until its roots threatened every raft," he retorted. "It took a week to dig it all up and cut it in lengths, then drag it to the fuelman. Now you propose to have—how many of these trees around the village?"

"Twenty-nine. I left my big one in the corner of the garden. I've had it for four seasons. It's my friend."

The councillors conferred among themselves for a few minutes, while Balink seemed ready to burst with glee. Hadn't she said the weaver's garden was getting out of hand? Maybe if the council put a stop to it, he would quit bothering Doen to come and help in the garden every spare minute.

"Has he *really* made a miniature tree?" Koalee asked. "From a tall tree?"

Balink nearly shook with her laughter. "The joke is, I believe he actually has. He's been growing one of these for four years now, and it doesn't get any taller than his house. A tall tree would have taken over the village by now. I don't understand what he did, but it worked."

"What good are they?" they heard Dyra asking.

"What *good* are they?" The weaver was incredulous. "Shade and beauty, of course!"

"Even if they don't grow big roots and destroy the village, it's very important that we are able to see each other's rafts," Dyra told him. "Sometimes our safety depends on it."

The miller's wife glanced at Yansa. "Thirty trees? I won't be growing any more if that's what's worrying you. I've something else going in my garden now."

"Well, we can't let them die," Lenk said.

The lampman was standing close to Yansa, listening to the conference. He looked closely at the coins he had received for his lamps, and then looked at the price posted on the weaver's stall. Courageously, he stepped up. "I'll buy a tree," he said.

The council watched the weaver hurry away with the lampman, carrying an earth digger and a tree. "I hope you have plenty of water on your raft," he was saying. "These little ones need plenty of water when they move to a new home."

Koalee nudged Dyra. "I'd like one, Dyra. High sun of the house, for shade."

"We won't be in that house very long."

"Somebody will be."

"I promised you another seed tree as soon as we get to the new house," Dyra tried.

"Seed trees are spindly compared to the weaver's trees."

By the time the weaver returned, his stall was one of the busiest at the market. The basketmaker was taking two trees to flank his raft. The musician wanted three. A shopkeeper was persuading council to put four along the middle street behind his shop, allegedly to shade the picnic ground. At that point, the weaver withdrew four trees from the market, announcing his intention of putting them on Doen's land, to shade the weaver's street.

"How fast do they grow?"

"How tall will they be?"

"Will we be able to climb them?" The last question came from Belm.

The doctor surprised everybody by asking for seven trees. He would plant them behind his raft, he said, in the hope of cutting off some of the smoke from the lime kiln, and he might plant some across the trail from the teacher's raft, to give shade to the infirmary. At the look on Koalee's face, he turned to Dyra.

"Come along, Dyra. If you're going to live next door to me, you must have trees as well. The kiln is a bad neighbour when the wind is wrong."

"Trees won't help. Besides, I've brought two trees for the raft I'm on now."

"Four more!" said the doctor, preparing to buy them for him.

That forced Dyra to buy the trees, and set the onlookers laughing. The morning was hardly begun, and only two trees remained in the weaver's stall. It struck Koalee, as she watched the weaver trudging up the slope beside the doctor to begin the planting, that it was the first time she had ever seen a local stall take attention from the traders on market day.

She re-appraised the traders' stalls now, noting that the miller's wife was giving close scrutiny to all of the brightest coloured merchandise. It was interesting that the traders seldom put their humdrum items on view. There were kegs of tar behind the counters, and honey, and bags of salt. Which reminded her, it was time she did her food shopping. She would come back later and look at the lace. Meanwhile, she'd decided to buy a piece of the white root and a few other roots, patronize the berry stall, and buy a supply of salt. She would have to call Belm and Nila to help her carry it all home.

"Are you interested in sharp, fine knives?" asked a trader.

Koalee felt like retorting, "Our own metalsmith makes the best knives to be found," but instead she said, "No. All I want right now is salt."

He turned to get the salt, and Koalee noticed that the handsome young trader who shared his stall was leaning on his elbows on the counter, with a far-away look in his eye. Koalee just had to turn to see where he was looking and found that he was watching Bekra. The herb woman stood on her raft, leaning against her shop with her hands behind her back, returning the trader's smile. She was wearing a dress of the brightest red Koalee had ever seen. It dawned on her that the singer was aware of the game. He dropped the gentle nature song he'd been singing and began to sing a love song instead.

Koalee paid for her salt and quickly nabbed the miller's wife. "That dress Bekra is wearing is your dyed cloth if ever I saw it!" she said accusingly.

The miller's wife gave Koalee her most innocent smile. "It's not as if I sold her orange. Red isn't my colour, is it? She isn't hurting my effect."

"But why did you do it? You constantly refuse to sell your dyed cloth. What did Bekra do to deserve this?"

The miller's wife winked. "It's once in a woman's life, isn't it?" she asked.

"You knew? About the trader? There is something happening there, isn't there?"

The miller's wife grinned. "Of course I knew. If you'd had your eyes open last big market, you'd have seen it too."

"I wasn't here last big market. Nila was sick."

"The market musician saw it. He sees everything, says nothing, that man."

"Do you think there'll be a wedding?"

"I don't know," said the miller's wife. "It all depends on that red dress." She went off chuckling aloud.

She has a heart of gold, that woman, Koalee thought.

A new wave of excitement took Koalee's attention. Kezel had arrived, with a single trail runner full of eggs. Last time there were five. She wondered if Radd had spoken to him about taking so many.

There would be no problem finding the children now. They flocked around the eggman like moths around a street lamp.

Koalee looked at the eggs wistfully. Should she or shouldn't she? Radd would be unhappy if she did. She checked her shopping basket and the two string bags she was carrying. Koalee could not resist eggs. "I wouldn't waste it," she muttered to herself.

"The biggest and best for the Chief Councillor's wife," said Kezel, unpacking a beautiful blue egg for Koalee. Then, with the same graceful gesture, he reached for another and said, "And its identical twin for her sister."

Koalee turned to find Flon standing right behind her, carrying one of the weaver's trees. Flon had dressed her hair around her finest comb and she was, without doubt, giving the eggman the benefit of her brightest smile.

"Why aren't you in the shop?" asked Koalee.

"Koalee! It's market day."

"All the more reason. People might want to buy glass." Before she could say something more critical, her sister darted away.

Koalee sighed. "Here, Nila," she said, handing her daughter a coin. "Go and buy two fish from your Uncle Syl and two peas from the peaman, then bring them right home. We'll have them for the noon meal."

On her way home with her food purchases, Koalee noticed that Bekra had left her post, and that the young trader was whistling the tune the singer was playing. Hoyim was deep in conversation with another trader. The two set off together toward the raft behind the market stalls where traders stayed while they were in the village. What could Hoyim possibly want at the trader's raft? She must remember to ask him.

Koalee did her second tour of the marketplace on her way to afternoon infirmary, so the family didn't see her next purchases until evening. She *had* been frivolous, purchasing a piece of the coveted creamy lace from the rootman's widow, a pair of enamelled hair clips for Nila from the traders, a new belt for Hoyim with his name carved into it, from Romo, and she had a prize for Belm. She'd also bought some special ink that was said not to fade, for Dyra.

Koalee considered the ink quite a piece of luck. She'd happened to hear the portrait painter discussing paint and pigments with the traders, because they often brought him colours he couldn't make locally, and it occurred to her to ask about ink.

"Do you like it, Dyra? Are you pleased?"

Dyra drew fine lines with his pen, commenting that it was a darker brown than his own. "We'll know in ten years whether it really holds its colour better than the ink I made," he said. "This was a very nice thought, Koalee. What did you buy for Belm?"

"It's out here."

They found a splendid feather kite tied to the gate, which brought welcome shouts from Belm. Koalee had won it as a prize for archery.

"Now see what I bought you," said Dyra.

"The comb cover! I saw this. The miller's wife pointed it out to me. Oh, it's so beautiful! The trader said they weave quills from a bluebird's feather. Just think. I wonder if I could learn to do that. Oh, Dyra, it's too expensive."

"It's about one-half of one of the old man's lenses—but think how you'll look at tonight's dancing. With all the fine women I've seen around the village today, I wanted the Chief Councillor's wife to keep up with the competition."

Hoyim was the last of the family to arrive for the evening meal, and he had the latest news on the weaver's trees. Apparently no one had purchased the last tree. The weaver had tried hard to persuade the baker to buy it, and the baker would have nothing to do with it because he was sure it would grow into a giant like the last one so, in a final spurt of humor, the weaver donated the tree to the meeting house. He was even now planting it on meeting house land, right beside the baker's raft.

The family laughed heartily at the news, but Hoyim's next item was not greeted so lightly.

"And guess what Aunty Flon is doing with her tree?"

"Putting it beside her raft, I suppose."

"No"

"She's putting it out by the peaman's bridge? It would be nice there."

"No."

"Oh, she's given it to Mother and Father. It would be fine shade behind their house."

"No. You can't guess. She's putting it on her raft."

"What do you mean, 'on'?"

"On her raft," Hoyim grinned. "She's having Tuje build a tub for it, and she'll fill it with earth, and put the tree on her raft. The weaver assured her it will grow in a tub."

"I'll have to put a stop to this," Dyra said, looking as if he intended to rush out that very minute. "A thing like that will unbalance her raft in a free-floater. This is council business."

"No, it won't, Father. It won't unbalance her raft. You haven't heard the half of it."

"What's the rest of it?"

"She's putting it right in the middle of the raft, and Tuje's building the house around it. Like this."

With his finger, Hoyim sketched a house around a central patio. "She's going to have a garden in the very middle of her house," he explained.

"Every rain will flood her out," Koalee scoffed.

"No. There's a drain system to carry rain away—and no holes in the raft, Mother. Tuje hasn't taken leave of his senses. In fact, Tuje's delighted with the idea. It's a new way of building. He can invent all he likes."

"Stores go in the center of the house," Koalee said firmly. "He can't design a house to float with a tree in the middle of it. Nobody can."

"Well, don't worry about it," said Hoyim. "Aunty Flon will run away with Kezel tomorrow anyway."

"Hoyim, I don't want you to ever say that again," said his mother.

"If she runs away with the eggman, well and good," said Dyra, "as long as she doesn't invite the eggman to come and live in the house around the tree. I don't think he's the sort of grassman I want to see living in the village." Hoyim was enjoying himself tremendously.

"Can I be first in the washing room?" he asked, as the meal ended.

"I suppose so," said Koalee absently, still concerned over the news of her wayward sister.

"But don't be long. Belm and Nila need to wash also."

"Well, you see," said Hoyim, "the widow has a guest. A niece from Gozer's village."

"I saw a young girl with her at the market today, but I didn't meet her."

"She's a nice girl."

"So you've met her?"

"Yes. Her name's Ajist. I've asked to walk with her to the dancing."

Koalee thought Dyra was going to swallow his ink.

VIII

Koalee smiled to herself as she reflected on the events of last evening. What a market day it had been indeed. The musicians had played with more spirit than ever before. Flon and the eggman danced as if they were possessed by fairies and elves. Bekra, flushed to match her dress, danced with the young trader and then stood holding his hand while her father announced in his stumbling way that they would be married.

Since there was no dolenter, a councillor must step forward and ask Doba if it was a promise in Truth. Yansa enjoyed these ceremonies, so he performed the role.

"Does Truth tell you?" Yansa asked formally.

"Truth tells me," said Doba.

"Then we give our blessings to your daughter and to this young man."

"Where will you live?" Hryn asked, hurrying to greet them.

"In the big village!" said Bekra, her dark eyes dancing. "The big village none of us has ever seen."

"Where the master doctor lives," said Koalee, proud of her knowledge. "High sun- setting sun from the tall woods."

"Twenty days' march," said the trader.

"But what will Bekra do when you are up trail?" asked Brond, who was taking some time to understand it all.

"I'll run a shop," said Bekra happily. "And I'll make a lot of money, because four thousand people live in the big village. Can you imagine that? Four thousand people?"

"She will come up trail with me sometimes," said the trader. "She will visit you, and on the return trip she'll go back with us."

The trader's name was Ryjra. As Koalee sat weaving thistledown into a soft blanket, a wedding gift for Bekra and Ryjra, she put her mind to memorizing his name. A huge fly landed on the window, shutting off most of the light, and she got up and shooed him away. Then her mind went back to the dancing and all that had happened there.

Hoyim had behaved perfectly. He danced with Ajist, but not too often, and he was attentive about getting treats and juices for her. He was polite to the widow. He introduced Ajist to all of his relatives, explaining very carefully, Koalee noticed, who they all were.

Ajist was a charming girl. She did not smile readily, but when she did her smile was quick and appreciative. Her hair was long and light, her skin fair, her body slender and graceful. Her blue eyes had a slant, and a look of deep concentration. She reminded Koalee of someone, but she couldn't remember who.

"Find out who she is," Dyra had whispered. So Koalee attached herself to the widow. Ajist was not really the widow's niece. She was her sister's niece. Ajist was the dolenter's daughter.

Koalee was delighted with the news, but when she told Dyra, he was distressed.

"Hoyim isn't yet fourteen," Koalee reminded him, "and he has no trade. What's more, the girl must be at least fifteen."

Dyra considered. "Well, then. We must invite the widow and the girl to the evening meal tomorrow. It will be expected. We should prepare to know her better."

"It's too soon for this!" Koalee complained.

But it made her proud that Hoyim had been walking out for the first time with dolenter Tokra's daughter, and such a lovely girl. Far more respectable than her hopeless sister, dancing with eggmen and building her own raft. With the *tree* on it.

Really, thought Koalee, breaking her yarn, I wonder what this village is coming to.

"Koalee! Doctor wants you!"

Koalee sprang up and ran to the door. "The singer behind the market," the messenger boy told her. "Doctor says hurry."

"I don't know if there's much either of us can do," the doctor said as soon as Koalee arrived. He pointed to some pieces of forbidden toadstool lying on the dirty, cluttered table. "I tried to force down an emetic, but he can't swallow. It may have been hours. The lampman came to check on him because he didn't hear any music this morning."

"How could any grassman mistake one of these for a kloro?" asked Koalee.

"I don't think it was a mistake."

"He wouldn't take Life?"

"He didn't have much reason to stay in Life, did he?" remarked the doctor, looking around the one-roomed house, still filthy from the flood. The only furnishings were the table and chair, the stove, and a mattress on the floor on which the musician was lying. The doctor rolled him over and pushed his forehead hard against the floor.

"Nothing makes him throw up," he said. "I'm sure it's too late. The poison will have done its job by now."

Koalee felt the man's pulse. It was very weak. "Doctor... I feel so ashamed. Here he was, living all alone like this, and we didn't do anything."

"Now stop that. The miller's wife tried hard to give him good food and some comforts, but he wouldn't take anything. He must have been as happy here as anywhere, or he wouldn't have stayed."

Koalee felt the musician's brow. "He's cold."

"He's gone."

Koalee found some rain water in a vat on the raft; she heated it and bathed the body of the singer. There wasn't even a complete blanket in which to wrap him, so she went to her parents' house and borrowed one from her mother.

Koalee couldn't remember when she'd felt so depressed. There was something about the singer behind the market which permanently haunted her. He had represented so much mystery, and there was that strange quality about him—that awareness that the miller's wife had mentioned. Koalee wept when she realized they would never hear his music again. In comparison, what the village musician played was cold, and too measured. The whole

147

village would mourn and, for the first time in nine years, the singer behind the market would not be there to help bring them through the sadness. She must see the widow as soon as she got home and cancel this evening's visit. It would not be expected under the circumstances. Dyra would be sending for Ajist's father now, for the rites.

"Koalee..." She was glad to see that it was the lampman standing in the doorway.

"He's gone from Life, then?"

Koalee nodded.

"I knew as soon as I found him. I knew it was too late for the doctor, but I had to try."

"You were a wonderful neighbour to him."

"I liked him. He wasn't like anybody I ever knew."

"I guess we all felt that way."

"The miller's wife liked him too. He was all right if you got to know him. Neglected himself something terrible, but he was all right just the same."

Koalee was glad to have the lampman's company. "Do you know anything about him?" she asked. "Did he ever tell you who he was or where he came from?"

"Not a word. Ask him that, and he'd go silent. All I have of him is his songs. Look, Koalee. I never told him I did this. I don't know what he'd think..."

Shyly, the lampman drew a little roll of papers from the inside pocket of his coat. "I wrote down his songs. He never saw me do it."

Koalee reached for the proffered papers. "This is a treasure," she said. "If the musician can remember the tunes and write down the music, we'll be able to keep it forever."

Koalee turned to the next song and looked suddenly puzzled.

"That's one he never sang in the market," said the lampman. "He always sang it in here, real quiet, like he didn't want the village to hear him. He'd sing it around the time of the evening meal, late in the summer."

But Koalee *had* heard the song. Reading it, she knew for the first time who the singer behind the market really was. Before she could collect herself, the doctor came back with the diggers.

"I'll come," said the lampman. "He had no relations. I'll be at his grave. I will tell the miller's wife. She will be his mother."

"The Chief Councillor will be his father," said the doctor.

"Last night he played and sang as I've never heard him sing before," said Dashe, the rootman's son, who was one of the diggers.

Tears streamed down Koalee's face as she went to tell the widow. This morning she would be at Lenk's house doing the cleaning. As she approached, she saw bedding airing on the line and the widow's "niece" sweeping the raft. She found the widow in the storeroom.

"I've come with a cancellation due to mourning," she said.

"Who has gone from Life?"

Koalee told her. "We will have the visit after the rites. Are you too busy right now? May I talk to you?"

The widow was gracious. She ushered Koalee into Lenk's small visiting nook.

"I know who the musician was," said Koalee, "Do you?"

"Yes. He was my cousin."

"And you told no one?" Koalee asked, shocked.

"I told Gozer. It was no use telling anyone else. He didn't know me. He didn't remember. I really don't think he knew who he was, or where he was from."

"He was a metalsmith, wasn't he?"

"Yes. A fine metalsmith. I don't think he remembered that, either. It was fortunate he had his music. It kept him alive this long. Koalee, how did he die?"

"The doctor thinks he may have taken Life. It was poisonous toadstools."

The widow nodded. "Yes. Well, when the messenger goes for Tokra, the news will reach Gozer's village. He had many friends and relations there."

"I wonder why he chose to live in this village."

"We think perhaps because it was closest to the old village where it all happened. But we don't know where he was those four years before he appeared in the marketplace. Maybe wandering in the tall woods. Or among the ruins?"

"Shouldn't Gozer's village hear at once? Won't they want to come to the rites?"

"No. They will hold their own rites. How did you find out, Koalee? Did he leave a note somewhere?"

"Do you remember how we went back to the village after the mower, and spent the night there? And there was a big meal for everyone, after the burials?"

The widow shook her head. "I have little memory of that day except pain."

"A young musician sang to us after the supper. He took up his quidda and sang a sad song of farewell to the village and his family. The lampman has been writing down his songs. That song is among them."

For the first time, tears swam in the widow's eyes.

"It took both our minds," she said. "Only it took my mind for just a day or two, and I got mine back. His didn't go so quickly, but when it went, it went forever."

"I will leave you," said Koalee. "I am sorry to have brought sadness."

"You won't have noticed," said the widow, "how puzzled he looked when he saw me. It was the same with any of Gozer's villagers. It will always be a mystery, how he remembered his music but nothing else."

"I can't understand why I didn't recognize him. Or Dyra either."

"He wasn't the same man, Koalee. The metalsmith you heard singing was tall and broad and strong, with dark brown hair. The man who came here four years later was thin and bent, with hollow eyes and lines in his face and grey hair. I hardly knew him myself. He was only twenty-nine and he looked fifty."

"The burial will be within the hour. The lampman thought the miller's wife would be his mother..."

"Let it be," said the widow. "The man who lived behind the market was friends with the miller's wife and trusted her. He didn't know me. I'll explain that to Ajist's father. He will understand."

The rites for the singer behind the market were very beautiful. The village musician had written down the music to the grassman's farewell as well as Koalee and Dyra and the lampman together could remember it, and he played and sang with so much emotion it was almost as if the other musician were back with them again. Koalee heard the last lines with such pain in her heart she thought it would break:

> *Oh, Life, keep my village*
> *In store through the years,*
> *And let me return*
> *When I've shed all my tears.*
> *Then nothing will vanish, nothing will die,*
> *And we'll walk with my lady,*
> *My baby and I.*

※ ※ ※

Tokra stayed in the village for several days after the rites and Dyra got to know him better. He was a fairly young man, not quite as old as Lenk, though a slight stoop and the lenses he wore made him look older. His expression was filled with such happy expectancy he could appear naïve as a child, but behind the innocence there was maturity and wisdom.

"You maintain a raft behind the meeting house with nobody on it," he said to Dyra.

"It's a raft for a dolenter. The people speak often of finding a dolenter to come here, but I've been satisfied with you. You come when we need you. I had bad experiences with the one at our old village."

"You're afraid a dolenter will turn the people sour and tell them Life is angry. Gozer has told me."

"I don't think a dolenter should run the village. I think council should run the village. That's how it is here, and it's a happier village."

"I agree that it's a happy village. It's happier than Gozer's village, but that isn't because you have no dolenter. It's because you and your councillors are easy people, Dyra. You know how to let people think and act for themselves, and yet you keep the village functioning. Please don't repeat this to anyone, but Gozer is too bossy, and he's getting worse. I think the villagers will ask for a new councillor soon."

"That's too bad. He has been a fine leader."

"You are a leader, Dyra. Gozer doesn't hear his councillors any more." Tokra smiled. "As you said, the dolenter is the dolenter and the council is the council. There is a young hunter in our village with eyes as clear as yours. His name is Runya. He has talked to me often of philosophy, and he understands the oneness of Life. He prays before he kills, do you know that? So he will never kill to no purpose. I would like to see him become Chief Councillor."

"You are like an elf sometimes."

"I study the old religion."

Dyra looked embarrassed. "I owe you an explanation, Tokra. The truth is, my wife and half the villagers are pressuring me to get a dolenter."

Tokra laughed aloud. "You're afraid you may give in to them? The grassman's way is a good way, Dyra. I think your changes here are good. But young people need to be surrounded by the Way, the complete Way. Having a permanent dolenter who is there when rites need to be held, who is there to hold meetings to remind us of the meaning of Life, to pray with the people when there is trouble—who is there for them to come to talk to, like the young hunter comes to me... It's all part of the total Way."

"Koalee and I were just saying it's as if our young people are changing too fast these days. They seem to be losing tradition."

"Dyra, can't you take a hint? I've been telling you that I'm discontented in Gozer's village and that I like it here. What's more, my daughter likes it here very much. And I'm sure my son would. He is just the age of your son and he wants to be a dolenter, too. I thought that by the time he is ready, Gozer's village may have gone through the bad times and he could be their permanent dolenter. We'll see."

"Are you saying you would run away from a village that needs you?"

"No. I've watched this process for over a year now. I've talked and

I've discussed and I've suggested. It's no good. It's a kind of growing pain they have to go through for themselves. I would go there and hold meetings, as I have come to hold meetings for you. Gozer has been making children of his villagers, and now they're expecting me to do their thinking for them. If I leave, it may help them to think for themselves."

"Will you be able to get permission to leave?"

"Yes. Gozer can be flattered. I may suggest he runs the village so smoothly that a permanent dolenter is not needed, and that your need is greater, having had no dolenter since the beginning. Would that be too much of an untruth? But first I need your permission to move on to that vacant raft."

Dyra was going through quite an inner struggle. He liked the dolenter, but old fears still lingered.

"I will pray to Life," he said, "and talk it over with council and with my wife. I will let you know at this evening's visit."

The widow and Ajist were coming for the meal, so Tokra was to join them. Koalee hurried Ston through his exercises with unusual haste and spent the rest of the day cooking all her special dishes. Nila and Belm were scrubbed and combed. The table was set with the best dishes, and Koalee placed a tiny glass of water at each place and laid a moss flower beside it. It was a tradition from the old religion, and she hoped the dolenter would understand. Hoyim came out of the washing room looking like a sunbeam.

The visitors arrived exactly on time. The dolenter was warm and friendly, the widow gracious and beautiful, Hoyim blushed when he saw Ajist, and Koalee could see why the girl attracted him. She was wearing a dress of blue and violet, with a wreath of paper flowers around her hair. On her wrist she wore the two glass bracelets Hoyim had made.

Koalee thought for an instant she would lose her breath. So that was it. Now she knew who Ajist reminded her of. Ajist looked like Violet. No wings, of course, and no antennae, nor did her eyes have quite such an exaggerated slope or that characteristic look of the wild things, but it was definitely Violet she resembled.

So Hoyim had already given her a gift. That was not tradition.

Things were moving too fast. It was a good thing that she and Yansa and Lenk had managed to persuade Dyra to accept Tokra's offer. And Hoyim had walked out with his daughter! Koalee was too happy to be worried about glass bracelets any more.

The talk during the meal was lively. Koalee decided to bring up the subject of Ajist's resemblance to Violet, and she and Dyra talked of their days in the woods. Their children had never heard a detailed description of Violet before, and they listened in wide-eyed wonder. Then the conversation veered to Balink's father-in-law. Now that he had dug up and sold his trees, the weaver had mossed his entire garden. He'd puzzled everyone by creating a small hill in it, similar to the slope on which the village was located. And then, with Doen's help, he cemented in a garden pool shaped like Hoyim's Lake. The weaver was painstakingly carving models of every house and shop in the village, all to scale. Even the street lamps would be there.

"The weaver is amazing," Hoyim explained to Ajist and her father. "There isn't anything he can't do."

"Except, the fussier he gets, the more help he wants from Doen," said the widow. "Balink grows very tired of it."

"Just think, we can take a stranger to the weaver's garden and show him the whole village, right there. He's even making models of the trees."

"The wind will carry it all away."

"Oh no," said Belm, who passed the weaver's garden daily on his way to and from school. "It's all cemented to boards and the boards are buried under the moss."

"He said he got the idea in the flood," said Hoyim. "He was wondering how the village looked to the elf when he was scanning."

When the meal ended, the widow helped Koalee with the washing up. Hoyim and Ajist sat on the top step of the stair in animated conversation.

Dyra took Tokra to his workroom to show him how lenses were made, and to tell him that the council had accepted his offer—and that Dyra himself was happy about it. The new dolenter would teach the children the old religion, and discuss timely topics such as the implications of the way of Life of the eggman. Finally, their discussion turned to the history Dyra was writing. The dolenter was very enthusiastic. When he left, he was carrying Dyra's, *History of the Settlement*, as well as the first chapters of Dyra's own book.

"I have a feeling this is going to be my village for Life," said Tokra. "I want to know all about it and the people in it. So see that you have another chapter ready for me in a few days."

But it would be a little while before Dyra could settle to write again. He and the council had to inspect Tuje's plans for the ridiculous house Flon wanted. Also, it was time to collect the drot. Custom dictated that he must be present when Yansa tallied up the record books. The order for magnifiers for Gozer's village had to be completed. And then there was the expedition to the tall woods to consider.

IX

Plans for the expedition to the tall woods materialized quickly. After Ajist and her father returned to Gozer's village, hoping to get permission to leave, Hoyim could be persuaded to come up trail. When Dyra approached Koalee about it, she hesitated, feeling it would be irresponsible to leave Ston's exercises to the doctor, but the doctor was willing. And there was that other matter on her mind—the tall man. She decided that a journey to the tall woods was in order.

In the end, a large party set off. Dyra's entire family went, right down to young Belm. Koalee's sister Pora and her husband went, as did one of the hunters and the smith's son, and others. The basketmaker decided to come too; he hoped to collect some of the rare coloured grasses to weave partitions for his house.

The official artist had been painting a portrait of the miller's wife. On the evening before the journey, she made a mysterious visit to Dyra's and asked to see Hoyim. She shoved her portrait into his hand.

"I don't know why I'm doing this," she said, "but the fuelman said I should, and you know the fuelman's hunches. He said you'll need it. Be sure to pack it with you."

Hoyim was mystified. But he did know about the fuelman's premonitions, and Nila insisted that he put the portrait in his trail runner.

"What use could it possibly be to anybody in the tall woods?" he wondered.

"You'll see," was his sister's reply.

Koalee made the usual preparations, noting that it was reminiscent of that other time. Except this time, they would be well protected by a large group and wouldn't be breaking trail into new land. They had a home to return to. She reminisced for a moment about that other home, the first home Dyra built for her. She thought of Lenk's wife and of Tuje's twin, and the day they fell victim to the four-legged shadow, of the old meeting house where Hoyim was accepted into Life, and of her grandmother's mirror that she hadn't been able to bring.

Would it still be there, she wondered. Or would the mower long since have destroyed their house and everything they'd left behind? She wanted to ask Dyra if they could go all the way back to explore the old village, but she knew he would never agree. It would mean risking too much danger for no good reason. They left at dawn with four trail runners, one with room in it for Belm should he grow too tired. Koalee carried her bow and took her station as one of the guards.

"Good trail!" shouted the villagers who had come to see them off.

They moved rapidly, and though they stopped to rest and spent an hour over their noon meal, they reached the temporary shelter by mid-afternoon. It was there that Hoyim was injured. A grasshopper, zooming in at full speed, hit the side of his leg. Hoyim doubled up, moaning, and Koalee had difficulty persuading him to let her examine it.

"No break," she said with relief, "but you are going to have a terrible bruise. Look at it swelling, Dyra. We've no way to cool it. Nila. Belm. Dig me some stones and bring them quickly, while they're still damp on the bottom."

The children ran to carry out her orders, and their Aunt Pora went with them. Koalee settled Hoyim comfortably among blankets in the space under the shelter, and laid his leg on the cool damp stones, finally burying it in roots and earth.

"Now, when you start to feel warm we'll do this again," she said. "It may help to take down the swelling."

"Will it keep him from walking?" Hent asked.

"I'm sure it will. It's going to be bruised from ankle to knee."

"I guess it's the trail runner for you for the rest of the way," Hent told Hoyim.

"No," said Hoyim firmly. "I weigh almost as much as a man. I won't have you pulling me. Just leave me here with some food and a flask of dew. Maybe by the time you get back I'll be able to walk."

They had to admit, reluctantly, that Hoyim was right. There really wasn't room on the temporary raft for them all to stay, even for one night, at least part of the party could push on to the tall woods before evening. The hunter volunteered to stay with Hoyim, but Hoyim insisted that he would be perfectly safe in the shelter. After all, it had been his home away from home twice a week for a year now. He even had a book stored there, and some paper and markers. If his leg stopped paining, he would be able to entertain himself well.

"Stupid grasshopper," said the smith's son. "They never watch where they're going. I wonder more of us don't get hit like that."

"And he didn't even knock himself out," said Belm. "If he had, we could have eaten him."

Hoyim's leg was soon a dark blue-purple over much of the limb, and far too painful to allow him to walk. Koalee checked it thoroughly once more, concluding that it was not growing worse. So the party decided to proceed up trail.

Hoyim saw them off bravely. He was not worried or afraid about staying at the shelter, but he was broken-hearted. He'd wanted more than anything to visit the tall woods and see the raft his parents had built there, and perhaps catch a glimpse of the fairy Violet they'd talked about. It was a bitter disappointment, but all he could do was wait until they returned. He hopped to the edge of the raft and eased himself down to the stone steps his mother had built, and there he settled with his book, to read for a while. He had his bow beside him and a supply of seeds in his pocket, and calculated that he wouldn't have to move until hunger told him it was time for the noon meal.

※ ※ ※

He had only read a few pages when he became aware of a pulsing in the earth, and realized that the raft was trembling. The pulsing became a regular beat, as if a heavy being was approaching. His senses leapt to attention. Hoyim had never seen the walking shadow, but he knew instinctively what it was. He knew he should hop down from the steps and hide under the float space, but he couldn't make himself move. He tried to tell himself that a storm was coming, but he knew it wasn't a storm. The sky was blue and the wind was calm. Then a great shadow blotted out the sun, darkening his book and the stone steps, stretching across the grass woods before him.

Hoyim could not have explained what made him react as he did, but he pulled himself up on his good knee and peered up over the edge of the raft. A dark monster stood there, huge and broad and high as the tall trees. Hoyim fought to keep from panic. His eyes looked up and up and up, and after a minute he was satisfied that he was in fact looking at a tall man. No grassman had ever seen a tall man as close as this. Was he safe? What would happen? Could the tall man see him?

A voice so deep and loud it almost burst Hoyim's ears blared from the tall man's mouth, but Hoyim couldn't understand what he said. What he said was "Another one? No one will believe this!" but Hoyim had never heard the English language.

Well, there was no point in cowering on the stone steps; his father would step right up and offer his hand. Painfully, Hoyim crawled up on the raft and got himself to a standing position. He held out his hand, preparing to bow.

"You couldn't shake my little finger," said the tall man, and Hoyim covered his ears. "Does my voice bother you? I'll try to speak softly."

The tall man got right down on the grass and looked closely at Hoyim and at the shelter.

Hoyim tried to manage a smile.

"Are you hurt?" asked the tall man. His breath swept over the raft like a hot summer wind, an evil-smelling wind. Thinking he would suffocate, Hoyim turned his face away.

"Hurt?" the tall man repeated, and when he saw that Hoyim didn't understand, he pointed to his own leg, and then to Hoyim. Hoyim nodded. He raised his trouser leg and showed his bruises, then pointed to a grasshopper on a nearby grass tree, indicating that a grasshopper had flown into his leg. The man nodded and looked sympathetic.

Hoyim was thrilled. He was actually communicating with a tall man! But what now? Ah, the portrait of the miller's wife. He fumbled in his backpack and brought out the picture, holding it up for the tall man to see. The tall man frowned, then reached into a pocket and brought out a giant pair of lenses like those Dyra made. When he had them on, he looked carefully at the portrait.

"Well, I'll be darned," said the tall man. "I swear it's my friend from the flood. Is she your mother? Have you lost her? I've been looking for her myself."

Hoyim had another idea. He hopped to the shelter and returned with his drawing paper and markers. Very quickly, he sketched a map of the trail and Hoyim's Lake and the village and the tall woods, pointing to the spot where they were.

"Intelligent little fellow, aren't you?" the man remarked.

Hoyim pointed to the village on the map, and then pointed up trail toward home.

The man shook his head. "This is too small for me, son." He drew a huge book of blank paper from his pocket and laid it down in front of Hoyim, indicating that he should draw the map on that. The pages were much longer than Hoyim himself, and his markers made a very fine line, but he managed to reproduce his map, making a series of marks to represent houses in the village, and pointing to the shelter to make the man understand what they were.

"So you live in a town. What else can you tell me about yourself?"

Hoyim was thinking fast. He pointed to the shelter and named it in the grassman's tongue, and then he did the same with his leg and with the paper. Then he pointed to himself and said, "Hoyim."

"If I sound like a roaring bull to you, you sound like a mouse to me," said the man, but he had the meaning, for he pointed to himself and said something that sounded like "Jon."

Hoyim held out his hand again and said, "A pleasant day, Jon."

The man rolled over on his back on the grass woods and laughed loudly.

"How many of you are there?" he asked when he had regained control. He pointed to the houses on the map with a tiny twig, and then held up his fingers and counted them.

Hoyim nodded and wrote the number, but it meant nothing to the tall man, so he then drew five marks and bundled them within a circular line, and then did it again. He indicated that the bundle would have to be repeated twenty-four times to number the people in the village.

The tall man seemed to understand. "I can't imagine how you survive."

Hoyim was now extending the map to show him Gozer's village and the number there, and the man looked more and more amazed. "Are you all over the earth?"

Hoyim made a gesture with his hands to show the tall man that his breath was much too overwhelming, and the tall man understood and laughed again.

"I'm sorry. Everything about me is too much for you, isn't it?" he said.

For some unexplainable reason, Hoyim laughed with him. He felt an undeniable friendliness and good will coming from the tall man. Then he returned to his paper and drew the tall woods and pointed up trail, pointed to his sore leg, pointed up trail again, and then made eight more people marks and two small marks entering the tall woods.

"Are you trying to tell me your companions have left you?"

The tall man pointed his twig at the portrait of the miller's wife, pointed to the group in the woods, and looked at Hoyim questioningly. Was he asking if she was there? Hoyim shook his head and pointed to the village.

"She's there? She got home safe then. I was afraid the wind would blow her into the water. I shouldn't have left her there, but frankly I didn't know what to do and I thought I was imagining it. She came as a surprise, to say the least. Also, you and I have a problem, young man."

Hoyim was getting none of this, so he stood uncertainly, wondering what to do next. It occurred to him that if the man understood a map he would also understand a lineage chart, so he sat down to draw out his father's and mother's families, his own family, the families of Lenk and Yansa, because they were councillors, and he finished with Dyra's brothers and sisters and their families, then his relatives on his mother's side.

"I don't understand these marks," said the tall man.

Hoyim could guess what he had said, and he was ready for him. He pointed to his own name on the chart and to himself, and then he pointed to his parents' names and those of Nila and Belm, and pointed once to the little group in the tall woods.

"This is your family you've listed then," said the tall man.

After a moment the man wrote something on another piece of paper, pointed to himself and said, "John." Hoyim decided that he must have written his name. Then he followed Hoyim's lead and drew a map, indicating the tall woods and making a mark on a spot some distance high sun- rising sun from there. That must be where the tall man lived.

"Let's get you to your people," said the tall man. "Now, what can I carry you in?"

He picked some grasses and wove them into what was obviously a crude basket—and Hoyim knew absolute terror. All he had wanted to do was to make friends with the tall man. It had never occurred to him that the tall man might steal him and take him home. He hastily stuffed his markers and the miller's wife's portrait into his backpack and put it on, and then snatched up his book and papers and hopped toward the shelter. He knew it was well within the tall man's power to lift him up, shelter and all, but at least he could retrieve his flatbread and nut meat. He might be stolen, but he had no intention of starving. He drew his knife and made hasty scratches on the floor of the shelter, to tell his family that a tall man had carried him away.

"Don't be frightened," said the man.

Hoyim was growing used to the voice, and he knew it sounded kindly.

"I'd love to take you home for a pet for the kids, but you wouldn't last long with our dogs and cats around. No, I'm only going to return you to your family. They can look after you better."

He pointed to the little group of people on the map, and to the shelter, and indicated that if he took Hoyim from the shelter and placed him in the grass basket, he could transfer him with ease to his family in the woods. Hoyim understood what he meant. It meant putting a great deal of trust in the tall man, but to refuse the offer might make the tall man angry and ruin the beginnings of this friendship. He indicated his willingness to go by gathering up his belongings, locking the door of the shelter, hopping to the basket, and climbing in. He tested the basket to make sure it was strong enough to hold him.

"I see by your clothing and your pack that you know how to make things well," said the tall man. "It's a mystery to me why nobody has ever seen you. Or maybe they don't tell. I didn't tell a living soul that I saw the woman in the picture. Who painted her, by the way? That's some artist. I wish I knew whether it's best to tell about you or not. Maybe you're safer with nobody knowing. I won't tell anyone. They'd think I was unhinged, and my wife would never believe me."

The tall man was forgetting to hold the basket steady. Hoyim hung on for his life as the basket tossed with every huge step. When the tall man's attention returned to him, he looked abashed.

"Sorry about that. I'll be more careful."

Even when he paid attention to the basket, the tall man's lurching strides made it sway until Hoyim was seasick. Turning green, he lay helplessly in the bottom and parted two grass stems, and was sick.

The tall man noticed that.

"What's this? Sick? Steady now. We're almost there."

He set the basket gently in the palm of his outstretched hand and tried to balance it as he walked. Hoyim was grateful. Then he realized that the light had changed, and that there were tall trees above him. They had come so fast! How could anyone travel this fast? Why, his family hadn't had time to reach the tall woods yet. Then a horrifying fear struck him. Had they been on the trail? Had the tall man trampled his family? His relatives and friends? He pulled himself up and peered over the side of the basket, hoping by some miracle to see them all.

Something struck him from behind. He was tackled around the waist and borne aloft, right out of the basket. A bird had him! Hoyim thought he knew now what it felt like to faint.

"It's all right. I've got you," said the eggman.

Hoyim found himself sitting on a broad branch of a tall tree, with the eggman beside him and the tall man staring at him at eye level.

"I rescued you," said Kezel, adjusting his ropes. "You're lucky I was swinging by."

"I wasn't in danger. The tall man is my friend. He was bringing me to my father." The eggman became aware that the tall man was watching them, and now it was his turn to look afraid. Hoyim looked at the tall man and shook his head, to show how unexpected it all was.

"Tarzan, too?" the tall man was muttering.

It was doubtful which of the three was the most amazed.

"This is a fix," said another voice. They looked around to see the elf Radd emerging on a nearby branch.

"What's happening?" asked Hoyim once more. His leg was paining dreadfully from all the jostling, and he was afraid to move for fear of falling from the tree.

"Nothing's happening," said Radd, "but if you're going to bring tall men trampling through the woods with their big feet, we'll have any number of accidents."

"I had to get to know him. I had to find out his plans."

"I know his plans. He was planning to run sheep on the land where you live, but now that he's met you he's got a problem. Right now he's trying to figure out where he can fence the land to keep you and the villagers safe."

"My father said if we could meet them and talk to them, they would stop harming us."

"Your father doesn't know the tall men as I do. You're just lucky you're dealing with this one." Radd almost added that it was the neighbour of this tall man whose horse killed Lenk's wife and who wiped out Gozer's village, but he reconsidered.

The tall man was wiping his brow. Tiny men who carried backpacks were one thing, but when they had golden hair and appeared from nowhere, that was something else. The eggman was in a similar stupor over the tall man. It occurred to him that he might just throw a noose over a branch and swing out of there, but when he looked up at the branches above he suddenly lost his confidence.

"I don't think I'll gather any more eggs today," he said.

Hoyim realized that the eggman was displaying fear where he himself had shown courage, injured leg and all. Suddenly the eggman lost some of his stature. Hoyim looked at the tall man and gestured that he wanted to be put on the ground. The tall man obligingly let him step onto his hand and lowered him gently down. Hoyim then proceeded to point to the tall man's feet, back to himself, and then to the floor of the woods, to remind his new friend that he would have to be extremely careful where he walked. The tall man nodded with understanding.

"I'm used to field mice," he said. "They move so fast they get out of the way. You can't scamper like that, can you?"

"He knows," said Radd. "He says he'll be careful."

"Do you speak his language?"

"I read his mind. I asked him if he stepped on anybody on the trail, but he didn't come by trail. Your family are all safe. They'll reach the hollow tree by noon. I'm sure they'll camp there. They'll be hungry for a meal."

Through signals, Hoyim conveyed to the tall man that he would follow the elf back to the trail, and the tall man nodded and prepared to follow them at a safe distance. Kezel was still up in the tree.

Hoyim found a branch suitable for a crutch, and Radd tested the footing for him. That way they made good time. The tall man was worried about his leg, though, and offered to put him back in the basket. Hoyim pointed to his stomach and rejected the offer. The tall man laughed, and the woods echoed with the sound.

When they reached the hollow tree, Radd showed Hoyim the room where he'd slept as a baby, and the one above where Golden first appeared.

"It was in better condition then," he said. "It will rot away soon."

Hoyim had an overwhelming sense of coming home.

"I seem to remember this place," he said. "Is this really where the fairy gave me a diamond?"

"You have a good memory."

"No. My parents told us the whole story just a few days ago."

They settled in the clearing in front of the hollow tree and held a three-way pantomime discussion about the possibility of learning to communicate. When Hoyim and the tall man had taught each other the names for earth and trees and flowers, and each item of clothing they were wearing, they decided that it would be possible to learn to write letters to each other. The tall man got Hoyim to write down several of the signs the grass people used for common words, and wrote his own signs beside them, and then Hoyim copied the list on his own small piece of paper.

Radd, who had been serving as translator, explained a few principles about how the English language worked, and promised to give Hoyim an Elfin-English dictionary. It was decided that the hollow tree would serve as a terminal where they could leave messages. Hoyim didn't know when he had ever been so excited.

"I hear them," said Radd.

Hoyim had forgotten that his family were still up trail and realized they were about to get a shock.

Radd caught his thought, of course. "I'll go and meet them," he said. "Otherwise the surprise may scatter them to the winds."

He met the expedition at the edge of the woods. "I trust it was good trail," he said.

"It was good trail," said Dyra, "except that my son was hurt by a grasshopper. We had to leave him at the shelter."

They couldn't imagine why Radd smiled at the news.

"I apologize, Koalee, for not coming to you with the news you wanted," said Radd. "There was no chance to make contact until today."

"What's this?" asked Dyra.

"Oh dear," said Koalee.

"There's no need for secrecy, Koalee," Radd said. "What the miller's wife began, your son has finished."

"My son?"

"He's here before you. The tall man brought him."

"A tall man!" Belm cried.

Belm, running ahead, was the first to spot the tall man. The others, entering the clearing by the hollow tree, were too dumfounded to speak.

X

ALL WATCHED in silence as a trembling Dyra stepped forward to speak with the tall man. Through gestures and Hoyim's maps, and with the help of Radd, it quickly became clear that communication was indeed possible. Dyra relaxed. He had only his intuition to go by, but he was sure the tall man was to be trusted. After they'd spent some time together and practiced saying everyone's names, the tall man assured them that he knew where their village was located and promised to keep it safe. Then he stood up carefully, extended his hand, and shook it in the air as if he was shaking Dyra's. Dyra imitated the motion, and the tall man understood. Then Dyra bowed in the grassman's formal two-handed greeting, and the tall man imitated him.

Hoyim hobbled to the hollow tree and pointed to the charts and the hidden room, reminding John that at some future time he would find written messages there. The tall man nodded and smiled. Then he looked around, counting heads to make sure no one was underfoot, and waved to the grass people. They all waved back, calling, "Good trail, tall man."

So, John thought to himself as he left, it had not been his imagination. The tall man was feeling better than he had since the flood. It was the strangest thing he'd ever seen, but at least he knew now that they were real.

"Now then," said Dyra, turning to his wife, "I want to know about this 'contact' Radd was making."

Koalee looked to Radd, then back to Dyra, wondering where to start.

"Dyra," she said, "much as I'm proud of Hoyim—and he deserves a great deal of credit for what he's done today—he doesn't deserve all the credit."

"Who does then?" a puzzled Dyra asked.

"The miller's wife. When she went to ground on the rocks..."

"Yes?"

"She met the tall man. He picked up her house." Here was a sensation.

"You knew this?" said Pora. "And you didn't tell?"

"You had no right to keep a secret like that, Koalee!" Dyra said. "Think how dangerous it could have been for the village. I can't imagine why you didn't tell me." He sounded more serious than Koalee had ever heard him.

"Do you get the feeling the tall man can be trusted?" she asked. "That he won't harm us?"

"Yes, I do."

"So did the miller's wife."

"She had no right. It was up to council."

"The council wasn't there to meet him. The miller's wife did. She is not a fool, Dyra. She knows people."

"This is surprising. My villagers taking it on themselves to make decisions like this."

Koalee knew what was going on in his mind. He was wondering again if he gave the villagers too much freedom—and again he was renewing his faith in their ingenuity and reliability. Koalee grinned broadly, and Dyra grinned back.

"And you think she deserves credit because...?"

"She remembered that you told us to make friends with the tall men. She made friends with him. I think she's the reason he came back today. I think she's the reason he accepted Hoyim and was good to him."

Dyra was silent. Koalee added, "I mean that, Dyra. We had lots of time to talk when we were floating on the raft. She broke the trail, believe me."

"I can't understand why all of you kept it secret. This must be the biggest story in the history of the grass people! By rights she should have come home bragging to the whole village about it."

"She thought it might stir up a lot of trouble that didn't need stirring up."

"Meaning?"

"She had an intuition that he was peaceful. She thought any meetings should be unplanned. The way she and Hoyim met him."

"It felt safe to speak to him," said Hoyim. "And you start to think seriously of what will happen in the future."

"*Are* you thinking seriously of the future?" asked his father lightly, not expecting an answer.

"If you're referring to me, Father, yes, I am. I believe I've chosen the right trade."

Hoyim knew his family would be surprised, and he enjoyed it.

"You've chosen a trade and not talked about it to us?"

"I was going to. As soon as I was sure. Ajist thinks it's a wonderful idea."

"I'm sure you won't mind telling us what it is?"

"I'm going to be a printer."

"But Hoyim, there's no…"

"…no print shop in the village. That's just it. It will be all mine, and I don't need to be trained. There's a book about it at school. It's something I just feel I know."

"But will there be work for you?"

"There will be work. The traders say there is no print shop between the end of the settlement and the big village. They can bring me plenty of orders. The young people want me to print the songs the singer behind the market sang, and they will buy them. Gozer's village will buy them. And then there's your history of the village, Father. Why send it to the big village to be printed? I can do it at home and sell copies of it."

"Son, you're apprentice age. Not the age to run a business."

"Uncle Syl will help me. He says he hasn't enough to do. Especially in the cold season, when he can't fish."

"So you've talked to Syl."

"I had to have a place for my printing press, and Uncle Syl has a room in his house he doesn't use."

Pora's husband was beaming. "This means a lot of paper orders for me, doesn't it, Hoyim?"

Hoyim nodded.

Koalee couldn't cope with his transition from a son with no sense of purpose to a son who seemed to think he was sixteen. Yet he had shown how brave he was today. "How do you 'know' you can do this?" she asked.

"I like charting and lettering. I like to work with spaces on paper. I like to communicate. I think I proved that today."

"The tall woods have gone to your head," said Dyra. "What you print will have to be approved by the council. You cannot have right of trade until you've passed apprentice age."

"I accept that."

Radd stepped forward. "Hoyim has made the right choice," he said. "He will learn the language of the tall men and even be able to print letters for them."

Hoyim nodded.

"Right choice or not," said Dyra, "a boy just turning fourteen cannot run a business."

"Like I said, Syl will run the business for three years. Syl has time."

"Where are you going to get the printing press, Hoyim?" asked Hent practically.

"The print is ordered, along with plans to build the press. Tuje will build it. I sent the order with the traders." Hoyim saw his father's expression and added. "I saved my trail money. Tuje will wait to be paid until I do my first orders."

"I am very pleased that you've done so much planning on your own, Hoyim, but it was impolite and untraditional to do it behind my back, and your mother's."

Koalee added her own rebuke. "You told the traders. You told Ajist. You told Syl. It appears you told half the village but not your own family."

"I had to do it this way. Anytime I tried to talk to you, I got confused. I was always afraid you'd tell me what to do, and I had to find my own way."

Dyra nodded, and a few moments later, as Hoyim discussed paper with Eltos, he put his arm around Koalee and looked up into the trees. "At least it wasn't a bird's nest in the top of a tall tree," he said.

"He's too young. He'll need so much help."

"I don't think so. Once Hoyim has set his mind on getting somewhere, he'll go straight there. Remind me, when we get back, that the village must give a formal banquet for Hoyim and the miller's wife."

They camped for the night at the hollow tree, and in the morning they divided into two parties. The trail men and the basketmaker went high sun to check on the state of the trail and to do what collecting could be done there. Dyra's whole family proceeded toward the old raft, promising to rejoin the others at the hollow tree.

"I don't think Hoyim needs to go there any longer," Koalee remarked, picking her way among the leaves. "I don't think there are any old spells ruling him now."

"But I need to go," said Dyra. "I've reached this place in my book. I want to refresh my mind."

※ ※ ※

Nila walked with Pora, marvelling at how much her aunt resembled her mother. It also struck her that Pora's face lacked something her mother had. It wasn't just that Koalee was older. She had some kind of open curiosity about life.

"I was fifteen," Pora was saying to her, "and Syl was your age. Flon was seven, and I guess Hent was eighteen. How old were you when we came, Hent?"

"Eighteen. Because we were the first wedding in the village, remember?"

"And you didn't know where you were going at all?" Nila asked.

"No, we didn't. All we knew was that your father and mother were out there somewhere in front of us, supposedly finding us a safe place."

"And there was nothing there at all?"

"Nothing at all. Just Hoyim's Lake, where we caught up with them, but it didn't have a name until that day. Oh, and your father's raft. He and Lenk had been up there and built that raft. There was no house on it—just a temporary shelter. That's all there was."

"If we had Dokrimalitzla, the elves would have led everyone to safety before anybody was killed," Nila remarked, thinking of the stories she'd heard of the destruction of the old village.

Pora smiled. "It is forty-one years since our last Dokrimalitzla died, Nila. Many say there will never be another."

"Oh, but there will. If the grass people keep faith with Life."

This time Pora laughed. "What makes you so sure?"

"I've seen him," said Nila, and Pora realized that her niece could be a very perceptive child. She was also a very beautiful one, with delicate features and her father's intelligence in her blue eyes.

Puzzled about what to say next, Pora managed, "You've seen him?"

"Yes. I see things. He's very tall and his hair is bright gold. He's so beautiful. I saw him standing among leaves and flowers, with the sunlight all around him like a mist."

"You saw an elf."

"No. I saw Dokrimalitzla."

As if she didn't wish to be questioned any more, Nila ran off to join Belm, and Pora stepped up beside her sister, to relate what she had just heard.

Koalee didn't register as much surprise as Pora expected. "She's a bit uncanny," she said. "She does see things, you know, and they turn out to be true."

Pora felt as if the woods were shivering through her whole body. "Could it be true, Koalee? Could the grass people be getting another Dokrimalitzla?"

"I've heard that elves once prophesied that the next Dokrimalitzla will be the seventh son of a seventh son. Not even the basketmaker can produce one of those!"

※ ※ ※

When they finally found the raft that Dyra and Koalee built for their first night in the woods, they were disappointed. The fallen tree was still there, as well as the giant tree behind the hollow, and the remnants of the stone fire pit they had constructed. But the raft was in ruins. The pyles had fallen, and one had sunk out of sight. What was left of the raft was propped against the fallen tree.

"Well, it's time we got here," said Dyra. He and his brothers-in-law set about sinking new pyles immediately and reconstructing the raft, while Koalee tidied the fire pit. Smelling the old familiar woodsy odours, Koalee checked to see if the red fruit tree was still there.

"Oh, Dyra this was a thrilling place!" she called.

"We camped here," said Pora. "Remember, Hent? Most of us slept on the moss, and some slept over there. There was a ring of toadstools. Gozer put all the oldest people on the raft."

"You slept there," said her husband, pointing to a spot beside the stump. "Right there."

"How did you know where I slept? I was not your wife in those days."

He grinned. "You know I particularly notice anything beautiful. You wrapped yourself in the brown blanket, the one you use to stop the draft from the door in the cold season."

"How did you see so much?"

"I was one of the fire guards. I sat on that stump from midnight until dawn."

While the exchange of memories went on, Koalee inspected Hoyim's leg and found it no worse for the effort. Now it was his arm that was hurting, from the crutch.

It was not until the raft was rebuilt and they'd had their evening meal and were relaxing with tea, that Dyra and Koalee began to recapture something of the magic that had accompanied their first experience of the tall woods.

"We were afraid, do you remember?" asked Koalee. "It was all strange to us. So big and dark."

"And yet it was so beautiful and easy."

"I remember thinking I'd get lazy if we stayed here very long."

"We didn't get any chance to get lazy," said Hent. "Gozer had us organized. There were so many of us, we just took over the woods as if they were the do-lan."

"That isn't the way," said Dyra. "You don't take over the tall woods. You become part of them. If a man lived here all his life, he would end up moulding on a pile of leaves and Life would use his substance to bring new life within a day. A grassman seems so insignificant in the tall woods."

"Oh no! You feel bigger and more important," said Koalee.

"Look what the tall woods have done to the eggman," said Pora.

"I saw Kezel looking pretty small today," said Hoyim. "The tall man frightened him half to death."

"It's strange he hasn't joined us."

"I wonder if the woods gave him that air of independence he has, or if it just comes from living alone," said Dyra. "If a man lived long in the tall woods, it would affect his thinking. I feel so much closer to Life here, and everyday worries don't seem to matter. Why don't we come here more often?"

They all looked puzzled.

"We live our whole lives so tied to one another in the village, continually going along in our same routines. It would free our minds and renew our faith in Life if we could get away to the tall woods and just spend a night or two here on the raft."

"Travelling vacations," said Hent, savouring the idea. "That's what my wife called it when I told her I was going up trail to get away from my shop for a few days."

"It's a dangerous luxury, Dyra," said Koalee, "and we don't need it. There is enough variety and change in the village."

"Yes, but you just took a voyage!" Hoyim reminded her, and everyone laughed.

"No one in our village is so busy that he couldn't take four or five days to come to the tall woods. We could take relays. Just little expeditions like this, coming in turns. The raft would be kept up then and the trail and resources brought back..."

"Dyra, that would not work," said Koalee. "Do you realize the village would never be the village then? What would it be with an expedition away all the time? 'Oh, the weaver's son has gone to the woods this season. The shop raft is closed. The fuelman went with the expedition. Nobody on your neighbour's raft. It would spoil the village, Dyra."

"But if their minds were rested and brighter? If they felt happy and free? Wouldn't it be worth it all?"

"It is the kind of question the dolenter should ponder," said Eltos. "Koalee may be right about the changes it would bring."

"Koalee has never liked change," said Dyra, giving her a loving smile. "She likes tradition. She has kept me permanently cemented in like the pyles so I can't drift away in a flood."

"And a good thing too," said Koalee. "But I haven't always kept you cemented in like the pyles. If I had, we would never have camped here in the first place. There wouldn't be any village."

Dyra laughed and kissed her. It occurred to Hoyim that he had never seen his father kiss his mother in front of other people before. There was something about the tall woods that was making them carefree and young.

Nila and Belm had spent every moment since their arrival exploring the plants and insects, finding things they'd never seen before. Now their father called them and ordered them to bed, mentioning the fact that the birds would waken them very early in the morning, and there would be no sleep then.

"Anyway, if we want to see Violet, that's the most likely time to do it," he said.

Morning did come early. Koalee had had the foresight to put some firewood into the shelter, where it kept fairly dry for cooking the morning meal.

When their seccar and gruel was finished, Dyra suggested that everyone follow him on a short expedition to where they might find Violet. They went off single file toward the lake, including Hoyim with his padded crutch.

Dyra had guessed right. Violet was swimming, and there was a beautiful fairy with her who must be Golden. The fairy boat was anchored farther out in the lake, its sail catching the rising sun.

Violet saw them and tried to ignore them, but they saw her signal to Golden to notice what was on the shore. She continued to enjoy the water, but then, to their amazement, she swam toward them and walked up on the beach. She shook herself and gently opened her wings. If she was, as Radd had said, 'a day or two older,' it didn't show. She was the same slender sprite, and except that her bathing costume had flowers of blue and gold, she looked exactly as she had the morning Dyra first stumbled upon her swimming pool. She looked at them with the same disinterest. The tilt of her head reminded Dyra again of a disdainful seed bird who happened to notice you nearby.

Her glance focused on Hoyim, and there was a flicker of recognition in her eyes. She turned and kicked aside the folds of a garment that lay on the shore and stooped to pick up a pair of twinkling crystal bracelets. She slipped them on, and with a slight smile she walked up to Hoyim, and clashed them lightly together before his eyes.

Hoyim laughed.

"Hoyim!" said Violet, and her own laughter tinkled through the woods, sudden and unexpected.

Then she turned as suddenly and, dropping the bracelets back on the dress, returned to the water.

"She *is* like Ajist," Hoyim admitted. "But Ajist is prettier."

"Aren't you going to introduce us?" asked Pora.

"You don't introduce people to Violet," said Dyra. "I said we were coming to see her, not to visit with her."

"Will she think it impolite if we stare at her?"

"I don't think so," said Koalee. "You stare at fairies the way you look at butterflies and flowers. Because they're beautiful. Because they're part of the scenery. I think they like to be admired."

"Violet liked that," said Nila. "What you said just now."

"How do you know?"

"I heard her thinking. Didn't you?"

"No, but I am beginning to think you have the gift!" said Koalee.

They all sat down to watch the swimmers. After a while they noticed a figure stand up in the fairy boat and wave to them. It was Radd. In a moment he was beside them. "Violet is happy that you came to see her," he said.

"Does it matter to her? Really?"

"Violet has her ways. Kezel is gone, by the way. Something gave him a fright yesterday. I don't think he'll be back."

"No more eggs," Koalee sighed, but Dyra was grinning.

Radd fixed his gaze on a tall tree, and said, "It's late in the season, but I'll see if I can get you an egg, Koalee." He disappeared.

Violet had had enough of swimming. She shook herself dry once more and stepped into her dress. It was a shimmer of shining tissues that matched her wings, and on to her toe went the familiar ruby ring. She slowly fanned her wings to dry them, and shook out her long hair and moved into the shelter of a spreading tree. There she stood, looking down into its roots.

Whatever she was watching caught the sunlight, and flashed light. After a minute she flew, and disappeared into the tall trees. The grass people noticed that Golden had gone in the opposite direction and was dressing on board the boat. So she hadn't gone away with the eggman. Perhaps she liked the boat better.

Koalee was curious about the object that twinkled so brightly in the roots of the spreading tree. She made her way over to it, and cried out excitedly, "It's my grandmother's mirror!"

There was no mistaking the heirloom, which had hung on her cupboard at the old village. Koalee had known the mirror all her life. It was made by her grandfather, the old glass-maker, and across the top it had a beautiful design cut from stained glass. It had broken her heart to leave it behind. It had broken her mother's heart too, but when her parents came they were also too burdened to carry it.

"What will I do?" asked Koalee.

"Why, take it, of course," said Hent.

"But Violet has found it, and she seems to like it. I can't just go away with it. She would be angry."

Radd hadn't found any eggs. He returned and stood listening to the conversation.

"You must take it," he said. "It's yours."

"Violet wouldn't like it. I wouldn't want to make a fairy angry."

"When I tell Violet it was your grandmother's mirror, she will understand. She has some sentiment, after all. You know the lace necklace she always wears? That lace is made from hair from the heads of all Violet's relatives. The new border is made from Golden's hair. Violet will understand. It is *a* mirror Violet likes, not this particular mirror. Maybe you could give her another in its place."

None of them knew that Violet was squatting on the bough above their heads, listening, with her hand on the hair lace collar. Her eyes suggested that she was thinking in that quick, instinctual way she had.

"It is for you, grasswoman," she said suddenly, and then flew down, looked carelessly at the mirror, and walked away.

"We will bring you a mirror in its place," Dyra promised, "the very next time a grassman comes to the tall woods. It will be left right here."

Violet didn't answer.

"She knows you will," said Radd. "You keep your word."

"How did my mirror come here in the first place?" asked Koalee.

"Traders brought it. They'd been rising sun to see if there was anything left at the old settlements worth saving, and when they got this far, Violet took a liking to the mirror and bought it. I believe it cost her an amethyst. No matter. Violet is never short of jewels."

Koalee went back to the raft hugging the mirror, then sat down on the moss and cried. Then she packed the mirror safely in layers of soft moss between two firm pieces of bark. "Trail runner or backpack," she said to the mirror, "you're going to be treated like pure gold all the way home. My mother will cry too. And this time you'll hang between the portraits of my parents, with Dyra's parents and the children all around you. You'll be a centrepiece in our house."

When they returned to the village, the news of the meeting with the tall man raised such excitement that no one could stop talking about it.

The banquet for the miller's wife and Hoyim was the most unusual the village ever hosted. No one had ever seen a tall man close up before, and they didn't know quite how to treat this event. Was it a triumph, the end of a disaster, or perhaps a celebration?

In the end it was decided they would erect a monument. The metalsmith went to work making a lettered tablet to be embedded in a specially carved pyle. The pyle was to be cemented in, and surrounded by stones. The problem was where to put it. Some wanted it by the bridge over the main drainage ditch; others thought it should stand at the entrance to the village near the first street lamp. Some believed it belonged beside the school.

The councillors finally decided on the entrance to the village. The miller's wife lived there, and it would be nice for her. Also, strangers travelling through the village would be sure to see it.

The entire village gathered at the new monument. Dyra made formal speeches of thanks to the miller's wife, and to his son, for reaching out the hand of friendship to the tall man. He said that this was only a beginning. No one knew what the next development would be, or what the future held. He called on any grassman or woman who fell into a similar situation to carry on the good impression made by these pioneers.

The miller's wife told her story. Hoyim told about the language problem, and how he came upon the idea of drawing maps and lineage charts. Once the elf brought the promised books, they could learn the language of the tall men and begin to communicate. The papermaker described his impressions when they came upon Hoyim seated beside the tall man in the woods.

And then Dyra told of his attempt to reach an understanding. Following that, he read the tablet aloud:

"The miller's wife of this village was first to meet a tall man in the thirteenth year of Dyra, when her house went to ground on a rock and he picked it up and smiled at her..."

The miller's wife, clad in a dress of the brightest purple and biggest puffs the village had ever seen, stood nodding and beaming in a way that made every heart glad.

"Twenty days later Hoyim the printer, son of Dyra the lens maker, met the tall man at the temporary shelter up trail to the tall woods, and opened communication with him by gestures and drawing maps and lineage charts. Love Life."

The dolenter Tokra then spoke of the importance of these events in the perspective of the long history of the grass people, saying it held out hope for the years to come. By that time the children were growing tired of speeches, so the dolenter made his short, in order that they might go to the picnic ground for the banquet.

It was a rather quiet and serious occasion. They had not yet recovered from the loss of the singer behind the market. But neither Hoyim nor the miller's wife felt slighted. They had been given the honour that was their right, and were made much of by everyone.

Bekra's wedding followed soon afterwards, when the traders returned from their journey. This was a much livelier occasion. Bekra had spent time arranging her gifts and belongings so they would fit into her trail runner and not be too heavy to pull, but most of her time had been spent preparing the herb raft. One of the hunter's daughters was going to take it over, and she had scant knowledge of herbs. Bekra spent many days teaching her, explaining how to recognize herbs, how to price them, and how to measure and weigh. It would have been a tragedy if there had been nobody who knew how to sell herbs.

Koalee finished the thistledown blanket and offered it, assuring Bekra that it weighed very little and she would be wise to leave another blanket at home, if necessary.

A woman in Gozer's village wove fine silk from the thread of caterpillars. Doba sent a messenger there and had a length of it delivered for his daughter's wedding dress. It was a creamy, golden colour that shone in the sunlight. Bekra and her mother made the dress ankle-length and full, with insets of lace in the sleeve puffs.

The day of the wedding dawned bright and warm, and the rites were held under the spreading trees where there were plenty of flowering trees for the ceremony.

"Is this a wedding in Truth?" asked the dolenter of Dyra's father.

"This is a wedding in Truth."

The question was repeated to Doba, and then to Kyb, and the answers were the same. "From the earth and the sun comes Life," said the dolenter, and he walked solemnly to two flowering trees that flaunted golden blooms, bending one blossom until the pollen showered upon the other. "When Life comes, cherish and guard it well,".

Bekra and her trader faced each other and joined their hands.

"Keep the Way of the grass people," said the dolenter. "Love each other. Be faithful. May you be long in Life."

Dyra noticed that Hoyim was standing close to Ajist and looking particularly serious all through the rites.

"Truth tells me, too," he murmured to Koalee, as the ceremony ended and people began to move informally about.

"No grassperson marries at fifteen anymore," said Koalee.

"But they can. It is tradition. And Hoyim now has his trade," said Dyra.

"He can't even begin his printing until the traders come back in the spring. He'll only be fourteen then. Don't hurry him, Dyra."

"I won't hurry him, but if it's the Truth it doesn't matter if he's fifteen or thirty-five, does it? That's his partner, Koalee. I have no doubt about it."

The rest of the day was spent in feasting and visiting, with many jokes and admonitions to Bekra and the trader. A bee had been seen buzzing around the yellow flowers as the dolenter bent them. This was considered to be the greatest of good luck at a marriage rite, for it was a sign of marital happiness and many children.

In the evening there was dancing in the street of shops, and even the children stayed to the very end. A tired group of villagers progressed along the Market Street with Dyra and his family, Dyra carrying Belm, who had fallen asleep. Creu and Koalee were discussing the wonderful news that Ston had been seen standing up at the wedding, and the equally wonderful news that he had been adopted by the cobbler's widow and was moving to the raft where the singer behind the market had lived. There he would be handy to the cobbler's widow, and she could come over to feed and nurse him, and keep his house clean. She was used to caring for an invalid, and looked happy about the arrangement.

Hoyim was telling Romo the leatherman that as soon as he made his first money from printing, he was going to buy mouse furs from the tanner, and get the leatherman to make him a good cold weather coat with embroidery all over it—the kind Aunt Creu could do.

Hyrn had seen Flon's new house, and that started a flurry of conversation.

"She has her water storage vat right in there beside the tree," he said excitedly. "If it rains she can have a shower right in the privacy of her house. Imagine that."

Laughter sounded behind them, and they realized it was Flon.

"I moved into my house today." Flon stepped up beside her sister. "A wonderful wedding, wasn't it? There will be another one quite soon."

"Another?" asked Koalee.

"Mine, I'm marrying Tuje."

"You're what? Flon will you ever learn that it is tradition to talk some things over with your family before you make plans?"

"I thought you'd be happy to know it's Tuje."

"Of course I'm happy it's Tuje. I love Tuje. Lenk's our best friend."

"But Tuje deserves better than me?"

"I didn't say that. Frankly Flon, I was afraid you might marry the eggman."

"Koalee! I don't want to live in a tall tree!"

"You seemed to be making a fuss over him every time I saw you together."

"I love to tease you Koalee. You have no sense of humour."

"Humph!" said Koalee. "Who is to have your fancy new raft, now that you're marrying Tuje?"

"We are. Why do you think Tuje built it?"

Koalee stopped walking. "Flon, a grasswoman moves onto her husband's raft. He doesn't move onto hers."

"Oh Koalee," said Flon, "You are so traditional."

PART 3

THE SEED

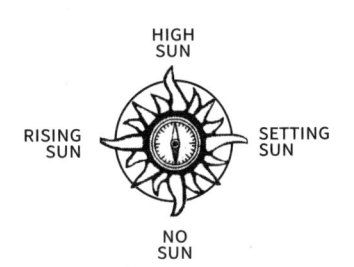

```
          HIGH
          SUN

RISING   ☀   SETTING
  SUN         SUN

           NO
           SUN
```

I

"Look Hoyim! What's that?"

Ajist was pointing to a dark coloured disc that lay beside the stairs.

"I don't know. It looks like a seed."

"The wind must have brought it. I never saw a seed like that. I'm going to plant it and see what happens."

"No Ajist, don't. You know how Father feels about strange trees in the village. If it turns out to be a tall tree…"

"The old weaver would plant it."

"He'd know what it was in time to pull it up if it was going to get too big."

"The portrait painter might know what it is. He sometimes paints trees."

"He's busy today. He's painting a picture of Father and Mother to mark Father's twentieth year as Chief Councillor.

"Then I'll go ask the weaver. No, I'll go and plant it beyond the bridge. It can't do any harm there. It might not grow anyway."

"Yes, plant it with the spreading trees," said Hoyim, "And we'll see what comes of it."

Ajist got a trowel and a dew flask and set off for the spreading trees with her find, while Hoyim made his way to his print shop on the back street. His father-in-law Tokra had written a book about the old religion, and Hoyim was setting it up and slowly publishing it, page by page. But today it would have to wait. He had just received an order to print a lineage table for a family in Runya's village who had nearly twenty households in their kin.

Runya had been in charge of Gozer's village for more than three years now, ever since the villagers insisted upon the resignation of the shopkeeper who had kept the village in turmoil with his arbitrary leadership. Ajist's father was happy about Runya, the philosophical young hunter he had picked out as a potential leader years ago. Relationships between the two villages were good.

Gozer, now past sixty and still a strong man, had accepted the changes silently. He was a man of tradition, after all. The villagers had the right to insist upon the cessation of his councillorship, and Gozer felt that he had perhaps been in charge too long. He had no regrets. He had led both villages to the safety of Dyra's new land, he'd broken trail to his own village, and he'd seen his villagers through flood and famine. Only Life knew if he would be called upon to serve again.

Though it was early morning, most of the shopkeepers in Dyra's village were already busy about their rafts, polishing windows and setting out displays. The baker, who always began work two hours before sunrise, was bringing his first loaves out of the oven. The smell was so hearty that Hoyim hurried past, lest it make him hungry. His Uncle Hryn was lighting the potter's kiln.

The metalsmith's children were coming out to play. "Stay under the float space, mind you!" their mother called to them. "Wheelers have been circling around."

Hoyim looked up automatically. There were indeed wheelers. He couldn't imagine why he hadn't heard the warning bell. He hurried his steps, hoping that Ajist would remember to check the sky. He could see the guard on the high tower, with his bow trained on one of the wheelers. If the bird came too close, it wouldn't stand a chance.

Hoyim's print shop was in the musician's old house across the back road from his Uncle Hent. The musician had moved to the other end of the village. There had been many changes during the past years. Five new rafts stood no sun of Hoyim's house, along the new trail. On the raft immediately no sun of Hoyim lived the portrait painter's son, who was promised to cousin Pettis. As Hoyim climbed the stairs to his shop, he saw Hent's son scurrying by on his way to work. His cousin was proving to be the best glassman in the family, and helped free Syl to go fishing.

Hoyim stood a moment longer. It occurred to him that one day the village would grow too large to keep the warm intimacy they knew. It was difficult to find anyone to marry who wasn't too closely related, so more strangers must inevitably come to the village. If they fit in as well as Ajist...

Even as the thought came to him, Hoyim knew that Ajist didn't fit in. People liked Ajist—perhaps they loved Ajist, as he did—but he knew they described her as different. She was polite and friendly, but there was a remoteness about her. It wasn't just that she had some of the dignity people associated with Lenk's widow; it was her habit of halting to study the minute details of some irrelevant thing, like the peculiar seed she'd found this morning. It was her tendency to sit for long periods of time, gazing at her surroundings. Ajist had practically relieved Doen of the role of chief assistant in the weaver's garden. She was also firm friends with Tienna, the portrait painter's wife, who had long been considered the oddest woman in the village. What bothered Hoyim most was that she had little to do with Balink.

Balink, Lenk's daughter, was a favourite of his mother's, and he couldn't understand why Ajist shouldn't love her too—but they had nothing in common. Balink, hale and healthy and athletic, found Ajist fragile and slow of movement, and grew impatient with her. It puzzled Balink that Ajist said it didn't bother her that she and Hoyim had been married five years, and still had no babies. Balink now had four children. Ajist drew enjoyment from intellectual discussions or observing the natural world. Balink's interests were externalized. She responded to the villagers and everything they did, and she expressed her feelings immediately.

Once, when the widow went to visit Runya's village, and Ajist needed advice about a domestic matter, Hoyim had suggested that she ask Balink, but Ajist appeared almost frightened.

"To tell the truth, Balink overwhelms me a little," she said simply, and went to ask the portrait painter's wife instead. When he brought the matter up again, she said, "I am shy, Hoyim. Didn't you realize that?"

Hoyim sometimes wished Ajist would be more like her father—warm and friendly, and able to meet the villagers easily. His mother felt the same.

"It's strange you should have married a girl like that," Koalee remarked.

It wasn't said critically. Koalee had stood by Ajist from the moment she met her, and never lost her sense of pride that Hoyim had wed a dolenter's daughter. It was a pity there was no grandchild yet, but Nila was sixteen now and had been walking out with the son of Rels. There would be more opportunities.

Hoyim looked up once more to check on the circling wheelers. These were new ones, and did not know enough to keep away.

The kiln keeper's youngest boy was coming down the back road, pulling his trail runner.

"Keep your bow in your hand and your eye on the sky," Hoyim warned him.

"We take turns," the boy explained.

"That's the right idea," Hoyim said. "What do you do to fill your time at the shelter?"

"We build." As Hoyim gave him a curious look, the boy added more softly, "It's a secret."

"Does my father know?" Hoyim asked.

"Oh, yes, council knows. They said to keep it secret. We're building something Tuje designed."

"You'd better get on," Hoyim said. "Good trail."

As Hoyim entered his shop, he wondered where the trail boys would fit in after their year on trail ended. If there was to be a trade for all boys in the village, the village was going to have to grow. And if it grew...

Hoyim shook his head and tried unsuccessfully to concentrate on a page of the lineage table. So he went to his writing table instead and began composing a letter to the tall man. The trail boys would carry it on their next trip to the tall woods.

Hoyim had met the tall man on three occasions since their chance meeting at the temporary shelter. The elfin dictionary of the tall man's language, a gift from Radd, was a great help—but what helped most was the mutual good will between the tall man and himself. The tall man took the trouble to send Hoyim's own letters back to him, correctly written, so Hoyim could learn how the words were placed. If Hoyim failed to grasp a meaning, he had only to return it marked, "I do not know," and his friend would write the troublesome passage in simpler form. After seven years of struggle, Hoyim could read and write English well enough to express many of his ideas. With painstaking care, he composed his letter:

"The trail boys go today. I am late. I send this to the tree when they go again. I considered long and consulted with council to obtain permission to say what I propose. Is it time you tell another tall man of our village? If you go ill is there one to know and protect our village? You will choose one to tell with extreme care. I wait to discover what you say to this. I now print Tokra's book of the Way. When the book printed I send one to the tree. The miller's wife asks again to say to you greetings. She does not forget. She smiles thinking of you. Hoyim"

When the letter was finished, Hoyim copied it onto a large roll of paper, using a brush that made thick, black strokes. Then he returned to work on the lineage table.

※ ※ ※

The wheelers were still circling. One of them dipped too close to the guard tower and met the guardsman's arrows. It fell on the burial ground, and the bell rang twice: "Wheeler down. Must be cleared away." Volunteers would soon be there to carve the carcass into manageable pieces and bury them. The useful oil would be saved, but grass people never ate the flesh of a wheeler, it was unpalatable.

Ajist heard the bell, but paid no attention. She was too excited about the unusual seed she'd found, and perhaps was the only person who was unaware that a second wheeler was still present—and that she was the most vulnerable. When Ajist came to the end of the new bridge road, she crossed the peaman's road and passed setting sun of the fuel raft to reach the spreading trees.

At last she found a clear spot with soft black earth. Planting the seed, she poured in all the water from her dew flask. She worked happily, thrilled by the magic of growing things, and the mystery of this particular seed. She tried to envision what the tree would be like.

Then she started for home, swinging the trowel in her hand.

The morning was so beautiful that she decided to proceed to the weaver's to tell him; he would enjoy the story of the strange seed. A field mouse scampered by her toward the school. An instant later, an ominous shadow fell across her. With a bloodcurdling shriek and a frenzy of flapping wings, a wheeler pounced upon the mouse, right between her house and the school raft. The buffeting wind took her breath away.

Ajist went cold with the terror of knowing that it could have been her. She heard the death squeal of the mouse and saw its blood; then the great wings rose, and the horror was above her again, bearing the mouse away. Ajist screamed in sheer panic, she felt certain that her home had been destroyed. And then she felt nothing.

When she came to, she screamed again. Someone said, "It's all right, Ajist. You're safe. It's all right."

Shaking, Ajist realized that she was lying on the ground beside the road, and Balink was bending over her.

"What a fright you had!" said Balink.

"Our house! Did it hit our house?" Ajist panted.

"It can't have. Your house is still there, but it sure hit the school. They all ran out to see what happened. Someone said they saw you throw your trowel at it!"

"Right in the village. They never land in the village." Ajist tried to sit up.

"You lie still. I've sent Kren to get the doctor. Didn't you hear the warning bell?"

"I heard two bells. I knew a wheeler was down. I didn't pay much attention."

The widow hurried toward them. "I heard screams, and a wheeler. Ajist, dear, are you all right?"

The portrait painter's son came running down the trail, calling, "It hit my house! Did it hurt Ajist?"

"Look, everybody, I'm all right." Ajist was embarrassed by so much attention. She tried to sit up but sank back again, dizzy. The widow sat down and took Ajist's head in her lap. Balink went into her house and returned with a pillow and blanket, and a drink of water.

"I don't deserve all this attention," Ajist mumbled. It troubled her that Balink should find her in such a vulnerable position.

The old doctor never ran, but there was a spring in his step as he rushed along the high street. He ordered that Ajist be moved into Balink's float space, since it was the closest shelter, and then examined her with his usual cheerful assurance. "It never pays to get too close to a field mouse," he cautioned her. "Don't feel bad that you fainted. I'd have fainted too. A wheeler landing in the village—that's enough to make us all faint."

He asked Ajist many questions about how she felt physically and how her appetite was recently, and he examined her pupils carefully. He studied the condition of her skin and took her pulse, then finally gave her hand a pat, saying, "Young woman, you're going to have a baby."

A baby! Ajist tried to sit up in her excitement, but the world still spun. The widow gently pushed her back.

The widow called to Balink and told her the joyous news.

"Kren has gone for Hoyim," said Balink. "Well, now that you're going to have a small one to look after, Ajist, maybe you'll be more watchful of wheelers."

Ajist appeared hurt and Balink was sorry that she had said it.

"That was an unnecessary remark," said the widow in a controlled voice. "You should apologize to Ajist."

"I'm sorry, Ajist," said Balink immediately. "I speak without enough thought sometimes."

The doctor ignored the remarks. "You will eat and sleep well," he told Ajist. "Lots of salad green and fruit. Tea of redberry leaves. Between Koalee and the widow, you'll be well looked after. You will let me know if you get sick at all or have any pains. You and Hoyim are very lucky. The whole village is lucky."

Just before Hoyim arrived, Balink put her hand on Ajist's shoulder.

"I'm so glad you're all right, Ajist, and it was brave of you to throw your trowel at the wheeler!"

The doctor had said that Ajist should rest in the float space until evening, and then Hoyim could take her home. The widow and Balink vied with each other to prepare tempting dishes for her noon meal, and Balink kept her small ones in the house to prevent them from bothering Ajist. But when Hoyim returned to his print shop and the widow had gone home to catch up on some housework, Balink came back down to sit with Ajist.

"Ajist, I haven't been very friendly to you," she said. "You know that. I sometimes pretended to be busy with the children, but I could have been much more neighbourly to you. Did you ever wonder why?"

"I just thought we were different kinds of people."

"No, it's more. I was jealous of you."

"You, jealous of me? Whatever for?"

"Over the widow. You know my mother was killed by the four-legged shadow when I was only ten, and it wasn't many days after that Dad decided to take us up trail to find Dyra. We had to leave our school, we didn't know if we'd ever see the villagers again. That was a hard time, Ajist."

"It must have been terribly hard."

"Then Dad met the widow from Gozer's village and built her house, and from then on she was constantly there. It wasn't like having Mother again, but she cooked for us and made our clothes and looked after us if we were sick. If we had problems, she listened, and she gave advice in that calm way she has. The widow gave me confidence. I depended on her. She was mine—the foster mother who belonged to me. I thought I was pretty special to her, and then you came..."

"Balink, I didn't take the widow from you."

"But can't you see how it looked to me? See how she came running to you when you fainted this morning?"

"She'd have come running to you, too. You're her daughter, Balink. She's interested in everything about you. She talks about you all the time."

"I know, but she and I are so different, and you're so much like her. That's what I noticed right away when you first came to the village. You have her poise and manners. You seem to fit together like pieces of a puzzle. I even thought you looked like her."

"I don't at all!" protested Ajist. "She's my uncle's sister-in-law. She isn't my real relative, any more than she's your relative."

"I know. But then Hoyim fell in love with you, and Dyra and Koalee made such a fuss over you. I love Dyra and Koalee, and it was as if you took everything I cared about and needed. I didn't want you in my house. I didn't want my husband and children taking a liking to you, either. I guess I supposed you were destined to take everything that was mine."

"You could have had me for a friend."

"Well, I'll try that. I can be more help to you now than the widow or Koalee, despite what the doctor says. The widow never had a child, and Belm is twelve. Koalee will have forgotten how."

"Koalee has helped many a baby into the world in those twelve years."

"True. But look at the babies I've helped into the world!"

They laughed together.

"Do you know what Hoyim said?" Ajist asked, changing the subject. "He said we'd see which grows biggest, the seed I planted by the spreading trees, or the seed he planted in my garden!"

Balink laughed heartily.

"Biggest or not, this one will be the best!" she said, tapping Ajist's belly.

※ ※ ※

News that Hoyim and Ajist expected a baby was soon all over the village. The soon-to-be grandmother Koalee set right to work weaving a light soft blanket of thistledown. Aunt Creu was decorating a tiny coat with intricate embroidery. Powa, the great grandmother, was making useful diapers and sleeping robes. Friends and relations on both sides of the family excitedly began preparing anything a baby and its parents might need. It was no more than would have been done for any baby, of course. New babies were a very special event in the village, but no doubt there was something a little extra-special about the Chief Councillor's first grandchild.

"It will be born in the cold season," said Hoyim, and he went out to the tannery to order the softest mouse fur to be made into a cover robe.

"I suppose he'll be a printer, Hoyim?" his father asked a little wistfully.

"He'll be what he's suited for," was the reply. "And if it's a girl, the next one will be a boy, and one will be a printer and the other will be a lens maker, to please you."

"A girl lens maker?"

"Why not?"

"I know I'm old-fashioned, Hoyim, but if girls apprenticed they couldn't be at home learning from their mothers—and how could they learn gathering and preparing? How would they learn spinning and weaving and sewing?"

"Is it so important?"

"Yes, it is!" his mother cut in. "I didn't begin to study with the doctor until Belm was five, and I'm sure I learned a great deal more than if I'd been an apprentice at fourteen, because I had experience. If you want your girl to be a lens maker, Hoyim, wait until she has learned some crafts and had some time with her young children. She has lots of time left then."

"You're both so traditional!" Hoyim laughed, but Ajist added gently, "They're both right."

"No, they're not," said Hoyim. "Grass people are only making use of half of their talents, expecting all girls to stay at home and learn crafts. Maybe some of those girls would be inventors or great councillors."

"Then they will do that," said Koalee firmly, "or raise a family. They have the right to choose."

Dyra was looking very reflective. "I've thought about this, son, and I'm not sure I know the answer. But I do know the question, and that's important."

"What's the question?" asked Ajist, fascinated.

"The question is, 'Which is most important, the mind of a

grassperson or the village in which they live?'"

"Why, it's the village. There is no argument," said Koalee. "The village is survival. The village is the Way of the grass people. Without that, we are nothing."

Hoyim was still ready to argue. "Isn't Father saying, then, that in order to keep the village as it is, we are sacrificing the individuality of our women?"

Ajist's eyebrows lifted. Dyra shoved aside the book he'd been reading, and stared at Hoyim. "We don't 'sacrifice' people, Hoyim. We all have a job to do. We live for the survival of all, and for the good of all. That is the way. Are you reading Tokra's book or are you merely printing it?"

"If that's what you believe, why did you talk to me when I was young about the individual creative mind and its rights?"

"Because we need individual creative minds to improve our way of life."

"Hoyim," Koalee cut in, "I've done a lot of thinking at the spinning wheel."

"Mother, you're not really helping. Here I am, trying to free grasswomen to apprentice, and you keep agreeing with father."

"I never felt Nila was properly trained in crafts," said his mother. "Sometimes I had to go to the infirmary and she'd be left spinning without supervision and made mistakes."

"Mistakes are glar, but they are how we learn. We don't need some of our home crafts any more," said Hoyim. "We buy cloth from Doen. People specialize now. Nobody but Father makes lenses, do they?"

"Listen, Hoyim," said Dyra. "The old weaver likes to grow a garden, so he grows a garden. When he isn't building, Tuje likes to prepare food and make designs, so he prepares food and makes designs. Your mother likes to care for the sick, so she cares for the sick. Men or women, every single grass person is important to the village. I'll tell you something. When you were a baby and we were in the tall woods, I told your mother I was going to have her do all the hunting, because there's no shot like her in the whole village. Do you know what she said? She said she wanted to have another baby and stay at home to look after him. If we hadn't had Nila, she'd have gone hunting, and we'd have eaten a whole lot better. Our people do what they want to do, and what they're good at, and the important thing is that they do it without doing any harm to the grassman's way of life."

"If my daughter wants to apprentice, I'll see that she has the chance," said Hoyim hotly.

"You can't do that without permission from council," his father retorted.

"Dyra, that's not true!" said Koalee.

"It's true if Lenk and Yansa and I say it's true."

"You do, and I will protest until that decision is overturned," said Hoyim.

"And I might join you," said Koalee. "That's the first time I've ever heard your father say a thing like that about council."

"I spoke hastily," said Dyra. "It's just that it bothers me to hear my son talk so much about such upsetting changes. Especially since I know the people are bound to consider him for a councillor when I die or resign."

"You run things for your generation," said Hoyim. "I would have to run things for mine."

"No, Hoyim," came Dyra's quick response." A councillor doesn't run things for his generation. He runs things as a trust from all the grass people who have gone before, and for all the grass people who come after. You learned that at your mother's knee, and you learned it in school, too. That's the way, Hoyim. Wait until you have wisdom. Any grassman or woman is free to choose a trade."

Ajist spoke gently, trying to smooth over the disturbance. "If my daughter wants to be an apprentice, and her father wishes it," she said, "I'm quite sure I can find time to teach her other things in her spare time. Grass people aren't that busy in their days."

Dyra smiled at his daughter-in-law. "That's another lesson for Hoyim to learn," he said with better humor. "Women hold the wisdom of the grass people."

Koalee smiled and brought the teacups. "That's because we have time to think while we're busy working," she said.

The conversation turned to more relaxing topics, but Hoyim felt disappointed. His father had belittled him for his youth and lack of wisdom. Hoyim was twenty, and he knew that Dyra was only twenty-two when he became Chief Councillor of the village.

II

THERE WAS A GATHERING at the water vats out by the spreading trees. It hadn't rained for many days and there was no dew in the mornings. People were growing desperate. The vat by Doen's raft was dry, and so they were coming from all over the high street and the new trail. Yansa had deputized Dashe, the rootman's son and sent him out there with a recording book to keep track of how much water each person took.

"Do you have to do that?" asked Dyra's father, as he watched "one finna" marked off beside his name.

"Council thinks so," Dashe told him.

"It is a disgrace to a grassman's honour," said the old lens maker.

"It's for the sake of fairness."

"It's ridiculous," said the fuelman. "It's going to rain in three days."

"You know that for certain, do you?"

"Of course I know it. I wouldn't say it if I didn't know."

Everyone stared at the fuelman for a moment. There was something so practical about him that it was hard to see him as clairvoyant.

"I wish I had more faith in your hunches," said Flon.

"Watch for it," the fuelman grinned. "Three days."

Kyb was filling her dew jars and carefully closing the spigot. "Doba says if it doesn't rain tomorrow, the berries are going to dry up."

There were worried shakes of heads.

"Two adults and seven children," said Dashe officially, checking off the basket maker's wife. "You can make two trips, Ma'am."

"With baby binders to wash?"

"The basketmaker plans to start his own village!" Rels teased.

"I won't say anything about that," laughed the basketmaker's wife. "At least you get your own water."

"This is different," said the peaman's wife. Quietly, she went ahead to draw water for Ston as well. The cobbler's widow was dead, and Ston had moved back to his old raft, where he was caring for his own needs with a lot of help from Lenk's widow and the peaman's wife. He had even gone back to helping Lenk and Rels whenever they had a job that could be done by a seventy-seven-year-old man with one useful arm.

Syl's wife, Deeka, was a bubbly little person with a merry laugh. "Syl has plenty of water," she said. "Did you hear about his boat?"

"Yes. It sank."

"It didn't sink. It happened near the shore and he managed to pull it in."

Hryn had sauntered up to the group. "What are we discussing?"

"The bird that pecked a hole in Syl's boat yesterday."

"I don't know how he survives, sitting out there on the lake half the day. Bait for wheelers, I've told him so many times. But fishing he will go."

"Have you heard what he's going to do now?" asked Deeka, opening the spigot for her turn. "He's going to build a shelter on a raft, and anchor it on the lake. Right on the water. Then he'll use the bark boat to go back and forth."

"Don't forget," Dashe ordered. "No drinking this water unless it's been boiled. Doctor's orders."

"And no unnecessary washing. Yes, I know," said Rels as he turned to go.

Creu looked worried. "This is serious, isn't it?"

"No," said the fuelman. "It isn't serious. It's going to rain in three days."

There was general laughter, and Flon and Deeka set off together toward Lenk's Way. Deeka carried her water up to her home, and then wandered across to Doen's raft to tell Balink the news.

Balink was trying to weave, but her youngest was making it

difficult, crawling about the foot pedal and tugging at the strands. The oldest two of Balink's children were in school. Her girl, Naj, was nearly five, and this one, the baby, was just toddling.

"Now see here," Balink was saying. "Your father may be the best weaver in the world, but that doesn't mean you have to start learning all about looms before you can properly walk."

Deeka's giggle made her look up. "I give up," she said. "The widow wonders why I let Doen make all the cloth. Well, this is why. I'll put him in his play area, and we can talk while I get something ready for the noon meal. Do you know why the vat is dry, Deeka? Doen's father has been sneaking over here at night and taking whole finnas of it to water his garden."

"If Council knew that…"

"They wouldn't do anything. They never say a word to the old man."

"But when he puts his garden ahead of the good of the village, he really should be stopped, shouldn't he?"

"Do you think I should tell Dad?"

"I wouldn't," said Deeka. "Not unless he starts emptying all of the water vats in the village. Then he can be stopped."

"He'll start on the meeting house vat next. It's closest."

Deeka changed the subject. "Balink, I have three pieces of news."

Balink smiled in anticipation. "One is that Syl is going to build a shelter on a raft and leave it on Hoyim's Lake. Another is that the fuel man has prophesied rain in three days."

"Balink! How did you know all that? Well, you don't know what the third thing is, because you weren't at the water vats to hear about it."

"There is an overnight guest at the tea house."

"Balink! You're spoiling all my surprises."

Deeka had been more than a little excited about that last piece of news. Since the sweet-shopkeeper's death, his wife had sold the shop and opened a tea house on the basketmaker's old raft. It was the first time the village had a place where one could stop in for a pastry and a cup of tea, and it still caused comments about extravagance if you were seen coming out of the tea house. The owner had also hung an unobtrusive little sign saying, "Sleeping Room," in case a traveller or a guest in the village should be in need of accommodation. But no one had stayed there until now. Deeka was quite deflated.

"Balink, honestly! Where did you find out?"

Balink took pity on her and nodded toward a bag of meal lying on her table.

"Oh. So the miller's wife was here."

"The miller's wife is huffy with me, but it didn't stop her from telling me all the news, just the same."

"Why is she huffy?"

"About Doen bringing in a dyer."

"No, no, dear!" Little Naj was at the loom, trying to throw the shuttle. Balink set out to distract her with a doll.

"The miller's wife is never huffy for long," Deeka said. "Did she know who is staying at the tea house?"

"Somebody from the big village, named Mev. He told the tea mistress he is visiting villages to see what they are like. Isn't that strange?"

Deeka said, "I'll go on over to Hoyim's and see if Ajist has heard the news."

"If you hear any more about this Mev person, come back and tell me."

Deeka turned back as she was about to leave. "I'm knitting a cuddly for Ajist's baby. Can I come work in your float space after high sun? I like it there."

"You are welcome, but why doesn't Syl build a floor in your float space? You could have a vine corner too."

"Syl's too busy with boats and shelters that float."

※ ※ ※

"Twenty-nine vats," Dyra counted, "and only six of them near the houses. It won't do. We have to have more vats before the next rain."

The council had spread a map of the village over Yansa's pottery table, and were studying it closely.

"Lime kiln's working day and night making mortar for the new mill," Lenk reminded them. "We can't build vats and the mill too."

"And we can't stop work on the mill."

"There's the barrel maker in Runya's village," Lenk suggested. "What if we had him build five or six, and spared enough lime to cement them in?"

Hryn came in to pick up some moulds. "I don't like to interfere," he said, "but the metalsmith says he can make a pump powered by wind that could pump enough water from Hoyim's Lake to keep the whole village."

Dyra stared at his brother. "Do you know how much we'd have to raise the drot to pay for a pump like that?"

Hryn said, "We'd need a big storage vat in high ground. Something could be worked out." He went out carrying his moulds, and the three councillors stood staring after him.

"There isn't enough metal in the village to make such a pump," said Yansa, after a moment.

"We can discuss it when the mill is finished," said Dyra. "Meantime I agree to Lenk's idea of buying barrels from Runya's village. Now, about the gunmaker's house..." They discussed plans for what to do with houses that had sat empty for a few years. "If we made it policy to tear down any abandoned house on the low street, people might agree to build somewhere else. All the small rafts are gone."

"Not the tea house. She loves her location. And not the lampman. He won't move."

"I say we suggest to the lampman that we take down Runya's little shelter and bring his own house up here. There's a street lamp on the trail, just like he has at home."

Yansa was shocked. "It's never been our policy to tell a grassman where to live."

"I don't mean to push anybody," said Dyra. "I just considered..."

"I'd miss the low street," Lenk mused. "All the first rafts in the village are there. What about your old raft Dyra and the metalsmith's house? They're not only the first in town, but they're also among the best. It would break my heart to see either of them torn down."

"We should keep them, for history's sake," said Yansa.

"I could rebuild them," Lenk offered.

"Do that!" said Dyra, enthusiastically. "If we rebuilt them on Dyer's Road, someone would use them. At the rate the village is growing..."

"Too fast," said Yansa. "There will have to be a new one soon."

At that moment, Yansa's wife bustled into the room.

"I've been to the tea house," she announced, "And I think you will all be interested in what I have to say."

"This is a meeting of the council, we do not have time for gossip," said Yansa.

Yansa's wife looked over the trio present. "It is, indeed. Well, I've got something for you."

Conscious of the importance of her errand, she dug into a pocket inside one of the petals of her skirt, and drew out a letter which she handed to the Chief Councillor.

"It's a note from the tea mistress," Dyra explained, "with a letter attached from her lodger. What lodger?"

"Aha!" said Yansa's wife. "Don't I say all the time that you three have no idea what's going on right under your noses?"

"Come now!" said Yansa.

"The lodger came to the village late last night," Yansa's wife explained. "The lampman told him he could find a bed at the tea house. The tea mistress is so proud! She's made money on her sleeping room at last."

Dyra opened the letter.

"'To the Chief Councillor and Council of Dyra's village: I introduce myself as Mev of the big village we call Karep, twenty days' march high sun—setting sun. I request permission to spend three days in your village, to meet and talk with you. It is my purpose only to study village life. I will not interfere.'"

"He's very formal," Lenk remarked.

"What does he mean, 'study village life'?" asked Yansa. "Village life is the grassman's way. Doesn't he know the grassman's way?"

"It's strange," Dyra agreed. "I guess we can't criticize him for not getting permission to spend the night in the village when he arrived so late. It's a good thing the tea mistress has a room to let."

"It *is* a strange thing," said Lenk, reading the letter for himself. "Has he come alone? I wonder why he didn't come with the traders."

"He's been to many villages setting sun," Yansa's wife explained, "and now he's going to visit all the villages to end of settlement."

"If he's visited that many villages and still needs to study village life, he must be dull-headed, that's all I can say," said Yansa. "Any child could learn the grassman's way faster than that."

"I'll start the noon meal," his wife announced, going through the doorway to their living quarters behind the shop. "Will you be on time?"

Yansa looked to Dyra for an answer.

"Yes, yes," said Dyra absently. "He'll be on time. I suppose we should all go to the tea house and make him welcome."

"Not when he wrote to us," Yansa added. "We should send a letter in reply."

"I will write the letter," said Dyra, taking pen and paper and settling himself to it.

"I can't wait to meet this Mev," he said. Suddenly he laid down the pen and looked at Yansa. "Yansa, do you think it's time we three resigned—as a council, I mean?"

"What made you wonder that?"

"I don't know. I don't feel very decisive lately. I seem to be losing my hold on it. Sometimes I feel as if I am tired of it all. Twenty years is a long time to be Chief Councillor."

"The answer is no. I don't think it's time to resign. All we need is a new challenge. Something besides new mills and water vats."

"Every now and then I feel as though I can't keep up to my son and his generation. They may ask for a change."

"Change is not the grassman's way," said Yansa firmly. "Continuity and consistency— those are the grassman's way. And that comes from the permanent council, as long as they can do the job. And you can do the job, Dyra."

※ ※ ※

News of the lodger had reached the back street, and Hoyim was already setting type for a newsletter to send to the other villages no sun.

"A stranger named Mev arrived by night from the big village twenty day's march..." he began, and then he stopped. There was no point in starting to write until he knew what the story was about. He returned rather reluctantly to the dolenter's manuscript and began to set another page. At noon time he would leave the shop early and walk through as many streets as he could, to see what he could glean regarding this Mev. A lodger in the village who was nobody's relative, and known to no one, was news indeed. Come to think of it, nothing like this had happened in his memory.

"His trail runner is light as air," said the villagers. "His coat is cut so. He has a finger ring." All Hoyim had to do was listen.

III

It was true that the stranger's coat was cut differently. His hair was cut differently, too, and he did have a finger ring. It was gold with a green stone, like melted leaves.

He bowed to the councillors and took their hands two at a time, in the formal grassman's greeting.

"I am honoured that you granted me an interview so soon," he said.

The councillors were ill at ease. They didn't understand a stranger who had come such a long distance with no purpose save to "study village life", but they appreciated his good manners.

"We make you welcome," said Dyra warmly, and introduced the councillors.

The stranger bowed again.

"My son, Hoyim the printer," Dyra continued. "He has requested permission to stay. He sends news of our village to other villages."

The stranger gave Hoyim the single-handed greeting and asked, "Do you send your news to the big village of Karep? I don't recall seeing such a newsletter."

Hoyim flushed. "I didn't think anyone in the big village would be interested in reading about our village."

"Oh, but we are! We are grassmen too. That's why I have come. To get to know my fellow grassmen better."

"Have you met the tall men?" Hoyim asked, wondering why he had blurted it out. The stranger raised a quizzical brow. "I have seen them and I have heard much about them, but met them? No."

"Do you know if they know of the village of Karep?"

Mev hesitated. "No, I think not," he answered. "Have you been to Karep?"

"No. No one in our village has been there save the doctor and Bekra. And the cornman's son, but he has not yet returned."

"Have they not told you? It is located within a cliff. It isn't easily seen, except for some houses in the area near the city, and the gateway is far too narrow for a tall man to enter."

"In a cliff?" Dyra was shocked. "Not in the grass, under the sky?"

"It is often necessary to sacrifice for the sake of security and convenience."

"How do you get dew?" Hoyim asked.

"I never got dew until I came to the small villages. Our water is piped down from a spring in the next crevice."

"I don't think I'd like that," said Yansa. "It is good to start the day in the dew before the sun is up."

"I hope you will forgive my son," Dyra cut in. "He has grown accustomed to asking questions."

"He is welcome to question me as much as he wishes," said Mev. "I will answer, but in return I hope you will agree to answer my questions."

The councillors nodded amicably, and Dyra suggested that they begin that afternoon with a tour of the street of shops. Mev could speak to the craftsmen themselves, finding out how they prepared their materials and practiced their skills.

"I warn you, some methods are secret," he said. "We don't insist that craftsmen tell any of their secrets."

Yansa nodded agreement. There were ingredients in his glazes that he hadn't even revealed to Hryn, nor did he intend to until he was on his death bed.

"I quite understand," said Mev.

"May I ask one more question?" asked Hoyim. "Are there really four thousand people in Karep?"

"Oh no. Over six thousand. We had four thousand people six or seven years ago. The big village has half-doubled since that."

"Why?" asked Dyra.

"Why? Why, because people have babies and newcomers arrive. It just naturally grows."

"I meant, why do you allow it? We are already thinking of starting a new village for our young people. There won't be places for all of the young folk in the village. If it gets too big, we won't know each other."

"It that important? To know each other?"

The councillors looked at each other, mystified.

"This man *does* have to study the grassman's way," Yansa whispered to Lenk.

Like an echo of Yansa's comment, Dyra was saying, "It is the grassman's way," with the kind of assertiveness that revealed Dyra's leadership. He ushered the visitor out of the meeting hall and lightly changed the subject.

"Other questions occurs to me," he continued. "If your village is protected inside a cliff, how do your small ones learn to be wary? Do they grow up unaware of the signs of rain? What about cats and longbeasts? Do they learn to watch for wheelers?"

Now it was Mev's turn to look puzzled. "Any grasschild knows that," he said. "It is instinctual."

"I don't agree," said Dyra. "I think these have to be trained. They have to be sharply developed in the setting of nature, as a blade must be sharply honed on the stone."

"You are an educated man." Mev sounded both impressed and confused, as if it surprised him to find such a man in a small village.

"I have read and written considerably," Dyra replied, "and I pride myself on knowing how to think. I would also like you to meet our dolenter. He is my son's father-in-law. He has written a profound book about the religion and way of the grass people. When my son has published it, there will be copies for sale in the big village. The dolenter's name is Tokra, and his book is called, *The Way.*"

"Interesting," said Mev. "Genius is all around us, is it not? We have a very large library in the big village. You must come to see it."

"I avoid trail," said Dyra honestly. "I am needed here, and I don't have much reason to toy with the dangers of trail."

Lenk and Yansa were following close behind. Lenk spoke up. "You must be brave to march for twenty days up trail all alone."

The visitor turned his head slightly to answer him. "I have been 'specially trained'," he said, "and I have a gun that spits fire."

The councillors were shocked.

Hoyim said, "But..." and stopped himself.

"Have you not heard of such a weapon?" asked Mev.

"Oh yes, we've heard of the powder that explodes," said Dyra hastily. "The reason our gunmaker is leaving our village is because he wishes to experiment with making such guns, and we have a rule here. There are to be no weapons that spit fire in the village. If you have yours with you..."

"I do, of course."

"Then I must ask you to deliver it to me at once, to be locked away. It will be returned to you when you leave. It cannot be in your possession here. It is the rule."

"I will comply, of course. The tea mistress is preparing mid-afternoon tea, and I wish to invite you all to share it with me, as my guests. I will turn over the gun at that time."

Hoyim knew that the invitation had been arranged for the councillors only, so he drew back.

"I must spend some time in my shop, I am afraid," he said tactfully.

It was decided to tour the mill street before going to the tea house, and Lenk felt that they hastened through his workshop a little too rapidly. Mev had seen many a carpentry workshop, and it didn't seem to interest him greatly. He was more alert to some of the fine furniture being made in Rels' workshop. They looked in briefly at the old mill, and the abandoned gunmaker's shop.

"Why have you forbidden the firing guns?" asked Mev. "They are much more deadly than pebble guns. There's far less risk of life to a grassman up trail with a firing gun."

"That's the reason," said Dyra. "We fear them. A grasswoman or a child could be accidentally killed by one of them. They also cause grass fires."

"And they're noisy," said Yansa. "The gunmaker bought one from the traders to study it and you never heard such a noise."

"I have heard it many times."

"We couldn't put up with that. It's an ugly noise. Worse than the cry of a water wheeler. It makes the ears go pop."

Mev looked amused. "I see," he said.

He showed much interest in what the metalsmith was doing.

"May I enquire about prices and about how much business is done?" he asked Dyra.

"Enquire, by all means. If a craftsman wants to tell you, he will. If he doesn't, he won't. We don't interfere."

"You don't control prices?"

"The women negotiate. If a craftsman prices something too high, they just won't buy until he lowers the price."

"But if you don't know how much money a man makes, how can you tax fairly?"

"We don't tax on the basis of how much money a person has. We have the drot, that's all. Every apprentice and every grassman and woman pay the same."

"Yes, that's what I'm told in every village I visit." Mev sounded as if he thought it was a very old-fashioned idea and turned his attention to examining a fine silver bell on a chain.

"I should like to purchase this for my wife," he said after a moment. "I am buying her a memento of every village I visit, whenever I find something worth having. It is compensation because I've been away so long."

When he was told the price, Mev said, "You charge too little. In villages nearer to Karep, I have been asked more for less."

"Money is not important," said the metalsmith, "as long as it's enough for me to buy silver from the traders, so I can make more."

The visitor paid, put the bell in his pocket and turned to examine a diagram which was pinned to the wall. "Are you designing a pump?"

"No. I copied it from a book. What I am doing is studying how to make it larger and stronger, so it would pump finnas of water up a slope."

"Can your people build stone ducts?"

"They can build anything of stone."

"You'll work this out. I like to see this. Shows ambition, and change."

The councillors exchanged glances behind Mev's back, and Dyra suggested they move on to see the papermaker. Mev expressed surprise that they had a papermaker, but when he was reminded that they also had a printer, he nodded.

"This is the husband of my wife's sister," said Dyra.

Mev seemed unimpressed by relationships, but he was excited about some multi-coloured paper being prepared.

"It is a partition for a baby's room," he was told.

"The craftsmen are working today just to let you see them," said Yansa. "Because of the water shortage, the papermaker and the metalsmith will be delaying their work and putting in their days at the new mill instead."

"Oh, am I holding you back from important projects? I'm sorry. I don't wish to interfere at all."

"We can spare this much water," said Dyra. "It's only for today. Now, next door is my sister's husband, the leatherman. A very fine craftsman. As soon as you have seen his shop, we'll go and have our tea."

Romo explained that there was a tannery out in the do-lan where he got his skins, and displayed the coat he was making, and some fine samples of Creu's silk embroidery. The sturdy belts and dew flasks, which were so necessary to the village, didn't seem to interest Mev, but he was delighted with the fur-lined sleeveless jackets, with their brilliant floral designs.

"I will buy nothing today," he said. "Leather is heavy. If I can still pull my trail runner when I return from end of settlement, I will want one of these jackets."

As they left the shop, Mev said to Dyra, "Your brother-in-law is indeed a fine craftsman."

The tea mistress fussed over their tea until it grew ridiculous. She had even placed a sign on the door saying that the shop was closed, which she took down the minute she saw them approaching the stair.

"It was to keep the villagers from coming to tea and troubling you," she explained.

Mev surrendered his firing gun without any complaint, and the councillors inspected it gingerly. Dyra took the gun and borrowed the tea mistress's trail runner, so he could keep it out of sight, and ran home along the shopkeepers trail, cutting across the meeting house grounds to the infirmary. The doctor had locked cupboards for some of his medicines and instruments, and this would be the best place to hide the weapon.

The doctor wasn't busy.

"Why is it you never told us the big village is in a cliff?" Dyra asked, as the doctor opened the lock and stowed the gun in the cupboard.

"There are many things I haven't told you about the big village. Why would I talk about their ways when ours are so much better?" The doctor looked at Dyra steadily for a moment and then gave a little shrug and locked the cupboard.

"Bekra has told you," he said.

"Oh, Bekra said something about a cliff, when she was home, but I thought she meant 'under a cliff'—you know." Dyra gestured to indicate a village sheltered by an overhang. "That's the way Koalee interpreted it too, and anyone who talked about it afterward."

"Yes, that would be nice," said the doctor. "A wall of protection at your back and the sun before you. There are some houses along the sides of the basin, but then you enter a protected way through the rock, and there is a metal gate that they lock up at night to keep out the ground animals—especially the longbeasts. If you don't come in on time, you have to ring a bell and the gatekeeper opens the gate for you, if he isn't asleep."

Dyra was having difficulty visualizing the place. "But where could there ever be such a cave?" he asked.

The doctor smiled. "They call it a cave, but it is a huge rock pile," he explained. "Like the stoneworks high sun. The tall men built a structure there, in the side of a high place. When it fell in ruin, it settled to form a giant cave. Our own people built the entry."

Dyra realized his mouth was open. "You should teach this to the school children," he said.

"Sunshine is for grassmen," said the doctor grumpily. "Not ceilings of rock. And if you'll take my advice, you won't let this visitor talk to the school children. It wouldn't do them any good."

"Everyone should know the truth."

"You're right, but if the big village ever came here, or you ever went to the big village, I think you'd wonder too."

"It appears the big village *has* come here, and I hate to look stupid before him. Can you tell me a few things? How does this water get piped in, for instance? How do they see in there?"

The doctor laughed, and indicated Dyra should sit.

"There is plenty of light. There are cracks between the rocks that admit sunshine and rain, though they have rain shields if it's too heavy. The light reflects from the rocks. It's all on levels, you see. There are shelves around the cavern. Some of the high streets are flooded with sunshine, and so is the marketplace near the gate. They have many more street lamps, of course, and they light them sooner in the evening. They grow gardens in there. Parts of Karep are very pretty."

"Do they need rafts?"

"They have no rafts. Karep can't flood, because of the drains. The water you asked about—there's a spring and they built a duct. The water pours into a vat just inside the gate. Pipes lead from there to each of the levels, and people get their water at spigots."

"How big is this vat?"

"Oh, as long as from here to the dolenter's house."

Dyra's eyes widened. "Someone could drown in it! A child."

"They could, if they were silly enough to jump in. They keep a net over it. Children can be taught to stay out of a vat, just as they can be taught to watch out for wheelers."

"I didn't have it visualized right at all. Do you wish to meet Mev?"

"I'll meet him when the rest of the villagers do. I'm in no hurry."

"I must go back," said Dyra, rising. "I pictured the big village as exactly like ours, only many times wider."

"There are houses in the valley in front of the cave that form a village nearly as large as ours. It's nice there, free-floaters and all. But the people are spoiled."

"Spoiled?"

"Some things are too easy, Dyra. There isn't any struggle with Life, and Life loses its magic. Money and shops come to mean too much. There's too much wasted time. It's too crowded. The air gets foul unless the wind reaches the right crevices for ventilation."

"How do they dispose of wastes? They surely can't bury them in rock?"

"Men are paid to collect wastes and pull them up trail to the place where they dump them."

"Food wastes? People's wastes? They dump them?" The doctor nodded.

"Who would want such a job? It's one thing to clean up for your own family—but for everybody?"

"They are paid. The big village pays much more to workers than you ever imagined."

"I have to go," said Dyra, "or I will appear impolite. I want to hear more, how they get food for instance."

"Another time," said the doctor.

Dyra took his leave and went down the street of shops, remembering his conversation with Bekra when she came home to visit her parents. She told him her house was "on a ridge", and he'd assumed she meant the peak of a hill. When he asked her if there was danger from wheelers, she looked at him strangely and said, "Wheelers can't get in, Dyra." How foolish he must have looked to her.

Dyra felt more confident in Mev's presence after his talk with the doctor, but by the time he rejoined the tour they had already been to the cobbler's shop and were examining Hent's glass. He apologized for his tardiness.

"I've been learning that small villages place less value on time than we do in Karep," said Mev.

"Oh, we value time very much," Dyra answered. "That's why we don't believe in hurrying through it. It's like a field of flowers. If you go too fast, you may forget to notice them."

"I never considered that. Time like a field of flowers. That's interesting."

They spent so long at the glass-blower's and at the weaver's, and in Yansa's shop, that it took the rest of the day to finish the tour.

"The tea mistress expects you for the evening meal," Dyra told the visitor. "You are tired. We will plan nothing for this evening." He laid out the plans for the next day. "...and we mustn't forget to inspect the school and see the portrait painter and the basketmaker, and some of the houses, especially Tuje's, which is different..."

"And the weaver's garden," Yansa prompted.

"Oh, yes! The weaver's garden. Our tannery and our corn area are too far away, but we could visit the pea trees..."

Mev held up his hand. "I have seen plenty of pea trees."

"Then we'll spare our legs. Next evening there will be a gathering of the entire village for a banquet, and the musician is preparing a concert. Some of the children will sing."

"Many villages have made me welcome," said Mev, "but I can honestly say I have never had a finer welcome than you are giving me. I am very impressed by Dyra's village. Very impressed."

He raised no objection to Dyra's proposals, and during the tour he was more than willing to have Hoyim along. But Mev asked so many questions that they found it difficult to insert their own questions about the big village. Mev wanted to know all they could tell him about Runya's village, the next one he would visit, and he was interested in their school system and their social life and their welfare. How often were markets held? What produce did the traders sell here? What did they buy? He was tremendously interested in their government. He asked about the drot, the paid workers, the bookkeeping, the system the councillors used for reaching decisions, and something he called "control".

"What do you do," he explained when they asked him, "if a villager harms another villager, or steals from him, or does something very wrong?"

"They don't, of course."

"Why 'of course'?"

"The village is like family. No grassman would harm another grassman."

"It has been known to happen," said Mev.

"I suppose it has; I've read of it. Well, we would handle it as grassmen have always handled it. A grassman like that would be put out of the village, and if the sacred book permitted, he might take his family with him. He could never return."

"Do you never think of punishments? A fine? Making him do a day's work on the streets?"

"But we all work on the streets. That is no punishment! That is voluntary, and we enjoy it. We love to work together to keep the village clean and safe," Dyra said patiently.

"And nobody gets out of line? You don't even have guards."

"Of course we have guards. We showed you the tower."

"No, I mean guards to watch the grass people. To see that they're behaving themselves. To bring them to you for punishment if they're caught doing wrong."

"Do they have such guards in the big village?"

"Yes, we do."

"That's terrible!" the councillors were shocked.

"Children doing wrong are taken to their parents, or to the teacher or the dolenter, depending what they've done," said Lenk. "By the time they're grown, they have learned not to do wrong. It is not manly or womanly to make trouble for your village. It is glar."

"Who would need guards to keep watch on children?" said Yansa. "It's up to the grassmen and the grasswomen. That is tradition."

Mev accepted these declarations quietly. Dyra noticed that, although Mev might differ from them and state his opinions, he never belittled them or argued with them. He seemed to respect their point of view, especially Dyra's.

"He's flattering Father," Hoyim told Ajist later, "I don't know why, and I suppose there's no harm in it, but I wonder if my father sees through it."

As for Koalee, she was disgusted by the whole affair.

"I don't understand you, Dyra," she said, fretting because she had to miss infirmary in order to cook the visitor's supper and for the banquet. "Who is this man? Is he a hero? Has he done the village a favour? Or is he merely passing through? It's because he's from the big village, isn't it? You're impressed. Dyra, you've never been impressed by anything unless there was some reason for it. If a visitor came down from two villages no sun and spent a night or two at the tea house, would you and Yansa and Lenk walk your feet off taking him all over—and invite him to a meal, and hold a banquet and concert for him? I wish the singer behind the market was alive. He'd be making up a very funny song about this. I just know he would. I wish I could write a song."

"This is different, Koalee."

"What is? Is it his fancy clothes? Is it because he wears a jewelled ring?"

"That is an unkind thing to say," said Dyra.

"I'm sorry."

"He wrote a formal letter to council. I told you that. He wanted to study our village. If a visitor from two villages no sun sent us a formal letter with a similar request, we would do the same for him."

"I just hope you're not getting into something, that's all."

"What could I possibly get into?"

"I don't know, but I know the doctor doesn't like what's going on. He knows the big village and how they do things there."

"You'll meet him and see for yourself."

"I have seen him, and I didn't much like him."

Koalee had been unable to resist the temptation to walk with the teacher's wife down the street of shops when they knew the councillors and their guest would be about. She added, "He looks too smart to me."

"Intelligence is no handicap."

"I didn't say 'intelligent'. I said 'smart'. It's not the same thing."

Dyra sighed. "Be cordial to him this evening when he is a guest in our house."

"Of course I will. And I will be very anxious to hear what Ajist's father has to say about him afterwards."

Hoyim and Ajist were invited to the meal, and Hoyim managed to ply Mev with quite a few questions about the big village, and get some answers. When Koalee asked several things about the health of the people, she found that he knew almost nothing about it. He knew of the master doctor there, and he had been in the infirmary for treatment, but he didn't know how many assistants the doctor had, and he'd never met the cornman's son.

The cornman's son had been in the big village for two years. After three years as the old doctor's apprentice, he had gone to Karep to complete his training, planning to come back to Dyra's village and take the aging doctor's place. Two years in Karep, and Mev had never met him? The big village must be a very strange place indeed.

Mev couldn't answer any of Koalee's questions about how the elderly were cared for, or what grass people knew about treating their families for illnesses. How could a man live in a village and not know these things? Had he no caring? Koalee wondered.

"Do people share?" Hoyim asked. "If they siphon off a melon on a hot day, does everybody get a share?"

"Six thousand people? You're joking! The melon juice would be sold in the shops, and if you wanted it, you would buy it."

"Everyone has money?"

"Well, some more than others. I don't think anyone starves."

"Don't you know?"

"Hoyim, no one can 'know' six thousand people. I think that's what you find hard to understand. In the big village, we know our own families and our friends and neighbours. Some of our neighbours. It's not the same."

"Judging by what you know of doctors' assistants, how will our cornman's son be living?"

Mev laughed. "Probably outside. I've had experience with cornmen's sons before. They take one look at the cliff and go out and raft themselves a house in the valley."

"There must be exciting things to see in the big village," Ajist remarked. Koalee had noted that whenever Mev looked at Ajist, his lips curled into a smile, like a small one wore when stuffing himself at the tea mistress's market table. Certainly expecting a baby wasn't doing Ajist's beauty any harm, but Mev's expression was not proper. Koalee was glad that she had sent Nila and Belm to have their evening meal with Hryn and Neev.

"Many exciting things!" Mev was saying. "You must come to see it. We have a travellers' house much bigger than your tea house."

"And you can get meals there?"

"You can get meals there, and tea there, and if you aren't satisfied, there are two other places where you can get meals."

"People open their homes, as the tea mistress does?"

"No, these are places of business. One of the eating places has twenty tables as large as this one." There was that fawning smile again.

"Who prepares the food?" asked Koalee.

"People are paid to prepare. But none of them prepare as well as you, Koalee."

Koalee gave a tiny smile, but Dyra thought he saw an odd expression cross her face. Did she think Mev was trying to flatter her? Dyra suddenly became more alert.

"What do you eat?" Hoyim asked.

"We are grassmen! Loaf, nut meat, berries, soups, gruel, cakes, roots, puddings, grubs, peas, grasshoppers, tea, seccar, eggs—if we can get them. Everything!"

"Kloros?"

"Yes, kloros!"

"Seeds?"

"Seeds. Birds. Grass animals."

"Birds and grass animals?"

Mev laughed. "Only if a hunter kills them. Not if they're lying dead."

"But grass animals are too big to pull, and they have too much meat. It would go bad," said Dyra.

"With six thousand people? Dyra, the men who carve meat could sell three grass animals a day. The people love meat."

"But grass animals don't hurt the grass people," Hoyim protested.

"You will think us impolite," said Koalee quickly, "to question a guest in this way, and not allow him to eat."

"I am growing used to it. The farther I get from Karep, the more questions I am asked. I suppose it will be like this from here to end of settlement."

"I am surprised that our doctor hasn't told us very much," Dyra remarked.

"I," said Ajist's father, "am not."

Koalee hastened to pour tea, but she took careful notice of what the dolenter had said. When Dyra left to escort Mev back to the tea house, she asked him, "Well, what do you think?"

"I think the same as you, Koalee," Tokra replied. "I think he wants something here. I only wish I was certain what it was."

Koalee nodded agreement. "What kind of person do you think he is?"

"A person who has forgotten the grassman's way. Unfortunately, visiting villages is not going to help him find it again."

"It is too far from his thinking."

"It is too far from his heart."

IV

On the third day of Mev's visit, like a nod to the fuelman's prophecy, it rained. Joyfully, the men put on their rain capes and waders and ran to uncover the water storage vats. It was not a driving rain, but steady. When it began Dyra was just leading his sightseeing party up the stairway to Tuje's house. Tuje had joined them, for he loved to show off his design. Flon had prepared sweet cakes and cold juice, but since it had turned cold and wet, she hastened to put water to boil for hot seccar instead.

The house was still the talk of the village. Dyra, who had worried about how it might float, was proud to show it off. Entering the house, a person could see right through to the other side. There was the tree, flourishing in the midst of it, with flowering shrubs at its base. Tuje and Flon had placed a bench beside it, so they could enjoy their garden. It was true that they could stand in there and take a shower.

"This village is full of creative people," Mev exclaimed. "The basketmaker's house is beautiful. Your portrait painter is excellent. The weaver's garden and that marvelous miniature village, and now this. It is an outstanding village, Dyra. Truly an outstanding village."

His audience glowed, and Dyra took pains to explain how Tuje had balanced the house by placing a storeroom on either side of the garden.

Mev appeared more impressed by the minute. "I really mean what I say about this village," he said. "I have never found a small village with so many people doing so many interesting things. Grass people are generally people of tradition."

"So are we!" said Yansa. "Oh yes, we are very much for tradition."

"But you follow tradition in a free way. I wish all villagers could live in this village. By the way, I saw a strange thing when I took a little walk rising sun of the tea house this morning. That monument..."

The bell on the guard tower began to ring, and even Mev knew enough to fall silent so they could count the signal. The bell kept on ringing at a rapid pace, and the grass people stared at one another in suspense. When the bell passed ten, there was no doubt. It kept ringing and ringing, until every grassman, woman, or child in the village felt the dread. *Dangerous animal.* They could do nothing now but watch and wait, and pray that all of their neighbours were safely in their houses. What if it was a large animal? What if it tore a house down with its claws? The bell continued to ring.

From where they stood, Tuje's windows allowed them to see across Lenk's Way to Syl's house, and, to high sun, the raft of Dyra's father. By stepping into the room rising sun, they could get a view up the middle street, and across the weaver's garden right up to the high street and the play area. What if the animal didn't leave, but curled up beside the meeting house to sleep, the way that cat had? Past incidents crossed their minds. One of the trail boys, a hunter's son, was taken by a longbeast just as he entered the village at dusk. The time Ston met the cat. The cornman's baby, plucked from the float space by a wildbeast before they could get to him. After that, the cornman moved to the country. The miller's wife lost her sister that way, long, long ago. She never talked about that, but everyone knew.

The bell stopped for a moment. Would the guard ring the all clear? No. It began again, wild and relentless.

"I should have my firing gun," Mev remarked.

"We don't shoot if we can help it," said Dyra quietly. "Not in the village. If we missed, it would madden them, and if we did kill, a house could be damaged when they fell. Oh, Life! Look there!"

On the raft across the way, a child not more than two appeared around the corner of his house. It was the smith's grandson with a toy in his arms, his fine blonde hair blowing around his head.

Lenk was already down Tuje's stairs and running for the

neighbour's raft. Past fifty, Lenk was still strong, but not as fast as he had once been. Dyra's heart gave a thud.

"Oh, Life!" said Flon. "It's a longbeast. Help him!" Flon was crying, hugging her baby close. Tuje stood in the doorway with his gun in his hand.

"Oh, Lenk!" Dyra bit his knuckles. There was nothing he could do. The longbeast was on the high street, and they knew it had seen Lenk dart across the road for it paused. Then it streaked like lightning across the weaver's garden and crashed through the float space.

Fortunately Lenk was up the stairs and the child, seeing him coming, had run to him. Tuje fired. Lenk grabbed the child, the longbeast's teeth came so close they filled the world. Afterwards, Lenk couldn't tell what he did. The watchers said he leaped and rolled, child and all, and did a backward somersault through the door. Tuje fired again.

Creu came out on her raft and screamed deliberately to distract the longbeast.

"Creu! Get in! Oh, Life, make her get in!"

But the longbeast was on the raft, pushing at the door. Creu screamed again and ran inside to safety.

"I want that beast," said Dyra. "Flon, give me your bow." He stepped out onto the raft.

"Life be with me," he said. "Tuje, you get the throat, and I'll put out his eye."

Creu came out again carrying a gun, but now the longbeast sprang for Tuje's raft. Dyra had no time to shoot. He backed through the door, dragging Tuje with him. Creu fired once, then again ran for cover. Dyra's father was shooting from an open window so Tuje did the same, and Creu ran out to fire another stone.

They never knew who killed the longbeast, but when it fell they ran out on the rafts and peppered it with arrows and stones until the job was done.

Mev had watched the entire thing with a kind of fascination, as if it was happening in some other place and had nothing to do with him.

The child's mother was badly shaken. "He opened the door himself," she explained, wanting them all to know that she hadn't abandoned him. "I had no idea he was out."

"It's a good thing the door was open," Lenk told her. "I had no time to open a door."

"We have a new hero," said Dyra admiringly, holding his friend's shoulder.

"A councillor is never a hero," said Lenk. "If you'd been closer to the door, you'd have gone, and you know it."

The tower rang the all clear. Yansa deputized Dashe to head the clean-up team, and he soon had ten men at work. Tuje joined the crew, but Flon insisted that the councillors and their guest be seated and relax over a cup of seccar.

"Thank Life we have no mourning," said Dyra simply.

Outside, the day was still dark. The men worked in the drizzle and mud, hacking the longbeast's body into pieces, glad that the shower would wash the blood away.

"You were asking something when we heard the bells," Dyra reminded Mev, unable to remember what it was.

"That monument at the entry of the village. It was dark the night I arrived. I hadn't noticed it before. What does it mean?"

"It means that the miller's wife and my son were first to meet the tall man. I met him in the tall woods as well."

"There are those in the big village who claim to have met tall men," said Mev, but he added, "They are not very jubilant about it."

"My son carries on valuable correspondence with one," said Dyra, wishing that Hoyim was there to speak for himself. "As we understand it, the tall man has claim to this land and he gives us protection."

"That is amazing and it sounds hopeful. Hopeful indeed."

Flon, still shivering from the terrifying episode, was looking out the window at the men at work. "He can't give us protection from longbeasts," she said.

"That is a danger grass people have faced since the beginning of time," said Dyra quietly. "Life has its reasons. It's not as hard to understand as the mower." He turned to Mev. "You have heard, of course, of the mower."

"I have run from the mower many times up trail. Why do you think the big village is in a cliff?"

"I had figured as much," said Lenk. "My son Rels and I discussed that last evening. Would we want to give up the sky and live in a cave to keep safe from the mower? We've been safe from the mower in this village for so long that you stop asking yourself that question."

"I never stop asking it," said Dyra. "I escaped the mower twice, and I would escape the mower again, one way or another. But I'm not sure I could give up the sky."

"I could!" said Flon. "If it's life or death for Tuje and me and for our little ones, I'd go and live in a cave."

"You can't mean that, Flon," said Dyra.

"Flon may be the honest one," Yansa reasoned. "I'm growing older. I don't want to have to change my ways. But Life calls us to struggle to preserve Life, and maybe sometimes we are forced to change."

"Then if the mower ever comes here, I can expect to see you in Karep," said Mev. "A wise decision."

Dyra's cheeks burned. In his mind, his thoughts thundered. *No, it is not! The grassman's way is a sacred trust, and if you have a choice between going from Life and giving up the Way, you cannot give up the Way.* He had questioned many things and changed many things, but not that. He bit his lip. It would not do for the Chief Councillor to insult their guest. When he regained control of his feelings, he simply said, "Grassmen will survive. Lenk has just proved that. You are all placing survival ahead of the Way."

Lenk, a sensitive person, had seen how angry his friend was. "I believe the rain is stopping," he said gently. "Perhaps we should go about our business now and let Mev rest before the banquet. He goes up trail tomorrow."

Dyra seized the suggestion gratefully, and they took their leave.

Because the moss was still wet from the rain, the banquet had to be held inside the meeting hall. The children had no place to run and play and grew restless. After they had eaten, they were sent outside, wet or not, in the charge of older brothers and sisters, and told to stay out of puddles. It was a useless warning, of course. When it was time for the concert, children were stripped and scrubbed dry and put into warm cuddlies for the rest of the evening.

Mev watched it all with an amused smile, and when he noticed that Dyra was carrying Flon's child, he said, "The children wouldn't be here, in the big village."

"Not at a banquet and a concert? Where *would* they be?"

"At home, watched over and put to bed by their grandmother or some neighbour."

"Then the grandmother also wouldn't be here?"

"Not likely. It's crowded and noisy at evening gatherings in Karep. Old folks don't like to be out that much. It's different here, I suppose it's because there are no strangers."

"No," said Dyra, and tears almost filled his eyes. "There are no strangers."

The dolenter called order. Dyra handed the baby back to Flon and stepped up on the dais, where he spoke of the honour of this visit from Mev, and invited Mev to make a few remarks.

Mev spoke extremely well, in a clear voice. He said that he had visited many villages but had received no welcome to equal the welcome of Dyra's village. He commented upon the happy, quiet life of the villagers, the traditional arts and skills and, in particular, the interesting people and unusual talents of those he had met in Dyra's village. "In the big village where I live..." he continued. The doctor leaned forward with a slight frown, as if apprehensive of what the speaker might say next, but Mev simply said, "...we seem to have lost the closeness and companionship that you take for granted. We are constantly seeking new ways of organizing our village to try to overcome this difficulty. When I return to Karep, I will make a report to council of all that I have seen. But in the meantime I travel on to end of settlement. On my return I will ask permission to spend a night here again. I will feel I am among friends."

Cries of "Yes!" and "Good speech!" and "Well said," were heard, but Mev suddenly appeared startled. His eyes were focused on the doorway of the meeting house. Dyra turned and saw to his surprise that Radd stood in the doorway. Koalee had seen Radd too and hurried to greet him.

Dyra felt a peculiar prickling in his brain. Radd only came to see him when something was wrong. Some disaster must be pending.

Mev was speaking quietly in Dyra's ear, "That elf shows up almost every time I make a speech in a village. What does he want, do you suppose?"

"I'll find out."

But Dyra didn't have to ask the elf about it, because thoughts poured into his head.

That man is bringing change, Radd was thinking, and you will want to resist. It may be a matter of the quality of Life, or of Life itself. Would you be able to move with changes and still keep the grassman's way? You must consider it, Dyra. It is urgent.

Can you help us? Dyra asked silently.

I don't know. I'm afraid the timer is set.

Dyra excused himself and picked his way through the crowd to reach Radd's side. The elf looked as youthful and healthy as ever.

"He has disturbing news," said Koalee.

"The tall man you know. He is ill," said Radd.

Dyra felt as if the entire world had just passed through his body, dropping heavily down past his entrails and into his feet.

"Will he go from Life?"

"I can't predict that, Dyra."

"How can that be? If a man is to go from Life, is that not the most certain timer of all?"

"It is no longer so with the tall men. They have miraculous medical cures."

"Then they have really taken Life into their own hands. Is it not dangerous?"

"As it would be dangerous for you to lead your people into such a culture as that." Radd gestured toward Mev.

Dyra signalled the elf to step outside where they would not be overheard, and gave Lenk the sign to introduce the musician and get the concert started.

"You once told me you were helping me because the Way of the grass people was a better way than the Way of the tall men. Tonight you asked if I could move with change, and still keep the traditions."

"Yes."

"If it had to be like that, would you still help us?"

"No. I couldn't, Dyra, because you would lose the ability to hear. That's what's wrong with the big village. Instinct and intuition—they have been lost. When you tried to tell him that, he couldn't even understand what you meant."

Radd smiled. "I would like to stay for your concert, Dyra, but there are contacts I must make."

"Thank you for coming Radd."

"I will let you know what I find."

As Radd slipped into the darkness, Dyra heard his niece Pettis starting to sing. He hurried back inside.

"Well?" asked Mev.

Dyra had forgotten Mev's question. "Oh," he said, thinking swiftly. "He brought news that the tall man we know is ill. It will be all right."

Dyra wasn't quite sure why he lied to Mev. Radd had spoken of much more, but some instinct told him to keep silent. The news of the tall man worried Dyra more than he cared to admit. If he was to go from Life, would some other tall man take his place? Would the mower...?

In front of Dyra, Nila and Rels' son were listening to the music with deep concentration. Belm was with a group of older children near the dais. They would likely be next to sing. Koalee sat on a bench with Creu and Pora, thrilling to every note Pettis sang. Gathered together were Hryn and Neev, in one tightly-packed group were Hoyim and Ajist, with the widow and Balink, Doen and his parents, Flon and Tuje and their youngsters, Syl and Deeka.... Everywhere Dyra looked were beloved kinfolk and friends.

He wondered, as he looked over the assemblage, if they knew how much he thought about them all, and how much he cared for their welfare. The burden of being Chief Councillor was very heartfelt tonight.

Yansa was seated with his wife and Koalee's parents, enjoying the concert. Dyra became aware that the doctor and the dolenter were standing close to himself and Mev. He could feel their silent support.

The miller's wife was asked to do her dance. She got up on the dais in a dress cascading with bright, blue ribbons and did four or five steps. Then she stopped and said, "There. That's all you get from me tonight. I am seventy-four years old tomorrow. I haven't the wind for it any more. A young one will take my place."

There were groans of disapproval, but she held up her hands and said firmly, "This is how it will be." She gave one of her broadest smiles and sat down. It was the end of something they had known and loved since long ago in the old village. They had been told the facts in her straight forward way. She wouldn't be teased into dancing for them again.

When the concert ended, Dyra felt someone nudge his arm. He turned and saw the lampman. "Torall wants to see you, Dyra."

"There's no need to escort me," said Mev, overhearing. "I know the way by now. I'll see you in the morning?"

"Oh, yes."

Mev bowed. "It has been a fine concert, Dyra. Just as I expected. A pleasant night."

"A pleasant night to you."

Dyra found Koalee and asked her to walk home with the doctor. Then, quite unprepared for another problem, he singled out Torall, the hunter's son, and told him he would walk with him and hear what he had to say.

"I am thinking of leaving the village," said Torall.

Dyra felt a wave of shock. "Why? Is there something wrong?"

"I know why the gunmaker left. I would like to follow him."

"We need you. Without you, the market will be thin. Your father is too old and this would leave only one hunter. And the guard tower... Who would take your turn? Koalee has had to take shifts in the past, but she is the doctor's assistant now."

"I want to use the firing guns, Dyra. I will go, with or without permission, unless the rule against the firing guns is changed."

Dyra's jaw hardened. "You will not give an ultimatum to council," he said. "Whether you go is your affair. Whether we change rules is *not* your affair. We do only what is best for the village."

"It is better hunting and safer for the hunters."

"Our hunters have remained safe for many years, no doubt safer than if a fellow hunter was spitting fire through the grass."

"It is the new way, and new ways are better."

"Tyad's husband prefers to use the bow. It is silent. Firing guns will frighten the prey away. We disagree. There is no need to argue."

"Bows are old-fashioned. I don't wish to go, Dyra. I have relatives in this village. I know there is no one to take my place."

"As I mentioned, my wife has done guard duty in her day, but the doctor has need of her skills."

The young hunter smiled, "I hear she has put up a target by the lime kiln to keep in practice."

"Yes she has and I will take your request to council," Dyra promised. "There is not likely to be a change in policy, but we will give the matter consideration. That is your right. You will do the same I trust."

"I have considered. New ways are best." Torall would not be moved.

"Chief Councillor Runya is a hunter himself. He uses the bow. He has a rule against firing guns, too."

"I don't seek permission to go to Runya's village."

Dyra felt that his influence was under serious threat. What could he say to convince the young man? Torall was two years older than Hoyim, but in many ways he lacked Hoyim's maturity. It crossed Dyra's mind that he should mention the legendary Nanta, whose myth constituted an ideal for young grassmen, but Torall was neither traditional nor sentimental. No, there had to be another approach.

"Have you considered the danger of grass fire from sparks?" he asked.

The hunter looked startled. "I hadn't thought of that. The gunmaker didn't mention it."

Dyra let the idea linger a bit more, then smiled and held out his hand for the single-handed greeting. "I hope you decide to stay," he said warmly.

"I apologize for trying to push council," said Torall. "I know you do what is best for the village. I hadn't thought about fire. I withdraw my request to leave until I have looked into it further."

The two exchanged smiles, and Dyra went back along the path feeling optimistic. In the morning, he would have to handle Mev's firing gun again. He must inform him that Runya also had this rule. It would be best for all if Mev would admit to having the gun as soon as he entered the village, and turn it over for safekeeping.

Runya would not be surprised by the visit, as Dyra had been. Mev didn't know this, but Runya's boys had gone up trail bearing a message to give him fair warning. They had also taken a personal message from Dyra to Gozer. Dyra wasn't sure why he'd done that, but it had suddenly struck him that ever since Gozer ceased to be Chief Councillor he had seldom bothered to contact him. It would be unwise to let the older man feel that he had lost Dyra's friendship.

The entire village came to the meeting house grounds to wish Mev good trail. Mev exchanged bows with each of the councillors, said a few fine words, adjusted his shoulder straps, and set off no sun at a brisk walk with his weapon in his hand and his trail runner laden.

Hoyim took it all in, thinking of what he would set in type for his newsletter, but his mind was working on other concerns. In his heart he was close to panic. If the tall man was ill, how would he go to the hollow tree to get messages? Could the elf help? Could the elf have been mistaken? What if the tall man went from Life?

"Mev took off his finger ring before he left," Hoyim's mind was composing, "because he said bright flashing things attract birds. Grassmen could learn much from Mev. He knows the big village, but he also knows trail, and when he has completed his tour, he will know much about small villages as well."

It was second nature to Hoyim to think about translating the story into English, but he stopped himself. Would the tall man ever read another of his messages?

Staring down at the path, Hoyim went slowly back to the print shop. Once there, he took the biggest piece of paper he could find and printed on it in huge letters with his brush. *"Do not go from Life. Please. Hoyim."*

Then he tacked the poster to his wall, bowed his head, and said, "Life, let him see this message. He cannot go to the tree. He must know I am praying for him, as is my father."

He and his father had decided to tell no one except the councillors and Koalee. Not even Ajist knew. The tall man might be all right. There was no reason to alarm the village. Even if he died, had they not been safe here before they met him?

Ajist was unaware of any crisis. She and the portrait painter's wife stopped to chat with Balink and then, noticing that the old weaver was in his garden, went to wish him a pleasant day. He was staring down at his miniature village.

"I am going to take it all up," he said.

"Not your village!" the women protested.

"It has been here too long. Everyone has seen it. It has been praised by the man from the big village. What future does it have now?"

"You will store the little houses away, and then put them back in the garden another time?"

"No. I will give them to the fuelman to help keep us warm through the cold season."

"Oh, no!"

The old weaver smiled. "I am getting old and tired," he said, "and sometimes I'm too stiff to bend over. You know that. If I go from Life, or if I grow too old to work in my garden, I don't want someone else destroying my village. I wish to do that myself."

Ajist shook her head.

"I have told my wife and I have told Dyra," said the weaver, "that if I cannot work in my garden it is to be yours."

"Mine?"

"Yes, this is to be Ajist's garden, and your small ones will play here."

Ajist was at a loss for words, so she gave her friend a hug. "But if it is to be my garden, I wish to keep the village!"

"Small ones will soon tear it up."

"Oh, no! Children love the village."

"You will find it takes a great deal of repair, and you will grow tired of it and wish to take it up, but you won't feel right about that because I will be gone from Life and you won't be able to ask my permission. You will decide you'd rather have moss and the garden pool and the shade tree and the flowering trees, but no village."

"No, I would want it to stay the same."

"Nothing stays the same. No, this is mine to destroy. If you want a village, you must build your own."

Ajist turned to the portrait painter's wife and was surprised to see that Tienna seemed to understand. Still puzzled, Ajist turned back to the weaver. "Let me help you, then," she said.

"No. This is my task. You will come back tomorrow and help me level the hill and lay the new moss."

Ajist left reluctantly. "I could cry over that," she said. "Surely he'll keep some of the houses. I have room on a shelf in the storeroom..."

"You heard what the weaver said," said Tienna. "You must build your own."

"Has he got permission from Dyra to do this? The councillors are all so proud of that village."

"He doesn't need permission."

"But it's silly, rebuilding a village that is perfectly good as it is."

"Then you must build something else."

"At least he could give me one little street lamp." Ajist frowned. The two sat down in the portrait painter's garden and gazed off across the drainage ditch. On the opposite bank, a grass animal with young sat up on her haunches and nibbled at something as she appraised the grasswomen. But her young were frisking away, so she didn't sit for long, but scurried to round them up and squeak instructions at them as they ran for a hole.

"She's teaching them about our village and telling them not to dig here," said Tienna.

"They never do, do they? I often wonder why they leave our villages alone."

"Would you like to tunnel up out of the ground and hit your head on a raft? Grass animals are too smart for that."

There was shouting beyond Ajist's house. Through the float space they saw Balink racing up the high street. Balink was not going to take this philosophically, as Ajist was trying to do. Balink was looking for Dyra, and if she couldn't find him, she would go all the way to the new mill and get her father, the weaver had to be stopped.

Dyra was in his shop making lenses and could see Balink's point of view. He sent her running for Yansa, and the two converged at the weaver's garden at almost the same moment.

The little village was a shambles. The old man had already dug up most of the boards to which the buildings were fastened, and they were lying about in disorder, though he had not destroyed any of them. Nor would he. When the councillors tapped at the door, the weaver's wife told them that he had come in complaining of being very tired, and had fallen asleep. She didn't wish to disturb him.

The weaver never woke again. He died a month later, still asleep, and never heard that Ajist had carefully saved every miniature house and raft, every water vat, every toy tree. Only one street lamp had been broken in half in the upheaval.

"Life can be very unpredictable," said Tienna.

In fact it was Violet who had saved everything. She had flown over just as the weaver took up a tree chopper to begin the work of demolition and, knowing what was about to happen to his life, she had prompted him with the full powers of her psyche.

"You are feeling very tired, grassman," said Violet. "Lay down the tree chopper for now and go inside to sleep."

The next morning Ajist told Hoyim that she had had a very unusual dream.

"I was standing in the weaver's garden, and it was just as it usually is, the little rafts all in place. I noticed that the flowering trees were different, but nothing else was changed. Then a fairy came up to me. She looked so much like me I thought I was seeing myself, but she was younger and her eyes were dark, and she had wings, of course. She said, 'It is for Hoyim's wife.' That's all. 'It is for Hoyim's wife.' And then she disappeared."

"How very strange," said Hoyim. "Violet was in the village yesterday. She stopped to talk to Tienna. It sounds as if you dreamed of her, but you've never seen her. Well, if she's given you the village, just don't ever try to thank her. She doesn't want any thanks. Did she notice you were going to have a baby?"

"Hoyim, you can't notice it!"

"Violet could."

"The funny thing is, I wasn't going to have a baby; it was already there. It went through my mind very clearly that the baby was in the house—the weaver's house. It was a girl, and her name was Denza. But Hoyim, that's not all. Denza was a baby in the dream, but there were two more small ones with me. They were boys, and they were twins."

"Do you believe dreams come true, Ajist?"

Ajist reflected for a moment. "Nila says they do. But they don't come true *all* the time."

Hoyim whistled. "I'd sure like to know if this was one of those times!"

V

VILLAGE LIFE was never dull. As soon as the metalsmith heard that his old house was to be rebuilt on Dyer's Road, he announced his intention of moving back to it when it was ready. That meant there was to be a vacant house on the back road, the ideal place for a craftsman. Who would take it? A topic like that could keep minds occupied for days.

Mev returned from end of settlement, still enthusiastic about his tour and showing no signs of fatigue. He bought the fur-lined jacket, which he had promised to buy from Romo, and he called people by name as if he hadn't met nine villages full of people since leaving them. He spent a night at the tea house to the great satisfaction of the tea mistress, who felt that her reputation for hospitality depended upon it.

"I *may* be back after the cold season," he told Dyra confidentially, in a tone which seemed to convey some deep meaning, but made no attempt to explain himself.

The traders arrived three days after Mev left for Karep, coming for the last big market before the cold season. There were four traders in the party as usual, and a woman. As soon as they entered the village, everyone knew that Bekra's husband was not among them, but Bekra was.

Not only Bekra, but a trail runner loaded with all of the worldly possessions she could pull, and her three-year-old daughter. The child was beautiful, bearing a close resemblance to her handsome father, and within moments she had charmed her mother's old friends and relatives.

"Quickly! Quickly! Fetch Doba and Kyb. Get Brond! Tell Doba that Bekra has come home with his granddaughter!"

"Where is your husband, Bekra?"

"He didn't come this trip." She turned away, then cried, "Brond!" Bekra ran to embrace her brother, and soon Doba and Kyb were hurrying up the market street.

"Can we go home now?" Bekra asked. "I am very tired."

"Give me the trail runner," said her brother, and set off with it as though it were a feather kite. The news travelled up the street of shops until Dyra was alerted that his niece had come home on a visit with her child.

Bekra was overjoyed to see Dyra and Koalee. "Uncle, do I need permission to stay?" she asked.

"Stay?" Dyra was baffled.

"I'm not going back to the big village. I want to stay here."

"Of course you don't need permission. You're one of us, Bekra."

"She wants to stay with us," said Doba, but he was obviously torn between joy at having his daughter and granddaughter there, and his feeling that something must be wrong.

"Ryjra is all right?" Koalee asked.

"He's fine. He may follow me. Koalee, will you be at home in the morning?"

"Yes, unless there's an emergency."

"I wish to have a talk with you."

"Then you will come."

"Is the village to know that you wish to stay?" asked Dyra.

"I've visited before. Perhaps by the time the traders return from end of settlement, there will be some change. I won't talk to the village about it until then."

"What will Ryjra do here?"

Bekra hesitated. "That's undecided."

"You might buy back the herb raft. The hunter's daughter is to marry Runya's son, and they wish to live in Runya's village."

"I have money. I'm tired, Uncle. I will think of such things tomorrow."

"We'll leave you," said Koalee. "Come early."

Bekra arrived soon after dawn. Dyra and Belm had not yet come in with the dew. "Can Nila help Father in the stall today?" she asked. "It's just until we have our talk, and then I will help him."

Nila was happy to have an important job to do at market and would have been off down the street of shops without her gruel, but Koalee saw that she ate it. Bekra said nothing of importance until Dyra and Belm had returned and then left again.

Koalee poured a cup of seccar for her visitor but didn't press her to talk. When she washed the breakfast dishes, Bekra quietly helped her dry them, then sat down with the cup of seccar and immediately burst into tears. After a short time, she dried her eyes and regained her composure. "Koalee, I don't know what is happening to me. It's the big village. It's *all* because of the big village. I wanted to talk to you first. Maybe you can help me think."

"Think about what?"

"I have trouble talking unless it's about business. You know that and you know my family."

"You have another family now. A fine husband and a beautiful daughter."

Bekra began sobbing again. "I may have left my husband."

Koalee's body jerked in such surprise that she nearly fell back from the stool. "That's impossible! A grasswoman does not leave her husband."

"I may have."

"What do you mean, 'may have'? Either you have left him or you have not."

"We had problems. Not at first, but you know Ryjra is away for sixty days twice a year. He would come home, and it got hard to talk to each other. We grew apart. I was unhappy when he was away. He blamed me, saying I knew he would be away when I married him. It's different in the big village, Koalee. There's nobody I can talk to like this. I knew some of my neighbours a little, and the girl who helped me in my shop, but I didn't know much about them or their families. So I couldn't trust them."

"I believe you, Bekra. We've heard much about the big village of late."

"You buy *everything* there, even a friend! Nothing is free. I think less of money now than before I left for Karep. It is not important any more to me. I didn't realize that Karep is in a cliff. No sky. No fresh air. No grass, and it's a long way out to them. That is not my village, and I know none of the people."

"It wasn't what you expected?"

"It was exciting at first! When Ryjra told me about the swimming place, and the dining houses where you can pay to have food brought to you—and the concert hall... Oh, it's exciting, Koalee. But after seven years you've seen all of that. You want family, even my family."

"I cannot understand," said Koalee honestly. "Dyra and I have rarely been apart. Just a night or two, once in a long time. I can't imagine what it would mean to have your husband away from you for nearly half a year. I'm trying to put myself in your place."

"That's why I came to see you. I knew you would try."

"Whatever the difficulties, it may not be possible to leave your husband. The dolenter gave you the trust when you married to follow the grassman's way. You must do that, Bekra."

"It is not the grassman's way to live in a hole in the rocks where children are saucy and people try to cheat you when they buy in your shop and where men..."

Bekra stopped and sobbed again.

"Men?"

"Ryjra has a friend. I don't like the way he looks at me and touches me. He does not have the respect a grassman should have for a woman. I told Ryjra, but he would not give up this friend. He said I would get used to the way of the big village, that I'm too old-fashioned and scared. He said the women of the big village would know how to stop him without offending him."

Koalee grew pale. "Bekra that is a terrible thing."

"More terrible than you think. They interfere with each other's wives, the men in Karep. They are not like grassmen at all—some of them. When...this friend...knew that the traders were coming on this trip he said to me. "So Ryjra is to be away for sixty days," and he made a kissing noise. Koalee, I don't like to talk about this."

"You are not going back to Karep," said Koalee.

"Oh, that's not the whole story. I told Ryjra I would come home this trip, and I told him why, and he did not believe me. Finally, I said I would take my daughter and never come back. I said I would not have her raised in Karep. We had such a fight then."

Koalee was thinking fast. "You said he might follow you."

"I said he could. I said, 'Jarin and I will go to my father's house in Dyra's village. What you do is your affair. I will be happy if you come too...'"

"And he didn't come."

"He was so angry he sent another man in his place and stayed in my shop. He has no craft. If he came here he could run a shop. He must give up trail trading. It's like that, Koalee. Either he gives up trail trading and comes here, or I will never see him again."

"Do you love him?"

Bekra hesitated. "I loved him very much when we understood each other. When he didn't know how afraid I was and how serious I was about leaving, I knew he wouldn't protect me. He wasn't sensitive to me as a grassman should be. I am not being hysterical, Koalee. My daughter will be raised under the sky among men who know how to properly love their wives."

"This is a matter for the dolenter, as well as Dyra. What happens now? If you were a widow, you could be adopted. If you were unmarried you could go on with your herb raft. But this rarely happens." Koalee was thinking quickly, but Bekra was ahead of her.

"There is a rule in the sacred book. I looked it up. It is treated like an interference. If he left me, he would be put out of the village. If I left him, I would be put out of the village."

"But you weren't put out of the village, were you? You left it."

"I don't count that as my village, Koalee."

"Then if they have to put you out, you can go to Runya's village, and we can visit."

"Koalee, for a woman who is usually traditional, are you considering breaking rules?"

"I think this is different. You are here because you were faithful to your husband, not the other way. Anyway, we are more willing to adjust rules now. I don't think Dyra or the dolenter will put you out, Bekra. Also, there is one thing we must remember."

"What is that?"

"Ryjra may follow you. If he loves you, he may give up trading."

"Koalee, you have reassured my mind. I've got it said at last, and now it's clear. Let's go to market. I'll get Jarin and let her see her grandfather's stall, if Mother hasn't already taken her there. Will you do one thing for me? Will you tell Uncle Dyra what I told you, so I don't have to go over it again?"

Koalee promised that she would, and they started down the street of shops. Bekra took a deep breath and said, "Oh, the wonderful air!"

"It was dusty in the dry season this year. We had cloths over our faces."

"It's such a long time since I've been out under the sky in the early morning. These twenty days up trail have been a dream. In Karep the air is horrible every day. Chilly and still except in the hot weather, and then it's airless. Rich people have houses where the drafts from the crevices meet, and they have the cool spots in summer."

"Can't anyone build there?"

Bekra shook her head. "It costs too much. You pay for space."

"*Pay* for space? I don't understand."

"No, you don't, any more than you could understand people who don't get up at dawn and go out for the dew."

"I knew they didn't go for dew. But why don't they get up at dawn? It's the good part of the day."

"They don't sleep at night. It's noisy."

Koalee couldn't understand that either. Of course there were celebrations in the street of shops, but everyone in the village would attend something like that. Nobody would be trying to sleep. Certainly Karep was a peculiar place.

"The cave echoes," Bekra told her. "The wheels of the trail runners clash on the stones, and so many voices shouting. The workmen grind stones and cut crevices, sometimes late at night. Crowds coming out of the concert hall..."

At the middle street they exchanged greetings with people on the shop rafts, and ran into Flon and Deeka, who had heard that Bekra was home. There were happy welcomes.

"It's so good to be home," said Bekra. "You can walk down the street in the big village and not see one person you know."

※ ※ ※

Bekra's appearance so soon after Mev's departure had kept interest in the big village strong, but not even Hoyim was prepared when Dashe, the rootman's son, announced suddenly, "I will go to Karep."

"Don't be foolish."

"I go to see for myself. It's all anyone talks about since Mev was here—Karep." "How will you get permission?"

"My excuse will be to visit the cornman's son," said Dashe.

"I'm with you," said Torall. "I want to get a firing gun and see how it works. I will guard trail."

"We'll have to travel fast in order to be back for harvest," said Dashe and, because Torall was married, he added pointedly, "We travel without women or children. We go with backpacks and hunt what we eat."

"I'm going with you," said Hoyim. "I must see for myself."

"Why do you go?" asked Brond, who could never follow a quick decision.

"Because something is happening Brond, some kind of change. I don't understand it, but I feel it in the air and I want to know what it means."

The three young men appeared before the councillors. Each had hastily equipped a belt and stuffed a backpack with a blanket, some meal, and a little salt. They carried their weapons in their hands. The councillors agreed that the young men could go, they were free to make that choice, but must exercise the usual caution.

"This will be the lightest trail in grassman history," Dyra remarked when they were gone.

"Not really," Tokra murmured. "Nanta went up trail with no pack at all."

Dyra reflected on the fierce independence of the frontier leader

Tokra had known during his childhood and remarked, "Nanta would be sick if he could see what is going on."

"Have grassmen really changed so much in twenty-five years?" Tokra mused.

Drya shook his head. "I think we've grown very fond of comfort. When I try to picture grassmen living without the sun..." Then he laughed.

"You're happy, Dyra," Yansa remarked.

"Our young men are showing initiative."

※ ※ ※

Hoyim and his companions made rapid time until they reached the first village high sun of the tall woods; there a heavy rain delayed them for three days. They were impatient, but it turned out well. They stayed on the traders' raft, and the young women of the village took turns bringing them delicacies to eat. Dashe, still unmarried, found a young woman who interested him greatly, and the others saw little of him during their time in the village. They laughed to see him splashing through knee-high water in the direction of her house.

"They'll need a rootman when the new village opens," he told them. "I'm going to go there and raft a house for a bride!" Dashe turned a backward somersault in his glee.

As the son of a Chief Councillor, Hoyim paid a formal call on the Chief Councillor to bear greetings, and was surprised to find himself bombarded with questions about Mev. What had Mev done? What had he said?

"The resistance starts here," said the Chief Councillor. "I have met with chief councillors for four villages setting sun. They all say I'm mad to oppose them."

"Oppose who?" Hoyim asked.

"He didn't tell you? Of course not. He didn't tell me, either, but we get visitors from Karep here. You don't?"

Hoyim admitted that their visitors from Karep had been restricted to Mev himself, and the return of his cousin Bekra. "Traders never talk to us about such things," he added. "They're too busy in their stalls."

"I can't find out exactly what they're up to," the Chief Councillor told him, "but there are rumours. They seem to be building a strong government in Karep. It looks as if they mean to make their Chief Councillor the superior authority over all the councils in all the grass villages."

"They can't!"

"They can't? Grassmen can't live without the sun. Grassmen can't lie to one another in untruth. Grassmen can't live without the Way. Did Mev impress you as the kind of grassman who cared about the Way? Did he, young man?"

Hoyim looked closely into the eyes of the wise, old councillor and shivered. "Why?" he asked weakly. "What benefit could there be in such a government?"

"Oh, they have much to say about benefits. They talk of bringing trade and security to the villages."

"Trade and security?"

"They mean they want to get all the products from us they can possibly carry, to feed and clothe the people in Karep. At least that is how it looks to me."

"This man—their Chief Councillor—are you saying he wants to set himself up as Dokrimalitzla? He can't."

"I'm sure he knows that. Only the elves can find Dokrimalitzla, and there hasn't been one in close to fifty years. That's the problem, perhaps. He sees a vacancy."

Hoyim was thinking fast. "I am not old enough to remember Dokrimalitzla," he apologized, "so I know only what I have studied. My father-in-law was taught by a dokrimalenter, and his teacher received his title from the Dokrimalitzla."

"Of course. He would have to."

"But Dokrimalitzla wasn't an authority over Chief Councillors. Not as I understand it."

"You are correct," the host confirmed, "He was our reminder to keep the old religion and not to break with the Way. He represented tradition and unity of the grass people in the Way. He had to have the extra sight, and he was the link with the elves."

"The prophecy tells that the next Dokrimalitzla will be the seventh son of a seventh son. This man in Karep—he isn't, is he?" Hoyim asked anxiously.

The old councillor gave a bitter laugh. "No. He has been known to say that he doesn't believe in elves."

"What does he call himself, this man?"

"Brecort."

"Then Brecort will have to be told!" Hoyim exclaimed. "When you say 'resistance starts here', do you mean that farther up trail they approve of these things?"

"As I said, no statements have been made. It is rumour, but rumour from good sources."

"And the villages setting sun are not responding to these rumours?"

"The closer you come to Karep, the more support you will find for Karep. It has always been like that. Traders reach there first, and they get the fine things from the big village you will never see no sun. They often go to Karep to work. It's as if their eyes are turned setting sun, never rising sun."

"Do none of them dream of moving to end of settlement and learning to live as true grassmen?"

The councillor shook his head. "I would very much like to talk to your father, and the other Chief Councillors, but it isn't a good time for all the leaders to be absent from their villages. If Brecort would make a definite statement—if they would come out honestly and say what they plan to do—then we could take a stand. Secrecy is something new to me. I fear it."

"Secrecy is a game in our village, of guessing apprenticeship and sometimes love."

"That is the grassman's way, not secrecy of this kind."

"But you are speaking out."

"And taking a risk. The neighbouring villages setting sun are displeased with me. For a grassman's village to be cut off from neighbours is hard."

"You're certain of the support of your villagers? They won't ask you to resign?"

"Those who love Karep have already gone there. Those who remain are grassmen." The councillor was confident in this fact.

Hoyim was aware that he had no official right to be speaking of matters of council, and that he had already far overstepped his boundaries, but an idea was gnawing at him.

"My print shop is mid-way from here to end of settlement," he said. "My newsletter goes rising sun regularly. We could set up a depot in the tall woods. If your trail boys could travel that far, our trail boys could bring printed messages to keep you informed, and we could get news of you."

"Printed messages are slower than word of mouth."

"My newsletter is brief. That way, every village gets exactly the same message." The old man nodded. "You are indeed a Chief Councillor's son," he said.

Hoyim left pleased with the impression he had made on the Chief Councillor, but also exceedingly apprehensive. This "change" Torall talked about was more than a feeling. It might turn out to be the most disturbing thing that had ever happened to the grassmen. He wanted to talk it over with his companions, but as the Chief Councillor had said, there was nothing definite. Anyway, Dashe was much too excited to be bothered with these serious matters. He said a warm farewell to his intended and went up trail singing.

"You offered her the gift of Life and she accepted!" said Hoyim. Dashe merely grinned.

"There's news for your newsletter!" said Torall.

But Hoyim was secretly hoping that the paperman was making enormous quantities of paper because his mind was composing a newsletter about this trip that might turn into a book.

※ ※ ※

At the second village they were received warmly, but when Hoyim questioned them about Karep, they became defensive.

"We've heard of you grassmen rising sun," they said. "You should open your minds. Don't be so stubbornly traditional. Only last week a deputy from Karep spoke in our meeting house about the future. There is to be a fine village house in Karep where Chief Councillors will stay when they go setting sun to meetings."

"Meetings?"

"You can't expect Karep to make arrangements for us without telling our councillors what is going on. It will be much better. The more produce we send to the big village, the less we have to pay for what the traders bring. And then there's protection..."

"Guards will be sent," a hunter explained. "Well-trained marksmen who can keep a village safe and give us time to hunt. It will cost us drot but..."

"Do you mean the villages have agreed to pay drot to Karep? Is that what you're saying?"

"Yes, just as villagers pay drot to the village. They are going to send workmen from Karep to build more guard towers, and there is even a rumour of a supply of fencing so high that dangerous animals won't be able to get in. The new government is concerned about the welfare of grass people everywhere."

"What happened to the idea that grass people can tend to their own welfare?" asked Torall.

Hoyim's cheeks were burning. Never in his life had he met a grassman with the audacity to suggest that he should plan for the welfare of another grassman's village. Grassmen helped another grassman when he needed help, because he was of the same village or a neighbouring village, and everyone knew one another. What right did these people in Karep have to talk about what Chief Councillors would or would not do?

At the third village the reception was the same, even slightly hostile. That night, on the traders' raft, the boys felt nervous. Hoyim closed the door and window carefully before he could settle to talk with his friends about what they had heard.

"I don't know what it is," he said, "but I feel a kind of anger. They want us to agree with them and I think if we don't agree, they won't like us."

"Are they trying to take power away from village councils?" Dashe asked, coming back from his dreams.

"My father would never allow it," said Hoyim firmly. "You know in the old village where I was born, they had a dolenter who dictated to everyone. There was no freedom. My father had enough of that. He will never live like that again."

"What should we do, Hoyim?" asked Torall. "If we keep on asking questions, we could make the people angry. If we don't, we aren't going to learn what's going on."

"We could turn into listeners."

"And know nothing?"

"That's the idea."

So the young men decided that for the rest of their journey, they would plead ignorance and make no statements. "Yes, we have heard Mev speak, and we heard some proposals," they would comment, if the new government was mentioned. "Of course, we don't know enough about it to have an opinion."

Dashe seemed too preoccupied to be much concerned, but Hoyim knew that, in spite of his new love, the well-organized mind of the rootman's son was logging and storing all their experiences with his usual precision. He would serve as a reliable source of information later on. As for Torall, the hunter's son, he reacted to everything emotionally and could hardly keep his temper. At night, camping on the traders' rafts or in the branches of spreading trees, he would complain about the arrogance of some of the grass people they were meeting.

"'Grass people' they call themselves! No grassman would look down on another grassman the way they looked down on us today."

At the twelfth village as they were drawing close to Karep, they settled down on the traders' raft for the night, only to be disturbed by a peculiar scratching at the window. It was very dark, and the boys were frightened. Before they could light the lamp, the door opened and two young men entered.

"Please be quiet," they said. "We are friends. We want to talk to you grassmen." Their names were Hilt and Lydyl, and they had both spent time in Karep.

"Our villagers are blind," they said. "They're being given promises of wealth and security, and in exchange they want to turn over their right to govern themselves. There is no resistance in these villagers.

All the resistance is in Karep itself, and all those who are not in sympathy with the government are afraid to speak out, because anyone who does so has his permission cancelled and you don't see him in the big village again."

"Is the Chief Councillor mad?" Torall asked seriously.

"I think they're all mad," said Lydyl, "with power. Karep is a big village, and they have many councillors. They collect a big drot, and they're growing rich. They've figured out a way to get bigger and richer, that's all."

"At the second village, they told us the Chief Councillors from all the villages are to go to Karep to have a voice in what happens."

"It's a lie. Oh, they will go to Karep, that's true. But have a voice in what happens? I doubt it," Lydyl replied. "I worked for Brecort as a confidential clerk. Believe me, Hoyim, I know the plans. Brecort is not a good grassman. He appears to care for nobody but himself. He doesn't know Truth."

Hoyim nodded. "And he thinks he's Dokrimalitzla. What position does Mev hold?"

"Deputy. He thinks he's going to get a promotion for bringing in the villages rising sun. He wouldn't be so pleased if he knew the plan is to make him a District Superior and send him away out to end of trail!"

"'District Superior'. They even have new titles."

"They have anything they like."

"How can the grassman's way be safe without tradition?" asked Dashe. "What do the dolenters say?"

"Dolenters have no power in Karep."

"Of course not," said Hoyim. "Their power *is* tradition. That's the only way it will work."

"When you reach Karep, keep your eyes open but say nothing," Hilt advised. "Mev has them believing that the villages rising sun are ready to fall into step, and the less they know of resistance, the less wary they are going to be."

"What are your plans?"

"To find a way to topple Brecort. If all else fails, I guess we'll gather up the grass people who want to be free and go rising sun." Hilt laughed.

"We are going to the tall woods next," said Lydyl. "We want to find the elf Radd."

Hoyim shook his head. "If he wants to find you, he'll find you. If he doesn't, there's no point looking for him."

The two young men shrugged, and then slipped away as quietly as they had come.

VI

STILL THERE WAS no news of the tall man. Dyra knew the miller's wife was accustomed to receiving messages from him and that she was beginning to wonder what had happened—so he decided to tell her. He was also considering making it public knowledge that the tall man was ill, but something held him back.

"We might speak to the fuelman," the miller's wife suggested. "He might *know* something."

For an instant Dyra pondered acting on the suggestion, but he stopped himself. The fuelman's hunches were often trustworthy, but here was a situation which might be too serious for hunches. He couldn't help but feel that, after twenty years of relative safety and prosperity, his village might be entering a time of adversity.

After Tokra consulted his books of rules and philosophy with respect to Bekra's situation and discussed them with Dyra, Dyra shared his worries about the tall man. Tokra advised against relying on the fuelman's hunches.

"This is Life, Dyra," he said. "It is not in our hands."

"When the old village was in danger from the mower, the elf warned me. Don't you think he would warn me again, if there was new danger?"

Tokra shook his head. "The elf knows the direction of Life, but a grassman can't predict what an elf will or will not do."

"I'm frightened, Tokra. I can't explain it. It's as if I know some disaster was coming. I've had dreams…"

They were interrupted by Koalee, who stomped into the kitchen, put her bow in its place, and removed the bundle of arrows from around her neck.

"I *missed*," she announced, obviously disgusted.

"You missed the bullseye or you missed the target?" Dyra asked good- humouredly.

"I missed the animal."

"You didn't shoot at a grass animal?"

"This was a different kind of grass animal. You'd have shot too. It was heading for the mill where all the men are working."

The bell began ringing in a frenzy. As they crowded to the window, they could see the wildbeast moving up over the crest of the slope, away from the village. In a moment the bell sounded the all clear.

Koalee released a deep breath. "I had pebble ice shivering up my back. I have never been so terrified in my life."

"You're a brave woman, Koalee," said Tokra. "Not even Nanta would have shot at a wildbeast unless he absolutely had to, and Nanta was the most skillful hunter who ever lived."

"You should write a book about Nanta," said Dyra.

"I'm thinking of doing that, and about my parents, and all the people who lived in Nanta's village. But it will soon be fifty years since I was born, and my memory may not be true. I must journey there soon and talk to the old people. It's time I visited my mother again. I can go with the traders, and that's ironic. It was really the traders who broke Nanta."

"What do you mean?"

"He resisted things. He only let the traders in because they brought salt and tar. When his people began to buy fancy metal and wear shoes, he was disappointed, as if everything he believed in was going to disappear. He didn't understand craftsmen and business, and he wouldn't change. He just gave up and resigned and died."

"A Chief Councillor has to change," Dyra commented. "I've certainly learned that." He then delivered his official news. "Koalee, Bekra is going to stay."

"I thought you'd see it that way."

"The grassman's way has to be strict," said the dolenter, "but it doesn't have to be cruel. I believe that rule we've been discussing is one of those things that was added to the sacred book."

Koalee was reaching for a plate when all of the dishes on her shelves began to rattle. Suddenly the whole house was shaking.

The bell pealed again, but it was drowned out by the sound of thunder that seemed to come up from the earth. Dyra grabbed Koalee and pulled her beneath the table, and Tokra dived down beside them. Moaning, they covered their ears. Tokra began to pray. Thunder beat upon the earth, as if caused by giant drummers. A shadow fell across the window, blotting out the sun, and then passed as quickly as it had come.

Shaking, Dyra crawled out from under the table and ran to the window. There it went, a great shadow moving down the slope beyond the burials, a monster so tall it hid the sky. It was as large as the spreading trees, with huge hair-like branches blowing about it. The shadow stopped, and then turned back toward the village on legs like the trunks of tall trees.

We are finished, Dyra thought. Fate closed in on him, sucking away his breath.

The monster's head stretched down and nuzzled a grass tree. An eye the size of a water vat stared at Dyra. One of the enormous legs moved again, and again the earth trembled. The head was raised, stretched upward so high that Dyra could no longer see it from the window. Then the giant figure shook and went rapidly down the slope, with a noise as horrendous as before. As it died away in the distance, Dyra listened for the bell again, but it didn't sound. Instead, the sounds of what seemed like the whole village screaming, filled the air.

Dyra raced toward the guard tower; the doctor was ahead of him. The guard tower was down. It was Torall's younger brother standing guard, scarcely more than a trail boy.

"Oh, Life!"

The cry came from Hent, who was first to reach the scene. The young guard had not fallen, but was trapped between the ladder and a broken post, halfway to the ground. The bell had broken loose and lay nearby, unharmed.

"Tuje, be careful! It's not safe!"

But Tuje had leaped for an upright and was edging his way up to the trapped guard. "All your ropes, quick!" Syl ordered. "And a coat. Hurry." He was knotting ropes and rigging the coat so that it could be used as a sling to lower the youth.

Dyra steadied the post Tuje had elected to climb. Syl tossed the end of the rope over a cross-beam and made it secure.

"I have to tie him and let the ladder go," Tuje called down.

"Don't jolt him," the doctor ordered. "Tie him to the ladder. If we get four or five men, we can lower it from this end and bring him down easy. Work fast, Tuje."

"It had a tail or something," Hent was saying, still shocked and bewildered by what had taken place. "It went *swoosh*. I think it must have been its back foot that hit the tower, just once. Just *once*."

"Some of you men raise the bell and see if you can ring the gathering," Dyra ordered. He had to know if everyone was safe, and the villagers had to know the cause of their fright.

"The first one went over the hill, and left a trail of gale-force wind," someone said.

"The second one... the teeth! It felled a dozen grass trees with one step. We can show the place. The breath...!"

No one was listening. Tuje had finished roping the hunter's son and was chopping through the wood that wedged the ladder in place. Hryn waited, ready to catch the ladder as it began to fall. The women gathered. Hent's wife said quietly to the doctor, "I brought some brandy, and bandages." Tyad and Powa stood with the old hunter, praying that his son would be brought down alive.

The wood gave. There was no cry from the young guard as the ladder was lowered to the ground, he was unconscious. The villagers watched in silence as the doctor checked him for injuries. Gently, Rels and Koalee undid the ropes holding the young man in place.

"He has a broken arm and some broken ribs," the doctor announced, "and I'm afraid for his thigh. He'll be all right. He's a very lucky young man. Koalee, you know what I need."

The doctor went ahead to set the arm on the spot, and when the guard had been placed on a stretcher and carried to the infirmary, Dyra collected the villagers.

"It was the four-legged shadow," he told them. "They are animals I have seen, using my telescope, kept by the tall man. If we have to move our village to a safer place, we will do so. If any of you wish to go to Runya's village for a time, you have my permission. In the meantime, we thank Life it passed by. What we have to do now is forget about the new mill and help Lenk rebuild the guard tower."

"I think it was frightened by the flags," said Hent. "The wind fluttered the flags and it jumped, and then it turned and ran away."

"There's an idea," said Dyra. "If the flags on the flood markers frightened it, perhaps we could frighten it even more if we erect very tall flag-posts at the corners of the village."

"Do they eat flesh, Dyra?" asked the basketmaker's wife nervously.

"They do not eat flesh," was the answer. "But if they walk through the village..." "We'll show you the footprints," said Lenk, looking solemn and pale. The men from the mill led the villagers out to the burial ground to show where the giant hooves had fallen.

It was true. As many as a dozen grass trees had been bent to the ground and broken by just one step. Even the combined height of three grassmen failed to span the space.

"This is what happened to your family?" the papermaker said to Tuje. It was more of a statement than a question.

Tuje nodded. "We don't want that to happen ever again."

The young men fanned out across the burial ground, looking for more impressions, and when they found one in soft soil, Hryn lay face down along the edge and measured the depth along his arm. He whistled softly. They studied the mysterious humps made by the monstrous feet and ran back and forth comparing the marks.

"It's wider than my house," said the lampman softly to the miller's wife.

"We will pray to Life that it remains afraid of the village," said Tokra.

"And we will pray for the trail boys," said the kiln keeper.

"We will pray," said Flon quietly to Ajist, "that it doesn't come at night."

Ajist was pale. "Hoyim and the others should reach the big village today," she murmured. "If only there was some way to tell them not to start back."

※ ※ ※

The first thing the young travellers saw as they approached Karep was a group of marksmen practising on a target range. They all had firing guns.

"Are these the guards they talked about?" Torall wondered. "While I wanted a firing gun, I wouldn't want to see strangers standing on our guard tower with one of these."

"I disagree with it too," said Hoyim. "My father is right."

The instructor looked surprised when they approached him. "No, we're not the guards," he said. "Guards practice once a week."

"Then you're the hunters."

"We don't have many hunters in Karep. The government encourages young men to learn to use firing guns. The best of them will have the chance to go up trail, and they'll be paid well. So of course everyone wants to be selected."

"Up trail?" Hoyim asked.

"When we build defences at the small villages, they will have to be manned with guards."

"Can I practice?" asked the hunter's son.

"Have you permission to stay?" the instructor inquired.

"I haven't been into the village yet."

"Sorry. You'd have to have permission."

"Am I permitted to buy a firing gun and practice for myself?"

"As long as you do it on a marked range, where no one can be hurt," the instructor replied.

"You can't take it home with you," Hoyim reminded him.

"If I decide I don't want it, I can sell it before we leave," Torall explained to Hoyim. "If I decide to keep it, I'll leave it in the tall woods."

"You won't be able to afford a firing gun," said Dashe. "We should have brought more money. I can think of a hundred things I want to buy."

Hoyim's mind was occupied with all the things that could be

learned in Karep. He asked where they would find the salt mine, but upon learning that it was over eleven hreds from the village, he decided against it.

"Let's see the village in the valley first," he suggested.

"Let's not," Torall retorted. "I want to get into the cliff and go straight to an eating place."

Hoyim didn't argue. Even the rafts in the hollow looked different, somehow, from those in the villages. There were more people on the streets. The young men entered a paved road that was walled with rock. A sign told them they were entering the big village. They heard it before they saw it. As Bekra had said, there was a din of voices and wheels, and all sorts of movement. The three travellers stood in the gate, thrilled at their first sight of the crowds.

"It's like big market every day!" said Dashe.

The gatekeeper asked them to sign a register. When they explained that they would not be seeking permission to stay in Karep, he informed them that some facts would be needed regarding the length of their visit. As they stood discussing whether to write down "three days" or perhaps "four days", a guard approached. He was dressed like the instructor they had seen on the target range, in leather jerkin and laced shoes, and his belt was equipped with a standard grassman's knife. He was not carrying a firing gun.

"From high sun?" he asked, without smiling.

"We come from rising sun," said Hoyim quickly.

The guard's manner seemed to change, and he appeared wary. "In that case, I'll need you to answer a few questions."

Hoyim glanced at his companions, aware that it might be best if they had one spokesman. They caught his meaning and stepped back. As Dyra's son, official business was Hoyim's affair.

The questions made Hoyim angry. Why should a guard in Karep want to know if they had spoken with councils in the villages rising sun? What did it matter if they had attended any public meetings? They hadn't, but Hoyim felt it was only right to complain about the question.

The guard was polite about his resistance. "You men from small villages don't understand the problems of keeping control in a big village like this," he said lightly. "We've had to cancel permission too often lately, because we've had a few people spreading discontent."

The guard asked about the Chief Councillor at the first village high sun of the tall woods. Had he said anything at all about Karep?

It went against Hoyim's nature to utter even a half-truth, but this entire procedure had made him extremely wary. He looked steadily at the guard and informed him that the councillor in question had spoken of plans to bring more trade and possibly defenses to small villages.

"This is the rumour we heard at every village we passed," Hoyim added.

"He voiced no opposition to the plans?"

Hoyim was glad that his companions had not been at the meeting.

"He would never have spoken to young men who have no official authority," he replied evasively.

To Hoyim's surprise, the guard didn't seem suspicious of his answer. Had he told such a blatant half-truth in his father's village, the villagers would have seen through it at once.

It was the next question which almost broke through his defense. Had they met two young men named Hilt and Lydyl?

Torall was standing where he could signal to Hoyim without being seen by the guard, and he began to mouth, "Don't tell!"

Hoyim was about to follow Torall's advice and lie openly, but a sudden hunch told him that the guards might already know about the clandestine visit in the dead of night.

"We did!" he said, breaking into a smile. "They were travellers going rising sun. They came to see us just two nights ago. They said they'd had their permission cancelled, and they wanted to know if there were any places for young men at end of settlement."

"Did they tell you what they planned to do at end of settlement?"

"One of them said he had been a clerk. We told him there weren't many councils in the small villages employing clerks, but he might find work keeping books for tradesmen. The other was a builder. It will be easy for him to find a place."

The guard looked them over cautiously, appraising their packs and the knives at their belts, and then said briskly, "We hope you'll enjoy your stay in Karep."

Hoyim felt as if he would collapse.

"Hoyim!" said Torall in disbelief once the guard had departed. "You were telling untruths as if you did it every day."

"If we really stay here four days, I'm afraid I will lose the Truth. I already understand why Mev is what he is."

No one but the guard seemed to have noted the coming of the three young men. As they stood gazing at the market stalls, a trail runner laden with red meat passed them on the run. Before they could appreciate that, a second trail runner followed, carrying the same burden. Another came toward them, heading out the gate. A child had apparently lost his mother in the crowd and began to cry. Two ladies dressed smartly swished past without looking at the newcomers.

Hoyim felt very uncertain, despite the fact that the guard had approved them. He caught the attention of an elderly man and said, "Pardon me. We signed the register and saw the guard. Is there anyone else we should see to obtain permission to spend a few days in Karep?"

The man looked puzzled. "Oh, you're villagers. If you signed in, you don't need permission. Just money."

It proved to be true. The first thing they did was ask directions to a place where meals were served. When they learned how much the meal cost, they looked at each other helplessly. It took a third of the money they had brought with them.

"I'm afraid to ask what a bed will cost," said Dashe.

Hoyim and Torall both gestured toward the gate. They would not be spending the night in Karep after all, unless the cornman's son had a place where they could stay.

The infirmary was a busy place, but the cornman's son was overjoyed to see them. He insisted they come back when it was time for the evening meal, and he would be free to join them. In the meantime they wandered the streets: climbing staircases carved in rock, studying the water system and all the places where the tradesmen worked, hunting for schools, finding the ramps where trail runners were pulled up to the high streets. They marvelled at the gardens, the ornate street lamps, and the brightly painted houses that had never been worn by wind or snow or rain. They saw the pool for swimming, and wondered at the clear water, but they all agreed that it was not as attractive as Hoyim's Lake. There were no smells of nature around it. The air in Karep was stale and unpleasant. The most exciting find was a series of lifts that allowed the wealthy people to ride up to their homes, rather than climbing. Next, Hoyim discovered the library and insisted upon lingering there, while his companions continued their investigations.

When they returned, they told Hoyim they had found the hall of government, and that it was very grand. If there was anything which could tempt Hoyim to leave the unbelievable collection of books and manuscripts, it was the chance to see the hall of government. All three hurried back. Hoyim insisted upon going inside, so the others followed him nervously. The room had a very high ceiling where a crevice let in natural sunlight, but the lower corners were aglow with lamps. The first thing to meet their eyes was a large portrait of a man.

"Perhaps he's the Chief Councillor," Torall whispered.

A clerk was seated at a table, writing. He looked up.

"I am Hoyim, son of Chief Councillor Dyra," Hoyim introduced himself. "Is it permissible to speak to council to carry greetings from my father and his council?"

The clerk looked startled. "Is that all? No one may speak to council unless council has established a time," he said. "And I am not permitted to ask council to establish a time unless there is a reason for it."

"I gave you the reason," Hoyim said. Whatever had happened to simple grassman courtesy?

"It is no reason at all," said the clerk.

Dashe tugged at Hoyim's sleeve, trying to get him to withdraw.

Hoyim stubbornly ignored him. "What if I said my reason was to ask the Chief Councillor to explain the new plans for the villages?"

Again the clerk was startled. "Are you officially deputized?"

"No."

"Then you're wasting my time."

"What if I said that I'm a collector of information? That by right of trade I have traditional authority to carry news to my village?"

The clerk looked taken aback. "Why didn't you say so? You're a printer, then?"

"Yes, I am."

"Wait." The clerk went to an inner room and was gone some minutes. When he returned he sat down at his table in a businesslike way and began to write.

"You may speak to council..." Hoyim took a step forward but the man held up his hand to stop him. "...on the morning of the day after tomorrow."

"But I don't think I'll be here then."

"You had me establish a time only to tell me you won't be here?"

"You didn't ask..."

"Wait."

Again the clerk retreated, and when he returned there was a middle-aged man with him. "I am in charge of the official printers," the man said. "There is absolutely no need for you to take council's time to ask about the new government. The information is all being printed and will be circulated to the villages very soon."

"Then I will print that, at least."

"Are you craftsman?"

"I have seven years' experience."

"We're looking for printers. How would you like to live in Karep?"

"Not at all! I belong to my father's village. My whole family is there."

The other smiled indulgently. "You are saying 'no' to a good opportunity. We pay printers well here. There can't be much money in printing in a small village."

"True. There isn't."

"Only the printers here in Karep are official printers under the new government, and so they are the only ones who will be paid."

"I live on what I can make by my trade. I will never starve."

"You may become subject to restrictions on what you print. The new government will be concerned about everything that goes on in the villages."

Hoyim felt his anger rising, and he could tell that Torall's was as well. He fought to keep his composure. "If I said 'yes' to your offer and became an official printer in Karep, would there be restrictions on what I print?"

"Of course! You would work for the new government."

"I couldn't say what I like?"

"Certainly not."

"You really *are* in a cave," said Hoyim. He turned and marched out of the hall of government, with his friends beside him.

VII

"WE FOUND SOMETHING else you should see," said Dashe. "Down that way."

"It's dark over there."

"Yes, but they have street lamps further on."

They went into a chasm in the rock. Beyond it there was less light and less fresh air. It was apparent at once that the houses were smaller and poorer, and Hoyim noticed that some of the women and children looked thin and pale. The drain by the water spigot didn't seem to be working, and a young woman coming for water had to wade up to her ankles through a pool.

"You need a raft," Torall called to her.

She smiled. "You're new here."

"Just visiting."

"Take my advice and go straight home," she said.

"Don't you like it here?"

"Would you? I'm from Nym's village. I'd be there yet, but my husband has a dream about becoming rich."

"What does he do?"

"Carries meal. At least he did until he hurt his shoulder, and now he's doing nothing. He promised to build us a raft in the valley, but of course he can't do that now, either. Not until his shoulder has healed."

"Did you know Bekra?"

"Afraid not."

"She had a shop. Herbs and crafts."

"I may have been in it."

"She's of our village. Dyra's village."

The woman waded out of the pool with her water.

"Thanks for talking to us," said Hoyim.

"Don't mention it. A pleasant day."

"Would you tell me one thing?"

"I will if I know it."

"What is the new government like? What does it plan to do?"

She laughed. "That's simple enough. They want to make things better down here in the low town. Or so they say. They want to bring more workmen and a lot more food and cloth from the country villages and make life better for the poor."

"That's it?"

"That's what I've heard. Sorry, I have to go. Have to heat this water and treat that shoulder."

The young men bade her goodbye and walked along several streets. On a flight of stone steps, they passed four elderly men who were just sitting, with nothing to do. They met two youths of about thirteen and wished them a pleasant day, but the boys turned away rudely and didn't reply.

"I want out of here," said Dashe.

"It stinks of wastes," said Torall.

"No wonder. Almost time for the evening meal and they aren't taken away yet."

"Maybe they do this section last, after the upper village is cleaned up."

"Here's a tea house! Let's rest."

Rather reluctantly, Dashe and Torall followed Hoyim into the tea house. It was small, but neat and clean, and once the tea mistress realized that they were not from the low town, she fussed to set their table properly. There was no one else around, so they plied her with questions and she answered willingly. No, she didn't mind the gloom. You got used to it. Why did she stay? It was cheaper than the other parts of Karep. Why be in the big village at all? She was a widow and nobody had adopted her. Adoptions were rare in the big village. She couldn't raft herself a house in the valley, and if she lived there she would have to perform all the tasks of survival, impossible to do alone. It was easier to live in the low town making cakes and serving tea. The villages? No, she was born in Karep. She really knew nothing of village life. Once a year she took an excursion outside to pick the herbs she used in her teas. It was much cheaper than buying them in the shops, and it allowed her to save a bit of money. It was also good for her health. The new government? She had no interest in politics. Of course she had seen the Chief Councillor. He was a nice man—good-looking and very intelligent. He knew what went on in Karep. He permanently stationed three guards in the low town. The old council stationed only one. That's what she liked. Young men without jobs had been fighting in the streets, they were restless and quarrelsome at times. There had been some thefts. It wasn't pleasant for a woman living alone, in a situation like that. She felt much safer with the new system.

They thanked the tea mistress for the tea and the conversation and went back through the section of houses behind the market place.

On their way to the infirmary, they had to pass the hall of government once more. Several men were coming out of the building together, talking seriously. Hoyim had an impression of long coats that curved to the back, like Mev's coat, of neatly trimmed hair and flashing finger rings and, here and there, a seal of office prominently displayed. Surely it was the council. He counted nine of them, and all but two came his direction and passed him on the road. Beside Hoyim, a stranger had stopped and inclined his head slightly as the men went by.

"You might have bowed," he said to Hoyim critically. "That was the Chief Councillor."

Hoyim didn't need to be told which man he meant, because the Chief Councillor was certainly the man they had seen in the portrait. He was, just as the tea mistress had said, a good-looking man, with dark hair showing some grey and a splendid walk. He had about him an air of vast confidence, and he looked happy, with the kind of happiness that comes of shutting the mind to anything that brings sorrow. He wasn't what Hoyim expected, and yet he had a feeling the instant he saw him that Brecort was not a man he could talk to.

He didn't look like a man who would listen. He looked like a man who believed he already had all the answers and could learn from no one.

Then came a surprise. Among the approaching councillors was a tall, familiar figure. He was talking and laughing with a companion in a relaxed fashion, and he didn't look at the boys from Dyra's village. Hoyim almost called to him, but he stopped himself.

"Did you see who that was?" asked Dashe, equally amazed.

"Kezel!" said Torall, as if he'd lost his breath.

"I wonder if Radd knows about that," said Hoyim.

"If the Chief Councillor has men like that on his council, it's proof that he has no love of Life," said Torall. "The eggman destroys Life without as much as a thank you."

"There is something else about the eggman," said Hoyim, with a slight smile. "He's a coward. I wonder if they all are."

He would have to tell the tall man about all of this.

They waited at the infirmary for the cornman's son, and watched the people streaming from the area of shops toward other parts of the big village. They seemed glad to be finished the day and going home, and all looked pale and tired—some as pale as the people in the low town.

"I couldn't work in this air," said Dashe. "I wouldn't stay in here overnight, even if I could afford it."

"I would," said Torall. "Just to know what it's like to buy a bed in the big village. But I'd rather keep my money."

The cornman's son understood their situation only too well. "I rafted a house in the valley," he said, "but since I came to live in the master's house, a new apprentice is living in my house. Tonight he'll stay at the infirmary, in my place, and you will be my guests in the valley."

They found the marketplace still busy, as people purchased what was left of the day's food at cheap prices. The cornman's son took advantage of it and bought food to take home for their meal. Some men came in pulling empty waste boxes in their trail runners; the smells wafted past and made them cover their noses. The last contingent of young men from the shooting range came in, a few hunters bringing meat and greens, some children who had apparently been playing outside in the sunshine—healthy looking children, almost like villagers, but not as shy. One of them playfully pulled the bell rope at the gate, even though the gate was open. Everybody was coming in, but no one else was going out.

"I'd have suggested we stay in for the concert, but the eating places cost..." began the cornman's son.

"We know!"

"We can still come back for the concert. My raft isn't far."

They greeted the idea eagerly and hurried so there would be plenty of time. There was so much to talk about. It would be another year before the cornman's son was able to come home, and he had messages for almost everyone in the village. It surprised him that there was so much excitement in the villages about the new government. He was too engrossed in his medical studies, he said, to pay much attention to politics.

"It's just another government," he said with a shrug. "Brecort has a reputation for intelligence, and he seems to have a very efficient organization. I have some newsletters he wrote about his plans for the federation. Remind me to give them to you before you leave."

"And you aren't worried about it?" Hoyim was amazed and disappointed.

"He may have some good ideas. He wants to improve trails and increase trade. He wants to encourage young grass people to come here to study. Above all, he wants to help the small villages achieve greater security. If he could protect you from animals and wheelers and the mower, shouldn't you give him a chance?"

Torall was red-faced with emotion. "He's not even looking after the people in his own village. We saw the poor streets this afternoon. I think he ought to worry about his own villagers and leave Dyra to worry about us."

A faint smile played about the mouth of their host, and then he said lightly, "There's no doubt that one of the reasons he wants to see grass people safe in the country is so they can produce more food for the people in Karep."

"You lived all your life in the country, and you can honestly sit here and tell us you don't think the new government is a threat to the grassman's way?" Hoyim was losing his patience.

The cornman's son smiled. "You think they've done something to my mind," he said. "I'm still a grassman, and I'll tell you this. Villages are villages, and the grassman's way will flourish. When the new government tries to get out there and make things fit their plans, they'll find themselves up against things they can't control. Let Brecort be snowed in once or twice. No, the worst threat I foresee is that his messengers may go into the small villages and sow discontent. That would be sad. Sad for Karep too. There are already too many people living here in shelter, forgetting how to fend for themselves. The master doctor has been trying to convince them that life in Karep is bad for the health, but they don't listen."

It was dusk when they got back to the gate, and they could hear the birds in the tall trees settling for the night. The cornman's son kept a wary eye.

"It's easy to get careless, living in the cave," he said. "You constantly have to remind yourself that you're out in the open, under the owls and the nighthawks. Did you notice we've no guard tower? This isn't really part of Karep, so the government doesn't pay guards. We just build out here and take our chances."

"If you had a flood and had to cut anchor, would they come to look for you and help you to pole home?"

"Oh yes, they'd do that. Now watch. Never enter the tunnel at night without first making sure there's no animal in there." He peered around the corner to make sure it was safe.

The road through the rock was lighted, but the gate to the city was shut. They didn't have to ring, because the gatekeeper was wide awake and on watch, and he let them in promptly.

"Paper rafts are afloat," the gatekeeper said.

The cornman's son said, "Good! We'll go."

He led them to the swimming place, and there they found a large crowd of villagers. Dozens of lights turned the area into day, and all over the water were beautiful flowers, rafts decorated with balloons and fans, and boats of many colours with fantastic sails.

"It's a children's contest," explained the cornman's son. "They make these themselves. Sometimes they're very beautiful, and sometimes they're funny. Over there is one of the flowers that opens after it soaks up some water."

Children were splashing in the water, rescuing rafts that were about to sink, and disentangling those that had caught together. A majestic ship topped by a bright blue feather was making its way the full length of the pool while its young owner on shore drew it along by a string, deftly keeping it from entangling with other craft. People began to cheer for him.

"He will win for navigation," a man remarked to Hoyim, "but that sluggish raft with all the flowers will win for beauty. You'll see."

Hoyim felt warm and tingly. It wasn't just that a stranger had spoken to him nicely, it was something about the crowd and the lights and the excitement. He looked out beyond the bright circle and saw the windows of homes twinkling up the slopes and far up on the heights. His eyes followed the patterns of streets, marked by shining lamps. The big village by night was an exotic place. He could learn to like this.

"We could do this on Hoyim's Lake," said Torall, and went to ask one of the children if it was difficult to fold the paper flowers. Before long, the children's teacher was summoned and was giving Torall a lesson in folding. The others gathered around.

"It's different," Dashe remarked, as they left the pool and made their way to the concert hall. "It's as if we could do anything we like here, and nobody would know. You feel so free." Even as he said it, they passed a guard standing by the roadside, watching the crowd.

"Your father mightn't know, and your intended mightn't know," said Hoyim, "but when did you ever see a guard with a firing gun keeping his eye on the people in our village?"

It made them uneasy. As they entered the concert hall, giving up another of their precious coins, they passed another guard.

"Pay no attention," said the cornman's son. "They are there to protect you from theft and to keep people from fighting. They won't do you any harm."

"It isn't right," said Hoyim. "Grassmen don't harm grassmen. When grassmen have to have guards with firing guns watching to see they don't hurt each other, they've lost the Way. They are not grassmen any more."

"Don't speak too loudly," the cornman's son advised in a hushed voice.

Hoyim lowered his voice. "Has it occurred to you that our children learn to make real rafts? What good will a paper raft do in a flood?"

"Look over there!"

The most beautiful woman they had ever seen was standing a short distance from them, talking to a middle-aged couple.

"Who is she?"

"That's Rayan, a very famous singer," the cornman's son told them. "She will likely sing tonight."

The young men could hardly keep their mouths closed. Rayan was tall and slender, with a great length of shining brown hair wrapped about an opulent comb. She moved with delightful poise, and her arms and throat glistened with fine jewels. Not even the widow had ever worn a gown that flowed about her with such graceful lines. Her slippers looked as if they were formed of silver lace.

"Rayan comes from a village far away high sun," said the cornman's son. "Sometimes she travels there and sings at small villages on the way."

"I can see more beautiful ladies from where I'm standing than I've seen in my whole life," said Torall.

Two young ladies overheard the remark and one turned and gave Torall a dazzling smile that made him flush.

"There's the Chief Councillor!" Dashe announced. "Is that his wife with him?"

"No, he isn't married," said the cornman's son.

Suddenly there was noticeable haste in the crowd to be seated, so the four young men found themselves a place on a bench.

"Is this hall a meeting house?" Dashe asked. "Does it belong to the village?"

"A man owns it. Some of the money we put in the box will go to the players, but most of it will go to the owner."

"*One man* built such a hall?" They looked around in awe.

"It was a cavern. Only the entry had to be built, and he hired stone layers for that."

"You mean he owns something that *Life* built and put here?" Hoyim was incredulous.

"He paid for it."

"We can't pay for something Life built. It isn't ours to buy. You think you can pay for anything here," complained Hoyim.

"We do! See where the Chief Councillor is sitting? You pay more to sit there."

"Look who's coming!"

The eggman arrived in a great flourish and a pretty young woman on each arm. For some reason Hoyim wanted to duck out of sight, but he was too late. It didn't matter. Kezel looked directly at the young men from Dyra's village, but it was obvious that he didn't remember having seen them before.

"Of course, I was only thirteen when he saw me," Hoyim murmured. "How could he remember?"

"He's become a snob, among other things," said Torall huffily.

"He's not all bad," the cornman's son remarked, and Hoyim frowned.

The concert was not as long as their concerts in the village. Music makers played three pieces, one of them very quiet and sad, and then a young man read from a book he had written and bowed deeply.

"He uses words well," said the cornman's son. But it was a story of the big village, and the others found little of interest in it.

A man and a woman sang together very nicely, and the crowd begged for more. Torall asked if it was a married song and was horrified to learn the couple were not man and wife.

At last the singer Rayan appeared, and she sang for the rest of the evening. Her voice was not as sweet as Pettis's, but it was very beautiful, rich and clear. Some of her songs were strange to the young men, though there were a few dancey village tunes that they recognized. She sang a song about Dokrimalitzla, and a murmur arose in the crowd around the Chief Councillor. The cornman's son stiffened a little. There was a slight hush when the song was over. Then the eggman stood up and led the cheer, shouting, "Well sung!"

"I've heard traders whistling that song," said Dashe. "Would she give us the words if we asked her?"

"Perhaps. I often see her at celebrations or the homes of friends. I will ask for you. If the song is printed, I will buy a copy and bring it when I come," promised the cornman's son. "I won't ask her tonight. She's always tired after a concert."

As the boys stood waiting for the cornman's son to speak to a man he'd helped through a sickness, Rayan herself stood not far away, receiving congratulations from the Chief Councillor and his party. A moment later a woman spoke to her. The singer must have been invited to a celebration, because they heard her make an excuse that she was much too fatigued. Another group of admirers surrounded her then, and Hoyim heard her say with more enthusiasm, "I mustn't miss a chance like this!"

"Rayan, you already have more jewels than twenty-five grasswomen could wear," Kezel teased her.

"Nevertheless, if the trader comes from high sun of the green lake..." Hoyim listened intently.

"I won't have you going down to the marketplace alone at this time of night," said Kezel. "If you won't call the jeweller to your home, allow me to escort you."

"Are they selling jewels at a celebration?" Dashe whispered, trying to make sense of what they had overheard.

"I don't think so. I think there are two different things happening." Hoyim replied.

The cornman's son returned and they started for the gate without hearing any more.

"I'll be honest; I didn't like some of the concert," said Torall. "Would Ajist want you to sing a married song with another woman, Hoyim?"

Hoyim thought not. "Their ways are strange, but interesting," he said. "Do they have a concert every night?"

"Oh no. You were lucky. Let's go see the late shoppers, and I'll buy a treat to take home for tea."

"I didn't see any of the traders," said Dashe.

"Looking for someone?"

A woman turned and spoke to Dashe flirtatiously. "W...would you know them?" Dashe stammered.

The cornman's son took his elbow and spun him away. He was laughing. "If you want to marry your new friend, you're not looking for her!" he said. "She's a different kind of grasswoman."

"What do you mean?"

"She lives by renting out a sleeping room to travellers."

"Oh, like the tea mistress."

"No. Not at all like the tea mistress. You see, she sleeps in it."

"*In the room?*"

It took them a minute to understand what was being said, and then all three looked shocked.

"If they've lost the Truth, they really have lost the grassman's way," said Hoyim solemnly.

They stepped into a shop to see what it held, but everything was too costly. They left the stall just in time to see Rayan and Kezel disappearing into a jeweller's shop. Before they could remark about that, they were surprised to find themselves face-to-face with a fairy. The lamplight shimmered on her wings and showed the pale oval of her face but, except for some sparkling touches of purple and crystal, her dress was lost in darkness. She gave a slight smile of recognition and said, "Hoyim! Go home and good trail."

She disappeared into the jeweller's shop.

Hoyim was paralyzed for a moment. Her sudden appearance and her uncanny likeness to Ajist had startled him, but the chief reason for his astonishment was that he had felt the powerful impact of her psyche in that brief encounter. The full meaning of her message, in all of its emotional shadings, had come across to him. In his mind her silent message resounded, *be patient*, look to the red valley and wait.

"Hoyim, do you know that fairy?"

Hoyim brought himself out of his stupor and smiled. "Yes, I met her a long time ago in the tall woods. Violet was never one to waste words," he said.

The young men had planned to spend four days in Karep, but there was no more money. They would stay the night on the raft in the valley, and then set off at dawn rising sun. It was not yet dawn when Hoyim woke to see the cornman's son bending over him, with his finger to his lips. He beckoned to him to get up quietly and follow, then led him outside and down to the float space.

"There is no one up and we won't be overheard," he said. "But speak softly just in case. Hoyim, say little when you return to the village about what I'm going to tell you. There is strong resistance to Brecort in Karep—much stronger than in the villages you passed on your way. There is really nothing to fear, but we don't want Brecort to be alert to what is happening. You may have guessed—Rayan is one of our key people. Her songs give us clues. If she sings of Nanta or Dokrimalitzla there are messages from rising sun. If she sings of evening, then it's setting sun. She gives away times and places and numbers, and no one has yet caught on. Rayan hears the elves, and she has direct contact with the elf Radd."

Hoyim nodded. "I would never have believed it of Violet," he whispered. "But what has Kezel to do with it?"

"I told you he was not all bad. Kezel will help the villages."

"But he's in the new government."

"That's right. He's the man with the power to cancel permissions."

Hoyim almost raised his voice. "You mean he's to blame for Hilt and Lydyl..."

"That's correct. He has power over everyone who comes and goes. It's very useful. Hilt and Lydyl are needed in Mekr's village for the rest of this year. They had to go."

Hoyim was stunned.

"He didn't fail to recognize you, Hoyim. He knew you were coming before you left the first village high sun of the tall woods."

"The fairies!"

The cornman's son grinned. "Brecort doesn't believe in the fairies! Will he ever have a communications network to top ours? Come, we'll get the dew and then wake your friends."

But Hoyim had one more question. "What good would fairies be against firing guns?"

The cornman's son frowned. "That is not yet decided," he admitted.

※ ※ ※

Rayan was usually tired after a concert, but tonight she felt as if she had used no energy at all. Her eyes sparkled and there was high colour in her cheeks. Still, she refused the usual invitations to late supper. She was about to join a neighbour from the heights for the walk to the lifts, when someone seized her elbow. She turned to find Brecort smiling at her.

"Allow me the honour of walking you home, Rayan," he said warmly. "You outdid yourself tonight! A wonderful concert."

Rayan thanked him and bowed to his company. People were turning to look. The two made a handsome couple—both tall and dark, both aglow with confidence. The Chief Councillor seemed to enjoy the company of women, but folks had seldom seen him with Rayan.

They were passing the tea shop under the cliff when Brecort suggested they go in for late supper. Rayan looked down at her dress, a full, sweeping circle of crimson petals over white.

There were red jewels around her neck and across her brow.

"I am in stage costume," she demurred. "It wouldn't look appropriate."

"I have never seen you more beautiful."

Rayan had to admit she felt flattered, and she agreed to the supper. When they had been shown to a table and had ordered their food, Brecort surveyed his partner as if she was worthy of the greatest painter in Karep.

"What's this I hear about you going up trail soon?" he asked.

"It is true."

"But the cold season is perilously close. Does this mean you won't be back until spring?"

"That's what it means. Yes."

"You never go away for the cold season. You are the light that keeps the cave warm. I should really refuse you permission to leave."

It was said lightly, but it needled Rayan. She disliked anyone holding authority over her. She had proved her right to make her own decisions long since.

"I didn't go home to my parents' village this summer. I miss village life. If I didn't live in a village part of the year, my energies would drain away. I couldn't sing at all."

"We certainly can't allow that to happen, but you have no idea how much you will be missed. I hope you have good trail guards?"

The tea mistress brought glasses and a jug of tea, which she set before Rayan. Rayan poured, assuring her companion she would be safe up trail.

"I will never understand it," Brecort murmured, "This romance with small village life that grass people insist on holding sacred."

"It is sacred. It is the Way. You know what is wrong with you, Brecort? You were born and raised in Karep. The Way was never part of you. It hasn't even touched you."

"Thank goodness, you're right. It hasn't."

A plate of crayfish meat and boiled white bark arrived, with yellow roots, crisp flatbread and sour seeds. Rayan wished she had more appetite for it. Why had she agreed to come with Brecort?

Brecort was not a subtle man, nor one to waste time. "You know, of course, that I still want you for my wife?" he said.

Rayan felt tears in her eyes, but she set her face and tasted the fish. It was excellent, and she caught the tea mistress's eye to let her know that. "But we don't agree," she said quietly.

"We agree on everything. We like the same people, the same paintings. The music— especially the music. We both like to look well and live well. We both like to have admirers. We are very alike, Rayan."

"We are very different. My heart is more than half-village. You haven't a grain of love for villages."

"I like villages. They are filled with fine people. I just don't understand why those people are content to live in them."

"You don't understand the freedom and independence which is the grassman's way. If you did, you would have abandoned this misguided scheme to set up a central government and dictate to the villages."

"'Dictate' is a very strong word."

"It is the correct word. The villages run smoothly because the men who run them know the people. They're familiar with both the advantages and the dangers of their areas. Without that knowledge there would soon be disaster."

"It leaves no room for change."

"Well, it does, but I won't argue about that."

"Do you think I merely want power for myself?" he asked.

"No, Brecort, I know you're not selfish. I am simply saying you are totally unfamiliar with village life. That should be enough to make you realize you are wading in unfamiliar streams, trying to make decisions for villages."

"We seem to end up here all the time—at an impasse over your precious villages." He was beginning to sound impatient. "You don't understand this issue as I do. Karep can't survive without materials from the villages. We need them."

"Karep is too large. If you haven't space to plant enough pea trees or find enough animals around the cave, then it is time the village divided. All the villages divide when there are not enough places for the people. The big village is unbalanced."

"Who knows what 'balance' means?"

"The villagers do. And the elves."

"Elves! There you go, Rayan. Another place where you and I don't exactly harmonize. Elves, indeed! When are you going to grow up?"

Rayan felt the warm spots on her cheeks blaze. She wanted to throw down her fork and walk out in a huff, but she calmed herself. "I suppose when you face the Truth," she retorted.

"I tell the truth. That is a very unfair accusation, Rayan."

"I know you tell the truth. Telling the truth is not the Truth I meant."

"I don't understand this other 'Truth' people go on about."

"I know."

"Let's not argue. Let's enjoy our meal."

They ate in silence for a few minutes and Rayan kept sipping her hot tea. The aroma made her feel more tranquil.

"You were rather defiant in your choice of songs tonight," Brecort remarked. "The entire concert was about small villages and freedom. I hope you weren't taunting me."

"I sing my own mood, Brecort. I wouldn't dream of taunting you from the stage. Believe that."

Brecort looked at her through the steam from her tea glass, enjoying the rich depth of the red jewels around her throat, the way her dark hair curved smoothly down each side of her forehead. There was no grasswoman on earth to rival Rayan. "Tell me something, then, as a friend."

"If I can."

"Is there a movement in Karep to have me replaced as Chief Councillor?"

"As far as I know, most of the people are extremely satisfied with you as Chief Councillor," Rayan replied honestly.

"Except you, then."

"Oh no. I'm extremely satisfied with you, too. There has never been a Chief Councillor made so many improvements or kept things running as smoothly as you do. I only wish you would close off the low town and settle those people in the do-lan. It is unhealthy and inhumane in that end of the cave."

"Aha! I caught you. You are telling me to plan for other people, and a few moments ago you condemned me for that very thing."

"Here you have the right. You are Chief Councillor. But you have no such right in the villages. You have gone beyond limits, and I will never agree with that."

"And you are angry that I have no woman on my council."

"We won't start that again."

"Is this why you won't marry me?"

"If you could face the Truth you would know why. You would open your eyes."

"So, unless I abandon my 'misguided' plans, you will abandon Karep and go live in your old village. Is that it?"

"A musician earns much less in a small village," Rayan said honestly. Then she added, "Karep was nice when we had three thousand people."

"I agree. It was."

"Stop taking them in."

"I want to protect them, just as I want to protect grassmen in the villages."

"Like I said, you were born and raised in Karep. To you, the do-lan is a place of danger that disturbs your dreams."

Brecort looked startled and Rayan pressed her advantage. "Forget that perception," she advised softly. "Grass people get their strength and knowledge from living in the do-lan. They do not need rescue. Only freedom."

"Will you marry me if I agree to your ultimatum and abandon the entire plan to take charge of the villages?"

It was impossible to tell, from his tone or his expression, whether he was being serious. "When you face the Truth, it will all become right," said Rayan.

"'When I face the Truth.' You might as well tell me again we are going to have a Dokrimalitzla."

"No, I'm not going to tell you that." Rayan suddenly burst into her widest smile. "I'm sure Dokrimalitzla himself is capable of telling you that."

Brecort stared at her. "For a moment there I almost saw what you see," he said, and shook his head. "One of the publishers wants permission to print a book about what would happen if Dokrimalitzla came back. It is apparently rather humorous."

"Has he right of trade?"

"Yes, but..."

"But, in Karep, publishers have no freedom. We'll argue about that another time."

"I'm sure we will. I could be perfect and you would still argue with me, Rayan. It's strange. I have never heard that you have a reputation for arguing with other people."

"Other people are not so stubborn-headed," she replied.

There was that devastating smile again. How could he be angry with Rayan? With a sigh, Brecort beckoned to the tea mistress and asked for sweets. Rayan asked for more tea. At least she was in no hurry to escape from his company. Brecort found solace in that.

"You go find Dokrimalitzla," he teased. "Bring him here to Karep and show him to me and I will bow to your wishes and forget about organizing the villages into a federation."

He thinks he is so safe, Rayan was thinking, trying to keep her smile innocent as possible. "You abandon your plans for the villages and I may consider becoming your wife," she replied, reaching out to select a sweet to nibble. Then she gave him a penetrating glance as she popped the syrupy morsel into her mouth. "Truth first," she said.

VIII

THE GATHERING BELL began to ring the moment the three young travellers were sighted entering Dyra's village. Villagers young and old flocked to the street of shops to greet them. At the meeting house, the boys were stationed on the dais so everyone could hear what they had to say.

They fell over each other in their eagerness to tell every detail of their visit to Karep, but had made a pact to say nothing at all about government until Hoyim could speak privately to council.

They began with the three days of rain which stranded them high sun of the tall woods, and there was great excitement when the villagers learned that Dashe, already twenty-six, had finally found his intended and would be married.

"You had no trouble up trail?" asked Lenk.

"Well, we met a cat on the way home, but Torall scared it away."

"He scared a *cat*?"

"Yes, with a firing gun. The noise frightened it and it ran away."

Dyra was concerned. "You haven't brought a firing gun into the village?"

"I didn't bring it," Torall assured him. "I left it in a safe place at a distance. In case, at some future time, I have need of it."

"Not in my village," said Dyra. "And the cornman's son? He's well?"

"He's busy and learning much. We didn't find Ryjra. His shop was closed, and we left a message on the door. Oh, Father! I saw Violet."

Hoyim didn't expand on that, because few of the villagers knew Violet. They explained how the big village looked, and how things were done there. They spoke honestly of their impressions about the low town, and the guards with guns. The water supply? The concert? The schools? It would take days to tell it all.

"Did you find people who will buy the books you print?" Tokra asked.

Here was a question Hoyim didn't want to answer. "I may run into some difficulty," he admitted. "I will say more after I give my report to council."

"What is it *really* like in Karep?" asked Koalee.

The young men looked from one to the other.

"None of us would wish to live there," said Torall simply and Koalee looked satisfied.

"It's confusing," said Dyra. "It sounds so beautiful and stimulating and then again it sounds so bad."

"There are pictures carved in the walls inside the concert hall. Pictures of tall trees and grassmen's homes on rafts, just like a real village."

"I didn't understand the big village," said Dashe, shaking his head. "They have such exciting things to do. They should be happy."

"But they aren't," said Hoyim. "They don't laugh and chat with a shopkeeper as we do here. They don't enjoy each other."

"No," said Bekra, who'd been listening closely, "They do not."

"Now there are five of us who have seen Karep," said the doctor, "and next year when our new doctor comes home it will be six. This should be enough to convince us we have a much better life as we are."

"It's the cave," said Dashe.

"More than the cave," said the doctor.

"It's more the love of money," Bekra suggested.

The doctor shook his head. "It is the necessity for organization. It's the size, because they don't know each other well and never will. There are far too many of them."

"They don't even have houses!" Dashe complained. "They crowd into rooms cut in the rock, like the honeycombs of bees!"

A gasp rose from their audience.

"Not all of them," Hoyim explained hastily. "What really troubles me about Karep is that the children are not learning the grassman's way. If these people become a majority, they will be the end of our way of life."

Dyra could see that his son had countless things on his mind that had not yet been spoken. "We'll talk later," he announced. "It's time these travellers get home to rest and spend some time with their families."

The three young men were shocked to learn that, while they braved the dangers of trail, their village had been threatened by the four-legged shadow. The guard tower had been re-built, and Torall's young brother was out of infirmary and at home with slowly mending bones. Torall hurried off to see him.

Dyra turned to Hoyim. "We'll talk in council in the morning," he said. "Meantime, the best way to preserve the grassman's way is to *live* the grassman's way. Have you greeted all your aunts and uncles and cousins? Be sure to greet Tokra. He has prayed for the three of you every day while you were up trail."

Ajist was looking tired, and eager to get Hoyim away where they could talk privately, but Hoyim knew that his father was right. He greeted each of his relatives before leaving with his wife.

Torall went hunting the next day with his firing gun, but Dashe accompanied Hoyim to the meeting of council. It was just as Hoyim expected. Whenever his own memory foundered, Dashe could remember every detail. He'd counted the number of young men they'd seen practising on the target range, the number of guard stations in the big village, the number of guards in the streets. He was nervous, he said, about the prospect of such guards coming to the villages.

"They claim to be training them to come and guard the villages for our safety," he told council, "but in Karep they stand guard on the people, to see that they behave. What if they decided to stand guard over us? What if the guns on the tower pointed at the village, instead of at the sky?"

Hoyim nodded, but council did not find cause to be overly concerned. "No grassman would ever do that," said Lenk.

"Karep is far away," said Yansa. "I don't know what you heard to make you develop such fears, but Karep will never send men to guard our village, much less *guard us*."

Hoyim thought he saw a look of more serious concern on his father's face, and he wished he'd spoken to Dyra alone before meeting with council. Lenk was so trusting, and Yansa so traditional. How would it be possible to make them understand? Especially when he had promised the cornman's son not to say too much. He began to direct his remarks directly to the Chief Councillor, telling him all about the meeting at the first village and the meeting with the two young men who visited the traders' raft in the night.

"They have passed this way," said Yansa. "They said nothing of any fear in Karep. What nonsense is going on high sun of the tall woods?"

"I have seen the hall of government, Father," said Hoyim. "I've seen the council. They are not our kind of grassmen. Not our kind of grassmen at all."

"We know that. We have met Mev."

"It's different when you're there. The way they talk about the villages. When you pass the second village it's like being in another civilization. They don't think of us as family. They think of us as..."

"Grass animals," said Dashe.

"Hardly!" Hoyim hesitated. "Well, maybe. We can collect the seeds and they will eat them."

"You saw Mev?"

"No. He was nowhere to be seen. He's their trail man. He'd probably gone on setting sun, or high sun."

"Kezel!" Dashe reminded him. Dyra was suddenly very interested.

"Oh, they've got Kezel on the council," said Hoyim hastily. "I don't think it's important. He didn't even recognize us."

"A strange grassman to have on council," Dyra mused. "If it's true that there are changes in the grassman's way, and if it's true that there is a threat to us in these changes, then I believe we need to pay serious attention to the situation in Karep."

"You should go yourself and see. Go at least to the first village high sun and talk to the Chief Councillor?"

"Hoyim, you will not dictate to council."

"But, Father, you don't understand! Not you or Lenk or Yansa. They want to take village government out of your hands. The Chief Councillor at the first village wants your support. He really needs to talk to you."

"It is your place to print. It is my place to worry about the village."

"And that's what I intend to do. Print. And wait until you read what I print! I am going to tell what I saw and heard in Karep. I am going to tell of the rude way I was treated in the hall of government. I am going to tell all about my talk with the Chief Councillor at the first village..."

"It is not your affair what a Chief Councillor says in any village."

"I have right of trade."

"You could stir up trouble, Hoyim."

"Oh, yes, I could! Father, you have no idea the trouble I could stir up. But I won't. I will be cautious. Nevertheless, when my newsletter goes to end of settlement, they will read things they never read before."

"Council will forbid this."

"A printer's right of trade is not subject to council unless what is printed is proven to be dangerous to the village."

"What you propose to do may be dangerous to the village."

"Not as dangerous as allowing people to sit believing that nothing is going to happen to disturb tradition. When the councillors rising sun read my story they will believe it. Runya will believe me. Mekr will believe me."

"Hoyim, you are speaking too loudly."

"Yes, I am speaking loudly! I will speak loudly with ink. Every grassman and grasswoman in the red valley will hear me!"

Hoyim was about to turn and march out of the meeting hall, but he caught himself just in time. Lenk's eyes, those friendly, loving eyes he had known all his life, were looking at him with hurt, telling him that his behaviour was glar. Yansa's pale eyes were misting, as if he was about to shed tears. Dyra was angry, but in control. Hoyim regained his own control.

"I apologize to council," he said. "I had no right. May I have permission to leave?" Dyra accepted his son's bow.

Hoyim walked away biting his lip, and Dashe stepped up beside him. "If they had been to Karep, they would understand," he said. "Don't be so impatient. He is Chief Councillor, and your father."

"There was a time when my father would have gone to Karep to see for himself. He was that kind of man, and I was proud of him for it. But I'm not sure he can handle what's coming."

"Dyra? He is wise, Hoyim, and he's a great Chief Councillor. He won't rush into something, and neither will Yansa."

"But they do rush into things in Karep. That's just what I mean. My father is going to come up against men who don't take time to think through the consequences. What if he has to be asked to resign?"

"It won't come to that."

"But if he had to, for our survival's sake? I don't think he *could* be asked to resign, that's one problem. When the new village is started, we'll lose at least six young men, including you."

"Hoyim, don't think about it. There isn't anyone in the village can do a better job of handling a man like Mev than Dyra."

"I was angry because they didn't trust me. They didn't really believe what I said."

"They believed us. You have to remember that Mev didn't do or say anything to make them suspect that he was more than just a curious stranger."

"Dashe, is it possible to tell an untruth when you don't say anything at all?"

"I suppose it is. We should ask Tokra."

"We can't say Mev lied to us when he was here, but he didn't tell the truth either, did he?" reasoned Hoyim.

"No, he didn't."

"That would confuse my father and the council."

"It would confuse us too, if we hadn't been to Karep."

When Hoyim told Ajist about his outspoken words with his father, Ajist was broken-hearted. "If your concerns for the village are real, Hoyim, you can only assist by helping your father, not by quarrelling with him," she said.

So Hoyim had a long talk with his mother, and Koalee told him,

"The problem is that you and your father have exactly the same sense of responsibility."

When he saw his father that evening, both had calmed down.

"I just needed time to think, Hoyim," Dyra explained. "You frightened us, bringing a story like that. If there is really a plan to overthrow the grassman's way, I want you to print everything you know. But keep your mind open to Truth."

Hoyim nodded.

"And hurry," Dyra warned him. "You will have to get the newsletter to end of settlement before the trail closes for the cold season."

IX

During the time when the three young men were on their journey to Karep, the monstrous four-legged shadows were seen twice more near the village, and once the thunderous beating of their feet came in the night. Parents held whimpering children and gasped for breath themselves, until silence fell again. But the villagers had to go on with their daily lives as before.

Bekra and her daughter stayed; she made plans to take over the herb raft after the hunter's daughter married Runya's son. Meanwhile the old weaver passed from Life and his rites were held. His widow was suddenly old and frail and wanting care. It was obvious she couldn't remain on the large weaver's raft alone, even with her son across the path.

Doen decided to build a sleeping nook for his mother in the weaving room, but he soon ran into opposition. His mother refused to move into his house, complaining that the noise of four children was more than she could bear.

Dyra received a call from Lenk's widow. Lenk's widow was the last grasswoman in the village who might be expected to approach Council, but she was there and Dyra gave her his full attention.

"Dyra, I hope you will not feel I am interfering," she began, "but please believe me— Balink and her mother-in-law are two women who should never live together."

Dyra had never thought about that. He frowned, wondering what the widow had in mind.

"You know Balink was impatient with the weaver sometimes," she continued. "She is even more impatient with his wife. The weaver's wife is a very fussy woman and Balink is— well, *not* fussy. I believe the weaver's wife is a bit antagonistic to Balink. I do not believe the children are the problem. I... This is between us, Dyra, but I found Balink crying. She doesn't want Doen to know how she feels. I thought you should know. I think it would be better if the widow came to live with me."

Dyra was aware that there was no great friendship between Lenk's widow and the weaver's wife, and he knew the offer was being made for Balink's sake. He deliberated carefully for a minute and then said, "You are generous, as usual. I will speak to Council, and I'm sure someone will suggest a suitable arrangement. Let Doen believe the children are the problem. He has accepted that. He is only concerned that his mother be where she is safe and where he and Balink can reach her when she needs anything."

Dyra was grateful that Lenk's widow had set aside her dignity enough to talk about such personal matters, and he thanked her warmly. Then, armed with her disclosures, he discussed this with Council. The solution came quickly. Yansa and his wife would adopt the widow.

The decision precipitated some shifts in the village. Work on the mill was suspended, since it couldn't be finished before the cold season in any event, and everyone went to work to take down the metalsmith's beautiful old house and raft it anew on Dyer's Road. When that was done, the metalsmith and his family quickly moved back into it. Arrangements were made to move Hryn and his expanding pottery business to the house the metalsmith had occupied on the back road. Hryn had been on the small raft behind the old sweet-shop, next door to Yansa. It was just right for the weaver's widow.

If she felt she had come down in the world by leaving her fine house to move in behind the shops, the widow said nothing about it. She didn't seem to care much any more. Yansa's wife began to make meals and take them to her new neighbour in a basket, and Yansa checked each night to see that her shutters were closed and her door latched. Balink insisted upon cleaning the little house and seeing to the laundry. Doen passed his mother's new home at least twice a day, as he went back and forth to work. She would not lack for her son's attention. Lenk's widow felt enormous relief. The next time she saw Dyra she nodded to him in mute gratitude. Only those two conspirators knew what lay behind all the shifts in the village.

Yansa had kept the weaver's money and record books in his lockbox, just as he kept his own, the lampman's money, and the money and record books of the village. Much had been turned over to Doen in recent years, but now they got together to go through it all carefully and Dyra was called to witness.

"I am going to bring Bekra here and teach her these things," Yansa told his wife later that evening. "If anything should happen to me, someone should know."

"A grasswoman has never looked after such affairs for the village."

"Bekra is the best possibility," was Yansa's matter-of-fact reply.

To his surprise, Hoyim was approached to see if he and Ajist would like to move to the weaver's house, since Ajist was to have the garden.

"My dream!" said Ajist. "We were in that house in my dream." She and Hoyim looked at each other and simultaneously broke into smiles and said, "We'll go!"

The weaver's wife commented, "The weaver would be pleased."

She didn't have room for much furniture on her new raft, so there was a sharing. By the time Hoyim and Ajist were moved, chill winds were blowing, seed trees were ripening and dying, and flowering trees had almost disappeared. The hunter's daughter was married in the meeting house because it was too cold to be outside.

※ ※ ※

The trail boys risked one last trip to the tall woods, backpacking their snow walkers just in case, and when they returned, they came to Hoyim's shop carrying a roll of the giant sheets of paper on which the tall man wrote his letters. Hoyim pounced upon it, shaking with relief.

"I have been ill and in our infirmary," the letter read, *"And am only now able to get around. I made a trip to the tree and found the letter*

you wrote many months ago. It is a coincidence that when I was ill I thought of those same things. I should tell someone about you in case something happens to me, but I feel I cannot tell. I can only show. My son is a bright boy and goes to our advanced school of learning. I will bring him and my wife to see your village. I have always wanted to see it. We will be very careful where we walk. Then I will show your letters to my son. He may know some professor who can be trusted. You forgot to tell me in your last letter if your corn man's son is doing well in his studies. I hope your parents and wife are well, and I hope your village is safe. While I was ill, my wife let horses into the area where you are. I told her to get them out. I have worried. When my son returns in ten days I should be better, and you will see us then. Warn your villagers. Your friend, John."

Hoyim put the roll of writing under his arm and went to find his father. Dyra read it eagerly, spreading the big pages on the floor of his workroom for want of a large enough table.

"This letter may have been ten days in the tree!" he exclaimed. "I will sound the gathering bell this evening and let the people know they can expect three tall people soon. But they cannot enter the village. How will we entertain them?"

"I have an idea!"

Hoyim busied himself supervising the welcome. Troughs were dug in carefully measured rows, and they were filled with the purple blossoms from the flowering trees that heralded the cold season. Children were sent from school to carry water to sprinkle the flowers. When the tall man arrived, the flowers spelled a purple "Welcome John" along the slope below the village.

The tall man smiled to himself. "We are here," he said quietly to his wife and son. "Don't move your feet. Be very, very careful."

"Whatever are you building silly little houses like this for?" asked his wife.

But she wasn't half as astonished as the grass people. They had been thoroughly briefed by Dyra and Hoyim, and most of the adults had seen tall men through a telescope. They had just spent two feverish days preparing for the visit—but when it came, they were not prepared at all. The usually irrepressible Flon was struck dumb.

Even Yansa was too paralyzed to speak.

Children choked back tears when the overwhelming shadows loomed up across Hoyim's Lake, and the beat of three pairs of giant feet shook the earth. The grass people had lined up on rafts as close to the entrance of the village as possible, but more than one lost his nerve and retreated to peer forth cautiously around the corner of a door or window. The bravest of the young men had scaled the market stalls and were lined up on the roof, where there was no retreat. Had John's wife been looking for them, she would have seen dozens of pairs of unblinking eyes staring up in wonder.

John got down carefully on one knee and waved his arm to indicate the beautifully crafted small buildings before him. His wife was about to ask him again why he had wasted his time on the project, when she saw the grass people.

The tall man's wife looked so surprised that Koalee was afraid for a moment she might faint on top of them. Fortunately, she recovered. John's son got down beside his father and asked to be introduced. Villagers who had never heard a tall man speak covered their ears at the sound.

"How long have you known about this? How come you're harbouring these little people? Where did they come from?"

"You'll hear all about it. Let's see everyone and everything while we're here. Okay?"

Lenk and Yansa were presented, and Hoyim managed to get it across that they were councillors. The tall man took Hoyim into his hand and showed him the lineage chart he had once made, and Hoyim delightedly pointed out all of his relatives listed there. It was at that point that those who had lost their courage found it again. They crowded to the very edges of the rafts, waving and standing on tiptoe in the hope of being seen. The trail boys slid from the roof of the market stalls and ran almost to John's feet, wondering if they, too, would get a chance to ride on the tall man's hand.

The monument commemorating the first meeting was pointed out, and the tall man turned to his wife and son and explained to them what it was about. Then John caught sight of a plump little woman doing a jig on the trader's raft. She wore a wildly-coloured dress of green and rose, with yellow puffs in the sleeves and a rakish comb like a cloverleaf. He held out the palm of his hand to her, and she climbed on and rose up toward his face, where they could be eye-to-eye. She gave him the benefit of her broadest smile and he smiled back. Then the tall man's son stood up and pointed a black box at them and made a clicking sound.

"Don't be afraid," said the tall man. "It's a camera. Picture. It takes a picture."

No one understood, so John went on to ask Hoyim to show his wife and son some of the things they made so well. Hoyim nodded and spoke to his father, and in a minute Yansa and Hent and Romo had run to their shops to bring goods to show. The tall people were afraid to touch anything because it was all so small, but John had brought his magnifying glass and they studied the objects in detail.

Hent offered a glass bottle tinted in pink to the tall man's wife. The tall man said, "But we have none of your money."

Hent shook his head.

"This is a gift. He wants your wife to have it," Hoyim wrote in large letters.

The tall man's wife was overjoyed. The glass bottle was about the length of her little fingernail. She had never imagined owning anything so delicate.

John thanked Hoyim, and then he pointed to the flowering welcome and repeated, "Thank you."

"They are so small. They should be under protection," said the tall man's son.

"They are. And as long as we own this land, they will be, if you can keep quiet. I trust you both."

"How long have you known about them?"

"About seven years."

"You kept this secret for seven years?"

"Would you have told if you'd been me? You'd have said I'd lost my marbles."

"You could have shown us."

"I wanted you to be old enough to understand before I did that."

"This is the most unbelievable thing I ever saw in my life. How do they survive? They should be under protection at the university or something. They should be in one big building where they'll be safe."

John shook his head firmly. "They are a highly developed and self-reliant people. They have a culture, and a very good one. Don't insult them by suggesting they be on display like monkeys."

"I didn't mean *that!*"

"Be careful. They read tone of voice and faces, and my friend Hoyim understands some English."

Hoyim nodded that he understood the last few words.

"Well, they have to live at all costs," said John's son.

"To my mind, *how* they live is a lot more important than just being alive," said John. "You haven't seen it all yet. When you know what I know, you'll be even more amazed. We should go, I can tell you more on the walk home."

John didn't want to kneel before the grass people talking to his son, he thought it would be overwhelming. But he gestured that he would like to walk around the outskirts of the village. There were many exclamations from John's wife as the three made the circuit, and then John pointed up trail and made imaginary handshakes in the air, and bowed deeply to the miller's wife and to Dyra and Koalee and Ajist. He gave a goodbye wave to all of the grass people on the rafts, and his wife and son did the same. And then the shadows retreated in the direction of the tall woods.

X

COLOURED LEAVES were falling. The trail was alive with trail runners, and the old mill worked day and night as people bought sack after sack of meal to store for the cold season. Most people kept needed supplies on high shelves in their storerooms, and they climbed up now and brought down the long snow knives, fur clothing, heavy blankets, the round snow walkers, and diggers. Women smiled over jars of preserves that would bring their families through half a year if necessary. Children brought home paper and markers and anything they might need, should it turn so cold that they couldn't go to school. Tools were sharpened, and men piled up wood. Women and children gathered sacks of raw fibre to be spun and woven. Every man spent a day with the cornman, cutting down the giant stalks and stripping off the golden kernels to be hauled to the mill. The fuelman's raft was as busy as the street of shops. The peaman uprooted the dead pea trees and hauled the last of the dried peas to the mill.

"I shall write *The Book of Nanta*," Tokra announced. "That should keep me busy."

"Ston will move in with me for the cold season," said Lenk. All others who were old or alone, or ill, would be accommodated as well.

Dyra hurriedly made snow lenses, trying to keep up with the rush of orders.

Bekra was almost sold out of herbs for colds and fevers. "Just in case..."

The leatherman brought home enough work to tide him over if

it happened that he couldn't reach his shop, and
that the cold season continually stank of too much suede.

The cold season had been on Dyra's mind when he settled on the slope no sun above Hoyim's Lake. The bank was high enough to provide shelter from the howling winds. It would take a very heavy snowfall to bury houses in the village. To setting sun, spreading trees sheltered the lower village, where danger from drifting was greatest.

Crews of grassmen went to work wrapping the houses. First the small extension platforms were bolted to the rafts. A trapdoor in each extension led via ladder into the float space. Next the giant canvases were buckled around the pyles and secured. Further structural precautions were made, and air pipes inserted in the second chimneys.

It was extremely rare for a grassman to lose his life in the cold season. The dangerous times were when high winds and snow whistled for hours or days at a time, and the banks became mountains. Then the only thing to do was to wait until the neighbours saw one's plight.

Giant animals prowled in the cold season. People could hear their yelps and howls in the night, their sniffing at chimneys. There was fear that their weight might break through and destroy homes, but it never seemed to happen. If animals began to dig in the snow, they would stop when they ran into a house. On more than one occasion animals had been responsible for opening the way for a snow-bound family.

When the houses had all been wrapped, the shopkeepers ran the great canvas worm from door to door, linking Yansa's shop all the way to the cobbler's, so that if a villager could get to one shop, he could get to them all. Tokra held a meeting to pray that Life would see the villagers safely through the cold season, and to express his thanks that there was no further danger from the four-legged shadow, and the tall man had renewed his friendship with the villagers.

Probably nobody in the village was more concerned about the cold season than Hoyim. His and Ajist's baby would be born this season, and he would have liked it to see the sky from the beginning.

"The fuelman says it will be a fine season for four months, and then there will be a very bad cold spell with much snow," Balink announced—but just in case the fuelman was wrong, all of the women converged for a party for Ajist, bringing their gifts for the baby.

"In case we get stormed in and can't get to you," they said.

"We have to get to her," said Koalee. "I won't have her having their first baby alone."

Koalee did get to her, and the doctor too, for the fuelman's prophecy was right again. For months there was just the odd skiff of snow that could easily be swept away.

Hoyim assisted at the birth, but almost fainted when he saw what he had. He was now the father of twin boys.

"One is Shad," said Ajist.

"And the other is Lundi," said Hoyim. "But Uncle made only one cover robe."

"I made only one cradle," Dyra's father moaned.

"I made only one acceptance robe," said the widow.

Only Aunt Pora was gleeful. She had knitted two complete outfits in sunshine yellow. "Who told you?" Koalee asked. "Was the fuelman having hunches again?"

"No," said Pora. "As a matter of fact, it was your daughter Nila who had the hunch. She told me."

※ ※ ※

Counting the gifts from Runya's village, Ajist had enough for four babies, but nevertheless there was a flurry to make things for the second grandson of the Chief Councillor.

The other grandfather, Tokra, knelt by the babies. He took their tiny hands and said, "I accept you both into Life."

"Does that mean there won't be a ceremony?" asked Ajist anxiously.

"Oh no. This is just my own private ceremony. Of course there will be a big gathering for these two sprouts in the spring."

As if it had been waiting for the babies to arrive, the cold season broke into the wildest storm there had been in years. Houses all the way up to the market street were drifted over, and men from the high streets crawled over the banks, finding the humps that indicated houses, and made sure the air pipes were clear.

The snow had settled in hard drifts that had to be sliced with long snow knives. Safe paths were created that allowed grass people to go from raft to raft on their snow walkers. But it was never safe to go out alone.

Teams of men helped villagers break through drifts, which blocked a doorway here and there, then all converged on the shopkeepers' trail and dug for hours.

Brond was by far the strongest man in the village and dug at a furious pace. Unfortunately, his father tried to keep up. Knowing that he lacked the keen intelligence of most grassmen, Doba usually tried to compensate by working extra hard at tasks he could do.

"Take it easy, Doba! You aren't a young man any more," said Dashe.

"They might run short of air," said Doba simply.

"We'll dig out this air vent and then take a break," said Dyra. "We should all go home and eat something."

Doba continued to dig.

"Come, Father," said Brond. "Come for hot gruel. You will work better after that."

"Halloo down there!" called the rootman's son into the air vent, and shouts greeted him.

It was only under firm orders from his brother the Chief Councillor that Doba finally stopped digging and agreed to go home for a break.

"You're wet through," Dyra said. "You're not the only grassman in the village to do the job, you know. Brond, tell your mother to keep him home. He has done enough."

"I must at least clear away the kitchen window for Kyb," said Doba.

As soon as they had eaten their noon meals, the men were back digging again. Doba had done as he was told, and not returned.

Hearing that the snow was packed hard, mothers allowed their children out to play. They slid down the banks merrily, but they too carried ropes and never went alone.

Balink had finished digging off her entire raft and started on the widow's.

"You do love hard work!" called Deeka.

Balink laughed, because Deeka herself was also shovelling snow. "Makes my cheeks red!" she called back.

The widow came out, wearing fur cover clothes and with a digger in her hand. "You do shout so, Balink," she said gently.

"The job is already done," said Balink. She gave the widow a hug, and the two went in together.

By darkness the village was dug out and Dyra was glad to relax by the fire and smell the dill loaves Koalee had baking.

In the midst of conversation, the door opened and the doctor came in with a grave expression on his face. "Dyra, Doba has gone from Life. He caught a fever while out digging. I didn't ask Koalee to come, because I didn't think I would need her. It was very fast."

The entire village mourned.

"Thank Life he had his little granddaughter at home before he went," some said.

Hoyim knelt by his twin baby boys and said, "I have lost my uncle. You will never meet him now. He was the kindest man, the most considerate man I ever knew."

It was Bekra who took her father's death the hardest. "Life must hate me," she said.

"Life hates no one," said the dolenter, gently laying his hand on her shoulder.

※ ※ ※

And then the cold season was over. The heavy snow pack melted gradually, and the moisture ran down the slope to Hoyim's Lake. After a few days of deep mud, the village began to dry.

Work on the mill had continued over the winter and would soon be complete. The miller announced his plan to move up to his new house on Dyer's Road.

Suddenly the miller's wife dug in her heels and refused to budge. "I will not go."

"What will I do with her?" the miller asked Council.

"What would happen if you took the furniture and moved, and just left her down there?"

"She'd stay. Surely you know my wife better than that."

"But she knows you must be close to the mill. You can't be climbing all the way up the street of shops every time you go to work."

"She knows. It does no good."

"Your wife is a sensible woman, and a co-operative one."

"Except for one thing…"

The meeting was at Lenk's house, and Balink had come in with her little daughter Naj to give her father a loaf she had baked.

"It's the dyer, isn't it?" she asked.

"How did you know that?"

"All the women know. The miller's wife was the best dyer in town. She was very proud of it. She wouldn't part with her dyed cloth."

"And the dyer…"

"…lives on Dyer's Road. They're even calling the new trail after him."

"She won't move there. She has said so quite flatly."

"She's been huffy with Doen and me ever since he invited the dyer into the village."

"Has she met him?"

"No," said the miller. "If he's on the street, she goes into a shop. If he's at the meeting house, she stays on the other side of the crowd. She'll have nothing to do with him at all."

"What if we persuade the lampman to move up to Runya's old raft? Will she come then?"

"The lampman won't move unless she does."

"Who is married to your wife? You or the lampman?"

There was a round of laughter, and the men all turned to Balink. "Can you do something about this?"

"I have to go!" said Balink hurriedly. She and her small one were gone.

"I swear even that child was laughing at me," said the miller.

Dyra leaped to his feet. "I have it! Brond needs something to cheer him up after his father's death."

"What in Life's name are you talking about?"

"Tell the guard to sound the gathering bell. I want every man with a trail runner at the miller's house, and we're taking everything up the street of shops. *Everything.*"

"It won't work. My wife won't go."

"She'll go," said Dyra.

None of the villagers could imagine why a message was going around the village that they were all to be on the street of shops just before the evening meal, but curiosity brought them. Even Kyb had come.

People looked around, trying to spot something unusual, but there was nothing. The men had kept the street busy that afternoon, taking trail runners up to the miller's new house—but they were all out of sight now.

Suddenly there were shouts of merriment. Soon the whole street of shops echoed with laughter.

"The miller's wife is being backpacked!"

Kicking and protesting between gales of laughter, the miller's wife was riding up the street across Brond's shoulder. She was the plumpest woman in town, but Brond was carrying her easily, and practically trotting with her up the street.

"Put me down! This is untraditional! Where do you think you're taking me?"

The miller's wife was trying to beat Brond about the shoulders, but she was laughing too hard. She could see everyone she knew standing about laughing with her, and she loved it. The miller's wife did like to be the centre of attention.

All the way up the street of shops they went, until they had passed Runya's old raft, with the villagers following. There, a sign had been erected, pointing to the new trail. It said, "Miller's Road."

"What's this?" asked the miller's wife.

"Your new home."

Brond was growing tired, but he carried on gamely all the way to the miller's new house, where the miller opened the door and ushered his wife inside.

The metalsmith's wife was there with a small, gentle woman who reminded the miller's wife of the lampman. She knew who the woman was, but she was in too good a humour to be angry.

The little woman said, "We made an evening meal for you and your husband. We want to be good neighbours."

"You are the dyer's wife," said the miller's wife, warming to her at once. "We will be. We have an interest in common."

"You and your family will sit down and eat with us now."

"How did you know you could get away with this, Dyra?" Koalee asked. "You took a chance, didn't you?"

Dyra shook his head. "I know the miller's wife," he said.

The lampman sidled up to Yansa and gave him an oblique glance.

"Well," he said with a sigh. "I suppose I might as well do as Council wishes and move on up to Runya's old raft."

"Then you'll go house and all," said Yansa. "Even your tree."

"But this sign won't do," said the miller's wife, contemplating the new sign at the crossroads. "With me up here too, this is definitely Dyer's Road, and when both our vats are steaming, then you'll see who dyes the best cloth!"

"We're to have a running competition," said the dyer happily. "I know I won't win. I have heard the reputation of the miller's wife."

"Go on with you!" said the miller's wife. "When you know me better, you'll know you can't flatter me. I'm nobody's fool."

She went out of her way to find Doen and to tell him, "You brought good people to town when you brought the dyer and his family." Then, at his surprised expression, she added, "Oh, I know I'm doing a turn-about. I made a fool of myself and I'm saying so, because I'm an honest woman."

"I know why the whole village loves that woman," Doen told Balink.

XI

THE TRADERS CAME in the largest party ever seen. Six of them pulled their trail runners into the village in the late afternoon before market day. The first to notice them was Pora. She had been in the cobbler's shop, being fitted for new shoes.

Pora couldn't help herself. She made her way straight up the stairs to the herb raft. "Bekra, your husband is here."

Bekra had heard the trail runners and seen for herself, but quickly retreated into her shop. "Yes, I saw him."

Pora was not bashful about taking another look. "He is coming straight here, trail runner and all."

"You will leave us?" said Bekra, hoping she didn't sound too impolite.

Pora had enough tact to realize that she should not be around. "Welcome, Ryjra," she said brightly on her way out as she passed him.

"I thought I would find you here," said the trader to his wife.

A smile began to break out on Bekra's face. "Have you come to stay?"

"I don't know."

"You don't know? Then we have nothing to talk about."

"I've brought things you left. Things I thought you valued. Will you come down and see?"

With a shrug, Bekra went down to the trail runner. The lockbox was half-filled with her treasures, and there were two bundles of her clothing and blankets.

"You gave up half your space for my things. You won't make

enough money this trip to survive in the big village."

"I believed you'd want them. May I see Jarin?"

"Of course. My father died in the cold season..."

"I'm sorry. I..."

"You are welcome to stay in his house with my mother and me and be with your child tonight."

People were staring from the shop rafts as Bekra ran up to close her shop door.

"Bekra's husband has come!" The news went quickly around the village. "Will she go back with him?" people wondered.

"The decision has been made," said Dyra. "She stays, with or without Ryjra. It is no longer our affair. It is theirs."

※ ※ ※

"When will you make up your mind?" Bekra asked, after a long silence.

"I will go to end of settlement and back. Trail is a good place to think. I have missed you. I thought until I saw you that I might persuade you to return."

Bekra shook her head firmly. "No. Jarin is happy here and loved. I will never take her back there."

"The schools are better."

"There is no better school than the village. You must know what is on my mind. I have mostly thought of two things. One is that you were in the country half of the year. I was not. You forgot that."

"I guess I didn't realize it, really."

"And I was the one who needed the country most. It is my home. The other thing I have thought—if you were not content to have the herb raft, we could find a village where they need a food shop. We could work together and have a good business."

"I have considered that too."

They had reached Kyb's raft. Jarin was playing in the float space with her toys. "Someone is here to see you," said Bekra.

Jarin's face lit up with a smile. "It's my daddy!"

"Does the big village have anything like this?" asked Bekra, and then wished her tongue was less cutting at times.

※ ※ ※

Since Doba's death, one of the fuelman's sons had decided to be berryman, and Kyb had the important task of teaching him the maze of paths through the spreading trees to the berry trees. Today she had gone with the fuelman's son out to look for grass berries, and it was hard for her to focus on the fact that her son-in-law had returned. But her happiness upon seeing him made up for her vagueness.

Ryjra patted her arm. "You are a good woman, my mother," he said softly.

The traders had brought messages from the cornman's son—one for his parents, and one for the doctor.

The doctor read his letter to Koalee. The cornman's son was now making rounds to the homes of patients on his own, and the master doctor was pleased with him. He was learning many new treatments and methods.

"Ah, I was hoping for that," said the doctor. "I hope the new treatments and methods are really better than what we know."

"This part is what I would not like," said Koalee, pointing to the passage where the cornman's son told of how they opened the bodies of the dead to see what had caused them to die.

"It is easy," said the doctor, "because you know you are gathering knowledge that will help others to live, but it isn't the most important knowledge. The important knowledge is how to use the health forces in the body—the forces that come from the mind. Attitudes. Attitudes, exercise, food, and breath—don't ever forget breath. Those were the basics the old master doctor taught me."

"Not rest?"

"Rest is an attitude. Posture is an exercise. It is all there, in the four principles." Hoyim and Ajist entered the infirmary, each with a baby in a backpack.

"Lundi has a cough," said Hoyim. "We thought we should bring them both."

The doctor examined Lundi and then Shad, and handed Ajist a package of herbs. "Make a very weak tea of this and give it to them lukewarm until the cough stops. This young man has a healthy chest. He'll be fine. What are these grassmen to be? Will one take after his grandmother and be my assistant? Will one be a printer or a lens maker?"

"My father has his own ideas," said Ajist.

Already Tokra had looked closely at Shad, and then pointed to him with a definitive finger, saying, "This is the one I will train to be a dolenter."

Hoyim laughed. "My sons will choose their own trade," he said, "as I did."

Tokra, on his part, was preparing for a journey. He had spent the cold season writing his reminiscences of life in the village of Nanta, and he felt it was time to travel there to visit his mother and renew his friendships. Since he preferred to go in the company of the traders, it was time to be on his way. The traders would not make another journey until the warm season was drawing to a close.

"You will keep safe?" Dyra reminded him.

"I will be safe," Tokra assured him. There was something different about his voice. Dyra had a peculiar feeling, and yet it wasn't a foreboding. It was more like the anticipation of something unusual and exciting.

Nila was standing beside her mother, with a secretive smile on her face. "Tokra has to go, Father," she said. "He has just set out on the most important journey of his life."

"Nila," said her mother. "Sometimes you talk like an elf."

The trail boys came to Hoyim's shop bearing another letter from John, and it contained a question which had to be answered.

"What are you building at the shelter where I first met you?" the tall man asked.

"Of course you may tell him," Dyra said when Hoyim showed him the letter. "I suppose you know all about it?"

"We saw it on our trip to Karep, but we promised the trail boys not to speak of it." Dyra smiled. "They've been enjoying the secrecy."

"We will soon start the new village?"

His father nodded. "Hryn brought it to council a year ago. He knows a second pottery is not needed in town, and he has asked permission to be one to start a new village. The cobbler can take an apprentice, and the cobbler's son will go. One of the hunters is restless. Runya has at least five men who want to make a new start. We have too many boys coming up to fill the apprentice places. It has to be, Hoyim."

"Yes, it has to be. Dashe plans to go."

"When the village officially open, Rels will go as Chief Builder."

Hoyim contemplated the loss. "Uncle Hryn and Rels? There will be too many holes in our village, Father."

"It is so each time a new village begins. It is the grassman's way. Rels will likely become Chief Councillor, with at least one councillor from Runya's village. A second new village may be started within a few years, between Runya's village and Mekr's village."

"There will be grassmen everywhere!"

Dyra thought of the four-legged shadow. "I hope so, son," he said quietly.

"Have I permission to write about it in my newsletter?"

"Yes. In fact I think it's time we took an expedition up trail and let everyone have a look."

The village turned out in numbers for the expedition. The guard tower was completed and two rafts were up on pyles, but so far only one held a house. The only people who had stayed in the house so far were Bekra and Jarin, and Bekra had kept silent. The traders had also been sworn to secrecy.

"Do you plan to live in this village, Tuje?" asked Lenk.

"No. But I was asked to plan it."

"You're as bad as the big village! Let the people build their own village."

"I am going to stay here," announced the cobbler's son, "and begin work on my raft. We may as well start now."

"Yes," said Rels with a sigh. "We may as well begin in earnest."

"Rels," said Tuje quietly. "Your woodworking shop?"

"It's yours. I'll soon have a new one."

"I didn't want you to leave the village."

"I didn't want to leave. But it's less than a day's march."

Balink was crying.

"The game is to have this up before the man from Karep has time to stop it!" Rels joked to lighten the mood. Those who overheard had a laugh about that.

※ ※ ※

"We are in need of new trail boys," said Dyra.

"A message must go to Runya's village," said Lenk. "Runya has young people who plan to come and join you."

"I will come for a while," said Hent's son. "You will need glass for the windows."

"Rels, put me up a raft right there, and I'll be back in a week to help build the house," said Hryn.

Rels marked the places Hryn indicated.

"Here is where we will build the lime kiln," said the kiln keeper's son excitedly. The kiln keeper's wife shed a tear.

"He is young to leave home," she said.

"Those boys will be all right," said Dyra proudly.

"Rels will be acting Chief Councillor," said the cobbler's son, "until our population is bigger and we can choose council."

"Very well," said Rels, who had expected it. He turned to Dyra. "You will tell Runya's trail boys to tell Runya we have begun."

"It's like a body splitting apart," said Balink.

Pora agreed. "But it's exciting, too, like a new child being born. Perhaps in ten years my son will come here. They will need a papermaker."

The rest of Dyra's villagers left the new villagers there, already busy felling trees. One of the trail boys stood proudly on the guard tower with his bow in his hand and his eye on the sky.

Back at home, Dyra arranged with the musician for a surprise concert in the meeting house, an attempt to dispel the loneliness that was sure to come. Pettis sang more beautifully than ever, and Tuje and Flon did a new married dance of their own invention—a delightfully silly one that made everyone laugh uproariously.

Everything the music makers played was lively, and there was more dancing than usual.

At the end of the evening, when the small ones were falling asleep, Creu's husband stood and asked for their attention.

"It is my pleasure to announce that over the past five years, I have taught my apprentice everything I know of leathercraft. There is no more to teach. My apprentice is now a craftsman."

To cheers and applause, the new leather craftsman stood, as surprised as the others. Only Council had known in advance.

Dyra came forward, smiling. "The announcement was duly reported to council," he affirmed, and held out both hands to give the young man the formal handshake. "Accept our congratulations," he said. "I now call upon the master craftsman to present you with the official statement of your status."

Everyone was anxious to see the new settlement and shake hands with the new craftsman. He was asked whether he would accept a party of celebration and when he would prefer it to be. If there was a possibility of another apprentice achieving status within a short time, it was customary to postpone the celebration to include the friend. They all knew why the new craftsman hesitated, but it would be impolite to stare at the portrait painter, still they wondered what he planned to do about his son.

The new leatherman excused himself. "These are busy days with the construction of the new village," he said. "I request permission to go there, as I need to build my house. I therefore wish to postpone celebration of my new status until the time of the wrapping of the houses."

There was another cheer. Everyone knew why he was giving them so much time. It meant there was a good chance that the portrait painter's son would be pronounced artist-craftsman. Then the sense of loss returned. The new artist, too, would probably move to the new village, and Pettis would go with him. Already Rels' wife and children were talking about their plans to move. That meant that the boy who had walked out with Nila would be going away.

"Wait and see," said Koalee. "If it is the truth, he will remember you. It isn't as if he was going to Karep."

Nila looked at her mother strangely. "Mother, the question of the truth doesn't enter into this. I am not destined to marry the son of Rels. He was my friend. We went to school together and he understood me best. I will miss him a great deal. That is all."

Koalee was momentarily taken aback, but she rallied. "It is good that you know," she said. "Only a grasswoman with a clean conscience knows the truth. But you are sixteen. Your brother was married at your age."

Dyra came in frowning. "It couldn't be happening at a worse time. Our village needs to be strong and unified with these strange new winds blowing."

"Trust Rels," said Koalee, "His village will be strong and unified and he loves you."

Dyra felt a tear in his eye. "Remember the day Lenk and his children caught up to us at the temporary shelter? I saw my own trail runner on the trail, and I knew it was Lenk. I don't think anything has ever moved me in the same way."

Koalee cuddled her head against Dyra's arm. "Rels was so young then. Fourteen. And he backpacked all his dad's fine tools, the whole way. Rels will make a fine Chief Councillor Dyra."

※ ※ ※

Soon afterwards the traders returned from end of settlement. Bekra anxiously watched her husband's face.

"You have won," Ryjra told her. "I don't know how I will fit into village life, but I am going to try."

"Will we go to the new village?" asked Bekra. "They need a food shop. We can take my mother there with us. You will be one of the men to build the village. It wouldn't be like coming as a stranger where everything is established. I can give Nila the herb raft."

Dyra gave them his permission to leave. "I expect they will make you a councillor, Bekra," he said seriously.

"Whether they do or not, I will fight Brecort's ridiculous plan," she replied.

Meanwhile, Tokra had not returned with the traders.

"He may return alone," Ryjra told Dyra, "or he may wait until the traders make another trip to end of settlement. He asked me to tell you that he is very happy and very busy, and that he prays for the village every day."

Unable to learn more, Dyra had to be content with that.

XII

THE TRADERS would hardly have had time to reach the tall woods after the big market on their way high sun, before Mev returned.

"I did intend to come earlier in the year," he apologized, "but there have been many conferences, and plans to lay. I request permission to speak to you and your people about these plans."

Dyra and his councillors exchanged glances.

"It is customary to speak first to Council," said Dyra.

"We in the big village believe that what I have to report concerns all villagers. I have instructions to let all the people know. It would only have to be told twice."

"We give instructions in this village," said Dyra firmly. "You will be expected to follow our customs or we will be forced to ask you to leave."

Mev bowed. "I quite understand. I meant no offense. It is just that I have been given authority to overrule local councils in such matters."

"That is impossible."

"No, it *is* possible. A new government has been formed in Karep, to have authority over all of the villages. There will be a federation of all grass villages."

"Ridiculous!" said Yansa.

"Without our knowledge and consent?" asked Dyra. "Is this what you want to tell the villagers? I'm sorry, there will be no gathering."

"I thought you were concerned with what is best for your village, Dyra. You are an intelligent and responsible man. I was proud to become your friend."

"My responsibility is to the village and the grassman's way."

"This village has been selected, on my recommendation, to be the central government for all the villages no sun of the tall woods. Representatives from all of the villages will come here for meetings. Your village will grow and thrive."

"I don't want my village to grow! And neither do my people."

"Now, that is what I have to ask your people. The governor in Karep believes that the form of government found in the small villages makes children of the people. They do not have enough voice."

"Our people speak to us whenever they wish, and we listen."

"I was impressed by this village. I was sure I could count on your co-operation."

"I am not open to flattery," said Dyra. "If I gave you a different impression, I am sorry."

"Dyra, I have approached this badly. I am enthusiastic. I thought you would be equally enthusiastic. Here is my seal of office. I am a governor's deputy, and I have the right to call gatherings in each village and explain why the new government has been formed—and how, and what, we want to do."

"We do not recognize such a seal of office." Dyra felt actual repulsion racing through his blood. "I trust you did not speak at the new village high sun," he said sharply.

"It was explained," said Mev coolly, "that they are not yet a village and have no council, that they are still under your councillorship."

Dyra caught Lenk's expression and saw that his friend was astonished that his own son would tell such an untruth, but Dyra was satisfied. Considering his tiny population and the early nature of his village, Rels had behaved wisely. Meanwhile, Dyra had his own to defend.

"This is my village," he said bluntly. "I pioneered it and established it. Lenk built it. Yansa has shouldered many a burden for it. If our people are dissatisfied with their council, they have only to ask us to resign. That is the grassman's way."

"It belongs to a past age. There are many grassmen now, and many villages. You know the dangers. It is not strength to live in scattered little groups. It is strength to have central communications, where people know all that is happening in the villages and where wise decisions can be made that would be best for all."

"Are you trying to tell us that somebody twenty days' march up trail in a cave knows enough about our village to make any decision at all, let alone a wise one?" Yansa asked.

"You misunderstood," said Mev smoothly. "You men don't force the people. That is not the grassman's way. Your Chief Councillor never makes a decision without consulting you, does he?"

"Well, rarely. In an emergency," said Lenk.

"No more does the central government plan to force you, though we will soon be in a position to insist. The plan is that no decision will be made without consulting representatives from all the villages. There will be a meeting in this village of those no sun of the tall woods. There will be a second meeting mid-way from the tall woods to Karep. The decisions from those meetings will be carried to a large meeting in Karep once a year and plans for the following year will be made."

"Plans? What plans? Will they decide whether we should complete our mill or build new water storage vats?"

"Well... Of course, there are many decisions that will need to be made locally."

"Yes, and quickly. By authority," said Dyra.

"But you see, the change is this," said Mev. "Villagers will no longer choose their councillors. The council will be assigned by the central government. That way we can be assured that the villages are being run by those who know and accept the plans."

The councillors were aghast.

Mev spoke into the silence. "I had recommended that this council be accepted as constituted. However, if you continue to react as you are, I will have to suggest some other arrangement."

"I struggle to keep my manners," said Yansa, "but I may become angry."

"It is all for your own good," Mev snapped. "What concerns the central government is strength. Increasing trade. Building defences for villages. Control."

"It is apparent that your—what's his name? Brecort. That he never lived in a village. By what madness does he think he knows how to make decisions for us?"

"You misunderstand again. He does not pretend to know enough to make decisions for the villages. That is why I was sent last summer. To get to know the villages and return with more understanding."

"Apparently you did not."

"We made you welcome in the grassman's way," said Dyra bitterly. "And this is how you return our hospitality."

"Dyra! I am not your enemy. I am trying to explain that the council in Karep are aware that they know little of village life. They admire what you know. They respect what you know. They intend to gather your representatives at Karep for meetings before any decisions are reached. The advantage of the central government is that they can balance the needs of the entire grassman community by learning what is going on everywhere, all at once."

"And to do this they would expect Chief Councillors—whom *they* approve—to journey for forty days a year up dangerous trail to spend goodness knows how long trying to reach decisions with a lot of strangers, about villages they never heard of, when they should be at home tending to their own villages? It is madness."

"If you will grant me the meeting, and let me present it to the people, point by point..."

"Lenk, tell the guard to sound the gathering bell."

"*Now?*"

"Now."

"But I am not prepared," Mev protested.

"We are none of us prepared. The gathering is now or never."

At the sound of the gathering bell, all of the villagers converged on the meeting house, young and old, babies and school children, hunters and shopkeepers. Only the cornman and his family, the tanner, and the fuelman's son out on the berry trail, were missing.

"This is how fast we can gather a meeting," said Dyra triumphantly. "Compare that with the year it will take to gather at Karep. And then merely spokesmen—not the people."

"What if the people disagree with you...?" Yansa began, aside to

Dyra.

"Trust our people." Dyra knew that he had the advantage.

"What did he mean they would be 'in a position to insist'?" Lenk whispered.

"It's just a threat," Dyra replied.

"I thought he was a refined man when we first met him," Lenk added. "He's a fool."

Right on schedule, Radd appeared in the meeting house door, and stood calmly watching Mev. It was the final straw. Mev was nervous, and his voice carried less authority than usual. He said nothing of the government, which had been formed in Karep, and instead began to talk of the weakness of the scattered villages, and of their potential to grow and thrive. Finally, he got to the so-called need for a central authority to make important decisions concerning all of the villages. He spoke of the government's experience in Karep of organizing large groups of people.

"I know how they organize in Karep!"

The voice startled everyone. Heads turned to see Bekra standing, her dark eyes flashing.

"If you have a question, perhaps you will be good enough to wait until I have presented my report," said Mev.

"No, I will not wait! Do you think we're fools, or children, that we don't know what you're saying? You want to set up this 'overall authority' of yours in Karep and organize all of the grassmen the way you organize there. I told you, I know how they organize. I have lived seven years in Karep."

"Then you will have useful experience..." Mev started to say.

"You should see *us* organize!" Bekra cried, her voice carrying to every corner of the meeting house. "You should see our men dig out a buried house in the cold season. You should see them take down the corn trees. You should see how they work with Lenk to build the mill or move a house. You should see how they laugh and smile and nod to each other, and understand without fighting and shouting—without Lenk setting himself up as if he was Life itself and telling them all what to do, while they sulk and complain and watch to see if it is time to go home for the night."

"Exactly what is your meaning, young lady?"

"I know how they organize in Karep, where foremen give men jobs they can't do and don't like to do, and then threaten to fire them if they don't do it. Where work has become a bad word and everything is by the clock and to some advance plan."

"Plans are necessary."

"Which is why this village must stay small. Plans may be necessary when you have a lot of strangers. They are not as necessary in a small village and everyone is known."

"We can be intuitive here," said Tuje loudly, and there was wave of agreement.

"What does 'fire them' mean, Bekra?" asked Dashe.

"It means you don't have your job any more, and you won't be paid. You get paid for everything. You *also* have to pay for everything there. If a man doesn't get paid, he won't work. There is no love in it. There is no sense of village responsibility in it. That is the kind of 'organization' he talks about. We don't need that, believe me!"

Ryjra's expression had changed from one of slight amusement at his wife's outburst, to one of pride.

"I expected no such breach of manners in this village," Mev shouted over the rising voices.

"I learned my bad manners in Karep!" Bekra retorted.

"The meeting is over," said Dashe, standing and preparing to leave. His father rose to follow him, then Flon and Tyad and the hunter. In a moment, the meeting house was half-empty.

"The meeting is over," said Dyra, with a shrug.

"That elf was here again. Where has he gone?" Mev fumed impatiently.

"I have no idea. You are welcome to spend the night in the village, of course. The tea mistress will expect you."

"It is early in the day. I will go to Runya's village."

"As you wish. I apologize for our breach of manners but yours is not the grassman's way."

Half of the village had followed Bekra to the herb raft, and she was standing on it now, answering their questions.

"Will the drot go up?"

"Will the drot go up! You can't imagine the drot they pay in Karep. Do you have any idea what it will cost to carry on this big organization he wants?"

"We can back Bekra in everything she says," Dashe shouted. "It is all true. The overseers shout at the workmen. People are not happy in their work. There are many poor people in Karep who don't look well fed, and their part of the cave is low and dark. Their children are saucy. Some of them steal. We don't want that here!"

Bekra nodded. The villagers shook their heads in dismay.

"We don't want the ways of Karep!" Bekra echoed, gesturing with her arms. "We will not live as they live in Karep."

"We are the grass people," said Koalee firmly. "And that is how it will stay."

"We should have listened to the young men," Lenk remarked.

"How could we have believed it?" asked Yansa. "It is impossible to believe. You look pleased, Dyra, in spite of everything. I told you all you needed was a challenge."

Dyra grinned. He had indeed been making decisions without hesitation today. Then the smile left his face and he sighed heavily.

"I can handle what I know," he said. "We all can. But what we don't know...There's something out there, something of which we have no experience. I sense a struggle ahead, a very serious danger to the grassman's way. But it is all so very vague. I wish Tokra were here."

"We may find out what's to happen soon enough," said Yansa.

"What's to happen is that if the big village tries to force this idiotic thing upon us? I will go and pioneer a new village where they can't find me," said Dyra.

Lenk laughed. "And I'll build it. The wind is rising."

Tienna the portrait painter's wife passed them at that moment and overhead Lenk's remark. "It is rising indeed," she said. "But so is the counter-wind."

"What did she mean?" Dyra asked, when Tienna was out of hearing. "My, she is a strange woman."

Yansa looked toward the lake and seemed to pay no attention to Tienna's remark. "Grass woods are bending, but not to the roots," he said.

Women were taking their small ones and hurrying for cover.

"I hope it blows Mev clean into the sky," said Dyra.

Dyra didn't expect to see any more excitement in the village until Mev returned from end of settlement, but when he looked out of his shop window the next morning, he saw a man coming from no sun. His body was not that of a young man, but he moved with ease, pulling a loaded trail runner as if it were empty.

"Koalee, someone's coming!"

Now Dyra could see that the man wore boots laced to the knee, and that his arms were bare and bronzed. His hair was thin and grey. His jaw was hard.

"Koalee, it's Gozer!"

They ran to meet him and gave the formal greeting.

"You will take tea with us," said Koalee. Gozer smiled his acknowledgement of the invitation and followed them into the house.

"You are welcome to stay here for the night."

"Thank you, but Runya's trail boys expect me at the raft. I plan to rest today and travel by night. I have business, Dyra, but I request that your council be present."

"I assumed you were here for a purpose. Did Mev speak in Runya's village last evening?"

"He spoke."

"I will get Yansa and Lenk," said Koalee.

Yansa arrived in a few minutes, but Lenk was harder to find. He had gone to chop seed trees beside the trail.

"The elf came ahead of Mev," said Gozer, "and warned us. It is a good thing, because Mev lied to us. He told us he had been welcomed here and that you and your villagers agreed to the federation."

"That is not so!"

"So the elf said. So common sense said."

Lenk arrived. Gozer greeted him and then continued. "The elf has gone ahead to warn Mekr and all of the villages rising sun. Not only that, but one of Runya's councillors also slipped away and is taking the trail ahead of Mev."

"It was good of you to come and tell us these things."

"I am deputized. Mev lied also about his authority. He told you the central government has been established and that he has authority over councils?"

"Yes."

"So he told Runya. It is not true. The elf says the central government has been organized, but they know they have no authority until all villages agree to the federation. Mev said they could 'insist'. He didn't explain."

"When the villagers rising sun find out about the untruths, do you think he may come to harm?" Lenk asked. "There could be reprisals..."

"No, Mev will come to no harm," said Dyra. "That is not our way."

"It is also not the grassman's way to be untruthful."

Koalee was busying herself setting out more tea and spreading loaf for the council.

"Koalee has been kind," said Dyra. "She has not said, 'I told you not to trust him.'"

"Is it wrong to be trusting?" asked Yansa.

"No. It is not."

"This man plays by other rules," said Gozer. "Now he must lose. He does not understand the grassman's way. He seeks power but doesn't know how to get it—certainly not among the grassmen. He thinks he can deceive us and divide us among ourselves."

"You are right. He has to lose."

"I understand power. I have had power." There was a momentary silence.

"I am older now," said Gozer, "and perhaps a wiser man than when they asked me to resign as Chief Councillor. I was arrogant. I know that. I began as Chief Councillor in an isolated village close to the nests of the wheelers by the tall woods. It was a dangerous place to live, and I learned to think and act fast. Then I led my people to the green lake, and finally all the way back again, together with your villagers, to begin the new villages."

"We know that, Gozer. We do not forget."

"I am a man for emergencies. I am at my best up trail. I accepted that. I gave the running of the village into other hands, and I do not want it back. But I want to serve my village."

"You say you are deputized."

"Runya wanted to come himself to talk to you, but he doesn't think it a safe time for any Chief Councillor to leave his village for any reason at all, as long as Mev is trying to win the people over to his favour. This is the first message."

Dyra nodded. "I had the same idea."

"The second message is that Runya intends to resist the idea of the federation."

"Hear! Hear! So do we!"

"If you entrust me, I will add your name to Runya's when I reach the villages high sun."

"Do you plan to go to the villages high sun?"

"My health is sound. Your message?"

"You may say that Runya and Dyra both intend to resist federation. What of the villages rising sun?"

"They are..." Gozer paused as if the word he was about to say failed to convey the meaning. "...restless," he ended, with a gesture to indicate that it was an under appraisal. "Your son's newsletter reached end of settlement before the cold season, and many a young man was ready to defy the snows and go to Karep to protest, but then the two young men came..."

"Yes, we met them. The young men who came from Karep?"

"They settled for the cold season in Mekr's village, and they have taught the people so much about Karep that the villagers know exactly what they are up against. One of them, it seems, actually worked in a confidential capacity for the Chief Councillor himself."

"My son had the impression that people in Karep who oppose Brecort are not anxious for the people to show any resistance. They believe it would put him on his guard."

"He *is* on guard. Only one of the traders would agree to carry messages this trip. They fear cancellation of their permissions. But a message came to Hilt and Lydyl that the resistance in Karep believes it is now time. Brecort must hear that he is unpopular in the villages rising sun. Runya has sent a younger deputy to end of settlement to learn everything. He sent me high sun because, according to Hoyim, the villages there will be harder to handle."

Yansa sat shaking his head. "This federation is foolish and unnecessary. They must be told," he remarked.

"It's dangerous," said Gozer. "The elf told Runya that they have many complex rules. No one will be able to make a decision until it has been passed in meeting in Karep. They want a District Superior rising sun to tell us what we are to do, and he will have no authority until he receives instructions from Karep. A village could burn or flood or die out while they sit deliberating, and the grassmen won't be able to do a thing. Not unless they break the regulations."

"And I suppose they would be punished for that," said Dyra. "The grassmen will lose the ability to make decisions. They will lose responsibility to the village. Our way will be ruined."

"I am surprised the elf didn't talk to us about these things," said Lenk.

"It was his plan, but then Mev changed his mind and came to Runya's village the same day, so the elf came ahead of him. He said Dyra would see the dangers for himself."

"I am coming to understand it," said Dyra.

"But they don't plan to make decisions of local importance, surely?" asked Lenk. "Mev hinted as much."

"Perhaps not. They make nothing clear," said Dyra.

"Now, hear the third message," said Gozer. "From what the elf tells us, the man Brecort has no intention of listening to Chief Councillors when he does get them to the big village, even when they are men he has chosen himself. It's all a trick to get them out of the villages and weaken their power, so the villages will have to turn to Karep for help. But, what if the villages got ahead of them?"

"Ahead of them?" asked Yansa.

"A plan to keep the Chief Councillors at home," said Dyra, thinking fast. "You know how Runya thinks."

"It is a brilliant plan!"

"What is it?" Lenk asked.

"Don't you see?" Dyra asked. "We already have a federation of villages rising sun."

"Runya said he could count on you," said Gozer.

"Was this discussed at Mekr's village?"

"It certainly was. It all rests on finding someone who is trail-wise and strong. Someone who can spend most of the warm season travelling from village to village to find out what the people are thinking. This grassman will represent all of the villages, and he will travel to the meeting at Karep to let them know what the villages wish."

"You," said Dyra.

"I need your endorsement," said Gozer. "That was the fourth message. I am authorized to go to the villages high sun with word that the villages to end of trail have formed a federation and that I am their spokesman. The trail boys are waiting to relay your son's next newsletter, letting them know your answer."

"Will it work?" asked Lenk.

"It will at least buy time," said Gozer.

Dyra was pleased. "Mev can't possibly come back until the next cold season is over, and by the time they discover that they are too late, that a federation has already been formed, it will take at least another year before they decide what to do."

Yansa was still cautious. "Has Mev met you?" he asked.

"He did last summer. This time I stayed out of sight," Gozer replied.

"Does this representative really have the power to tell us what we are to do?"

"This representative has the power to speak for all villages, or not at all. He has the power to say no to anything they propose."

"And he believes...?"

"He believes in the grassman's way. He understands the problems of running a village, and the rewards. He has no intention of letting men from Karep change that."

"He will not be corrupted by the big village?" asked Yansa.

Gozer looked at him scornfully.

"When the villages speak with one voice, they will have no chance to argue," Dyra mused.

"They will have no chance to divide us."

"But the villages high sun will never agree. And what of changes?

What if, by the time you reach Karep for one of their meetings, the villages rising sun have changed their minds about what they told you to say?"

"I may not need to ask for a meeting in Karep, I believe the villages will unite," said Gozer.

Dyra laughed aloud. "Mev will be kept so busy going back and forth with proposals...!"

"And if Mev says no...?" asked Yansa.

Gozer stood. He looked tougher, if anything, than he had the day he pushed the widow down the animal hole. "He will not say 'no' to me," he said. "I shall go sleep for a while. Tonight is a clear moon, so I will travel."

He took his leave.

"Do you not fear him Dyra?" asked Yansa. "Runya has given him a lot of power. He is not even a councillor."

"He does not deceive," said Dyra. "He does not divide. No, I do not fear Gozer." Then he smiled. "But Mev will, and so, I hope, will Brecort. And therein lies the brilliance of the plan."

"Runya acted wisely," said Koalee. "He has sent someone with strength and experience. Someone who isn't committed to local responsibilities, so he can be spared without weakening the village. Someone with the skill to be up trail for days..."

"And someone who understands what's going on," said Lenk.

Yansa scowled. "I see no value in a central government. They must be mad in Karep."

"Bekra says they love to organize for the sake of organizing," said Koalee. "For control. They think it's glar for grassmen to govern by intuition. They believe it shows inferior intelligence."

"Yes," Dyra agreed. "They also want something from us."

"Remember how curious Mev was about our produce?" Yansa asked.

Dyra nodded. "Next they will try to get us to agree by offering us money for our goods. Or offer to build our guard towers or high fences... I wish I knew what the elf meant when he said he was afraid the timer was set. He also said if these changes come to be, he won't be able to help us."

XIII

Ajist brought the news that her father had returned. He had come alone, and he was safe and healthy. Dyra found him in his float space, pounding roots.

"So, you have finally turned to the dolenter?" Tokra remarked, as if amused.

"I came to welcome you home."

"You came to ask me what to do about Karep."

"Well, both. You know I discuss everything with you. Gozer was in the village, going high sun."

"I know."

"Oh, he saw you?"

"No, but I know just the same."

"Tell me what he had to say."

"First, tell me. Your mother and your friends, they are well?" Dyra asked. "I'm surprised you returned alone but I'm glad you're here." What had happened to Tokra? He was like a delighted child.

"The village has never been in better health. Now, tell me about Gozer."

"Tokra, what if we found a man—one representative—who could travel from village to village and find out what all of the people really want? Someone who could then go to Karep to speak for us? That way councillors would never have to leave their villages, but could still communicate with Karep and let their wants be known."

"A federation of all the villages?"

"I didn't say that, exactly. Well, yes."

"Gozer could go to Karep and say, 'We thought your federation was such a fine idea that we went ahead and formed one of our own. We have already organized a central government. If you want to do business with our representative that is up to you.'"

"Ah, but with a difference. We wouldn't be treating them as they plan to treat us," noted Dyra.

"And who is to be Chief Councillor of this federation? Gozer?"

"We didn't suggest having one."

"It is no matter. You are still wrong."

"How can we be wrong? It's a brilliant strategy. It was Runya's idea and Runya is an intelligent man."

"And you are an intelligent man. Both of you are so smart that you only have to be faced with a new form of organization and you can learn it, even copy it."

Dyra felt something in his mind weaken.

"It's wrong," said Tokra. "It will not work."

"Why not?"

"I can't tell you that. You must think."

Dyra felt as if Tokra had smothered him with a feather kite. Long years ago, Radd said something like that. "I can't talk to them. They have to think."

Dyra had done a lot of thinking during those dangerous and exciting days when he was searching for the site of the new village. He had heard the thought network to which the elves listen. He had known.

The dolenter was chopping roots with a faint smile on his face, as he had looked a thousand times before, but Dyra realized that there was something different about him today. It was as if he had brought back from Mekr's village a great sense of peace. Dyra was aware of the sunlight falling across the table where Tokra worked, and an insect buzzing near the pyle. Suddenly the sky was more blue and all the smells of nature were sweeter. *Life.* What mattered except the grassman's responsibility to Life?

"You are looking for a political solution," said the dolenter quietly. "You are guilty of the same stupidity as that man Brecort in the big village. He lives without sunlight. Why follow in his steps?"

"Should I have asked Gozer not to go?"

"He will do no harm."

"Why does Life suddenly seem to be in harmony? At least for you?"

"Because a counter-wind is blowing. It will win, but only..."

"...only if the grass people return to the Way."

"Unless we please the elves, we live without the elves. That is Truth."

"I knew magic once," said Dyra.

"Not quite. You knew harmony. You will again."

"It's coming to me, as if the elfin world was right there behind the curtain of light at the end of the float space. Something happened at Mekr's village. Will I be able to discover what it was?"

"Is it going to be the way of Brecort?" Tokra asked. "Or the grassman's way?"

Dyra wanted to weep. "Do you have to ask? What blinded me? What made me deaf? Tokra, what *did* happen when you were away?"

"I guess I can tell you now. There is to be a ceremony here in the village after the next cold season. I am to be made dokrimalenter."

Dyra's head was spinning. "But you can't... I mean, you should be, of course. You have always been dokrimalenter in my view, but you can only be appointed if the grass people have..."

"A litzla."

There was a sunrise in Dyra's mind. In the back of his mind, Radd's voice was speaking—saying a line from nearly thirty years ago—*"Look to the red valley."* It took him a moment to find his voice. "The elves have found Dokrimalitzla."

A smile broke out on Tokra's face. "You remember my stories of my boyhood? About my best friend Ilva, Nanta's seventh son?"

Dyra saw it all. "Ilva has had a seventh son."

"He did, Dyra. Fifteen years ago. The Dokrimalitzla is Anodee, son of Ilva. Only the dolenters know, and the elves, and the fortunate grassmen who can hear the elves thinking. The boy has known from birth, but he wasn't told of it officially until spring."

"So Runya and the councillors have been planning to no purpose. Brecort is finished."

"He will have difficulty standing. If the grass people follow Dokrimalitzla as they should, they will leave the cave and return to Life."

"This Anodee... What is he like?"

"He is tall and fair like his grandfather, with eyes that see into the future as Nanta's did."

"Can I see him, Tokra?"

"He will come, when the elves say the timer is right. Probably when the earth dries after the next cold season. He will visit every village from end of settlement to Karep, gathering support as he goes. Hilt and Lydyl have planned it all, and the old elf Buko will be with him, the one who befriended me when I was a child."

"The people will follow Anodee?"

"They followed his grandfather, and Nanta was only a grassman!"

"What can I expect? I am too young to remember Dokrimalitzla. Should we prepare gifts? A banquet? Speeches? Will he let us know when he is coming?"

Tokra laughed.

"Dokrimalitzla announces himself quite dramatically."

"But how?"

"Dyra, you know as well as I do. For one thing, the elves and fairies will come back to the villages. They'll be dancing in your street of shops. You'll hear them laughing in the morning and singing in the evening. They'll remind us to be happy just to be in Life. The grass people are the grass people. The joy and harmony are ours. You must polish your windows and begin to see."

"As it was before the mower," Dyra murmured. "We can't get back to it, Tokra. We have seen death by the creatures and machines of tall men. We have seen our Way destroyed by our own people in Karep. We've lost too much of our independence, I think. Worse than that, I believe we've lost our innocence."

"Harmony is a state of mind," said Tokra.

"Maybe it's easier for you. Your world is the Way. Mine is administration, and..." Dyra hesitated.

"...and they are not as far apart as you imagined, are they?"

Dyra sighed. "I need something more to renew my hope, Tokra. A sign that nature is not angry—that Life is really going to smile on the grass people. I do not know if I believe that a grassman can save us, even one appointed by elves."

"Dokrimalitzla has been found and the elves are at work. You will get your sign."

XIV

THE TRAIL BOYS CAME BACK from the tall woods carrying a large flat package, and when Hoyim saw what it contained, he was so excited he asked his father to order a gathering.

The parcel contained three enormous pictures and a note which said, "These are not paintings. This is what my son took with the camera—the black box. They are called snapshots. They are for you."

There was a picture of the miller's wife standing on the tall man's hand, held before the tall man's face. Both were smiling broadly. There was a picture of the floral greeting Hoyim had arranged for his friend. Best of all, there was a picture showing much of the village, with the villagers lined up on the rafts and on the market stall, waving to their friend.

"It's a mystery," said the portrait painter. "A picture out of a box like that. I don't understand."

"He intended them for me," said Hoyim, "but they're too big for my house. They should be on the walls of the meeting house, for all to see."

"Put them high," Dyra advised, "in case the meeting house drowns."

The miller's wife stood awestruck before her photograph, while the lampman and the dyer and his wife stood with her.

Dyra decided the gathering was a good time to tell the villagers why Gozer had gone up trail to the tall woods. He was bursting to tell them that a young boy was coming who might convince the people of Karep to come out of the cave and return to the grassman's way, but it was too soon. He contented himself by answering questions about Gozer and the resistance.

Dyra couldn't help noticing the mood of contentment and happiness in the village, so tangible that it made him feel good to look into the faces of his friends and relatives. Deeka's rippling giggle was even merrier than usual. Balink and Flon were almost dancing as they moved. Koalee's smile revealed her dimples. There were people in the village Dyra had suspected of hearing the elves, and he took care to look at them all. One was his daughter, Nila. Others included the clairvoyant fuelman, and Tienna, the portrait painter's wife. Yes, it was in their faces. Surely they sensed something. But there was a quality of alertness about all of the villagers today—a kind of dawning awareness. Were they all starting to hear the elves? They were so lively and full of love that Dyra hated to tell them the gathering was over.

"Wait, everyone!"

The peaman called for attention just as they were turning toward the door. "I have something to show you that will complete the evening. Follow me. Out to the bridge, and hurry, before the sun gets too low for us to see."

A mystery? A secret?

"I saw it today when I came back from the pea trees. It's very beautiful," he said.

Eagerly, the villagers trooped along the middle street and Lenk's way, out to the peaman's road and the bridge.

"There," said the peaman, pointing setting sun of the spreading trees.

A glorious tree stood there, as high as the spreading trees, bedecked with giant wheels of colour in such a rosy red that when the golden rays of the lowering sun fell upon it, it seemed to burst into fire against the green.

"Oh, how splendid!"

"What kind of tree is this?"

"Where did it come from?"

"Ajist," said Hoyim. "Where did you plant your seed?"

"My seed?"

"Your seed. The day of the wheeler. The day we found out the twins would be born."

"My seed! So much happened that day, it went right out of my mind. I planted it here, I think. Right here. But that was over a year ago."

"Beauty develops slowly," said Tokra.

"Oh, Ajist, it is the most beautiful thing I ever saw," said Tienna.

"It's her tree all right," said Hoyim, going to where a seed pod hung low. "These seeds are going to ripen just like the one she found."

"Hoyim, just one flower is as tall as you are."

"Ajist, may I have one to plant by my raft?" asked Balink.

"First she must plant one by her own raft," said Flon. "No, she must plant two—one for each of the twins."

"This is Ajist's very own tree," said Koalee proudly. "Where did you get the seed, Ajist?"

"I don't know. It just blew in. It was lying beside the stair at the other house."

Lenk stepped up beside Dyra. "What are you thinking, Dyra? You've been staring at that tree as if you'd seen a vision."

Dyra smiled. "No," he said, catching Tokra's eye across the heads of the crowd, "I've just seen a sign."

"Now this is really worth discussing," said Koalee. "If the singer behind the market was still in Life, he'd be making up a song about it. I know he would."

Lenk's widow nodded. "Yes, he surely would."

Koalee was sure, as she walked with the widow through the sunset, that she could hear singing.

PART 4

THE PROGRESS

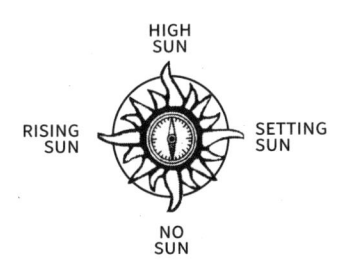

```
        HIGH
         SUN
RISING        SETTING
  SUN           SUN
         NO
        SUN
```

NILA'S DESTINY

I

KOALEE DECIDED NOT to mention the singing, sure it was a product of her imagination, but then she noticed that Hoyim and Ajist were listening with expressions of amazed delight. Deeka was bubbling, "Do you hear it too?" Tuje was asking, "Who's singing? What is that?"

At that point, Koalee admitted that she heard the lilting voices, like a chorus of birds who had suddenly learned a more beautiful tune than had ever been sung before. "It is not the ghost of the singer behind the market," she conceded.

"Don't you know?" whispered Tienna, but Koalee only shook her head.

"I can't see anything," Syl complained. "It seems to be coming from nowhere at all."

Dyra was standing completely still and Koalee was sure some of the colour had drained from his face. He was staring at Tokra incredulously. His mouth finally formed the words, "They have come."

Tokra nodded. "Of course," he said, just loudly enough for most of the crowd to hear. "It is the fairies, saluting the village for the first time. It is up to us to encourage them to stay."

No one moved until the song ended and a cascade of silvery laughter shook the spreading trees.

The remainder of the evening was a time of excitement throughout the village. The tree of the giant red flowers was discussed and re-discussed, also the return of Tokra and, by far the most important, the magic song. Every grassman, woman and child talked with animation—every one, that is, except Nila.

Nila had lingered by the spreading trees after the rest were gone. She arrived at home a little later than the others and kept silent, responding only with a slight nod when Dyra put a direct question to her.

"Oh dear," Koalee sighed to herself. "I'm afraid she is entering her dream time. She is sixteen, after all. It is to be expected. But she told me herself it is not to be the son of Rels, and I know of no other young grassman in the village who has ever been seen with her. Could it be one of Runya's trail boys, I wonder."

It struck Koalee that Dyra must have been very tired of her traditionalism, fighting it all down the years. Well, that was long ago. Now she could enjoy trying to out-guess her daughter until Life saw fit to reveal the plan.

Later, as she snuggled into bed beside Dyra, Koalee asked, "Are you aware our daughter has entered her dream time?"

"Did she tell you who it is?" he asked.

"No. Apparently it's a secret, so far."

"This is how it should be," Dyra remarked. "Life's greatest guessing game."

"Everybody in the village knew when we were going to be married."

"Sometimes they do; sometimes they don't. It's said that in the days of Dokrimalitzla nobody ever knew. There was just suddenly a wedding. Sometimes the couple hadn't even met each other, except through the network of elves. A magic kind of thing, eh?"

Koalee wasn't sure. "It sounds dangerous to me," she admitted. "Think how well we knew Ajist. I would hate to think Nila was going to be married to a stranger."

"Maybe we just need to learn more about this network of the elves," Dyra replied.

※ ※ ※

Nila had many lessons with Tokra before the cold season, as it was tradition for the grass people to be educated about many topics like history and etiquette before their wedding day. She brought home many books to study. One dealt with social traditions and Koalee was gleeful. Here was a book she would read indeed! It told exactly how to greet guests under every type of circumstance, the traditional use of bows and handshakes, the order of greeting when a band of relatives or councillors were present, how to proceed when visiting a village or welcoming strangers, behaviour at rites and rituals, how to phrase invitations, cancellations, thank-you's, farewells—everything was here.

"He is going to question me on that one," Nila remarked, seeing that her mother was enthralled. "I am to know it so well that I can pick out the serious rules from the ones that can be relaxed."

"Nila, are you to be married to a Chief Councillor?"

Nila grinned. "It is still a secret, Mother," she said.

II

KOALEE CONTINUED her studies. The cornman's son had returned from Karep with the traders and the village was jubilant. Not only was it exciting to welcome home one of their own after such an absence, but now there would be two doctors. Koalee feared secretly that she might not be needed any more, but both doctors insisted that she continue. The cornman's son planned to spend most of his time in the new village, but he would come back if the old doctor decided to retire one of these years.

Listening to the two doctors converse, hearing what the cornman's son had to say about his work with the master doctor in Karep, Koalee felt she was the luckiest woman in the village. It was so good to feel useful and needed. Sometimes it still bothered her that Hoyim hadn't wanted to become a lens maker but it was clear that Life had other plans for him. At least he was doing what he loved and what he did well. So was Dyra and so was she. Now, if she only knew what Nila was doing.

The weeks just before the cold season were always the busiest of the year. There were no widows or invalids to be adopted this year, but teams were already being organized to wrap the float spaces and every house had to be checked to make sure they had adequate supplies of food, fuel, and wax. Koalee made the rounds with the doctor to see that each house had a selection of herbs for the winter sickness, rubs for aches and pains, and a means of calling to neighbours should they need assistance.

There was a great send-off banquet for those who would go to the new village, and Pettis was married the same day, so it was a never-to-be-forgotten celebration. It was the young who had requested the new village and it was the young who would go there, so the party was planned by the young who would stay behind: Hoyim and Ajist, Balink and Doen, Tuje and Flon, and Syl and Deeka.

In the midst of it all, there were preparations to be made for winter crafts. Dyra was taking an inventory of his glass and other supplies, when Koalee entered the little sitting room, her arms full of rough thistle down and flax fibres.

"Winter spinning coming in," she announced. "Did you remember to put up the air pipe?"

Dyra groaned. "I knew there was something."

"I will help."

"No need. Lenk and Tuje are coming to see if there is any way they could put in the high window I'd like to have. It would illuminate the work table just right. They'll likely want to climb up for a look, so I'll ask them to uncover the chimney and work the top end. It will only take a few minutes."

Dyra sighed. Cold seasons were nice seasons, in spite of the danger and discomfort. Then he grinned again. Koalee, flitting around the house like a moth, now emerged from the storeroom with his fur cover robe in her arms and draped it over his chair. It was there permanently during the cold season, so he could wrap it around his shoulders if he grew chilly at his work. Next he heard her in the washing room. She had said she was going to put a blanket to soak early today so she could get it aired and dried by nightfall. She had also said something about stew for the noon meal, so it would not be long before he heard the big stew pot rattling. Koalee never stopped. She would be off to infirmary this afternoon, but not until she had accomplished all the busy household tasks she set herself. In came another box of down.

"I should make another thistledown comforter," she remarked.

Dyra knew what she meant. "I suspect we have all winter," he said slyly. "What do you know?"

"No more than you do, but it isn't likely a young man from another village will arrive in the cold season. A puzzle," Koalee mumbled. "Really a puzzle. I'm off now to see Kyb about some fur boots."

III

Belm decided to learn to knit and he mastered it as he mastered everything, with patient concentration. He had helped with the carding of fibres since he was old enough to hold the combs. During his trips on trail maintenance, he had gathered the fluff from the cotton trees and other materials his mother would use for spinning and weaving, so now it seemed only natural that he should make use of them. It would be welcome relaxation during the cold season, when work on lenses might be sparse.

He was seated on a stool beside the fire. He was seemingly oblivious to everything that was going on but missed nothing, of course. He had set himself the task of knitting new scarves for the whole family—the biggest, warmest scarves in the village. Being Belm, he would of course succeed. While he sat thus occupied, he could be asked to watch the stew pot for his mother, or the baking loaves, and he would remember to take them out on time. Sometimes Koalee wondered what she would do when Belm married and moved into a home of his own. He was becoming as indispensable to her as he was to Dyra in the shop. In fact, he was more use in the kitchen than Nila, and now Nila was sick again.

Koalee checked on her before leaving for infirmary. Nila was lying in her sleeping nook, gazing listlessly at the ceiling. At least she had no sign of chills or fever and the only stomach complaint was lack of appetite. She had hardly eaten anything for two days. Koalee had seen other young women behave this way during their dream time, but, with Nila, it had been a problem since earliest childhood. Sometimes a spell like this would pass off with a day or two of rest, but there had been other times—many of them—when the child moved rapidly from the state of lethargy to a raging fever and frightening illness. The spells hadn't been as frequent the past two or three years, and Koalee had hoped the girl was outgrowing them. Now the worry returned.

Nila's nook had no window, just a rotating air vent that could be opened or closed, and there was a sharp wind coming through. Koalee suggested that she close the vent, but Nila didn't answer beyond a shrug that apparently meant she didn't really care what her mother did with the vent.

"Will you come to infirmary with me and see the doctor?"

Nila turned her face toward the partition that separated her sleeping nook from Belm's. "I'm fine," she said. "I just need to rest today."

Koalee felt her brow. "I'll be right next door," she said.

Belm had overheard, of course. "I'll watch her," he promised. "If she gets worse I'll come and fetch you."

Koalee left reluctantly, hoping no one would come to infirmary today, because she wanted to consult with the old doctor about Nila's collapse. At first it looked as if she might not get the chance. They were busy for some time attending to minor ailments and then it was just the two of them.

"Now my friend," said the doctor, "You've been shuffling from one foot to the other ever since you got here today, waiting for a chance to talk to me. What's on your mind?"

"Have you time to listen?"

"I want to visit the lampman sometime before the evening meal. Get a look at his leg. That's all, as things stand right now."

"It's Nila. She's having one of her down spells again."

The doctor frowned. "Fever?"

"Not yet."

"I was hoping she was growing out of those attacks."

"Sometimes it's almost as if she makes herself sick. I mean, she goes to bed and doesn't eat; just lies there waiting to be sick. As if she feels it's her destiny to be sick. Does that make any sense?"

"Do you want me to come and see her?"

"She refused. Said she was fine."

"You realize this may be recurrent all her life?"

"But..."

"I know. I can't find any cause, but I have been working on a theory that could explain it."

"She's not a lazy girl. When she feels up to it, she puts almost too much energy into things."

The doctor nodded. "Nila is a seer, Koalee. Don't look so startled. You knew that."

"I know she has hunches. Sometimes visions. But a seer?"

"I'm sure she is. I knew a case once, when I was a student in Karep. She was a young woman too. She would go into spells of despondency and stop eating and sleeping. She would gradually get weaker and weaker and sometimes it would progress to fever, as Nila does."

"Are you saying it isn't her system? That it has something to do with her character?"

"Well, you said it yourself—sometimes it's as if she believes she has to be sick. There may be more to it than that. The woman I knew came to trust one of the doctors enough to talk to him about how she felt when she was ill. She was seeing and hearing things that would put any of us off our food. She knew when people were going to die or be hurt. She knew if a child was lost or if a man interfered with a woman. Sometimes she saw blackness beyond what one could imagine. She foresaw illness. She lived with fear and sadness until she was exhausted. As you say, Nila puts too much energy into things. So did this woman. But it was often mental energy, emotional energy. She wore herself out combatting the visions inside her head until she had no strength left."

Koalee stared at him with more concern than before. "You don't really think Nila..."

"I said it was a theory, Koalee. When she was a child I wasn't sure she had the gift, as it doesn't usually present many symptoms until dream time, so I didn't mention it. Now that she is a young woman, it looks to me as if it may be true."

"Yes, she has entered her dream time. Tokra knows she is to be married."

"I doubt that's the cause. It might temporarily aggravate a condition that has been there all the time."

"Is there nothing you can do? Or I can do?"

"If she hasn't come out of it by tomorrow, either she must come to me or I will go to her. Meantime I'll give you something to soothe her mind just enough to help her sleep. Might help erase any dark visions that may be troubling her. Remember, I didn't say this is it, Koalee. I said it's a possibility."

"She isn't crying."

"It might help if she would."

"May I go and check on her before you go to the lampman?"

"Go ahead."

"No change," Belm reported, as he concentrated on a purl. "She seems to be sleeping."

So Koalee went back to keep infirmary while the doctor made his call. Then she hurried home to begin the evening meal and prepare the special tea for Nila.

Nila was sleeping deeply when Koalee arrived home, and Belm was in the workroom polishing a lens under his father's supervision. Koalee quickly prepared the supper ingredients. Now, as she trimmed her wick and set her stew to heat, she was startled by the feeling of a presence behind her. She turned quickly, then let out a breath with relief.

"Forgive me. I continually seem to frighten you," said Radd. "May I summon Dyra? I want both of you to hear my announcement."

But Dyra was instantly aware of the elf's presence. He came into the kitchen, followed by Belm, and greeted his trusted guide. Radd broke the news then, so factually they wondered where their wits had been.

"Nila will marry Anodee, the new Dokrimalitzla," Radd said.

Why had none of them guessed? Nila knew, of course. Koalee clucked like a fussy bird and Dyra was astonished.

Radd asked, "Did you not guess why I watched over the safety of this family for so many years?"

"But you said it was because I was listening. You always try to help grass people."

"Then the question, Dyra, might be, why were you listening?'"

Radd smiled broadly and bowed himself out. "Oh," he said, as he turned to go, "Expect more visitors."

Dyra, Koalee and Belm could hardly wait for Nila to wake and discuss this wondrous news.

※ ※ ※

An ancient elf appeared in the kitchen early the next morning, just as they prepared the first meal of the day. He brought a gift of rare leaves for tea and Koalee found it difficult to remember her manners and thank him. They were all staring at the visitor in awe. He had none of the golden beauty that was Radd. He was short and wizened like old wood, but his large eyes held the depth and reflection of pools. There was an impatience about him that made him move in quick, jerky gestures, and at first impression it looked as if he might have a very short temper. In spite of that, there was an aura of friendliness and benevolence about him. Their silence did not discomfit him at all.

"I am Buko," he said. "I know all of you."

Dyra found his voice. "The elf Buko from the village of Nanta. Tokra will be so happy to see you."

"Tokra knows I am here."

"Forgive me," said Koalee. "You are very welcome. I will get you a spoon and bowl."

Buko advanced to the table and opened a bundle containing two pots of the freshest redberry jam they had ever seen. "From the wife of Mekr," he explained. "From Mekr I bring greetings to Chief Councillor Dyra and his councillors." He was holding out a bound scroll.

They noticed that his arms were long and he had slender, tapering hands with expressive fingers. His legs were a little bowed. His clothing was clean, but stained and frayed from long use. He was bearded, with elfin points to his ears, bushy brows, and thin lips that constantly changed his mouth into new and fascinating shapes. Of all his characteristics, it was the eyes which held attention. They were not old, like the rest of him, but young, brilliant eyes. There was the light of great wisdom there.

To their astonishment, Buko did not accept the offer of a seat at the table at once. Instead, he went directly to Nila's sleeping nook. "This young woman is to wake up!" he announced briskly. "Come, Nila. We are beginning the morning meal. No more sleep unless you are ill. You feel fine. You will rise and put on a blue dress and be at the table as fast as I can seat myself."

With that, he drew the curtain over Nila's nook and turned to the others. "I will train Nila in the basic concept of discipline for four days," he said. "It is fundamental."

Koalee's mind was racing. Hoyim's old nook had long since been made part of the workroom and the sitting room was full of her fibres. Where could she find a place for the elf to sleep?

Buko read her mind, of course. "I have chosen a nest in the spreading trees," he told her. "If I eat with you, I will bring my share. I want to spend time with Tokra, you will understand."

Nila appeared in a blue dress and took her place at the table. "Nila is not well," Koalee said weakly. "I just now made a tea from an herb the doctor gave me, to calm her and help her to rest."

Buko acted so rapidly that no one was sure, afterward, that they had seen his hands move. He seized the packet of herbs and stuffed it into his pocket. "It will do me no harm, but it is wrong for Nila," he said.

Nila wore a faint smile and she had colour in her cheeks.

I hope he hasn't put her under a spell, Koalee thought. But Buko was behaving so normally it was hard to think of him as one who could cast spells. He ate heartily. Long used to feasting at the tables of grassmen, he chatted of everyday things, asking questions about the village people and answering factually when a question was put to him.

Nila ate very little gruel and was making her meal of fresh water and seedcake. Buko seemed to approve. He opened his hand and dropped a fresh red fruit into Nila's bowl.

"At this season?" Koalee gasped, before she could stop herself.

Buko only smiled.

IV

Having Buko spend his time with them afforded Dyra's family an interesting four days. He reminded Nila to remember to contribute to daily household tasks and to set aside a portion of each day to read and relax. At the same time, he was kind and he often laughed with her if he felt that she was growing tense.

"You must balance your energy," he told her. "A brief rest can do you as much good as a whole day in your bed, if you will learn to let your mind slip into harmony. Put less effort into what you do. We accomplish more by moving steadily, without haste or pressure. Nothing should be taxing. Never forget, the elves have no word for work."

Koalee could sense Nila falling into the pattern Buko advised. She seemed less tense, less anxious to fill every minute of her time with activity, and she was more alert to the members of her family, more attuned to their moods.

When Buko had gone out to visit Tokra, Nila confided to her mother, "Buko speaks to me mind-to-mind quite often. You don't hear that. He says I have been interested in the pictures in my mind and the voices, and sometimes that has led me to neglect the world and the people around me."

"He wants you to be more outgoing?"

"He wants me to be both. I must be alert to what goes on within my mind but I must also be alert to the realities around me."

"You will meet many people," said Koalee. "Can you be alert to all of them without being exhausted?"

"Buko is teaching me to bring peace to my mind by an act of will.

He is showing me ways of breathing, ways of making my heart beat slowly. Even how I stand or how I smile can make the difference between being tired and being rested. It is all so useful, Mother. I only hope I can remember everything when Buko is gone."

Buko enlisted the help of Belm and spent one afternoon constructing a beautiful butterfly ornament with soft colours in its wings. They hung it over Nila's bed in her nook. "That will help you relax," he announced. "Something calming to look at, to take your mind off your plans and worries."

Tokra had told them of Buko's talent for design, so it didn't surprise Koalee that he examined her weaving patterns with great interest. He liked to sit and talk with a marker in his hand, entertaining himself by making vines and twirls on paper. "Ah!" he said, when he had happened upon one that pleased him, "It is a pattern for a rug, Koalee. You will hook a rug like this, to remember me. You will place it beneath your feet at the loom. It will be our connection."

Koalee was thrilled.

So cheerful and entertaining was the elf that they failed to see him as Tokra had described him—impatient and a little short of temper. It was only when he fell into discussions with Dyra in the evenings that the impatience emerged. Dyra was a rapid thinker, but it was difficult to think at elfin speed. Still, it pleased Dyra to realize that Buko's impatience was not so much with Dyra as with himself. He would sit at the table drumming with his fingers against his neck, just as Tokra had pictured him, but it was his own thoughts he summoned.

"You are wrong to envy the elves," he told Dyra. "It is true that Life gave the elves freedom from possessions. We can survive on foods that would be toxic to grassmen. Our bodies adjust to temperatures so we may sleep outdoors without cover on cold or wet nights when a grassman would perish. We can put our bodies into a sleep-like state such as the trees do in the cold season and live for months without food or drink."

"I really don't envy those things," Dyra said honestly. "I think I prefer possessions, but maybe it's because I'm used to them. What bothers me is that I can't do these things you talk about. I can't just move my body at the flick of an eyelash and find myself where I want to be. There are many things an elf can do which I cannot. When I think about that, I can't help but feel inferior."

"A grassman compensates for his shortcomings by building shelters, storing food, making clothing. You find new ways of overcoming problems of snow and rain. Life gave the grassman creativity so he might make use of all things for his survival."

"But don't the elves have creativity?" Dyra asked.

"Buko does," Koalee put in, joining them at the table. "Just look at the design he made for my rug."

"The creativity of the elf is not related to material things in a practical sense," Buko told them. "It is focused upon mind structures. This has been the essential difference between grassmen and elves from the beginning. The elf envies the grassman his skills with arts and crafts, but he scorns material things and will usually avoid a village where grassmen have moved too far from the natural life. The grassman envies the elf his mind structures and so, when he moves too far toward material crafts, he tends to close his mind to visions and voices. He ceases to look and to listen. Elf and grassman move apart."

"But it doesn't have to be, surely? Aren't we in process right now of trying to bring elf and grassman together again?"

Koalee was nodding as Dyra asked the question. Nila, concentrating on some sewing, was smiling. Belm came from the workroom and quietly joined the group.

"The separation does not have to be," Buko agreed. "Creativity is natural to grassmen and a good craftsman can work with his materials with open mind, seeing the future and hearing the present without letting the insights of his mind interfere with the relationship between his methodical brain and his hands. The grassman's brain concentrates upon what he calls the reality of the world. The methodical brain is not highly developed in the elves. We handle it by taking cues from the mind of the grassman. Only through mental communication can we comprehend the grassman's problems. We are better able to understand the problems of plant and animal because we are tuned to the same voice. The grassman, by increased interest in his 'reality', has been cutting himself off from the voice of Life."

"These are things Radd told me," Dyra remarked, "but it is clearer when you explain it."

"Radd is not a philosopher," Buko said factually. "When he has lived as many years as I have, his understanding will deepen."

"Don't forget," Nila interrupted, "that a few grassmen and women can still hear the elves thinking."

Buko nodded. "But of those, fewer still can hear the plants and animals. Nanta could. Tokra can, and Runya. And, of course, Anodee." Buko smiled broadly at Nila and actually winked at her. "It is the quality of awareness that is such a mystery to so many grassmen."

"There, it is just as I said," Dyra insisted. "The mind of the grassman is inferior, in spite of all his creativity."

"Not inferior, Dyra," Buko told him. "Only different. And, I might warn you, much more vulnerable."

"I will make us all a hot drink from powdered redberries," Koalee suggested.

"Not for me, thank you, Koalee," said Buko. "The sun has set. My nest is calling. I go rising sun tomorrow, but I will be here to wish you goodbye."

Buko was back so early the next morning that no one was awake but Nila. He had sent a thought message ahead to rouse Nila from her bed, and the two had a few moments to talk while they lighted the wax in the cooking stove and put water to boil.

"I have lived in the same village with Anodee for sixteen years now," said Buko. "If it was possible for an elf to have emotions, I am sure I would love him. He is a remarkable young man, and he is to marry a remarkable young woman. You may think it unfair that Anodee has had the advantage of sixteen years of our training while you have had four days. Have no fear, Nila. What we have begun will simply continue. You will be able to ask me questions whenever you wish, and you will hear my answers. Whenever you run into difficulties, simply think, "Buko" and I will be there in your mind. And remember your lessons. You must continue the discipline. If I sense you slipping, I will be here to prod you, even if I have to come back in person. That is a warning."

Nila smiled. Had Buko been a grassman, she would have given him a hug and kiss, but he was an elf. She tried to send him a thought message filled with her gratitude and trust, and she knew it was received.

Koalee had roused and soon the entire family were about the table, insisting that Buko stay for seccar and gruel. In the midst of the preparation, the elf disappeared.

※ ※ ※

For a few days, Nila felt she couldn't make a move without asking for Buko's help or advice. Finally she heard him saying, "You are free, Nila. Make your decisions. Plan your days. You will know if you need help. Or I will sense you need help and I will be there. Learn to stand alone again."

It grew easier and, as Nila gained confidence in herself, she found she wouldn't have to stand alone because Anodee was on the network, that warm, golden presence with an aura of love as wide as the world. They were allowed much more time together than ever before. Often they chatted silently for hours, and Nila found she could go about her daily work without losing touch with him at all.

"At first I wondered how I could deserve this," Nila told her mother. "I don't mean the honour of being his wife, I mean all the love and support."

"I imagine you will pay," Koalee suggested, "with responsibilities."

Nila sighed. "Oh, I am sure we will. He receives and answers more messages in a day than Father does in a year as Chief Councillor. He's already sharing a lot of it with me. But it is calm, you know? Since Buko's lessons, I find I can keep my mind tranquil through it all. Life will never allow more messages than we can manage. I am learning to trust Life to decide when I need to be listening to the elves' network and when I don't."

"If you get a message for your father and I, I hope you'll let us know at once."

"Of course."

"You know what you said a minute ago—about deserving the 'love and support'? An idea just came to me. If Anodee is able to hear the elves and act as a communicator between elves and grassmen, could it be that he gets his power from the grass people? I mean, not from the elves at all, but from us? From our love and support? Just identifying Dokrimalitzla—wouldn't this enable us to push him forward, make the elves take notice of him? I suppose I'm all wrong and I don't think I'm explaining it very well."

"Ask Buko," Nila suggested.

"Me? How could I ask Buko?"

"You have met him. You know him. Don't be afraid to try using the network, Mother. It is very simple. Just listen to your thoughts."

"That's what Radd used to say."

"Meantime, I do have an important message. A party from Karep are high sun of Hoyim's Lake. They will be here by sundown."

V

DYRA WAS HAVING a cup of tea in the kitchen and Nila joined him. She was looking tired and wan, the way she looked when she came down with one of her sick spells, but she made no mention of going to her bed. She moved a little slower and breathed more deeply, as if she was willing the colour to climb back to her cheeks.

Koalee was stirring something over the wax fire and Dyra saw her cast a worried glance at Nila. "It is all so unpredictable, and I am in too much excitement to begin to think," she remarked. "With marriage rites like this in the village—and in our family—there will be a huge crowd of people, Dyra. This will be more work and fuss than I have ever imagined."

"The elves will help, Mother," Nila reminded her. "And it is a long time until the end of the cold season."

Dyra realized what had been troubling him. It really hadn't been clear to him before— that his daughter was being prepared for marriage to someone she had never met and she might not be happy about it.

"Nila, is this marriage your wish?" he asked suddenly.

Nila seemed to understand what he was thinking. "The elves are not taking over, Father," she said. "This is simply the way it will be. The timer is set."

"But you? Your wishes should come first."

Nila smiled, though her customary energy was still lacking. "I am very happy about the marriage," she assured him. "There is nothing I want more than to marry Anodee. What is worrying me is that I am not just marrying Anodee. I am marrying Dokrimalitzla."

"Buko assured us you will know what to do and what to say," Koalee reminded her. "You have only to ask your network if you run into difficulties."

"But there will be so much travel; so many new people to meet. I will feel as if I am like the monument to Hoyim and the miller's wife, an object to be stared at."

"You will be loved," Koalee insisted. "The wife of Dokrimalitzla! Just think how important you will be to all the grass people."

Dyra's sharp ears had detected an unusual stir in the street and he went to the window to see what was happening.

"Your invasion has begun, Koalee," he said. "Visitors, and just when I was going to help the crew wrap our house and the infirmary." Dyra reached for a coat and prepared to go down to greet the travellers.

"It is the party from Karep," Nila called to him.

Dyra paused at the top of the stair to get a look at the newcomers. There were five men pulling loaded trail runners, but none of them seemed prepared to step forward as spokesman. It was the woman who appeared to be in charge, a grasswoman so beautiful Dyra thought he was going to miss his footing and tumble down the steps. She was flanked by two elves who had obviously been acting as her trail guards.

Dyra found his footing and prepared to greet her with the two-handed bow. "I am Chief Councillor Dyra," he said firmly. "I make you welcome."

Koalee had stepped to the raft and she stopped in amazement. The tall, dark-haired woman was not only shapely and of the loveliest colouring, she was an exquisitely graceful creature. Even in her dull cover clothes, dyed to provide protection in the do-lan, Rayan's beauty was astonishing.

Rayan offered Dyra the two-handed bow and introduced herself. Her voice, too, was arresting. "I request permission to spend the cold season in your village as the guest of Tienna, the portrait painter's wife," she said.

"That must be discussed with my council," Dyra was telling her. "A mere formality. I can assure you, any guest of Tienna's is welcome in this village."

"It is a short distance to the portrait painter's house compared to the trail you have followed," Koalee called down, "but the day is cool and you will be tired. Please come and join us for tea."

Rayan smiled acceptance and came up the stairs, but the elves bowed and vanished. Dyra was learning the identities of the men with the trail runners. Three had come as assistants to Rayan but the other two were bound for Mekr's village and requested permission to spend the night on the traders' raft. Dyra invited all five to join his wife and daughter for tea and then, rather reluctantly, he set off to find Yansa and Lenk. They would have to decide how to house these three men from Karep. No doubt the tea mistress could take at least two, but she would likely charge money. Maybe one could stay with Ston.

Nila stood when her mother introduced her to Rayan, but Rayan hastened to bow to Nila. "You were expected," Nila told her. "Rayan the singer. My brother Hoyim heard you sing in Karep. He has talked about it often. I think I know why you have come."

"Just at this moment I have come because your Mother has kindly invited me to tea," Rayan replied.

The five men gathered around the table, but Nila and Rayan took their tea to the little sitting room and made themselves comfortable among the boxes and bales of Koalee's spinning fibers.

"I am grateful to you," Nila said quietly. "You have come so far to help me. I am to watch you and listen to you and learn how to move and how to speak – so Buko told me."

"Ah, there is much more to it than that," said Rayan. "You will not copy my movement or my speech. It is true, I am used to being on stage with many people watching me, and I can teach you a great deal, but our task is to find your voice and your grace. I have not come to turn you into a copy of Rayan. I have come to find the great beauty that is in Nila and bring it out where the world can see it."

The words filled Nila with a new confidence. "Is it really there?" she asked.

"Oh, it is there. We will work on that for at least two moons before we begin work on your wardrobe. There is no point in designing clothes for a Nila who has not yet found her full expression."

"Then you will help me with my wedding dress?"

"Oh, we want your mother to sew that dress. It is her place. But Tienna is already drawing designs for other clothes, with help from Violet. Approval of the designs is my authority."

"I'm glad," said Nila.

"The last time we had Dokrimalitzla I heard that the fairies dressed his wife in wispy green and shoes of polished bark—woodsy. She was slender and brown-haired, looked like a sprite. We had no big village in those days. You are not a sprite and you are not woodsy. You are fair and you are serene. Already I am grasping an image of what you will be, but we have all winter. Let us simply enjoy our tea."

A warm smile of companionship passed between them and Nila felt more relaxed than she had for many days. They began to talk of music.

The young men at the kitchen table could be heard preparing to leave when Hoyim arrived, accompanied by his father.

"My brother is here," Nila announced with a smile, watching Hoyim extending his hand to the strangers. "He has a newsletter. Nobody manages to come up the street of shops without Hoyim hearing about it within a few minutes."

It amused Nila to note how fast Hoyim gathered his information. He seemed to be exchanging mere pleasantries with the young grassmen, welcoming them to the village, showing concern that the two who were going on to Mekr's village should have a safe trip, but by that time he knew who they were and where they were from, why they had come and where they were bound.

"Will you mind?" Nila asked her new friend.

Rayan grasped her meaning without question. "I am here to rest this cold season and my friend Tienna has kindly invited me," she said quietly. "I hate to deceive your brother, but it is not yet time to divulge our secrets."

"Oh, Hoyim knows," said Nila. "He talked to Buko. You don't have to worry. If something is to be kept secret, Hoyim will not put it into his newsletter. He is trustworthy. That is why he has right of trade."

Rayan stepped into the kitchen then, to bid goodbye to her trail companions and to thank them for their safe company, Dyra led them out. He would escort the three who were staying to their various accommodations.

Hoyim stood wide-eyed, staring at Rayan, until Koalee finished saying her goodbyes to the guests and nudged him sharply in the arm.

"We have been honoured by a visit from the singer Rayan," she said, and then, to Rayan. "My son Hoyim wishes me to convey his welcome. He has no voice."

For a moment, Hoyim had been transported back to the concert hall in Karep, overcome with awe at the beauty of the woman who wore the silver lace shoes. Now that he was seeing her in trail clothes, the fact that she was a grasswoman of substance and not a mere mirage took time to focus in his mind. A picture came back vividly of Rayan disappearing into a jeweller's shop, accompanied by Kezel. Violet had gone into the shop an instant later. Something popped into Hoyim's brain, some kind of connection, and he was trying to grasp what it meant.

"Forgive me," he said, finding his composure. "I didn't expect to meet the singer Rayan in my parent's kitchen. This is the greatest honour our village has ever known."

Rayan bowed. "You are lavish with words, Hoyim," she replied.

"Let me guess," said Hoyim, noticing that his sister was very at ease with their guest. "You have come to help Nila prepare for the ceremonies. Am I correct?"

"I have come because I needed to rest this cold season and my friend Tienna kindly invited me to come and stay with her," Rayan told him.

"I understand completely. Your visit to Tienna will be in my final newsletter of the season. I have received orders from Tokra and from Buko and from my father. My pens are to be sealed away in the doctor's lockbox if a word of the plans is leaked prematurely."

Rayan laughed. "Please add that I may be persuaded to give a concert when I am well rested," she said.

"My friends and I heard you sing in Karep," Hoyim told her,

beaming with pleasure at this news.

"And his stories have left us all agog to hear you," Koalee added. "I hope it won't be too long before you are rested."

Rayan liked Koalee. Busy, assertive, polite, and obviously proud of her expertise, Koalee embodied the best of the grasswomen.

"I will sing for you now, if you like," she said. "And then I really must leave to find Tienna."

"Oh, please," said Hoyim.

Nila and Koalee stood with their arms around each other's waists, hugging each other with joy. Rayan simply sang, without hesitancy, as if she were entertaining herself. Her song was *When I Go Up Trail*, about a young grasswoman dreaming of the day she might venture beyond her village and see more of the world.

The song took Koalee back to a young woman leaving her home with her husband and baby, to go into the unknown do-lan and found a new village, but it made Nila anxious. She had yet to go.

The cold season was mild. What snow there was fell two moons later than expected and there were many days when there was water on the ground when they were prepared for ice. It meant that visiting was easier and village spirits were higher. There was a concert in the meeting house when Rayan had had time to rest, and she sang two songs. Villagers who had never heard her sing were thrilled, and clamouring for more, but it was another moon before Rayan decided to give a concert on her own. By that time she was well acquainted with the musician and accepted as one of the village music makers. There had been many an impromptu concert at the musician's house, or at the portrait painter's, or at Dyra's. Dashe and Torall, proud to have heard Rayan before anyone else but Hoyim, acted as if she was their own discovery.

What Rayan was doing at Tienna's house was not so well known. Off on the edge of the village near the drainage ditch, the portrait painter's house had never been much frequented, so it was hard to find an excuse to go there now. It was known that the grassmen who accompanied Rayan from Karep had taken small bundles of clothing out of the trail runners and that the remainder of all three loads had gone with Rayan. Obviously, the bales contained a beautiful dress or two, because she had worn them at the concerts, but why would any grasswoman need three trail runners?

❅ ❅ ❅

Belm arrived later, looking hungry and carrying a bag of pastries from the baker's. "I know you are too busy to be baking," he explained, as he handed it to his mother. Then he reached into his pocket and brought out a small tie bag. "I saw Violet outside. She said these were for Nila."

The bag contained bright flashing crystal beads like the ones Violet wore around her neck. "I saw these in my dream," Nila explained. "I had the feeling it was a message from Violet. These will be stitched into the designs I am embroidering for the skirt. They are to represent dewdrops."

"Has Tienna approved this as part of the design?" her mother wanted to know. "Don't worry, Mother. I think Tienna gets a lot of her ideas from Violet. They have worked together for some time."

Belm set an extra candle on the table and they all stood around admiring the sparkle of the crystals in the candlelight.

"Without beauty there would really be no point in Life, would there?" Dyra remarked.

VI

IN THE MIDST of sunshine, a dark cloud passed over. Nila felt it first and her eyes looked strained with worry.

"Have you talked to Buko?" her mother asked, as they sat together sewing fine seams in pieces that would eventually be lining for a big skirt.

Nila nodded. "He will try to interfere, but an elf can't help if a grassman won't listen."

Nila said no more, so Koalee set her sewing aside and made tea, her usual remedy for problems. "Snow is going to fall at last," she remarked. "You can smell it."

"It won't stay—not this time," Nila answered. "It is coming down wet." She took her sewing to her nook, out of the way of the tea.

"It can't be pleasant, knowing so much of the future," Koalee ventured.

"Sometimes it is misery, but then I probably see more light and joy on the happy side than most people." Nila returned to the table and began to drink her tea. Koalee could see her breathing deeply. It was almost as if she was willing the tightness in her forehead to smooth and disappear.

"Do you know what it is? What is going to happen?"

"No. But I think I know who it is going to happen to."

The family was quiet that evening. Dyra went to the workroom to write but returned after a very few minutes to say his mood was not right. Koalee asked him if he would play Flon and Tuje's table game with her, but he shook his head. Belm played the quidda for them for a while, and then announced he would go to bed early. Koalee remarked he had chosen rather mournful tunes, but Belm only gave a hint of a smile and offered his mother a hug.

Grass people slept a little later in the cold season, when there was no dew to collect, but Dyra's family were wakened after a short sleep by a scream from Nila's nook. They were all up and running to Nila in an instant. She was moaning and crying in her sleep and it was plain she had had one of her bad dreams. Koalee sponged her brow and put an extra blanket on her bed. Satisfied that Nila had settled into a comfortable sleep, she returned to her own bed to try and get a little more rest.

※ ※ ※

Nila's mood of gloom lasted into the next day. It was time for the evening meal when Tokra appeared. He was carrying a letter which he handed to Dyra. "Runya has sent a messenger," he said. "Jukek sent a message to me, as well."

Dyra could tell before he opened the letter that it contained some tragic news. Everyone waited in silence.

"Oh, Belm," Dyra said, when he had read the letter. "It's your friend Gyten. He and his trail mate were practising on the shooting range and…"

"He was shot?" Belm filled in.

"No, not shot. It was a rangebeast. It took them both. Runya says, "We would not have known that happened had Gozer not been there to see it."

"It is some mistake," Belm exclaimed. "Gyten is my best friend."

"Belm, I am sorry, but it is no mistake," said his father.

Koalee beckoned to Tokra to sit at the table and she brought him tea. "I wanted you to know how sorry I am," Tokra told Belm. "Jukek mentions you in his letter and says how much your friendship meant to Gyten."

Realization was dawning on Belm, but he fought it away. "It's not possible," he insisted. "Gyten listened to the elves."

A visible shock passed through everyone at table. Tears were forming in Belm's eyes and Nila bowed her head. After a minute, Tokra realized that all eyes were fastened on him, questioning.

"The elves cannot control the timer," he reminded them.

"Gyten's timer was not set," Nila answered. "I have talked to Buko. He cautioned him."

"It would be a matter of persuasion," Tokra explained. "I have known it to happen many times. When one who hears the elves is with someone who does not, he may forget to listen and let his companion persuade him to go to dangerous places."

Belm could tell that Tokra was watching him, waiting for his reaction. "There is no blame," Belm said after a moment, and Tokra sighed with relief.

Dyra was thinking at his customarily quick pace. "How can the coming of Dokrimalitzla improve a situation such as this?" he asked.

"I recognize your concern, Dyra," Tokra replied. "We have expectations of a perfect world when we find Dokrimalitzla. Then a fine young grassman goes from Life and his timer wasn't even set."

"Dokrimalitzla is not yet in everyone's consciousness," said Nila.

"Ah, good for you, Nila," said Tokra. "The exact point I was going to make. Had both Gyten and his friend heard the elves, they would not have been on the shooting range at that time. I'm sure we can count on that. Dokrimalitzla makes the world safer because all of the grass people will come to full consciousness."

"Everyone will be listening," Dyra added. "It's what Radd has always said, 'They have to listen.' We can't tell them."

"They will all listen soon," Nila assured him.

"But not on time for Gyten." Belm's tears were beginning to run down his cheeks. Koalee stood beside him and cradled his head against her body, rocking him gently.

"They are glar to discuss such questions when you are in mourning," she murmured.

"No," Belm told her. "It is alright. I needed to understand."

"Love Life, Belm. We all love you, and we are all saddened by your loss," Tokra told him. "I will leave you now. When you wish to talk, you have only to send for me."

"I wish to go to the rites," said Belm.

"It is too late in the season," his father told him. "Snow fell yesterday and I sense more to come. It pains me to have to forbid you to go, Belm, but I must."

"The messenger? Has he returned?" Belm asked.

"He is not going to take the risk," said Tokra. "He plans to stay on Runya's raft for the cold season."

Dyra nodded, thankful to hear the news.

"I will speak to the musician," Tokra promised. "There will be prayers and special music for Gyten at our next meeting. These rites will be offered in the name of Belm, because he has lost his best friend."

Despite the gloom, Belm came around the table and shook Tokra's hand when the dolenter was leaving. "Thank you, Tokra," he said. "For telling us, and for being so understanding."

Koalee filled with pride. Belm was so strong and traditional. She had often wondered how she came to deserve such a son.

'I've just had a feeling,' she thought. 'Am I starting to be like Nila? But I've believed Hoyim might succeed Dyra someday, as Chief Councillor of the village. I think I was wrong. It will not surprise me if I live to see Belm the next Chief Councillor.'

She told Dyra about the feeling that night and he said, "I have the same hunch. I am also beginning to wonder when we will have a hint of his intended."

"He likes Naj," Koalee whispered.

"Naj isn't even in school yet."

"No, it is unlikely, I realize that. But there is no older girl who appeals to him that I have seen. I will try to learn what the miller's wife is thinking. She recognizes the Truth among the young people faster than I do."

"She had better be a good one," Dyra mumbled sleepily. "If she is to follow in the steps of this Chief Councillor's wife!"

Koalee sighed. "I will pretend you are serious," she answered. "This has been a tragic day and tomorrow will not be better, but Belm is making me very proud."

"And me," said Dyra.

VII

BELM WAS WELL LIKED in the village, and several people had met Gyten on his trips from no sun, so a mood of sadness lasted for many days. Hoyim set the story in print and made enough copies to send up trail at the end of the cold season. There was little for him to do now that trail was closed. No one had ordered genealogy tables. No songs were being printed. No one was writing a book as far as he knew. It was unlikely his father would finish one with all that was happening in the family.

Hoyim wandered up to his parent's house. He found Nila alone, studying one of the books Tokra had assigned. "Mother is at infirmary," she told him. "You will have seedcake and tea?"

"I will have seccar, if you don't mind," said Hoyim. "It is too cold to be outdoors today. I should have gone straight home and stayed there."

"I'm glad you didn't. It is pleasant to see you."

Hoyim nibbled thoughtfully at a seedcake. "Mmm. Mother didn't spare the honey."

"I made them."

"Aha! Nice work, too. Nila, there is something I want to ask you. I have been curtailed from printing anything about your marriage plans or what is to happen when the cold season is over. No—I'm not complaining. But what I wanted to say—is there to be no need of printers, then, when Dokrimalitzla is announced?"

"What do you mean, Hoyim?"

"Well, the elfin network will be in operation. News will be travelling in the air. And printers will apparently be in restraint until a story is already widely known."

"Of course there will be printers!" Nila told him. "Books will be written. Songs will be written. Facts will need to be written down. It is hard to transmit facts on the network. It is much easier to send feelings. Warnings. Sometimes appointments. Promises. You realize why the elves are so reluctant to tell everything, don't you?"

Hoyim nodded. "Curiosity makes people think. But this village goes too far sometimes with its secrets. It is sometimes not a good place for a printer."

Nila laughed.

※ ※ ※

Seven days later the village was greeted with the news that the Chief Councillor had another grandchild. This time it was a girl. "The most perfect little girl you ever saw!" Kyb bragged, as soon as she saw her.

"This is Denza," Ajist announced. "I dreamed of her, even before the twins were born."

※ ※ ※

When Nila's dress had been completed, it was pressed and hung in a protective bag of paper, soon to be followed by the one Tienna had made for Koalee. The rest of Nila's wardrobe would remain in the sewing room at Tienna's for the time being.

Koalee began to turn her mind to other matters. She liked to have things planned well in advance, but this time she was up against an impossible situation.

"Oh, Dyra," she moaned. "I'm sitting on excitement like a jumpy frog."

"Enjoy it all," Dyra advised. "The elves can be counted on to help us when we need them."

"But we don't even know who will be here. The village will be invaded, Dyra. Everyone from Mekr's village is sure to come, and Runya's village and the new village and who knows who else? How can I possibly plan food for people when I have no idea how many people there will be?"

"I was talking to the hunter. A bird roasted over a firepit will feed a lot of people. I'm sure Syl will bring fish. Put everyone to cleaning roots and making salads. The more people to work on a task, the faster it will be done."

"But loaves...? Even if every grass person in the village baked and the bakery worked day and night..."

Suddenly Koalee heard Buko's voice. She looked around to see if he had entered the house, but there was no sign of him.

"I am speaking to you mind-to-mind, Koalee," Buko told her. "You are to cease this fussing."

"But, our reputation for hospitality is in danger."

"It is not a problem. We will have a precise count of how many guests are coming to the village once they are up trail. That will give us plenty of time to prepare. If anyone arrives unexpectedly, they will be advised to bring their own food. The fairies arranged with several villages to save nectar and juice last season. Some was dried and some was preserved with honey. They will be bringing it with them. There was only one thing for your village to remember, and that was to have your young people gather five times as much chicory as they usually do and make sure the shopkeeper is well stocked with seccar."

"But it is too late! That should have been done before the cold season."

Buko laughed. "Then your young people were listening more attentively than you were. The shopkeeper has just been complaining that he has hardly room for all the chicory he stored."

Koalee felt overwhelmed, but she set her spine and put on a rather determined expression, as if she had known all along exactly what was to be done. "I am sure the tea mistress will be happy to bake sweet pastries and I am sure the miller will be glad to supply the meal," she mused. "If every family in the village cooked enough for ten or twenty people..."

She realized that Buko was no longer in her mind.

The cold season remained mild, though there was enough snow to bury Brond's house, and Dyra's father and the fuelman needed help to dig out. Almost everyone had winter sickness but recovered.

Tokra was bursting with good humour. Not only did he have a new granddaughter, he was full of the pending surprise. He had known about Dokrimalitzla for long enough that he felt almost as if he had engineered the whole plan himself. He visited everyone in the village in turn and then began again. He was having an evening meal with Hoyim and Ajist, where he usually enjoyed a little playtime with the twins, when Ajist broke the news that Tienna was designing a dress for Denza to wear to the ceremony.

She looked at Hoyim slyly. "It is to be her acceptance dress."

Hoyim looked startled. "Are you planning to accept Denza at the same time as the wedding?" he asked Tokra. He felt it was unfair, as if the baby was to take second place.

Ajist grinned. "Hoyim—our daughter is to be accepted into Life by Dokrimalitzla himself. The very first child to be accepted by this Dokrimalitzla. Can you imagine?"

Suddenly she was crying and hugging Hoyim, and he began to cry too. He was only beginning to fathom what was happening to the grass people.

Rayan gave a concert as the cold season was drawing to an end and it served as the signal for a period of great activity. Houses were unwrapped and worms dismantled with alacrity. Water vats and rafts were scrubbed and streets were cleaned until the pebbles shone. Without being asked to do so, the shopkeeper and the lampman set to work as soon as the earth was softened to erect new lamp posts on the street, hoping to double the number.

"We should have a dance," the lampman suggested, as they were fastening the braces and fixing lamps to the tops of the poles. Dyra was tempted to tell them there would be a very big dance indeed, but he kept his silence.

Doen stained his raft with fresh berry stain and oil and, as if by a signal, the other shopkeepers followed suit. Soon the village was looking new. The miller's wife cleaned the dead growth away from the monument commemorating how she and Hoyim had met a tall man, and she put down fresh clean gravel all around it.

When the pea trees were planted, Dyra organized a work party to transplant flowering trees in the hollow below the old mill. As he and Lenk stood surveying the transformed village, he remarked, "We will be festive!"

"You will be festive!" a voice echoed, and there was rippling laughter. A band of fairies flew over and dropped flowers around the new lamps. Tokra had written that, in Nanta's village, they would rescue a lost child. It was going to take getting used to, having fairies as neighbours.

What would they do next? When would they show up? At times the unpredictability troubled Dyra.

With everything that was on his mind, Dyra found less time to worry about Karep. Gozer had come back from his journey setting sun to report that the villages close to Karep had refused to recognize his status. They had laughed at the idea that the villages rising sun had formed a federation.

"Good," said Dyra. "Brecort will not be worried."

Still, now that the warm season was approaching, Dyra was nervous. What if Brecort *was* worried? What if he was to appear with his guards, his whole organization and impose his wishes without their consent?

Something must have troubled Brecort, because Mev came through the village as soon as the trail was open, and he was in an incendiary mood. What were the small villages thinking of, trying to form a federation? They had no right to take such action.

"And Karep does?" Dyra asked sarcastically. "By what right?"

"By authority."

"Mine or Brecort's?"

"That," said Mev, "is preposterous!"

"We are both Chief Councillors," said Dyra. "Equals in the eyes of grassmen."

"Brecort runs the big village. It is more challenging. Much more difficult. He has the support of many grass people. He also has far... far more experience..."

"As before, we disagree," said Dyra. "Our federation has no central authority. We remain equal. That is the way it will be."

Surely if a grassman had ever stamped his foot in anger, Mev would have done so. He did not return again, and Dyra was uncertain what it meant. Had Brecort given up? Or were plans for some new strategy going on at Karep?

When Buko returned to the village to see if he could be of further assistance, Dyra asked him about Brecort. The old elf merely shrugged. "Wait and see," he said.

The fuelman, following his own hunches, took a trek to the first village high sun of the tall woods and returned to report that Brecort had been sending his envoys setting sun instead of rising sun. Did it mean he was giving up, or was he trying to gain support in order to overcome the resistance? Dyra would have liked to know.

VIII

"Hammocks in the float spaces?" Dyra was skeptical.

"The elves will be on watch," Buko assured him. "It will be safe. You could put temporary cots in the meeting house. Every home should be prepared to open to all the guests they can hold. You will need cots in every bit of space. Of course, after they leave your village, anyone who follows up trail in the progress to Karep will be prepared to sleep on the ground. Only the couple and their official escort will have accommodations prepared in the villages. But while they are in this village, they should certainly be given places to sleep."

"The tea mistress has a room, but Rayan's escort are staying there. The traders' raft holds six."

Buko shook his head. "Hammocks in the float spaces," he insisted. "It is your only hope."

Buko had no more than arrived when it became obvious the village was to be favoured by the fairies. As Hoyim walked to work in the mornings, he was greeted by more of them each day. Dyra would come in with the dew and report great doings in the trees. Leaves would be shaking with laughter and not only birds were singing. It seemed as if the world was growing more beautiful. Everything was greener, brighter and more alive. The very bark on the tree trunks looked renewed. Was it imagination, or did the grass animals sit straighter on their haunches, watching with blacker eyes? It was hard to believe that some of the villagers still failed to notice these things.

When Pora saw the dress Tienna had designed for her, a dress like light, spring leaves, she began to realize what was happening.

"Nila, are you to be married soon?" she asked her niece.

"Yes, I am," Nila told her.

"But who? When?"

Nila ignored the first part of the question. "The day is not certain," she said honestly. "When he arrives."

Pora and her mother had to be satisfied with that.

The mysterious fever of activity, which had gripped the village at spring clean up time, was now channelled into production. Every shop concerned with food produced its limit and more. The tea mistress closed her shop because she had too much baking to do. Syl fished from long before dawn until long after sunset. There was a restless excitement in the air, a different feel to the breeze, a different sound to the birds, a sense of anticipation. Children played with glee.

Koalee gathered her family for an evening meal, including Hoyim and Ajist and the children, as well as Tokra. Nila was completely relaxed, putting everyone at ease. She was carrying dishes as if it was the most ordinary of times.

"How does she do it?" Ajist wondered. Belm, less reticent than the others, asked her.

Nila gave him a warm smile and said, "Destiny is destiny, Belm." There was no further explanation.

They had just finished the meal when there was a light tapping at the door and it opened to reveal Violet.

"You will all go to your homes now," the fairy ordered. "You will do nothing more, grasswoman, except to unlock your storeroom in the morning. Our people will tidy your house and take any food you have prepared to the banquets. Tienna and Rayan will help Nila dress."

Koalee had never heard Violet utter so many words before. Everyone at the table looked astonished.

"The marriage ceremony is tomorrow," Koalee said quietly.

Violet nodded, and gave them a look which told them without doubt that they were to obey her orders. Hoyim gathered up the twins, Ajist put Denza into the backpack, and they left silently with

Tokra. Violet closed the door and flew after them. Dyra and Koalee hugged Nila and bade goodnight to Belm and they all went straight to bed.

More than a hundred and forty guests spent the night in Dyra's village, but the Chief Councillor and his family were spared any knowledge of that. Elves met the travellers and guided them to homes where accommodations had been arranged. Many were taken to hammocks in the float spaces, as Buko had recommended. Food and hot drinks were handed out and the visitors went to sleep rested and content. It was all done so quietly not even Hoyim was aware, and he had trained himself to be alert to everything that happened in the village.

Early next morning a throng gathered on the shopkeepers' rafts. Grass people in their best finery were rolling up sleeping blankets and tucking them into trail runners, finding seats, arranging hair, and accepting steaming cups of seccar from attendant elves.

Rels had come, with a large contingent from the new village, and he helped his father build a bower in the moss near the meeting house. Fairies decorated it until it was fresh with vines and flowers. Hoyim, on his morning walk to gather the dew, wasn't sure whether he should believe what he was seeing. Most of the men of the village were setting out chairs and making benches on every raft and in every nook along the street. As soon as the seats were ready, they were being filled.

Hoyim hurried home to alert Ajist. They dressed the twins, put Denza into her new gown, and set off for the meeting house. Dyra and Koalee were coming down the Infirmary Trail, followed by Belm. Tokra met them and led them to benches directly in front of the bower. Rows and rows of chairs almost covered the short grass, and they were filling rapidly. Dyra's parents were there, along with Hoyim and his family. There were places for Creu and Hryn and their children. Koalee's parents and her brothers and sisters were all seated near her. Still, at least half of the chairs were vacant.

"What is happening? What celebration is this?" There were still a few villagers who didn't hear the elves and they raised curious voices.

Dyra was resplendent in a new coat that glowed like the sunset with embroidered flowers and leaves. Nobody mentioned it. Koalee was wearing the dress of soft golden yellow that Tienna had made for her, but no one mentioned that, either. All of the women took note of the pretty dresses the others were wearing, but no one was in a mood to chatter. Heads were turning, trying not to miss anything.

Buko appeared to take over the care of Shad and Lundi, and he sat down on the grass beside Ajist to entertain them. "Is he still travelling?" Dyra asked him, unable to contain his curiosity any longer. "He will be too tired..."

"He spent the night on Runya's trail boys' raft," Buko told him. "He was in the village, sleeping as soundly as the rest of you. You will see him soon."

The excitement was heightening. They could all feel it inside, as they would have felt the coming of a storm. The crowd had not been noisy, but now there was a breathless silence. They were all listening.

It sounded as if five thousand fairies were singing and the air was suddenly filled with the flash of wings. The song flooded the gathering—choruses bringing it to a crescendo on one side of the street, only to have it picked up by the voices on the other side—or down high sun—or up no sun. People kept turning, hoping to see where the music originated. Koalee leaned against Dyra, afraid she might swoon. Someone gave a surprised squeal of delight and they saw that it was Deeka.

Flon murmured, "Hush. It is so beautiful!"

Lenk and Yansa and their relatives were being seated behind the Chief Councillor's kin.

Dyra turned to smile in acknowledgment.

The singing grew louder and brighter until the grass people began to feel they might burst for joy, and suddenly there was a surge of activity in the street. A large group of young grassmen came swinging down from no sun. All of the young unmarried men from Dyra's village were there, as well as from Rels' and Runya's, and more that no one recognized.

Koalee found voice enough to say to Dyra, "And I was worried about how we would entertain them all."

Then the young girls came from high sun, tossing flowers to the guests, laughing and singing with the fairies. Fairies who had been hiding suddenly flew up from behind houses and trees and alighted in the street of shops, whirling in an airy dance. They began to dance among the young men and women and in a moment they were all dancing. Belm ran to join them. Then Flon and Tuje disappeared into the midst of the dancers. It was impossible to keep an eye on everyone.

The singing changed, from a lilty tune to one that was a little slower, and the dancers began to form into lines, following each other in graceful patterns. Spaces began to open among them. Suddenly, in the center of the great band of merrymakers, Radd stood facing Rayan. They bowed very slightly to each other. Elves began to form around Radd and fairies surrounded Rayan. Both Violet and Golden were there. Where had they come from? Had they just materialized?

Then Koalee gave a gasp and Dyra said, "Nila?" as if it were a question. The grandparents began to clap their hands with pride.

Could this beautiful creature really be Nila? Her hair was so bright it sparkled like strands of soft gold. There was a wreath of moss flowers around her brow. The petals of her gown were the pale grey of a shimmering mist, thickly embroidered with a design of flowers of the pink thorn tree. Her underskirt was gleaming white and a collar wide as her height and gossamer as cobwebs wrapped itself around her arms. Her shoes were a soft, quiet green that touched the street like a prayer exchanged with the earth. She wore finger rings and a bracelet that sparkled.

So much attention was focused upon Nila that it was a minute before people turned their attention to Radd. He was clad in his usual green and, as always, he was slim and golden and perfect, but there was another beside him who was taller and every bit as golden. The second figure wore violet and blue and he was definitely not an elf.

Dyra murmured, "Dokrimalitzla," and went forward, as Chief

Councillor, to welcome the visitor. Koalee went with him, and they were followed by Lenk and Yansa.

Radd held up his hand for silence. "I bring you Anodee, the son of Ilva, from the village of Mekr in the red valley. After fifty years, we have found Dokrimalitzla."

The people were all standing, unable to make a sound. Hoyim said to Ajist later, "I wanted so badly to cheer but my voice stuck in my throat. All I could do was wait for him to speak. I noticed the golden seal of office about his neck and the fact that he was wearing his belt, like any grassman, but it was like being in another world."

Anodee went to stand beside Nila and took her hand. "Thank you for my beautiful bride," he said. "Were it not for Dyra's village, this day could not have happened. Thank you for welcoming me and thank you to all my friends among the elves and fairies who have done so much to make this day possible. With their help, we have no fear for the Way of the grass people. I am young and I am inexperienced, but I have wise counsel. I promise you I will do my very best."

The cheers began then and dozens of people were crying. Dyra and Anodee exchanged the formal two-handed bow. Then Anodee embraced Nila's parents and accepted a formal welcome from Lenk and Yansa. Nila looked quite at ease.

Dyra noted that many of the people around Anodee resembled him and then it struck him that the new Dokrimalitzla was the seventh son of a seventh son. It was going to take a mastermind to keep track of so many new relatives. He beckoned to his own family to come forward and then he said to Anodee, "Please introduce your relatives first. You are the guests."

Grinning, Anodee began. Hoyim knew his father and mother would be relying on him to keep track of these new relatives and he wished he had a brain like Dashe, which could take in and record detail like a marker on paper. There were over fifty of Nanta's descendants in the party. Hoyim managed to focus on Anodee's parents and grandparents and he was sure he had each of his brothers and sisters on recall, but trying to keep track of their spouses and children was more difficult, as was the task of trying to remember all the aunts and uncles. Mekr had come. He was short and dark and looked very much the Chief Councillor. That made it easier. Hoyim was glad that two of Nanta's sons looked like Liba. Even so, he would request a printed lineage chart before this day ended.

He was aware of Ajist's father standing at his elbow.

"Have no fear, Hoyim," said Tokra. "I know the entire family connection well and I have it written down. You relax and enjoy the day!"

"Where have you been?" Hoyim asked. "We've been looking for you."

Tokra smiled. "I've been—behind the scenes," he said.

Dyra's clan was small by comparison, but he went through it methodically, explaining the relationships, and he felt that Anodee would not forget. Of course, if his memory failed, he had only to ask the elves.

When the endless introductions were over, complete with bows, handshakes and embraces, the people from Mekr's village were given the vacant chairs on the grass in front of the bower. This explained why the elves had left spaces in every row. Anodee's people were being seated at intervals through the group, where they could get to know Dyra's family. Shyness soon turned to familiarity as they waited together for the important event of the day.

Radd called for attention and announced, "You have come for a wedding but do not become impatient. There can be no wedding without someone to perform the ceremony. We are about to acknowledge that someone. For the first time in over fifty years, you are about to witness the creation of a new Dokrimalenter. Your dolenter, Tokra, has proven himself worthy of the title of Dokrimalenter. Only Dokrimalitzla can convey that title. Tokra?"

Tokra went forward and stood before Anodee. The latter went briefly over Tokra's life story, from his childhood in Nanta's village to the villages where he had served so faithfully as dolenter. He also spoke of Tokra's studies and of the books he had written. He went on to recite passages from the sacred book and to give prayers to Life. Then he said, "It is I who am honoured and it is with gratitude I convey the title of Dokrimalenter upon Tokra." He embraced Tokra and handed him the scroll of status.

The fairies were singing again, but their words were in the elfin language.

Anodee has authority, Dyra was thinking. He has command. And he is so young. What is it—sixteen? He doesn't look at all tough, really gentle. But it's as if he knows in advance just what to say and how. Whether he had been Dokrimalitzla or not, Anodee would have made his mark in the grassman's world. Tokra had said Nanta's eyes seemed to see far into the future. There was something more in Anodee's eyes; future, yes, but they were keenly aware of the present, too. His grandfather had been totally at home in nature, able to sense and predict the animal world with uncanny accuracy. Dyra realized that Anodee could do that with people.

Dyra also took note of Radd. He had never seen him look as he did today. Radd seemed eternally alone, as if he carried the entire future on his back. Today he looked as if he knew Anodee understood him and could share his burdens. There was a feeling of partnership there. It made Radd softer somehow, more like a grassman and Dyra liked that.

Nila had stood to one side of the bower, flanked by Rayan and Tienna, while Tokra's ceremony was going on. Now Anodee seemed to shed the weight of duty and become buoyant. He ran to Nila, took her hand, and called, "Now we have a grassman qualified to perform a wedding ceremony for Dokrimalitzla!"

"Oh, what a handsome couple," Pora murmured.

Indeed they were, and the entire assembly was proud. It was well that Nila had grown taller than her mother, because Anodee was as tall as Lenk, but they were both so fair and so well-formed.

Hoyim was thinking, Nila, of all people. My own sister up there, prepared to be married to Dokrimalitzla! He had never dreamt of the possibility. He turned to Ajist and whispered, "It's real, isn't it? It's really happening."

Ajist whispered back, "My father is Dokrimalenter. It was the goal of his life and he never expected to see it happen. We can believe this—all of it." She looked down at Denza and said, "Your very own

Aunty!"

Now everyone was quiet. Bumblers were tumbling among the flowers on the bower—naturally. Who would predict anything but good luck for this marriage? It was blessed. Still, it was particularly nice to see bees on the flowers at a wedding. They represented Life conferring best wishes.

Tokra's speech to the couple was filled with concepts of destiny and of the rewards that come to those who obey Life. He spoke of love and compassion, of sharing and of the burdens which were going to lie with this couple, faced with more responsibility than was usual for young couples. He spoke of his personal gratitude to Life and to the elves. Finally he turned to Dyra and asked the important question, "Is this a wedding in Truth?"

Dyra answered positively, in a clear voice.

Would Tokra also admonish the newlyweds to be faithful and to keep the Way of the grass people, as he would if this were an ordinary couple he was marrying? Yes, he would. Nila and Anodee were bound to the Way, as if there was nothing special about them at all. "When Life comes, cherish it." The ceremony was no different from the words Tokra had used when his daughter Ajist was married to Hoyim. Finally, the Dokrimalenter turned to the assembly, raised his arms and prayed, "Life, guard them and keep them safe. They have come willingly to do your bidding. These two young people have a value far beyond power. They are our hope for the future and our steady hold on tradition and the past. Life, bless Dokrimalitzla, and Nila his new wife."

The grass people were echoing, "Life bless... Life, bless." Almost everyone was crying. "One more little ceremony," Tokra announced, and Anodee stepped up to Hoyim and Ajist. "There is new Life," he said, and reached for Denza. "My new brother Hoyim and his wife Ajist are the parents of a very small grasswoman." Denza, wearing the soft dress Tienna had made for her, half-smiled. Anodee took her in his arms and walked toward the bower. He paused to look at her for a long moment and then said clearly, "It is with great joy I accept this child into Life. Her name, I am told, is Denza."

Now there was the long parade, as the relatives filed past to welcome Denza to Life and to congratulate Hoyim and Ajist. The strangers did not come, because Denza was so tiny and she would grow too tired.

Koalee put her arm around Dyra and laid her head on his shoulder. "It is too much, Dyra," she said. "Too much. What have we ever done in Life to deserve an honour like this?"

When Denza was back in her mother's arms, well-wishers crowded around Nila and Anodee and a time of merriment began. The mid-day banquet was spread on the grass and passed among the visitors who crowded the shop rafts. The music makers played to entertain the diners. Pettis sang. Nila and Anodee were pressed to sing a married song and, to everyone's amazement, they did so. When could they possibly have composed the song? Of course—the network.

Gifts were brought in. Anodee's people had brought trail runners of gifts for Nila and for Dyra's village. The fairies flew about pouring nectar, sometimes teasing a child, sometimes giving an old grassman a gentle pat on the head. There was so much happening it was impossible to follow.

When everyone had eaten well and seen the gifts, Rayan stood in the bower where the ceremonies had taken place and sang. Caught up in her magic, the fairy chorus began to sing again, and before long the young people had recommenced the dancing in the street.

Ajist was too tired to dance and Hoyim felt tired himself, so he wandered away from the crowd for a few minutes, down to the end of the street where the old mill used to stand. He gazed up at the last street lamp, looking so lonely now that the lampman's house was gone, and then he stepped off the trail to look at the cairn. There was the miller's wife.

"You too?" she asked, as if Hoyim would fully understand why she was there, looking over the inscription that told how she and Hoyim had met and befriended the tall man. "I was just thinking; I was the first one to make friends with the tall man. Now I have seen Dokrimalitzla. That is more than anyone can expect, really. Will I go from Life now, do you suppose?"

"We will all go from Life," Hoyim answered. "Don't be in a hurry about it."

Suddenly the miller's wife broke into one of her broad smiles. "I won't be. You can be sure of that!"

"It was all so beautiful," Hoyim remarked. "I feel a little sad about an occasion like this. I think about my uncles who would have loved to be here. And I was wondering how much the cornman managed to see. It would be a terrible thing, to lose your sight."

The miller's wife studied him for a moment. "You are too serious, Hoyim," she said. "You will come back to the gathering and enjoy yourself. Your baby has been accepted by Dokrimalitzla!"

"I have no right to feel morose. I know that. I should not fear happiness."

"You are in Life. That's all that matters."

Hoyim patted her plump arm and laughed. "You sound just like Lenk!" he said.

When he returned to the festivities, there was a lull in the dancing and his kin and Anodee's kin were taking advantage of it to get better acquainted with one another. Anodee and Nila were seated in the bower, with endless streams of well-wishers going to greet them.

Koalee sat basking in the beauty of the day as if nothing in Life would ever equal this.

She noticed that Balink's daughter Naj, now five, was standing near Belm, listening contentedly to the music makers, and she nudged Dyra.

"She is nine years younger than Belm," said Dyra.

"That is what I mean. It may be a long time before we have another wedding in this family."

"Koalee, you do insist on trying to out-guess Life."

"Nevertheless, if he decides one of these years that he wants to show Naj the workroom, be sure to let him. She may as well know what her future holds."

Rayan sang and Nila and Anodee held hands, feeling as if every nerve in their bodies was being played by the music makers. Rayan sang four songs and nothing else could be heard in the village, not even a bird. Even Shad and Lundi listened with rapt expressions, as if they accepted it as a treat meant only for them.

"I am afraid I may let go of responsibility," Dyra remarked. "I am a guest at my own daughter's wedding."

"Don't forget that it isn't because of us," Koalee said practically. "It's all because of Dokrimalitzla. Things may return to routine soon enough."

There was movement after Rayan's songs. People were inviting visitors to their homes, to rest and use the washing rooms. Chairs were being carried into the houses from which they had come. Elves were carrying warm water to the meeting house where they had set up a washing room for guests.

Dyra thought, not even elves can change the needs of grass people. What a nuisance we are. If only grass people could live like elves—no houses, no furnishings, no tools, no extra clothing, not even cooking pots. How tired the elves must be when they try to tolerate our burdens. But it's like the washing rooms. It is a fact we carry with us. We can't change and survive.

"We could simplify."

The voice startled Dyra because he knew he hadn't spoken his thoughts aloud. Anodee was standing beside him.

"Do you plan to teach us that?" Dyra asked. "Simplification?"

"I do not plan to teach at all. I will do as the elves bid me. Perhaps I will be able to live an example. We will wait and see."

Dyra said, "I am so pleased that you are in my family."

Anodee answered, "I am pleased, too."

As Anodee walked away Dyra wondered, now that the wedding was over, who would escort the new couple in their long journey to Karep?

※ ※ ※

The expedition set out on the second day after the wedding. Radd was there to arrange the order of the march. Without asking questions or prying into any trail runners, he was quietly assessing supplies and making sure everyone had a properly equipped belt. Trail guards were assigned places at regular intervals. "Keep alert," he reminded them. "We are here to teach grass people, not to do everything for you."

He was smiling. Dyra didn't remember ever seeing Radd really smile until the wedding day. "The weather is perfect," he remarked, when the elf came to speak to him. The day was bright and still, yet cool enough to be comfortable.

"One year ago there was a three-day wind that would have carried us off trail," the elf replied. "Do you remember? Then came such a rain you were afraid of a free-floater."

"So you chose this year?" Dyra ventured.

"Or perhaps the weather chose that year," was Radd's puzzling reply.

"I was only trying to find out whether you can change the timer."

"The timer is always set," said Radd. Then he stepped out of the line to speak to the gathering. "You are under protection of the elves as long as you are with Dokrimalitzla," he told them. "You will be safe as long as you remain with the progress, but do not relax your usual precaution. Grass people are to become more alert, not less so. Good trail!"

Radd led off, walking with Anodee's brother Hobay. Nila and Anodee followed, then Dyra and Hoyim. Koalee walked beside Nila, serving as trail guard, though they teased her about it and assured her that she could have trusted the elves. Behind were Anodee's brother Elsh and his sister Gleeda, Lenk and Chief Councillor Runya, then Rayan and her trail guards. Villagers were bidding a last goodbye to friends and relatives and the line was beginning to move. Already it held over eighty grass people.

"I feel younger," Dyra boasted. "I feel as if I weighed less than I did."

"You are turning into an elf," Koalee teased.

Dyra shook his head. "There's a curtain—a curtain that keeps a grassman from ever entering that world. But we can hear through it—and sometimes I think I may even learn to see through it."

"You don't want to be greedy."

"I don't think it's a matter of greed. I think it's a matter of how much the mind of a grassman can cope with in one lifetime."

"Anodee's mind can cope."

"Anodee was born Dokrimalitzla."

Koalee was quiet for a moment. "Life is in charge, as usual," she said. "We'll never be able to control the timer, but a thought just passed through my mind—will the day ever come when all of the grass people will be born Dokrimalitzla?"

Dyra stopped walking and stared at her. "Koalee, that is the most daring thing I have ever heard you say!" He looked proud and Koalee walked on with her head a little higher, waving her bow above her head as if it held a pennant.

HOYIM'S JOURNAL OF THE PROGRESS

DAY 1

WHEN WE REACHED the new village, most of the people rested, but Father and I went on a tour with Rels to see the newest buildings and find out if the shops were thriving. The pottery and metal work is quite unique.

In the evening, Mother and Rayan went to the target range with the trail boys to practice with their bows. Rayan looked as if she was amused by Mother, who is middle-aged and so small, marching along, bow in hand, but she was to have a surprise. No one has ever managed to best Mother on the shooting range and Rayan was no exception. She watched in astonishment as Mother split her wand as neatly as she might cleave a root.

There was no dancing and no concert. The villagers simply gathered around Anodee and asked questions.

"There are no plans," Anodee explained. "I take my lead from the elves. We will do this progress moment-by-moment and see what transpires."

"I asked, "What are we doing at this moment?"

Anodee's answer was immediate. He said, "Resting, there is no need to 'do' anything at this village."

He knows what he speaks of. He was casual, spending a while talking to each grassman and grasswoman in the village, just getting acquainted. He and Nila seem very popular. All who plan to accompany us up trail announced their intention. Rels' son plans to come and so do Bekra and Ryjra. It looks as if there will be eight. The village is still small. I know Rels himself is longing for the journey, but he has decided to put the village first.

Just before darkness fell, I went to the temporary shelter and ran up the stone steps Mother built when I was a baby. It was there I met John for the first time. The little shelter seems so tiny now. Rels followed me and assured me they will keep it in good condition. "The trail boys still use it when they are here," he said.

I reminded him that a grasshopper nearly broke my leg at that shelter, and we laughed. "We still don't have them under control," said Rels. "We will have to work on that!"

I asked him if he remembered it at the beginning, the day he caught up with Mother and Father, and he does. He said I could sit up, but I couldn't walk or talk, and Balink was my caretaker while Rels helped his Father and my parents to break trail. Tuje stayed with Balink, too. Rels said, "Yes, I remember it, Hoyim. I will never forget."

The incident left me with a horrible premonition that, should Brecort and his plan for the villages triumph, sentiment and tradition will be destroyed. A relic like the trail boys' shelter would be first to go. I sent up a prayer to Life: "Please support Anodee and wake the grass people to the Way," and I felt as if I had been heard.

There is a lack of haste to the progress and there are no small ones in the group, so we will have no undue worry. Nila and Anodee are guests of Rels for the night. Mother and Father will stay with Bekra, but it is a beautiful night and the elves are standing guard, so most of us will sleep in the float spaces.

DAY 3

We slept on soft moss at the base of trees and were wakened by the birds. The dew was saturating. We could bath in it and drink our fill. Everyone has dew bottles to the brim. Mother and Father danced to welcome the day and even the fairies enjoyed that. I am amazed at the delight my mother takes in the tall woods. I wish I had Ajist with me. I will bring her to the tall woods someday, when the children are older. Her spirit would be so at home here.

The sun had hardly begun to climb the sky when we abandoned

our leaf plates, soaked the fires well with dew, and set off rather informally for the first village high sun. We were sure news of our festivities would have reached there by now, but we were surprised. Or should I say *they* were. People came out to stand on their rafts, literally agape at the sight of so many grass people up trail. Fairies and elves! Like a migration.

The Chief Councillor stood on the stair to his raft and Nila and Anodee moved to the forefront. Father stepped up with them, as he would have to convey greetings as one Chief Councillor to another, before any other business could be conducted. I was beside Father, hoping the old Chief Councillor would remember me, and it was a joy to see instant recognition cross his face. "Welcome, my friend Hoyim, son of the Chief Councillor of the second village no sun," he said. "It is good to see you again."

I looked to Father to see what I should do and he nodded, so I made the two-handed bow and introduced Father. It was obvious the two of them would have liked to dispense with formal exchanges and talk to each other, but introductions were expected.

"I am Radd," a familiar voice said simply.

"I recognize the elf Radd," said the old Chief Councillor. "Are you responsible for bringing so many guests from your world?"

Radd told him he brought the most important guest to be hosted by a village in over fifty years, and the smile on the Chief Councillor's face showed he was not totally surprised.

"At last," he murmured. "It is not a false prophecy, then?"

"Anodee, son of Ilva, from the village of Mekr in the red valley. I introduce Dokrimalitzla and his bride Nila," said Radd triumphantly.

It looked for a minute as if the Chief Councillor was going to fall to his knees before Anodee, but instead he made the two-handed bow, called for his villagers to find food and lodging for the entourage, and ushered us into his house. Father and Mother followed Anodee and Nila. Belm and I came next. The Chief Councillor raised his hand to beckon to someone. "My councillors will join us," he said. "It is their place to be here."

"Then allow me," said Father. "One of my councillors is with us. I should like him to be present."

I ran to find Lenk.

By now we were a party of eleven, too many to crowd into the house, so the old man changed direction and beckoned us to follow to the meeting house instead. His villagers were watching the procession in awe. Seats in the meeting house were quickly arranged in a circle and we found places as a man and woman came around offering juice.

The Chief Councillor took a minute to consider what was happening. Then he asked, "Am I correct in assuming no word of this visit has penetrated to villages setting sun?"

Radd assured him he would have been the first to know, since it all began in the red valley.

"Hilt and Lydyl came through on their return from end of settlement. They said nothing."

"Nor will they."

The councillors were all properly introduced then, and everyone began to relax. The old Chief Councillor appraised Anodee carefully. "You are young," he said. "That is doubtless an asset."

"I will live long," Anodee replied.

"You will also appeal to the young."

One of the councillors was a ruddy-faced grassman, rotund and jovial. His hair jutted up over his brow rather in the manner of a fan. His voice matched his appearance, filled with humour. "Are we to be allowed in on the plans?" he asked. "Or do you have any?"

I think we all realized our thoughts had just been spoken aloud and there was general laughter.

"Not plans," Anodee told him. "A goal. We will encourage the grass people to return to the Way."

Lenk, with his customary naivety, asked Anodee if he thought he could talk them into that. Anodee said, "No, I don't think I can talk them into it. We are on the threshold of a new age. The grass people will begin to hear the elfin network again, as I do. I receive messages first and I will follow as the elves lead."

They were all concentrating on Anodee as if they didn't want to miss a hair on his head, a line in his jerkin. We were silent for a moment and then the old Chief Councillor nodded. "We forget the power of Dokrimalitzla," he admitted. "You look like a grassman—a fine specimen of grassman, but still a grassman. One does not expect magic, looking at you..."

My sister spoke up then. "It is not magic," she corrected him. "It is the network. We can be in touch with the elves and have wise counsel at hand, every moment."

"Because the elves can see more and see farther, they are more aware of consequences before action." It was my father speaking, and it sounded more like a question than a statement. Father is very willing to admit that he doesn't understand it all. He is learning.

Anodee nodded. "Most importantly, we can be in touch with the timer and we can be in touch with each other. We will gradually learn to follow again, so we go where we should go and do what we should do."

"It sounds simply like the Way in a well-run village," one of the councillors remarked.

"Aha!" said the Chief Councillor. "Have we not said the evil of Brecort is that he leads grass people from the Way. The big village—the changes..."

"The small villages work because they are small. The people know each other and care..." Father suddenly broke off.

Anodee smiled. "What the network does is put us in touch with each other and make us aware of what is good for each other. It will turn the entire grassman's world into a village."

It was as if the group released a collective breath.

"I have been a little afraid we might be in for a more rigid system," Father remarked. "Everyone in his place, like a colony of ants."

"The elves are too fond of variety," said Anodee.

"And the fairies are too fond of pranks!" said my mother.

"Our dolenter should be here," said the Chief Councillor, and the young woman who had brought the juice went to fetch him.

"The elves won't lead us from the Way?" asked one of the councillors. "We don't want to become the elves."

"The elves gave the grassmen the Way," Radd said firmly, "And no grassman can be an elf. Your methodical brain is too well-developed.

You indulge emotion. Believe me, no grassman can be an elf."

I was mulling over that when I realized Lenk was saying something about responsibility. "...for your family and the other villagers—responsibility for their safety and well-being," he said. "And that comes of growing up in the midst of Life—the dangers as well as the gifts."

"And that is what they do not learn in Karep," said the old Chief Councillor.

The dolenter arrived and was introduced. Anodee informed him immediately that a school for dokrimalenters was to be established at Mekr's village. If a dolenter was qualified and willing to spend two or three years..."

The dolenter nodded and the flash of his eye showed he welcomed the news. "Dolenters have lost all authority in Karep," he said. "And the attitude is spreading through the villages from setting sun."

"Perhaps better than rigid conformity," said my father. I knew he wouldn't be able to resist saying something like that. He still retains his resentment over the dolenter in his old village. I think Mother does a little now, too, but it took her years to admit it.

Anodee broke into a wide smile. Radd seized the moment and suggested the meeting break up. The Chief Councillor concurred. Then he asked, "Do I understand correctly that Rayan the singer is with you?"

We all nodded.

"A concert tonight!" he announced. "If Life favours us and Rayan is not too tired, perhaps she will be persuaded to sing."

"Some of your villagers will no doubt ask permission to accompany us in the progress," Radd told the Chief Councillor. "We try to keep down the numbers. About twenty would be acceptable, but they will have to be prepared to sleep on the ground. It will be safe trail. We have elfin guards—and Koalee."

No one had ever heard Radd attempt a joke before. It brought a wave of laughter.

DAY 4

Today we walked to the next village, it was dark as we approached it, so Radd lit a torch and handed it to Anodee. Then he stepped ahead of the procession and began to sprinkle the fairy dust he uses to light his path in darkness.

The fairy chorus sang, voices emerging here and there all over the village. Violet, looking her most mysterious and most exotic, fluttered down and led us up the street of shops. Villagers left their evening meals and dropped their tasks to crowd the rafts and gaze. Some began to clap. Others sang with the fairies, so our procession began to sing too, and a marvelous chorus greeted the evening.

I noticed at once that most of the villagers looked older. As the Chief Councillor at the last village told me, the young people are going to Karep. I wondered how a village could survive, that way. Who will wrap the houses? Where will the new small ones come from?

The Chief Councillor ran to meet us on the steps of the meeting house, brushing food from his coat as he ran. It was obvious he had been disturbed at his evening meal. His councillors joined him and Father and Lenk stepped forward for the formal greetings. It appeared there would be no speeches. An informal banquet on the grass was organized immediately and Anodee and Nila had a chance to get to know the villagers. There was no sense of pressure. Our young couple were congratulated and wished well. By the time darkness deepened, we had been escorted through the street of shops and been shown a spring of clear water of which the village was intensely proud. How we wished our village had such a spring! It gave rise to a river which flowed into the lake in the tall woods. That explains why the lake is constantly fresh. Hoyim's Lake goes down drastically in a dry season, but we have no spring-fed river leading into it. Life does not distribute favours equally, it seems.

"Is your village a safe place to live?" Bekra asked, and I knew she was hoping they would start talking about the plans for high walls and guard towers, but no one complained. They insisted it was very safe. Father mentioned that Gozer's village had been located on the other side of the tall woods, about the same distance away as this, and it was wiped out by the mower the year our village began. They replied that the mower had never come here.

Then Mother asked if they were well-provided by Life and they told us the tall woods provided every kind of berry. There were seeds aplenty, and lots of plants for building and for fabrics. They had the very best clay for pottery. They did have to trade for meal; there was no grain area.

"Aha!" Father muttered. "To be free of the mower, it looks as if you must go short of grain. It is a pattern, no doubt about it. Tall men who grow grain use mowers." He suggested that they plant their own grain. Six or seven hundred trees would give them a lot of meal.

Did they hold a lot of concerts and dances?

Not as often as they used to. The villagers were growing older. Many young people had left.

I took a deep breath and said, "It must be hard, keeping up with the work of the village, without strong young ones to do their part?"

"We miss them," one of the men answered. "But they earn more money in Karep and they send things home to us. It is satisfactory."

"No, it is not," said an outspoken woman who reminded me a little of Bekra. "I should have my own grandchildren in my own village, not growing up away off setting sun in a cave!"

Tuje broke into the conversation then, to ask if they had a place to swim or fish. "Only in the center of the tall woods, and that is two days' march up trail."

Father mentioned that it is the same distance to the lake in the tall woods from our village.

It is a long way.

Radd thought the serious conversation had gone on long enough. "We have a very famous singer in our party," he told the councillors quietly. "Perhaps your villagers would enjoy it if she sang for you?"

There was a joyful response and villagers began to erect lamps around the stair to the meeting house and set chairs on the short grass for older people. A fairy chorus seated itself on the steps and prepared to sing softly to provide Rayan's music. She sang until the stars were out. Nila and Anodee sat in the full light of the lamps, listening intently, and the beauty of the young couple was enough to make the onlookers forget they were real. Rayan seemed to be weaving a spell over the village, using the space between Dokrimalitzla and herself as a loom. I suddenly remembered that Rayan was a master of singing in code and I wondered what she was telling them. When would they find out about it? I doubted that any of them were able to understand a thing beyond her actual words at this time. Does the elfin network work over time-lapses, then? That must be it! I'll pass you a message now. You will recall it and decode it when the timer tells you to. I wonder if I dare ask Radd about that. No, Radd would give me an enigmatic answer if he deigned to answer at all. Perhaps, if I see Buko again… I'm determined to make some sense of this mind-to-mind network the elves use with so much ease. Radd can be so aggravating. He speaks as if he wants us to figure everything out for ourselves, but there are times when I feel he would be resentful if we knew what he knows, as if the elfin world must always be a big secret from grassmen, with or without Dokrimalitzla.

Hilt and Lydyl had anonymously arranged a room for Nila and Anodee, and rooms were offered to Father and Mother and also to Rayan, but the great majority of us slept in the float spaces. It rained in the night. Those of us who had cots or hammocks were all right, but others crowded into the meeting house and on to the trader's raft. Some got no sleep at all. Well, the elves promised us safety, not comfort.

DAY 5

We marched without fairy escort again this morning. We have to grow used to moving in and out of the elfin world. Nothing eventful, but we were growing so weary of nut meat and flatbread for trail lunches that Mother shot every grasshopper she saw on the way. We rolled them in leaves and roasted them in a firepit at noon time. It was a welcome feast.

While we were sitting in a circle eating the meal, I noticed Mother and Father watching Belm laughing with Nila and Anodee, and I saw them exchange a look of resignation. I think I know what they were feeling, because I felt it too. What will it be like when Nila goes to Mekr's village to live, as she surely will? I've never been away from my sister for any length of time. I'm afraid I'm really a lot like Mother. I don't appreciate change.

Later, I turned to Anodee, who was resting comfortably against a knoll. "The village we just left will soon need a lot of young people," I ventured.

"It will."

My mind felt very slow. I could sense that Anodee's mind was working like Radd's, encompassing many thoughts at one time, but I couldn't read what passed there.

"To live with Life, the important thing to remember is that grass people can occupy just so much space," said Anodee. "Grass animals and birds and insects have limits to their territory, too. Too many creatures, and Life will step in and put an end to them. Too many people in Karep isn't just a problem because they are forgetting the grassman's way; it is a problem because they are putting too much pressure on Life for food and materials. Brecort can solve that by bringing in more and more provisions just so long. There will be a limit."

I said, "If some of the people in Karep would return to the village we just passed..." He grinned. "My thoughts, too, Hoyim."

Nila joined us. "Stop thinking for a bit, Hoyim," she teased. "We have Dokrimalitzla. The network is alive. The grass people have guidance again. You can relax."

I said no more, but my curiosity was still unsatisfied. I'm not sure what I expected. That the pageantry and costumes would become brighter and more arresting? That people would be awed into following Anodee out of the cave? If everything is to be done mind-to-mind on a secret network, why are we all here?

Anodee picked up my last thought. He said, "We are the proof. When they see us, they know the grass people have Dokrimalitzla."

I asked him how it makes him feel, being Dokrimalitzla, and what he said really did surprise me. He said, "I am not Dokrimalitzla! I am Anodee, son of Ilva, I carry Dokrimalitzla, like a gift—a voice in my mind, an understanding in my heart. Sometimes I know messages are passing through to other grass people. Sometimes I don't realize it and only find out about them later. Or do I? Wouldn't it be interesting to learn that I have passed many messages to others and will never know what they were? Or why they were needed?"

I wasn't sure I should be asking so many questions, but my natural curiosity led me to another. I asked him if it was pleasant, passing the messages. He looked at me with that far-seeing expression in his eyes and added, "Or hearing them." Then he said, "No, it is not always pleasant, Hoyim, but there is so much more light. It is compensation for pain."

Nila reached out and laid her hand on his. I can see that she shares with him in a way that goes beyond anything I have known with Ajist. I could almost feel an understanding pass between them.

DAY 9

As the progress continues, the following gets larger. From what I knew of these villages, I thought they would be skeptical of any great throng heading for Karep, but the presence of Dokrimalitzla seems to wipe out their suspicions. Dozens of young people have joined us and the enthusiasm keeps growing.

Today we are at the sixth village. The Chief Councillor is a grasswoman named Hlor, a rather heavily built woman of my mother's age. She has an unusually large head, a friendly smile, and a manner that gives her easy authority. She has made a greater fuss over Nila than the other councillors have and presented her with a magnificent cover robe of dressed squirrel pelt. Then she rather startled the company by embracing Anodee and giving him a motherly kiss. Nila and Anodee took the attention gracefully, and then presented Hlor with a belt and carrying bag of the finest tooled leather. They were obviously the work of Romo, and it was the first time I realized their trail runners contained gifts for just such occasions.

DAY 15

It has been many days since I have written in my journal and I have lost a few pages to a sudden wind. I will have to content myself with writing more when we return to our village, after I have time to reflect on these events.

Nothing that has happened on the progress so far can compare to the surprise which awaited us at the eleventh village. We had started up the street of shops about time for the evening meal and a huge crowd moved down the street toward us. It took only a moment to realize that there were far too many grass people to belong to one village.

Father was walking in front of the progress with Radd, and I saw him look at the elf quizzically. Was this to be a friendly or an unfriendly reception? Then he recognized the two figures leading the oncoming procession. So did Mother and I. They were Kezel and Golden.

Anodee stepped into an open space and raised his arms as if to embrace them all. Cries of "Dokrimalitzla!" moved through the group and it sounded like a rising wind.

It took us all evening and most of today to meet and sort out these grass people. Most of them were burdened with backpacks and trail runners, looking as if they had loaded everything they could carry. Many had small ones riding on top of the loads or trotting along on their own tiny feet. There were babies in frontpacks, adding to the weight on their parent's shoulders.

"Suddenly I wanted to be home in my own village," a grasswoman said. "My parents are growing old. They will need us there."

"I was growing tired of stale air and the lack of sunlight. I just had to get back to the do-lan," said another.

Belm spent time making a count of the travellers and reported that he counted between six and seven hundred. That night, camps under the spreading trees seemed to stretch for hreds. More elves appeared, to stand guard, and Violet showed up suddenly. Overhearing Belm's count of the multitude, she told him, "As many have gone high sun and setting sun."

By the time Belm could ask, "What's going on here?" Violet had flown away.

I thought I could figure out what was happening. Most of these grass people looked poor.

They looked to me like the people who, like the woman from the water tap, lived in the dark dampness at the low end of the cave. But by what authority were they leaving Karep? Who would have given them permission to go? This didn't sound like something to which Brecort would agree. Were the elves getting them out? Taking them back to the sunlight and the grassman's Way? If I had truly believed in the plan, I would have been thrilled, but I just couldn't believe. It was all too unexpected and impossible.

Anodee and Nila were flitting among the newcomers tirelessly, as if they felt they had to meet every one of them, but Anodee paused for a moment beside me. "It's like getting a letter instructing you to move," he said. "Telling you where to go and when. I have been getting such instructions all my life."

"They actually hear it?"

"Sometimes. Sometimes they will just know. It will be their own idea. Suddenly to wake one morning and think, 'I am tired of it here. Today I leave Karep and return to my father's village.'"

With a smile, Anodee went on his way.

Bother! I thought. I should have asked him if they plan to clear everybody out of the big village.

I needn't have worried, because I heard Anodee thinking. Don't ask me that, Hoyim, he was saying. We don't have plans. It all depends on the elves and the timer and what happens when the thoughts and wishes of every grassman are weighed and considered. There are many, many factors...

But it's all so fast!

Yes, Hoyim. The network is fast.

My sister joined me then. "This episode was really Anodee's idea," she admitted. "You know that little game Tuje and Flon made up last cold season? With the little pieces you have to move around the table? Tuje played it with Anodee the other evening and Anodee checked with Radd and—well, you saw what happened."

"Move the grass people! Nila! That's coercion! That's as bad as what Brecort plans for us."

"No, it isn't," said Nila. "They will do as they wish, everyone is free to act and make their own decisions."

I could understand what she meant and, despite myself, I was laughing. "But what do they do now? Where do they go?"

Nila was gone. I heard her calling, "Trust the elves."

The next person I encountered was the tea mistress from the low town. She had told us why she was in Karep. She couldn't build her own house, wrap it for winter, get her own water and carry out her own wastes, and there was no one in Karep to adopt her, so she lived in the low town and earned her living serving tea. What had brought her to the eleventh village? She was born and raised in Karep. She knew nothing of the cold season and nothing of gathering food or watching for wheelers. I told her that, wanting to say, Go back where you will be safe!

"I got this letter," she said, reaching into her pocket and bringing out a piece of paper. "My sister remembered me. My sister left Karep many years ago to live in her husband's village. See, she writes that her neighbour has lost his wife and wants to adopt a widow who will share meal-making and caring for aches and pains in old age. There is no one in the village he wants to adopt, and she wants me to come and meet him. I am on my way."

I looked at the letter and saw with some surprise that it was from the second village this side of the tall woods. I told her, "There are many older grass people in that village. If this man doesn't adopt you, I have a feeling there will be no shortage. I am glad you are doing this."

She grinned and retrieved her letter. "So am I," she said. "It has been fun, running away."

"Running away?"

"Brecort and his council are on a tour of inspection of the salt works. We took advantage of that. It was easier to slip out when the guards wouldn't ask too many questions about where we were going or why we were taking so many possessions."

"The fairies are saying that close to two thousand people have left

Karep."

"And mostly from the low town. Just think how much money they will save on guards and waste disposal! They should have emptied out the low town long ago. I can't think why it took us so long to see it."

The day I met the tea mistress, I got the idea she was quite content in the low town, and I told her that.

"We are content with what we know," she answered, "Until something opens our eyes."

I asked what opened her eyes and she looked as if she wanted to tell me some very big secret but changed her mind. Perhaps she felt I wouldn't understand. All she said was, "My sister's letter, I guess. I don't know. Suddenly the world looked a lot cleaner and brighter to me and I wanted to be in it. Perhaps I can run a tea house in the village."

I asked her how many would go as far as her sister's village, but she didn't know, so I said, "If they drop away to stay in the villages between, I don't want you to go on unless you have enough people to guard trail. I mean that. If you're uncertain, I want you to wait in whatever village you are in until we come back, and we will take you safely to your sister." I thought for a minute she would cry.

"That is so good of you," she said. "You only met me once."

I said, "We are villagers. We are not citizens of Karep."

The day was coming to an exhausting close when I found myself face-to-face with Kezel. He said, "Forgive me. When you were in Karep... I had to pretend I didn't know you."

"I realize that," I said.

"I plan to stay with this group until they are all re-established or know where they are going. Then I will go setting sun for a while and build a raft in a tall tree. Maybe not quite as tall as I used to. I am a little out of practice."

"You don't plan to return to Karep?"

Kezel tossed his head in that carefree way he has and said, "Hoyim, I was in charge of permissions! If you were me, would you return to Karep? How would I explain why eighteen hundred people from the low town had to have their permissions cancelled, all on the same day?"

"But they ran away."

Kezel laughed. "I was responsible for knowing who lived there and who didn't, one way or another. No, my situation is not enviable now. Too bad. I did so enjoy the concert hall and so many of the comforts of Karep."

"You will survive."

"Of course."

"Have you any idea if these people are on a wild chase to nowhere or whether this intuition they follow can really bring them safely to places where they belong?"

"You have a printer's enquiring mind, Hoyim. Have faith in this. Don't doubt. Look at all the new partnerships that are being formed today."

We watched as they gathered in small groups and large, studying the map, comparing abilities. The first leader had mustered ninety men, women and families, and they set about listing and gathering supplies. Anodee discovered two more leaders and people were migrating toward them as if by some organized plan.

"What is wrong with no sun?" a voice asked.

"I wouldn't advise it," Father told them. "The best area rising sun is no sun of the high place, and we have already settled that. This side of the high place, the soil is poor and there is no shelter. Worse yet, you soon run into grain areas and that means the mower."

A few shook their heads and turned down the chance to open new territory. "I have grandparents in the red valley. I wanted to go there my whole life. Now I'm on my way." "I'm too old to build another house. I'm sure I'll find a village that needs a fuelman. I have been gathering fuel for the people who lived outside the cave. I like that."

One young man said, "I'm going back to Karep," and people looked at him aghast. "I'm a musician," he said. "I'm sure I could find a village that wants a musician, but then I saw that Rayan is going back to Karep, and I realized I'd never find a more exciting place to make music."

Father turned to me and murmured, "Perhaps there is a place for

Karep after all."

It was obvious, though, that, as far as the fairies were concerned, the do-lan was the best place to make music. As darkness fell and people planned where they might find a place to sleep, the fairies settled in the trees and their night song was soft and gentle as a lullaby.

DAY 17

People were more settled by the time we reached the high rise before the twelfth village. It was heavy pulling on the slope, and the rise also kept us from seeing the village until we were at the top.

Elsh and Hobay had taken the lead and I could tell, by the way they stopped to stare, that something was very unusual. When I saw what it was, I was speechless. Mother, who walked as a trail guard near Nila and Anodee, stepped up beside me, followed by Father.

Lenk had found the top of the rise. "I didn't believe it," he kept repeating.

"Have faith." Anodee reminded us.

"I suppose we have to ask permission to enter the gate," said Mother practically.

"I just wonder if there's only one gate," said Belm.

"Why didn't the people from Karep tell us about this?"

"They probably thought we knew. After all, he's been threatening to do it for long enough."

"They did tell us," said Nila. "Didn't you hear anybody say they slept outside the wall at the first village?"

The top of the rise was growing crowded and people behind us on the slope were calling to ask what was keeping us from moving on.

Bekra pushed her way to the front of the line and, as soon as she saw what had our attention, she turned, ready for battle and insisted, "Anodee, order them to take it down."

"They will do that on their own, Bekra," was the answer.

"This is preposterous!"

"All that, and then it isn't high enough to keep out a wildbeast,"

Father guessed.

"If a wildbeast got in," said Belm, scratching his head, "I'd want to be sure it got out again."

"I wonder if Brecort is able to admit he's made a mistake," asked Mother.

"Brecort has more than one lesson to learn," said Anodee.

"I hope we aren't going to run into that interfering Mev here," said Lenk.

Even as we stood pondering our discovery, the fairies rallied. They hastened to dress Nila and Anodee in arresting costumes, procured wreaths of moss flowers to drop on the grass people, and then, singing a rollicking chorus, they flew in a cloud of bright colours over the wall and threw open the gate. The progress marched in, the elves flanked Dokrimalitzla and his wife, and the villagers stopped what they were doing to stand mesmerized in the street. The guard on the tower rang the bell wildly and jubilantly, a signal that knew no code and had never been heard before. Small ones began to pour from a building that was no doubt the school. The Chief Councillor came bustling to find out what the disturbance was about.

"You appear inhospitable," said Anodee lightly, waving his arm toward the new wall, "but I know you are not."

Radd said, "If you are indeed grassmen, welcome Dokrimalitzla and his wife, Nila."

We were invited in and the welcome was lavish. Food and drink and offers of places to rest were proffered on every side. People began to dance in the street of shops. Rayan sang with the fairies. Anodee and Nila agreed to dance with the villagers and it was the merriest time they had had up trail.

"I signed the agreement," the Chief Councillor explained to Father. "The wall goes with it, you know. Brecort has promised fences and guard towers to all the villages."

Belm asked, "Did your own villagers build this?"

"No. Craftsmen came from Karep. They've finished and gone back now. At least I think they went back. A huge crowd of people passed on the trail two days ago, going rising sun. You must have met them. I thought I saw three of the masons leaving with them."

"If you don't like this, will you take it down?" Father asked.

The Chief Councillor looked puzzled. "Why wouldn't we like it?"

Father shrugged. "I just considered that it might make you feel as if you'd lost your freedom. Do you really feel safer?"

"I can't really say. We haven't had it finished long enough."

"I admit I don't like it," Father said, "But don't listen to me. Listen to your own intuition."

"Brecort's people don't seem to put much faith in intuition. They like to follow plans instead."

Sometimes I think my father is too gentle, but at other times he is quite forceful and I feel proud of him. He said, "Planning is the death of grassman culture," as if he knew he had the right answer. "At least it certainly is when it gets to the stage where people plan without consideration of all the surprises that can happen."

The Chief Councillor nodded toward Nila and Anodee. "This has been a most pleasant surprise," he said.

It was obvious to me that Father and the Chief Councillor had taken an instant liking to each other. They might not be in complete agreement, but they were going to get along well.

Father said, "Dokrimalitzla is bringing back the elfin network. It may not let you plan."

The Chief Councillor studied him quietly for a moment. "Something unusual is going on," he said. "All those people going rising sun, and now this. Are you saying none of you planned these journeys?"

"I am saying it is a little like being caught up by the wind. But it is a kindly wind. You find yourself going but you don't mind going at all. You will have to experience it to understand."

"Are the elves taking over, Dyra? Is there to be no place for chief councillors any more?"

"Of course there will be a place for councils."

"But if your villagers are listening to the elfin network and being wafted away by this 'wind' you speak of, how can you regulate the village? Will it be like dealing with the fluff from the golden wheels? You reach for it and it wafts away?"

"Village regulations remain the same," Father told him. "If a grassman doesn't like the way things are done in the village, he goes to another. The elves will simply improve his chances of finding the village where he truly belongs. Intuition."

Father turned to Belm and I and grinned. "I wonder," he said. "If Tuje and Flon had any idea what they were starting when they made up that table game of theirs."

DAY 20

The last lap to Karep, and the number of grass people in the progress has increased by ten or more. I led the way today, anxious and curious to see the big village again. It looked much the same as we approached. A few archers were practising on the shooting range. Trail runners were coming and going at the entrance to the tunnel. Below, the houses in the valley, perched on their high rafts, looked welcoming.

Radd encouraged the people to scatter, hunting for sheltered places where they could make camp before the size of our multitude became too obvious. He gathered our family and Anodee's relatives and led us to the house the cornman's son built. At the steps, he reached into his pocket and produced a paper.

"Hoyim recognizes this house," he announced. "It was the home of the cornman's son. When he returned to your village, he left a young doctor-in-training living here, but the young man now resides in the home of the master doctor in Karep. The cornman's son is giving the house as a gift to the new Dokrimalitzla and his bride, to be their home whenever they visit the big village."

In spite of his link with the network, Anodee had been kept ignorant of the plan, so he was as surprised as Nila, and they were both delighted.

"Our families will stay with us here tonight," Anodee said quickly. "We will be crowded, but that is good."

Mother announced her intention of going straight to bed and staying there until tomorrow, and Father elected to do the same. "I never did enjoy trail," he said wearily. They are always tired by the end of the day, but there is never a complaint out of either of them while we are on the march."

Before the rest of us had decided what to do next, Hilt and Lydyl approached from high sun, both wearing marksman's clothing including helmets. I didn't recognize them at first.

"We're being discreet," said Hilt. "We had our permissions cancelled, you remember." They asked Radd if it was true they would be going setting sun and were told they would.

"Be leisurely," Radd advised. "Make the appointments when you are told to make them. It will be a few days before Dokrimalitzla follows you. Be cautious. Brecort should be coming back from the salt works, and you need to avoid meeting him up trail."

"We'll be careful."

Anodee's family were keen to get inside the cave. Flon, Tuje and Belm were just as eager, and Lenk, surprisingly, elected to go with the young people. "Might as well see it while it's still there," he suggested.

"We must be inconspicuous tonight," Radd cautioned. "Not too many people, and go in small groups. Be quiet and orderly. No one is to know we are here tonight."

Rayan covered her head with a large-brimmed sunbonnet and slipped in with the others, managing to avoid the eyes of the guard. She had a large apartment cut in the rock on a high street, and she invited Bekra and Ryjra and the portrait painter to spend the night there. Then she asked me if I would like to join them for the evening meal and I was more than willing. I failed to get to the high streets on my first visit and I was eager to go.

The shops were closing and the lamps were lit. It was quieter than I remembered it. Rayan, looking very inconspicuous in her trail clothes, led us to the lifts. I remembered how I wanted to try out the lifts and hadn't been able to afford them. This time, I made sure to bring plenty of coins. There was a messenger boy waiting beside the lifts and Rayan dispatched him to buy a meal for five and bring it to her home. Then she took Bekra up to the high street and we three grassmen waited. When the lift came down again, we crowded into it just as the lift beside it descended and we saw two men run up and enter. I realized with a jolt that the tall, handsome one was Brecort. He was not in happy humour, so angry he seemed oblivious to the fact that strangers were riding in the lift beside his, quite capable of hearing everything he said through the bars of the cage.

"Where were the guards? Where was the gatekeeper?" he demanded.

"The gatekeeper went with them, Chief Councillor," said his companion.

"Then where was Kezel? The minute we're up there, you go back down and bring me Kezel."

"I'm afraid Kezel went with them too."

I thought Brecort might explode, but I tried not to look. This was too good an opportunity to miss by appearing interested.

"A lot of those people had no work," the second man suggested. "They were just mouths to feed."

"We did not have eighteen hundred people out of work in Karep. There were men to train as guards for the federation. They provided workmen for the building projects—new roads. We need these people. Where did they go and how are we to get them back? Send after them."

"Send who? Half of the guards in training were from the low town."

Brecort said something that sounded obscene.

"The master doctor said..."

"What has he got to do with it?"

The lifts were coming to a stop. Rayan had told us to get out at the second stop, so we opened the door and emerged. Brecort was apparently travelling higher, so I could hear no more of the fascinating conversation.

The portrait painter had been silently enjoying the lights spread below on the floor of the cave, but Ryjra had been listening. He grinned at me, and then took time to point out the street where he and Bekra had owned their shop.

Bekra was standing in Rayan's doorway to beckon to us, in case we missed our directions. The apartment was impressive: a kitchen, washing room, two sleeping rooms, and a fairly large gathering room with soft chairs. There were windows facing the street and a large skylight in the roof. When the meal came, Rayan spread it on low tables and poured delicious tea for us to drink. "Are you above suspicion, Rayan?" the portrait painter asked, when Ryjra and I had reported what we heard in the lift.

"I think so," she said. "The story was well-circulated that I went to my home village high sun to pass the cold season. I even informed Brecort personally. And I wasn't seen coming in tonight. I will hide here until Radd says it is time to announce my return. Brecort enjoys a concert. He will be glad I'm back."

Someone knocked at the door and I saw that Rayan and Bekra had an understanding. Rayan slipped into another room and then Bekra opened the door. We heard her tell a half-truth. "She may be here tomorrow," Bekra said. "I am here to clean her house and get it ready for her."

When the caller had departed, it struck me that the messenger boy who brought the food had called Rayan by name.

"Totally trustworthy," said Rayan, when I mentioned it. "He carries many messages for me. It was not an accident that he was waiting by the lifts tonight."

I was thinking, "Here I am in Rayan's apartment!" This amazing woman who took my breath the first time I saw her, she came to my own village for no purpose but to help Nila prepare for her new position, is no longer a distant star beyond our reach. She is a friend, someone we know, someone who has actually competed on the archery range against my mother. I have seen Rayan walking in cover clothes, pulling her own trail runner. I've seen her curled up asleep on the ground under a float space. Yet, in spite of the familiarity, she retains that essential grace that seems to be inbred. I wonder if there is a grassman anywhere... I wonder if Rayan ever married. What brought her to Karep? How long has she been involved in the plan to save the Way of the grass people? So many questions, and I can't ask any of them. Sitting there in her own home, watching her, it came to me that I knew of no one I would consider Rayan's equal except Radd, and I wondered if she was part fairy, after all.

DAY 21

Father and Mother were rested this morning and eager to see Karep. We left Nila and Anodee to spend some time alone and walked the short distance to the gate. Mother's eyes were round as she tried to see everything at once. The first thing we did was go to the sleeping place where Lenk and Flon and Tuje had all spent the night.

"Better than the ground," was Lenk's comment, "But the ground is sure cheaper."

Belm went off with Elsh and Gleeda to find the lake, but the rest of us made a circuit of the cave. When we came to the entrance to the low town, we found two men discussing the fact that several hundred houses were standing vacant in there.

"They should be torn down," one of the men said.

"A lot of the hollow wood will be good," said the other. "And steps and windows. Yes, they should be taken down."

Lenk's interest was piqued at once. "Is there any law that says you can't tear down a house?" he asked.

"Not if it's your own house, but these aren't our houses."

I asked, "Do you need permission to build a house in the valley?"

I wasn't surprised when he answered, "People do it all the time, but council keeps threatening to regulate the village."

Father said, "It seems to me the ideal thing is to take whatever is salvageable from these houses and get it out to the valley, where it can be put to use."

Lenk stepped into the shadowy depths of the low town to take a closer look, and Flon and Tuje followed.

I was standing there with Father and Hobay, all of us wondering if there was anything sensible to be done, when three grassmen walked up, obviously engaged in argument. I recognized one of them as a councillor who had been with Brecort the day we met them coming out of the hall of government.

"It's a waste," said one.

"It is stupid!"

"We'll never fill them again."

"Why not?"

"For one thing, the doctor is against it and the doctor does have some authority."

"By what right?"

"By right of threatening to close the infirmary if our actions endanger the grassmen. He's done that before, when he wanted his own way. The infirmary is one of the most valuable things in Karep. We can't risk offending the doctor."

Mother gave me a wide grin when she heard that remark.

"Ahem," said Father hesitantly. "As Chief Councillor of a village, I couldn't help but noticing your remark about waste. No one wants waste."

"What village?" one of the men asked shortly.

"It is Dyra's village on Hoyim's Lake, no sun of the tall woods. I am Chief Councillor Dyra."

"Haven't heard of it."

"No. It is half a moon's march."

"If you have a suggestion for how we can salvage five hundred wasted houses, I wish you would tell me."

"I can only suggest what I would do," said Father. "I would put workmen to the job of taking them down, carefully, and then I would take all the good wood to the valley and raft it. After that, people can start putting up houses on rafts. Your doctor could only approve of houses in the open air."

"We have no one to live in them. They are still wasted."

"Has everyone moved out of this part of the city?"

"There are a few left."

"I'd start with them. Get them to build in the valley and put all the wood you can salvage into storage. If people want to build, it will be there. If not, it would make excellent fuel."

"The grassman makes sense," said one of the men.

"My husband has long experience as a Chief Councillor," said Mother.

"We haven't enough builders to take down so many houses," one man grumbled.

"My best builder is with me," Father told them, "And so is his son. This is Hobay from the village of Mekr. They are all masters at training grassmen to build, and I am sure they would appreciate a little work." He stepped into the shadows and called to Lenk and Tuje and they were introduced.

"Do you want a job to do?" the councillor asked. "The doctor has ordered the low town closed. We have been discussing the possibility of dismantling the houses and rafting the best wood in the valley for future use."

Lenk looked happy enough to dance. "Get us a crew," he ordered. "They don't have to be builders. I can teach a man how to take down hollow wood fast enough. Come, Tuje. Let's not stop with the roof half on! I mean off!"

Flon had emerged with a look of disgust on her face, her initial impression of the low town, but she wheeled about and followed Lenk and Tuje, with the three men of Karep at her heels.

Father remarked, "I hope they don't think to ask if Lenk and Tuje have permission to work here."

Hobay said, "Permission or not, this is my chance to work with Lenk the builder and I'm on my way."

The grass people, who had come on the progress were making themselves unobtrusive as possible, camping at scattered locations in the valley. A few had friends or relatives where they could stay. Others had paid to live part of the time in Karep.

"We need all able-bodied grassmen," Radd told them. "If you are a builder, get to the low town and help Lenk demolish houses. Otherwise, follow me to the valley. I will show you the locations and you will start building rafts. We need large rafts, because we will be storing a lot of wood."

It was rumoured that Brecort was not happy with the idea of more people building in the valley. That he didn't see how he could control the coming and going of people who lived outside the cave, and he was also worried about pressure for guards and waste collection, both obvious needs, which he had successfully ignored for a long time.

Ryjra knew a lot of people in Karep, and he was able to glean bits of information about what went on in council. Someone had dared to suggest that the village in the valley form their own council and be independent. Brecort had answered carelessly, "Only as part of the federation." It appeared he was losing his perspective. Things were moving too fast for him, outside of his plan. I wasn't surprised to hear a woman tell Ryjra, "He's experiencing nightmares again."

I didn't have to ask how she knew. As soon as she had gone on her way, Ryjra explained. "That's his housekeeper. She's not adopted. She's just paid."

I said, "She is elderly. Has she no one to help her?"

"In this village? Probably not. She's blind in one eye, too."

Every time I see something I like about Karep; I see something else to make me angry. Karep is not right for grass people. Not right at all.

DAY 23

Lenk has had no shortage of workmen. Every man left in the low town suddenly wants to dismantle his house and move to the valley. Men who had no employment are eager to be on our list. For the past two days, you can scarcely enter or leave the city gate without running into loads of lumber headed for the valley. There are trail runners piled with windows and doors. Men hurry past carrying entire flights of stairs on their backs.

Father asked Lenk if he intends to finish the entire job, but Lenk says he'll work until Radd says 'Enough.' He said, "They know what they are doing now. They can finish the job very well themselves. There are very good builders in this village, but they weren't anxious to do the job at first. I think it's because it was their village. It was upsetting, seeing it being demolished so fast. It took outsiders to get them started."

This morning the news came that the pipes taking water to the low town were to be taken out and the water cut off completely. Not long after that, we received the greatest surprise of all.

Masons arrived to study the entrance to the low town. When the most valuable wood has been salvaged, the opening is to be sealed.

The cave will be smaller by a quarter, but it is a quarter not fit for habitation, and the people seem happy at the prospect. A large stone granary for storing meal is to be built where the opening has been. I was shocked to see Mev standing forlornly at the entrance, looking like a grassman whose last dream had been dashed to pieces. Recognizing me, he glowered as if I was responsible for all the destruction. Then he walked away without a word. I asked Radd about the plans for Mev, feeling almost sorry for Brecort's messenger.

Radd listened for a minute. "He hasn't found himself yet," was his answer. "There is a possibility he will be teaching school in a village away out setting sun. We won't hear much from him again."

DAY 24

We smuggled Rayan out of Karep this morning and kept her at Nila's house until her trail runners were ready and her trail guards assembled. Then she returned to the gate with enough pomp to assure that Karep would know she was back. None of us were seen with her, of course. When we were satisfied that she was properly reinstated, we gathered at Nila's for a noon meal.

"What has come over Brecort?" Belm asked curiously. "He's doing exactly what Radd would want him to do. Walling off the low town. Letting people leave the city without permission. Allowing rafts to be built in the valley..."

"He knows he has lost," said Anodee, smiling. "He thinks now he has had a wonderful new idea of transferring the low town to the valley and making an outdoor area for Karep. It's all you have to do, you know. Just drop suggestions. They will take root like seeds."

I said, "That's too easy. Something is going to go wrong."

"No," he said. "The elves are helping now."

"If you are quiet," said Radd, "This elf will let you hear what is going on in council. You may as well know the Truth."

We heard a councillor's voice first, clearly. "They say he's been seen in all the villages rising sun. Where he is no one knows. They say fairies and elves are travelling with him and guarding him."

Brecort gave a forced laugh. "You know how much credibility you can give to stories of fairies and elves. There is work to do today. Get everyone to the conference table and forget these ridiculous tales."

We heard the sounds of people seating themselves at a table and they were the sounds of serious people, but Brecort had not heard the last of the story.

"All those people from the low town? Their friends are saying they went to meet Dokrimalitzla. They say fairies came and told them to go."

Brecort made an impatient sound.

"And Kezel went with them," said one of the councillors sarcastically.

"Exactly. I warned you Kezel had a lot of interest in the elves."

"If I hear one more word about elves...!" Brecort snapped.

"If I may speak?" asked a councillor, and was approved. "A large group of grass people are visiting Karep at the moment. Some from beyond the tall woods. They are camped at the picnic place beyond the target range, but they have been coming to visit the village. Some have spent a night or two here. Some builders among them are helping with the new plans—to build rafts in the valley. I thought perhaps, with persuasion, we might increase our population again. A little bit, at least."

"Excellent idea!" said Brecort. "But be sure no permission is granted to a grassman unless he has a trade. We want no more indigents hiding in back corners refusing to work."

"Ahem," said the councillor. "We have no one in charge of granting permissions."

After a moment we heard Brecort say, "Truyp, you were in charge of supervising the low town. You will have few responsibilities now. I appoint you to control permissions."

I was amazed at what was being transmitted over the network. Not only did I hear what was being said, though it came to me softly, like my own ideas going through my mind, I was also aware of reactions and expressions. I could feel that Truyp was less than pleased over his new assignment, but he said nothing. The man who had brought up the subject of Dokrimalitzla spoke up again.

"That crowd of grass people beyond the target range? It is said they travelled here with Dokrimalitzla."

"I am losing patience!" said Brecort. "Not one more word about the imaginary Dokrimaltizla."

"But if he exists..." persisted the councillor. "It means he has authority over councils. It is in the sacred book. Authority over councils and dolenters."

"Old-fashioned ideas," someone commented. "We will just have to change the sacred book." There was some laughter.

"We have a lot of business today," Brecort announced, putting an end to the discussion. "The expansion of the village in the valley. With so many people moving out of the cave we are going to have to take responsibility for the village. We will declare it officially part of Karep. All agree? Newcomers will need permission to live there. We will have to do something about waste disposal and guards. They clamour for streetlamps too, and there should be a guard tower and a warning bell. In exchange, they will be required to pay drot."

No one argued, but a man added, "I think we should be arranging for two or three villages at a distance from each other, each responsible for its own services. Then claim the ones closest to the cave and charge them for walls and guard towers!."

It sounded to me as if the remaining councillors agreed completely with Brecort's plans and the rest of the meeting would be rather dull, but Radd kept us tuned in and we kept listening. As the meeting was coming to an end, we felt Radd flash a thought to one of the councillors.

"By the way," the councillor announced, "I understand Rayan is back. She will be rested and ready to give a concert tomorrow night."

We could almost feel Brecort smile, though we couldn't see him.

"Ah," said Anodee. "It is time."

DAY 25

As soon as we entered Karep tonight for the concert, I experienced some of the magic I felt when I first went there with Dashe and Torall. The cave at night has a fascinating mystery. The lights reflect from every shiny surface and sounds seem to echo in a less shattering way. People seem relaxed. There is more laughter than you hear during the day. Hundreds of grass people were moving toward the concert hall. To be sure, not everyone has left Karep.

The group from our village were standing near the doorway of the concert hall when Rayan appeared. She smiled but didn't stop. People were practically bowing to her as she passed. She hasn't been seen in Karep for many months and her appearance is obviously a joy and a relief. It struck me that Brecort may be the organizing brain that keeps Karep functioning, but Rayan is its soul. There is so much beauty in this woman: her mind, her manner, her talent. I still can't recover from the realization that I actually know her.

We sat close to the center of the hall and Father and Mother and Lenk began to gape at the carvings in the rock walls, wanting to know why they carve leaves and flowers when they could have been living among them. It is senseless and strange. We strained to see if everyone from the progress was managing to get into the hall and were able to pick out some faces we recognized. I noticed that the expensive seats at the front were being filled.

"Who announces the dancers and singers?" Father was asking, and I told him what I know. I never saw my mother staring so openly. She quite lost her composure. "They will think you are from the villages," I teased her.

"And proud of it!" she retorted. She has not lost her sense of perspective.

"Will Rayan sing the whole concert?" Gleeda asked.

I had been to one concert in that hall and I was to be the expert. All I could tell her was that, when I was here, they had readers and various singers.

Restless excitement was passing, smile to smile. Rayan was somewhere behind the stage now, with whatever other entertainers were to take part in the concert. We could sense a slight stir back there, but we couldn't hear or see anything. The man who 'owned' the concert hall strode down the outside row of seats with a grin on his face and gave a sign to a workman to light the stage lamps. Some of the lamps on the wall brackets were being extinguished.

Belm mumbled something about the lights at the back being bright and turned his head to look. He said "Oh!!!" The sound came out in a gasp and a few others who had turned their heads gasped with him. At the sound everyone began to turn, and astonishment seized the whole audience.

A host of fairies were flying above us, filling the vault over our heads, singing as they so often sang in the trees surrounding a village. The hall filled with their thrilling voices. Then elves were marching in, singing, all wearing bright leafy green.

I experienced the most overwhelming moment of my life and I knew that everyone from our village felt it too. It came of knowing exactly what was going to happen next, without having been told, yet in spite of knowing, it was a kind of suspense. We weren't quite sure. It was too fantastic to be true. How could we believe?

Then they were there. In the midst of the elves walked Dokrimalitzla and his bride. We thought we had seen those two looking splendid at their wedding and at some of the villages up trail, but never had we seen them like this. They were both in shining white with golden circlets about their heads. They wore golden shoes, necklaces of twinkling gems, and golden bracelets. Cloaks of rich forest green trailed behind them as they came.

Violet flew over their heads, carrying a bouquet of bluebells and lily of the valley, and scattering fairy dust. Her troop were emerging from the dimness of the mid-section of the hall to the brighter lights of the stage. Everyone was focused on Anodee and Nila as they approached the stage. Radd stepped out, side-by-side with Rayan, and they smiled at the audience and stood waiting to greet the procession. Violet touched down and stood close to Radd, and the moment Nila reached the stage, she was presented with the bouquet of bluebells and white lilies. Violet had been trying not to sneeze, but suddenly it came out of her like an explosion. Father muttered something about Violet reacting to bluebells. That sneeze made everything real. I wasn't having a dream. It was all happening. How could my sister stand there so calmly and gracefully, as if she had been doing something like this every day of her life?

Radd was saying, "We present to you Anodee the son of Ilva from the village of Mekr in the red valley, historically the village of his grandfather, Nanta. We have found Dokrimalitzla."

Rayan led the applause and it was well she did, for the people of Karep were stunned into silence.

Radd continued, "The bride of Dokrimalitzla—Nila, daughter of Dyra of the village of Dyra. Life for Dokrimalitzla and his own!"

A dam seemed to break. People were actually fainting. There was a wild blend of cries and sighs, laughter and sobbing. "The elves are with us! Oh, thank Life!"

Brecort stood as if he meant to march out of the concert hall. What was this? Some elaborate joke aimed at him because he didn't believe in fairies? Then the look on his face changed and he said, "But they fly..." He fell back into his seat just as Nila and Anodee were led to chairs on the stage and sat down, holding hands.

Then Rayan sang, her glorious voice reflecting from the highest reaches of the vault, and the fairy chorus sang with her, providing a background of sound beyond anything the music makers could have imagined. I am sure no one in that hall had ever heard such music. When Rayan paused to rest, the whole audience stood and cheered. Golden stepped out of the chorus to give Rayan a wreath of pink flowers, and Rayan bowed as only Rayan could bow, with dignity and charm. Mother was audible in her delight over it all and Father had tears in his eyes. Tuje and Flon had been swaying to the music and they patted each other's hands like small ones who were unable to contain their joy. Elsh leaned over my shoulder and said, "Sometimes I play the quidda. I wonder if I will ever dare to play it again!"

The fairies were flying around the hall again, sprinkling the luminescent dust Radd used to light his path in darkness.

"Drop the shields from your minds," Radd was saying quietly, and everyone sat in silence to listen to him. "Open your eyes and take the covers from your ears. It is fine to see. It is good to hear. It is your duty to listen. Dokrimalitzla has come to give guidance to councils and to dolenters. You will trust that guidance. Harmony is yours."

He bowed to Rayan and she came forward to sing again. We expected another fairy chorus, perhaps some song of Karep that would give full range to her voice, but instead she sang a village song, *Do-lan n' frlomlen* (grass woods are greening; life is renewed). The grass people from the small villages have sung that song countless times. As Rayan's voice swept through the first lilting verse, people were tempted to sing with her. But the chance to listen to Rayan was too precious. Even the fairies were silent. There was only her voice, taking us out of Karep, returning us to the grass woods where we belong.

Then, without warning, a second voice joined hers. It was a rich, man's voice and it blended with Rayan's as if they were two parts of a whole. Everyone strained to see who it was, and then Rayan, smiling like the rising sun, held out her hand and invited whoever was singing to come to the stage and join her. It was Brecort! He literally ran up the steps to the stage, put his arm about Rayan's waist and went on singing.

"They are turning it into a married song!" Mother whispered.

"The resistance is falling," said Father.

"The elves are truly back," Mother murmured.

Indeed they were, figuratively and in reality. Dozens of fairies and elves were on the stage, forming background music for Rayan and Brecort, and now they signalled to the audience to sing along. The hall rang to the old village song.

Nila and Anodee were singing too, but I noticed that Anodee was watching the audience carefully, his eyes taking in everything, concentrating for a second here, an instant there. Nila turned to nod to him as if he had spoken to her, but he hadn't spoken out loud.

Then Rayan was singing again, and we fell silent.

PART 5

THE BOOK OF NANTA

AS WRITTEN BY TOKRA, THE DOLENTER

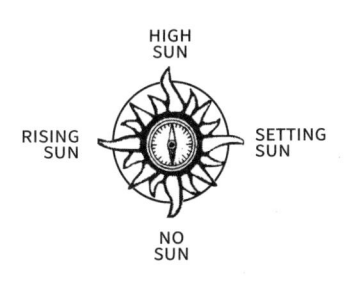

```
        HIGH
         SUN

RISING         SETTING
 SUN            SUN

          NO
         SUN
```

I

MY FATHER TOLD ME most of what I know about the early years of Nanta. He seemed to know more than my mother, who was backpacked to Nanta's village as a child of a year and raised there.

In Nanta's village little was said about the villages left behind. Nanta was bitter, I was told, and yet I find it hard to visualize Nanta as bitter. I remember him as a laughing, singing man. His voice was rich as a gathering of birds in a tall tree, and his laughter set the leaves to shaking. He was my boyhood hero, as he was the hero of every child in his village and for several villages up trail. It was known that he disliked influences from the older villages, and when a newcomer said anything about "how we did it at home", Nanta was likely to cut him short with a brisk, "You are in this village now," and if that was bitterness, I suppose he had it.

Nanta was born and raised in the seventh village no sun of the green lake where the red valley begins. He was orphaned at a young age; his father was killed by a mad beast, and his mother died in the cold season of a fever. His father had been a strong, brave man, whose chief occupation was collecting honey. Nanta and his two younger sisters were adopted into the family of their uncle, a hunter. Nanta left school early because there was a shortage of food, and his uncle needed help. He never did apprentice and knew nothing of crafts, but his skill with a bow was legendary. When he had been Chief Councillor of his own village for more than a generation, he was still referred to as "Nanta the hunter."

Nanta spent most of his time in the grass woods on the low

slopes of the red valley. They say he knew every bird that nested there, every animal hole, and every tree. It was as if he had been born a creature of nature and not a grassman at all. His breathing seemed to match the breeze in the leaves and his eyes were quick as a wild thing. He was fearless, yet had a hunter's caution, moving silently and reacting with lightning reflexes. When he bent the bow he struck true, and the table was always laden. Even as a young boy Nanta made money on market day.

When I knew Nanta there was grey in his hair and a beard on his face, but I have been told that when he was a boy, his features were handsome and his hair was golden in the sunlight. I think of him as very tall, but perhaps that is because I was a small boy. Nanta did stand nearly ten hands, though, much taller than the average grassman. Unless he was stalking prey, he was restless. He was happiest in the grass woods, and hated sitting at table through a long meal, and avoided lengthy polite conversations. After meetings and concerts, he always left alone rather than staying for discussion with the village young people. He preferred his own thoughts, and it was rumoured that he could talk to the elves in his mind. Since few grassmen could do this, the idea was passed off as a mere story. He loved Truth and had the look of purity and innocence about him that is seen in those of clear conscience.

Nanta was barely sixteen when the trouble came. It concerned Liba. She was fourteen, dark haired and beautiful, and her father was one of the village councillors. He stood up in public meeting and announced that Liba was promised to the chimney maker's son. But she was Nanta's intended. As a boy he had offered her the gift of Life and she had accepted. It was recorded on the Truth. Nanta was waiting only until he could afford a house before speaking for her. He was so stunned by the news that he nearly collapsed, but thought it over quickly, and went to the chimney maker's wife. She was his father's cousin and had been kind to Nanta.

"I knew it was not the Truth," she said. "I told my husband, but our son is so persistent that my husband fears for him. Our son is not behaving according to tradition and has confused everyone. I believe even Liba is confused. I will talk to her, Nanta, and see if she is facing the Truth."

Whether the chimney maker's wife spoke to Liba, Nanta didn't know, but when the meeting ended Liba approached him herself.

"My father acted in haste," she said. "I told him I was uncertain. Why didn't you speak for me, Nanta?"

"I have now. I have spoken to his mother and I will speak to his father and to your father. This is one promise which will be undone."

Nanta was confident that the promise would be undone once the mistake was clear. Surely if Liba's father loved the Truth as he did, he would hasten to make it right. But Liba's father seemed shut out from awareness and didn't absorb what Nanta said.

"I have given my word," he told him, "and my daughter has not denied it in a public meeting. A grassman and his daughter cannot go back on their word."

Nanta left in a rage and spent a sleepless night. The Truth was the rock on which he built his life. What could he do now? Where could he turn? He prayed to Life and tossed in his bed, then finally went out to pace about the raft. The night was dark, lit only by a sliver of moon and a few stars. When he heard someone whisper his name, he couldn't see who it was.

"Nanta, it's your cousin. Come down to the float space quietly." The chimney maker's wife was trembling. "My son's mind is unbalanced," she said. "When he learned that you spoke to Liba's father, he threatened to kill you. He will, Nanta. He means it. Please go away. Don't make my son a murderer. I love you both."

"No grassman will kill another grassman. It's impossible."

"No it isn't. He is not himself, Nanta. He has behaved strangely for a long time. You must save yourself. Please go."

"If I go, she comes with me," he said.

"Yes, I know. Keep her safe, Nanta. Keep both of you safe."

Nanta didn't hesitate. He put some food and clothing into his backpack, stuffing in his money and the sacred book. He equipped his belt with two dew flasks and his two best knives, roped a roll of blanket to his shoulders, took his bow in his hand, and stole silently out of the hunter's house. He knew the room where Liba slept—but her sisters slept there too, so he stood in the darkness below the raft and made the call of a night bird. They had often used this signal as children, and he prayed that she would recognize it. When there was no response, he tossed a light pebble against the window and gave the call again. In a moment the window opened and Nanta stepped into the best lit spot, putting his finger to his lips. Liba waited for him to climb the stair and come around to the window.

"We have to leave the village," he whispered. "He wants to kill me."

"Go together? We aren't married."

"There is a dolenter setting sun."

Liba looked at him for a minute. Then she passed half a dozen items of clothing out through the window, followed by a backpack and her shoes. While Nanta put the clothing into the pack, Liba slipped through the window. She came like that, with her belt over her sleeping gown, taking time only to put on her shoes and reach back through the window to snatch a blanket. As she closed the window, she heard one of her sisters stirring.

They went rapidly and quietly. It is said that they followed the broad animal trail that borders the valley ledge, and that they ran most of the night. By morning they had reached the eighth village, where Nanta bought a loaf from the baker and asked for the dolenter's raft, saying they had come for a visit.

The dolenter's name was Larsh. He was a young man of imagination and intuition, and heard their story with sympathy.

"But we cannot have marriage rites without family," he said.

"We can't go back," said Nanta. "I would have to kill him, and I cannot do that."

"I have never known of a grassman to lose his mind," said the dolenter, "but I know it is possible. In a special case like this perhaps I might proclaim the marriage and then journey to your village and hear your parents' vows."

"I have no parents. I am adopted. And we can't be sure that Liba's father would make the vow. My foster family would."

"You are honest," said Larsh. "I love the Truth."

Larsh decided then and there to marry the couple, and out of a dozen village couples summoned, Nanta and Liba were allowed to choose two sets of temporary parents who duly stated that it was a wedding in Truth. Then they produced a festive meal for a celebration.

"I have heard of this young man," more than one villager commented. "Nanta the hunter. He has a good reputation."

They wanted Nanta to settle in their village, and Nanta was considering it—but before evening, Liba's father arrived, enraged, claiming that Nanta had run away with a woman who was promised to someone else. The dolenter believed Nanta and stood up for him, stating that he would not have performed the marriage had it not been in Truth. But the Chief Councillor, anxious to maintain good relations between the villages, told Liba's father that they had been deceived and would surely not have sheltered the runaways had they known the facts.

It was that act which turned Nanta bitter.

"We don't need your shelter!" he said. "We don't need *any* village. We will start our own settlement, and no one will live there unless he can recognize the Truth. Your dolenter has asked my wife and me to keep the Way of the grass people. We will. Be assured that we will."

They left the village toward setting sun. Again they travelled by night, and it is said that in the night an elf came and told Nanta to leave the animal trail and climb into a hollow tree and wait there with his bow at ready until he knew all was clear. In that way they escaped a longbeast.

They slept in the hollow tree for a long time because they were exhausted. Then Nanta killed a grasshopper, which they roasted and ate with the rest of their loaf. By nightfall they reached end of settlement. Certain that no one had passed them up trail to bring news of the trouble, they asked permission to sleep on the trader's raft and purchased another loaf and a sack of meal.

"Just visiting settlements," they said.

They told no one their story, and in the morning set out setting sun before the villagers awoke.

My father knew the story well. He was a young apprentice in the village where Nanta and Liba were married, and was one of the youths who waved them goodbye, wishing them good trail. Not only that, but his parents (my grandparents), were the couple who took the part of Liba's parents at the marriage rites. My father knew that the young hunter and his beautiful wife had not returned and, like many other young people in his village, he was curious and worried for them. The dolenter prayed for their safety.

When a year had gone by and there still was no word, many believed them to be dead.

News came that the young man who had threatened to kill Nanta had taken his own life. The grass people shook their heads in regret that the young couple had been lost escaping from a threat which no longer existed.

A young hunter in the village, ripe for adventure, announced one day that he would go to end of settlement and then penetrate beyond and see if he could find any trace of Nanta and his bride. He, too, failed to return.

People were growing fearful and superstitious now about the grass woods, which lay beyond end of settlement, but Nanta's cousin and foster brother, the hunter's son from his own village, was certain that Nanta was alive.

"It is something I *know*," he said.

He gathered a search party, and by the time he left end of settlement he had six young men with him. Their intention was to search every trail for five days' march before giving up.

"It is madness," said the elders. "There is no hope that two young grass people would have survived alone in the wilderness. The young men would do better to stay at home and work at their crafts."

Two weeks later, five of the seven returned to end of settlement and they were laughing. They had found Nanta.

II

NANTA WAS NOT ALONE. Liba was with him, and so was a baby son, and so was the young hunter from my father's village. They were dwelling in a crude shelter with no raft, and living a life of untold freedom. There were no councillors to tell them what to do, no social rituals to be obeyed, no possessions to be maintained. They spent their days hunting and gathering and doing target practice, enjoying the beauty of nature. In the evenings they lit a large fire in the clearing and told stories or sang songs. Often the elves and fairies joined them, and there might be dancing. Nanta read from the sacred book and the elves would nod or disagree, depending upon the passage. One old elf was particularly interested, and he would comment, "Now, that's where the grass people have gone wrong," or "That's a distortion of the old religion!"

Nanta loved these discussions with the elves, and he loved competing with them at target practice. He took joy in the days spent collecting dew and berries and leaves for tea, of stalking prey in the do-lan, of running races with the young hunter, of holding his baby boy up to see a butterfly on a flowering tree, but mostly he loved Liba.

The two were blissfully happy, and that was a good thing because Liba was not very skilled. She was young and had not paid close attention to what her mother taught her. She could spin and weave plain, rough cloth, but knew nothing of fine weaving or patterns, and neither she nor Nanta knew how to build a good loom. When she made clay pots, most of them broke in the firing, so their dishes were ones Nanta carved from wood. Liba was learning to hunt and gather, but her cooking was bland. She did not keep her roots dry, and many spoiled. She could grind seeds and bake a batter bread which was crisp and good, but her loaves were often hard. Still, no one seemed to mind.

Certainly the worst thing about their living arrangements was the fact that neither Liba nor Nanta knew how to tan skins, and neither did their friend the hunter. When they wanted leather garments for the cold season, they killed two grass animals. They knew enough to scrape the flesh from the skin and to rub urine into the hide and smoke it, but the job was only partially done, so they permanently smelled of rotten flesh. They laughed about it and said they were used to it, and for many years Nanta took pride in wearing half-tanned skins. If he was up trail and became chilled, he had been known to kill an animal, scrape the skin, and cut out a rough garment on the spot.

Nanta's camp was about three days beyond end of settlement and very difficult to find. The first young man to follow had kept to the animal trail for a day and found no sign that Nanta had passed that way. He was about to give up and return home when his eye caught a mark on the trunk of a spreading tree. There was no broken trail, and for a day he searched for marks that indicated where to go. Wary lest the chimney maker's son should follow, Nanta had taken pains to obliterate the signs of his passing, but he'd left obscure marks, which only a hunter's trained eye would see. The young man on his trail was a hunter and he was successful.

He came upon the remnants of a campfire and charred sticks on which something had been roasted, and used the stone firepit himself, then roped himself in a spreading tree to spend the night. On the third day he came to a new animal trail and a marked pyle showing him which way to go. The trail eventually led him halfway up the slope of the red valley to a wide clearing.

The young hunter took a look at the view of the valley he'd left, the luxurious grass woods spread around him and the many berry trees, and smiled at the sight of a grassman's house and two people bending over a fire. This, he decided, was exactly where he wanted to live. He called out a greeting and got Nanta's permission to stay.

There he built a shelter on the ground, since Nanta assured him they were too high for floods. The hunter stayed, and when Liba had her child, he became its adopted uncle.

"I will go back next year," he said, holding the baby gently, "and bring my wife."

But before he could do that the search party arrived and the camp entertained them with hunting and games, with feasting and singing. Their guests were impressed.

All stayed for nine days, and the two youngest decided not to return to their old villages. They asked Nanta's permission to build shelters under the red spreading trees and remain. Nanta hesitated. He hadn't wanted to start a settlement—but then again, it would be to the advantage of Liba and the baby. What if something should happen to him or to their friend the young hunter?

"Who is Chief Councillor?" asked one of the party.

"Nanta," the hunter replied quickly. "He founded this camp."

"We have no council," said Nanta, "but this is my camp so that makes me head man. If this is to become a settlement, those who come must be ready to live by two rules. One is Truth. The other is survival."

The young men looked at each other, wondering if they understood.

"If anyone in this camp is ever found to be telling or living an untruth—to me or to any villager—he will be sent away at once. We have no possessions here, and thus no burdens. Everyone must be young and healthy, and his instincts must be quick. Our population will be small, even if you stay. Our lives depend upon each other. I did not bring my wife to this camp to risk her safety."

There were nods of agreement. "I name the hunter as councillor," said Nanta. "He has been here longest and knows our ways. Those who stay must swear to read the sacred book, and keep the Way of the grass people."

Five of the search party took the oath.

"The villages are growing crowded," said Nanta's cousin. "Young men have been talking of founding a new settlement. It appears that you have already done it. I think you can expect more villagers."

"I want no craftsmen," said Nanta curtly. "Tell them that. There will be no street of shops. We live by hunting and gathering. The women must be as active as the men."

Of the seven who had come, two remained in camp. When the other five returned to their homes, the three who took the oath packed their backpacks and weapons, and came with their families to join Nanta. They could take no trail runners, so nothing of value went with them: no fine dishes, no furniture, no metal, very little clothing. But they brought something of much greater value: the love of Truth, and the love of their families.

My grandmother was one of those wives and my mother, a child of a year, was on her back.

Her older brother of four years, my uncle, walked all the way.

III

My mother's name is Krand. She grew up in Nanta's village, barefoot and wild. There was no school, and though she learned necessary skills from her parents, my mother never read well. She knew nature and could have survived anywhere. She knew every plant that was good for food or medicine, and every plant that was poisonous. She knew every sign of wind or rain. She bathed outdoors in rain or in dew, and in fine weather she wore very little clothing.

Nanta and his wife had set the traditions for the new settlement. When shoes wore out, there were no shoes to buy. Though they could make moccasins for the cold season, they went barefoot much of the time. The men learned that they could move more quietly and quickly without clothing, and took to hunting with only a small apron of skin looped between their legs. Nanta fashioned belts that kept ropes and knives from making a noise as he ran, and all his villagers learned to do the same.

In the first years everyone ate together in Nanta's village, and all shared equally. However, as their numbers grew larger, it became easier to eat in the old way, as separate families. Nonetheless, food was still divided equally, so that all shared alike.

Nanta grew strong in his leadership, but never liked to be called "Chief Councillor". He preferred "Head Man." Young as he was, he had the advantage of his clarity of vision. He could look right into a grassman's eyes and know whether or not he was telling the truth. His ability to mind-speak with elves was no longer a secret, and the elves and fairies continued to love the settlement. They were constantly around, sometimes sharing in the food, and nearly always joining in the singing and dancing. The old elf Buko seemed to consider himself one of the villagers and slept in an abandoned birds' nest overhead.

Because they were trained to sharp instinct, many of Nanta's villagers also learned to hear the elves thinking. It was a great advantage because elves warned them if storms were coming, or if wildbeasts or longbeasts were around. They led the grass people to shelter if wheelers were in the sky, and often snatched up a baby if it had strayed or was in danger, and returned it to its home.

The legend of Nanta's village spread all the way to the green lake and beyond. Many disbelieved in its existence and held those who'd gone in search of it were surely dead in the wilderness. In one village the dolenter and councillors refused permission to any young couple who asked to move to Nanta's village. It became the destination of runaways.

In time Larsh, the dolenter who married Nanta and Liba, became concerned. Nanta was too young, he thought, to be Chief Councillor, and certainly the village was not being run according to grassman tradition. These villagers were all equally young and inexperienced. He decided they needed a dolenter, and thus he gave up his home and possessions to move there with his wife and children.

Nanta might have admitted a dolenter in any circumstance, but he certainly could not say no to the man who had married him. He even went so far as to build a raft for Larsh, the second raft to be built in the village. Both rafts were large. They could hold half of the population, and both contained large stores of food.

"Stores!" Nanta would scoff, if one of his villagers suggested that he might lose his stores in a flood. "Are you such a poor hunter and gatherer that you can't find more? And are the villagers so selfish that they won't feed you in the cold season?"

It became a mark of pride to scoff at stores, as it became a mark of pride to excel at games. In Nanta's village the games went on continually. Boys and girls raced and jumped, tumbled and climbed. There were target areas where men, women, and children practiced whenever they were free.

What impressed Larsh most was the harmony and good spirit with which the people lived. "We live in Truth," Nanta explained.

"And so you live in trust," said the dolenter, and he also began to participate in the games and hunt for his share of the food. Like the others, he took to running barefoot and naked up the grass trails. In the cold season he talked for long hours to the old elf Buko, and to Nanta, and to any other villagers who wanted to join them.

"You can even get used to the stink when he puts on those smelly skins," he told his wife, "because Nanta has such a pure conscience, it is like meeting goodness face-to-face."

Once in a long time one of Nanta's villagers would travel to the old settlements to find a wife or to shop. They didn't buy much, because they could take only what they could backpack.

In the seventh year Nanta himself came out, and his entire village with him. The village where he and Liba were married had begun to hold a great annual picnic with feasting and dancing and games, and there were prizes for tree climbing and archery and running. One just had to look at Nanta's villagers coming down the street of shops to know that the competition was theirs. The trail guards were constantly laughing as if the journey had produced no strain at all, and they exchanged positions as if by a signal that no one else could see or hear.

Nanta didn't go as far as his own home village because Liba's family and his own foster parents were all at the games. It is said that Liba's father apologized to Nanta, but that Nanta was stiff and formal.

That was the second time my father saw Nanta. My father was nineteen then, and still unmarried. He had apprenticed with the leatherman and specialized in making belts. He was fond of reading. He was not an active man and didn't take part in any of the games, but he had the grassman's love of social life and was in the midst of activities all day. He told me many times that it was the most exciting day he had ever lived. The whole village was in a state of merriment. Nanta would nod to one of his villagers to enter a running race, and the boy would finish the race while his competitors were only midway up the course. He would choose another to climb a spreading tree, and the boy would have it scaled while the others were still tying their knots. His women stood before archery targets with their bare feet planted apart and sent their arrows to the heart of the target every time.

The most difficult archery competition of the day was the one Nanta himself entered. The target was a small white speck on a tree, so minute that only the judges standing close by could see it well. Nanta walked so far from the tree that the onlookers stared in disbelief. When he loosed the arrow, it found the white spot. Those who had planned to compete against him stepped to the place where he'd stood and shook their heads, unwilling to even try.

Nanta won one of the fur-lined sleeveless jackets resplendent with rich embroidery that are so much loved by grassmen, and he put it on immediately and wore it. He seemed to be tremendously pleased.

Everyone from Nanta's village was winning. A school-age girl with black hair and shining eyes caught my father's attention. He noticed her expression as she accepted her prize for winning a race; it was as if she had known the prize was hers even before she left Nanta's village. My father had a premonition that the little girl would someday be involved in his life, and he remembered saying to himself, "It looks as if I'm to have a long wait."

He had seen Krand.

※ ※ ※

Nanta and his villagers came out to the games often after that and took home most of the prizes. The prizes were useful articles like belts, knives, or dew flasks. Sometimes there would be a jug of preserved berry juice or a tray of pastries. Those would be consumed at once because the people never carried away any extra burden. Occasionally a young man would complain that Nanta's villagers shouldn't be allowed to compete since no one stood a chance against them, but in general the others found it exciting. After all, Nanta was a grassman, with the same rights as everyone else.

In the fifteenth year, Nanta came to the games for the first time in three years. He was wearing a beard which made him look older, and he had grown even stronger and more confident in his leadership. He had six sons and a daughter, and he and Larsh were looking for a teacher for their village.

There were so many villagers now that only the best athletes had come to the games. Krand was there, and my father recognized her at once. She was sixteen that year, and she was winning at archery. "Yes," said my father to himself, and went to ask Nanta for permission to move to his village.

It was only because my father made belts, and belts were indispensable to grassmen, that Nanta accepted him. He was the first craftsman ever to gain admission to Nanta's village. He married my mother four months later.

"I must have loved your mother a lot," he once told me, "to have put up with this!"

The truth is that while my father could enjoy life in Nanta's village, he never really felt as if he was one of the villagers. As a craftsman and an educated man, he had little in common with the hunters, and they treated him as an outsider. The teacher they had found was able to give some basic knowledge to the children, but he was a dull man. Only the dolenter was of my father's calibre, and my father could hardly believe it when he found that Larsh participated in the games and ran naked with the hunters. He had known the dolenter before, of course, but my father was a boy of fifteen when Larsh moved to Nanta's village and they'd never had need of each other's company. The dolenter sometimes avoided my father at gatherings, explaining that he didn't want people to think they were setting themselves apart. But naturally it was known that they were close friends, and in the evenings often sat for many hours, talking of things the other villagers didn't understand. If the discussion was about the Way, Nanta and the old elf Buko would join them. Nanta's mind was keen, but he still bore his resentment of the old villages, and so he was disinterested in history.

"It is fine to know and it is finer to think," he would say, "but birds and insects and animals don't know and don't think. The mind of the hunter must be as free as theirs, or he will become their prey."

Nanta's village was still based on his two principles: Truth and survival. His success at keeping his villagers safe in dangerous territory was part of his legend, and his experience as a hunter was now so vast that he seemed omnipotent. He could take enormous risks and win, but to him they were not risks at all because they were based on the instinctual calculations that marked his genius.

If Nanta ever longed for civilization, what he longed for most was probably bread. There was no grain near his settlement, and they had no mill. They ate a good deal of flatbread made from seeds. When Nanta came out to the older villages, it was predictable that he would buy and eat several loaves and go home carrying a sack of meal. The other staples didn't interest him because there was natural salt near his village, and as for tar, the two rafts would float very well on tree resins.

As the years went by, there were signs that Nanta's self-sufficiency did have some limits. Once he attended a market and bought a shiny metal pot to take home to Liba, and another time he bought beautiful fine woven cloth for her to make dresses for herself and their daughter. Those who visited relatives in his village came out with horrifying stories of the barren homes in which the people lived, and, in contrast, enticing tales of the beauty of the village.

"They sit on piles of brush and skins and have no tables. Often they sleep on heaps of moss and furs. But they build good fireplaces and their houses are all of stone. They make screens of grass and put butterflies' wings in their windows. The pathways are paved with coloured stones, and flowering trees grow beside every house. Fairies bring eggs and nectar. The people wear necklaces of polished seeds, and children learn to write with sharp sticks on tablets of wet clay."

So the stories spread. Some were true and some were fiction. There were in fact only two houses of stone in Nanta's village, but by the time Nanta and Liba were in their thirties, the village was beginning to enjoy comfort. In the cold season, more time was spent at crafts. There was a potter's daughter among the wives who made beautiful pottery, though she had no shop. The "piles of skins" were more likely to be stuffed stools, and my father made many leather seats for chairs. Most of the villagers constructed benches and tables, and there were good mattresses filled with sweet-smelling herbs or padded with cotton. Looms went constantly because the women liked to have warm blankets for their children's beds, and much attention was given to their clothing for the cold season. In warm weather the children still ran naked and barefoot, learning more from the fairies than they did from the teacher.

Nanta had heard himself referred to so often as "the wild man" that he enjoyed being one. If a stranger came to the village, he was sure to let his hair hang long and leave it unwashed, and he might get into one of his half-tanned skins. Nanta loved to catch children off guard and trip or startle them, reminding them to be continually alert. His own eyes just grew sharper and keener. In the sixteenth year of Nanta, when he was thirty-three, I was born.

IV

I DON'T REMEMBER being confused by the differences between my father and the other villagers. To a small child, what is there, is there, and it is simply the world's reality. The villagers were tough people. The men went for dew on the chilliest mornings without clothing. They ran and climbed trees and wrestled with each other and lifted heavy things to keep up their strength. They feared nothing except longbeasts and wheelers, and pity one of them if he came within reach of one or two grass people with bows. I was not very old before I realized that I was proud of my village.

One of my earliest memories is of watching a villager who had a pet grass snake. It would sometimes be coiled around his feet as he stood talking to someone. All of the villagers were finely tuned to nature, but he was special. There were field mice that would come up to him and sit and wait to be stroked. He could talk to nature's creatures and they would listen.

I can no longer be certain that my memories of my early years in Nanta's village are in the right order. My grandfather made me a flute that made a pretty tune, and a fairy sang when I played. My grandmother had reverted to many of the traditional old ways and believed I should learn how civilized grass people lived. She reminded me to watch my father's manners and follow his example and she told me many stories of life in the village she had left behind. When there was meal, she made sweet pastries that still make my mouth water in memory. My grandmother died when I was eight and I wept until I thought my insides were raw. She and my grandfather had tended me when my father was busy at his leatherwork and my mother was out hunting. They were like second parents to me.

My father dressed traditionally and tried to maintain correct formality for special occasions.

"Beltman, you shame me!" Nanta would say, and he'd throw up his head and laugh when he saw my father bow to a visitor or heard him phrase a formal greeting. But Nanta liked my father and didn't seem bothered by the fact that he sat working in his leather shop while the others hunted for his food and saw to his protection.

When Nanta watched the boys at games, as he often did, he would call to one or the other, "You are your father's son! Show me your heels!" or "Your father could jump twice that high at your age!" When it was my turn he would say, "You are the son of Krand. Do you think she would be off target? That shot was glar. Show me you can do it right."

I did my best to keep up with the other children, but I was also my father's son and wanted to be in the workshop learning how to work with leather. I wanted to read as well as my father did. I knew that he had a certain contempt for the teacher, and I understood why. The teacher halted when he read and sometimes made mistakes. My father read smoothly and with expressive meaning.

Most of the boys had bows their fathers had made. My mother made my bow and gave me my first lessons. When I went up trail with the hunters, it was my mother who took me, or else my grandfather. One day the old elf Buko sat in the tree above me watching my efforts. He knew that I was unaware of more than half of what was going on around me. I shot at an insect and missed, when a bird that would have fed the entire village was perched on a nearby branch.

"You are not a hunter, grassman," said the old elf. "You must find out what you are."

It was several years before I did find out, and in the meantime I just enjoyed being young in Nanta's village. I remember one spring when the thaw left a lake in the bottom of the red valley; Nanta and his men built a raft and poled out on the lake and the villagers went diving from it. I remember the giant campfires that warmed the clearing in the evenings, and I remember the dancing. My father used to join in the dancing. He was good at that.

And oh, how I remember the fairies!

Larsh had been taught by dokrimalenter, but I don't think that was the real reason the fairies stayed around the village. I think they loved our village because the grass people there were so close to nature. We saw them every day, swinging from the branch of a seed tree or sipping dew from a rose petal, or taking a bath in a pool of water trapped in a leaf during a rain. When our people sang, the elves and fairies would often gather in numbers and sit about nodding to the music; if they liked the tune, they would join in or fly off humming it to themselves. They often brought eggs to the village. I remember one day when I was trying to reach a juicy pip of the pink thorn tree but couldn't, and a fairy flew past and picked it for me. She dropped it with a giggle right on top of my head. They liked fun and they liked to laugh. They took nothing seriously except an offence. We were all warned not to offend them and were taught how to get along. They were really very good to us.

When I was young I could hear the elves thinking in my mind but lost that ability when I left the red valley. Perhaps the elves were just too far away. Nanta could hear the elves all his life, and so could the majority of his villagers. An elf once prophesied that a descendant of Nanta would be Dokrimalitzla and save the Way of the grass people. Everyone said that was probably why the elves and fairies took so much interest in our village.

One thing I remember little of in Nanta's village was an emphasis on work. The villagers owned few possessions. There were just the two big rafts with stores. Nobody worried; if a house drowned, it drowned. Rafts were for wealthy people who had many things to save, and we were not wealthy people. It was glar to complain if you lost food stores, for it suggested that you were incapable of replenishing them. This attitude worried my father, who thought it a sign of foolish pride and a senseless waste when objects had been crafted with hours of patience and skill. My father did not defy Nanta, but he did build a stair inside a hollow tree where he kept his good hides and most of his completed projects, high above any danger of floods. Nanta knew about it of course, but never reprimanded my father.

There were no shops to be maintained, and no trails to keep. The only trail wide enough to accommodate a trail runner was a very short one that led to the burial place for wastes. At one time a villager made a trail runner with a canvas to be used for transporting wastes to the burial site. Every day or two someone had to fill that canvas with soapy water and scrub it out because it smelled and attracted animals. When they'd had enough of scrubbing, the people went back to carrying wastes in containers. Nanta allowed no one to bury food wastes beside their houses. He was conscious of safety, and his word had to be obeyed.

People fractured bones in the village and suffered cuts from thorns, but Nanta never lost a man, woman, or child up trail. We felt safer in that isolated village among those sensitive people than we would have in any of the old villages with their guard towers and warning bells. One afternoon a child barely able to walk went missing. Someone reported seeing it toddling up trail. The elves and fairies flew out to find it, and Nanta seized his bow and ran. An elf spotted the baby just as Nanta got to it. The child wasn't gone long, but had he been missing for days, he still would have survived. Many a time I saw Nanta go up trail with no pack at all—just the knife and rope on his belt, and the bow in his hand. He could travel faster than any grassman who ever lived.

V

By the time I was born, Nanta had seven sons, his complete family, though he had only the one daughter. Wreda was third in the family, very beautiful, and as tall as a man. I loved to watch her running with her golden hair flying in the wind. Nanta didn't allow women to wear their hair free if they were up trail or hunting, because it could blow into the eyes at the wrong moment and perhaps cost a life. On the day she was married, Wreda wore a red rope in her hair, and I remember how jealous I was. I thought I loved her more than any other, but I was too young to know.

Nanta's sons were handsome and strong. Two were shorter than the others and had dark hair, like their mother. The fourth son, Mekr, was one of the dark ones. He was a methodical person compared to his father, and lacked the quicksilver reactions so typical of Nanta, but that is possibly why he is able to organize himself to act as Chief Councillor of a modern village.

The other sons were tall and fair, good hunters, and proud. The two oldest both left the village. Nanta was not pleased about it, but he put up no real resistance. He would have been happier had they gone off into unbroken country as he had done, but they chose to return to the older villages.

The youngest of Nanta's seven sons was Ilva, who was less than a year older than I was. He was the most like Nanta of them all, and when I think of Nanta's eyes, I see them in Ilva, the same blue-grey eyes with distance in them, as if he knew all things. Nothing escaped his notice. He shared Nanta's trusting, naïve nature and, like Nanta, had exquisite skill as a hunter. Nanta was very proud of Ilva.

Ilva and I were friends. Like Nanta, Ilva had a considerate side, and found my quiet interests pleasant when he was in from trail. He took me under his protection and tried to help me with my hunting—but to little avail—so he settled for passing time with me at things I *could* do.

It's ironic that, under other circumstances, Nanta could have been an excellent craftsman. He carved toys for the children, lifelike birds and grass animals and dolls, and the table he made during his first cold season in the village was a thing of wonder. Ilva and I investigated it thoroughly. Nanta's family had grown so large that they could no longer sit around it for meals, but Liba guarded it jealously and used it to hold extra dishes and supplies. Today Mekr uses it as a council table, and it is the most traditional thing in the village.

I crawled about beneath the table with Ilva, noting how sturdy it was. The top had been made of half-logs, and from below you could see that they were still round and covered with bark, but the top itself had been smoothed flat with a chopper and knife. Beneath the table there was a shelf with a door, and Ilva told me not to touch it because his father kept his important papers there. All around the edges and down the legs, Nanta had made carvings. There were feathers, birds' heads, vines, and leaves. There was even a sun in a sky, shining through the branches of a tall tree. The carvings went all the way around each leg, and had been polished to the smoothness of glass. I found the underside of a leaf of a spreading tree, so lifelike it made me gasp. There was an aphid clinging to its surface, just as in life. I wondered if I would ever be able to reproduce detail like that. There was no need to ask Ilva if he could, because he could.

Ilva undertook to help me with my drawing. There was a shelter under a red tree, with a canopy to protect from wheelers, and it offered a magnificent view of the valley in three directions. Ilva and I sat there to draw, and often brought in leaves and flowers and seed pods, trying to copy them as realistically as Nanta could. My efforts were less than perfect, but I was happy. Except for the lessons in design my father taught me as he carved the belts, my only instruction came from Ilva.

One day Nanta himself came past the shelter and saw us. He stood watching in silence for a few minutes. I stopped drawing because I didn't think my work was good, but Ilva kept on. Nanta pointed to the smallest vein in a leaf and said, "See?"

Ilva saw. I would never have noticed the tiniest flaw in the vein, but Nanta had seen it in an instant. Then he smiled in satisfaction and left us. I realized then that Ilva did have a teacher, one who was a master of observation.

It seemed to me that I could usually tell what Nanta was thinking, as if his ability to absorb the world was matched by his ability to let the world see him. That crystal-clear self. Was this why the dolenter said he lived in Truth?

My most vivid childhood memories are not always of the exciting times, though we certainly had them, like the time a porcupine walked through the village and a baby was nearly killed when the animal knocked down the wall of a house. Animals went through the village often and we kept on the alert for them, but a porcupine was so big that it couldn't move among the houses without causing damage. Nanta suspected an animal trail was being made through the village and so he set the young people to work planting small trees to obliterate the trail setting sun. He was sure the porcupine would return the way it had gone, so every man and woman set about the task of knotting together all the hunting nets. When they had one giant hunting net, they suspended it from spreading trees rising sun above the trail and rigged cunning traps that would make it fall. All day the babies were watched and the older children told to keep away from that end of the village, but by nightfall no animal had set off the trap.

Instead of putting out the night bonfire as usual, they left it burning, with two guards to watch for flying sparks. Everyone else had gone to bed when a terrible commotion told us that there was an animal in the trap. The scene has permanently stayed with me as if it were a dream. My mother ran out with her bow; I saw her pause and plant her bare feet and draw the bow and loose an arrow, and then run on. People poured from all the houses, some lighting torches from the bonfire and holding them high, while the expert archers showered arrows into the captured animal by torchlight. The bravest ran right up with knives, and there were shouts of excitement and surprise. It wasn't a porcupine in the net but a longbeast, and it had almost succeeded in biting its way out of the net by the time the people killed it.

Nanta whooped in triumph and put his arm about Liba, shouting, "They say you can't trap a longbeast!" He and his villagers laughed the darkness away.

My father caught up to my mother as she was retrieving her arrows from the neck of the longbeast. "Krand, you take such risks!" he said. But I noticed that my father helped to rope the longbeast and drag it away from the village. I think he understood Nanta that night, and what he lived for.

As I think of it, it occurs to me that this may have been the last time I ever saw Nanta triumphant.

Things were beginning to change, and Nanta didn't change easily. Growing boys and girls had seen the older settlements and become curious about the shops. Some wanted permission to go and learn to make glass or work with metal, Nanta's two oldest sons among them. At first Nanta granted permission grudgingly, on condition that none of them come back to his village with their skills, but then there was pressure among the villagers to break trail for the middle-third of the way to the next village. Again Nanta was reluctant, for the stretch of unbroken trail marked only by hunters' signs had been symbolic of his isolation from outside. But his councillors overruled him, and so he dispatched a party to break the trail.

For many years the people of the next village had been in the habit of saying, "We aren't really end of settlement any more. There's another village three days setting sun, but there is no trail the mid-third of the way."

Traders would shake their heads and give up any hope of doing business there, but now that the trail was open, it was a different matter. Nanta's village was unmistakably dubbed "end of settlement", and on their next trip the traders arrived for the first time. They found no market stalls and had to trade from their trail runners, and they were met by a stern head man who told them they were being allowed to trade there only because his people could use improved salt and honey and useful articles like knives. He wanted them to keep all frivolous articles out of sight.

It didn't work well, of course. Villagers traded furs for pots and cutlery, and many asked the traders to bring shoes on their next visit. When the traders had gone, several items of jewellery were in evidence.

"The village is older now, Nanta," said Larsh. "The people want more comfort. It has to change."

"People who look at their shoes fail to see the wheeler in the sky," said Nanta scornfully. "If my villagers change into that kind of people, I cannot lead them."

I don't know if I was old enough to be aware of any change in Nanta, but because of my associations, I was made aware of it by hearsay. I never failed to listen to the long conversations which went on between my father and Larsh, and I heard them remark that Nanta would have to change or the villagers would ask him to resign. The villagers wanted craftsmen, particularly a shoemaker, and more people were building rafts to make sure their houses were up out of the wet in times of rain.

"You will go soft," Nanta warned them. "Your children will learn to think of possessions and forget how to smell the wind."

Nanta didn't laugh and sing any more, and the joyousness went out of the village.

I am sure they still loved the Truth, but they saw only improvement in their new interests and none of the dangers which Nanta seemed to see.

VI

I WAS TOO BUSY with my own affairs to pay much attention, for Larsh and Buko had discovered my intense interest in their discussions about the old religion.

Certainly, one of the most interesting characters around Nanta's village was Buko. The old elf was short compared to a grassman, with a long beard that came to a point. His eyes were the colour of brown autumn leaves, and keen. He could be impatient and sharp, and he had a habit of drumming on his neck with his fingertips if grassmen weren't thinking fast enough to please him. He is the same today, for elves live ten times and more the span of a grassman.

Buko was a busy elf, often coming down from his nest before the grassmen were awake, to collect berries or a fresh mushroom for his breakfast. He enjoyed children and often minded them if their mothers were busy. If young and inexperienced hunters went up trail, Buko was likely to appoint himself as their guide. Occasionally he acted as advisor to council. His imagination knew no limits, and he lent an elfin flair to many of the decorations which appeared on the houses. He usually ate the big meal of the day with the villagers, circulating from family to family. He never failed to bring his share, and the house where Buko ate was more likely than any other to have a fresh egg for dinner, or possibly rare dewberries ripened deep in the tall woods where no grassman could find them.

Long before I was born, Buko had recognized in our dolenter a grassman who was capable of comprehending the old religion, for not only was Larsh wise and intuitive, but his teacher had been dokrimalenter. So Buko set himself the task of being mentor to Larsh.

He always made a point of asking Larsh what he planned to say to the people, discussing it with him, and frequently he came to a meeting to listen. On one occasion when the dolenter was interpreting the sacred book, Larsh told us that the acceptance of a new Life by the village could not be observed in the cold season because it had to be accompanied by the initiation of the flowers. Buko stood and said, "That is not the true religion!" and walked off, flinging back the challenge, "Don't the snowflakes also live and die?"

I asked my father and the dolenter what Buko meant by that, and they told me that at one time the elves and grassmen had the same religion. The grassmen called it the old religion, but when the elves spoke of it they called it the true religion.

"But isn't our sacred book the true religion?" I asked.

Larsh looked at me very seriously and said, "I believe it contains some of the true religion, Tokra, but grassmen have added to it and taken away from it, until now it is nearly impossible to find out which is which."

I asked him why the elves couldn't tell us which parts of our sacred book were the real parts and he said, "That is exactly why I talk to Buko. Would you like to know what he's told me?"

I said I would and meant it. I was very excited about that. I began to spend more time with Larsh, listening to what the elf had to say about our sacred book, and when he was sure that I was serious about it, Larsh asked me if I would like to become a dolenter. I did want to, and my father and mother were pleased as well, so when I was barely twelve, I left the village school, where I had long since learned all the teacher could teach me, and set out on an intensive study of religion and the grassman's Way. I remember one evening when my father asked Larsh why he was so content to live in such a primitive village and run naked with the hunters, and he answered, "Because these people truly know the grassman's Way."

I realized with a thrill that there was something special about my village, and I wanted very much to understand what Larsh meant. I understood some things intuitively that I couldn't put into words. Perhaps Larsh meant that they knew everything in nature and lived with nature. Because my mother was one of these people, I knew the magic of being of one breath with butterflies and clouds. Then I wondered if he meant it was because the villagers were a happy, loving people. My mother's parents loved me, when they were in Life, and loved my brother and sister too, with such warmth. Family ties were strong, but the whole village was family. We could not eat if those of another household were hungry.

I was too young and inexperienced to know that in most villages grassmen had their own interpretation of the Way. It meant to be industrious, careful of possessions, and traditional in manner. Certainly, that was not what Larsh meant when he said that Nanta's villagers knew the Way, because that wasn't typical of our village at all. No, when Larsh spoke of Nanta's people keeping the Way, he must have been referring to the love and the family spirit—and the awareness of Life. I knew that it must have something to do with the fact that Nanta and so many of his villagers could talk to the elves in their minds. We seldom see an elf now. I think they feel ill-at-ease among modern grass people, but perhaps it is a problem of communication. Elves find it a waste of time to talk aloud at length because they know that the only true understanding is mind-to-mind.

As I studied with Larsh and Buko, I learned that the old religion had in truth been practiced almost in pure form by Nanta and his villagers, and this made my studies worthwhile. I had the very best of teachers. Larsh knew all there was to know of history and philosophy, and for the next few years my mind was so occupied with its intellectual interests that I may not have noticed that the fairies and elves were seldom seen around the village as often as they used to be.

The sense of mutual dependency was still strong in the village, but the sense of being members of one family seemed to be disappearing. People spoke of "your house" and "my house" and there was a new emphasis upon stores, and less insistence upon sharing. Hunters stayed home from trail to sink pyles and make wind guards. As the houses began to look more like the homes they had left behind, the women smiled and hung curtains and wove partitions, and they began to behave more like grass people everywhere. The women began to buy combs from the traders and wind their hair, and then, at the villagers' insistence, a cobbler was admitted to the village.

Just at that time two things happened which almost forced Nanta to open a street of shops. More than twenty years had gone by since the first influx of settlers, and now the old villages were going through another population crisis. Young people needed to find a new place to set up their trades. Nanta already had my father's leather shop and the cobbler, and a young villager had set up a tannery. The female potter had been doing such a trade that her home might as well have been a shop. It was no longer possible for Nanta to say in truth that there were no craftsmen in his village.

Then the dreadful news came that villages both high sun and no sun of the green lake had been destroyed by the mower and many grass people killed. Those who survived were seeking new places to settle. All the way through the settlements, people would tell them, "Go to end of settlement. They have a few craftsmen there. There is sure to be a place."

Nanta could not refuse admission to refugees.

VII

I HAD LEFT HOME before the tragedy of the mower. Having completed my training, I went two villages rising sun to the village Larsh had left behind, my father's old village, and there I began my career. But I found that elves and fairies were never seen there, and the people had no interest in "the old religion." I was restless to find people such as I had known at home, and so I took the long trail high sun to the green lake, and on the way I heard that Gozer's village near the tall woods was without a dolenter. I received Gozer's permission to stay, but I soon learned that Gozer's villagers also thought of the old religion as superstition. I remained in the village only one year but, brief as it was, my time there was worth the trail, for it is there that I found my wife, who has since gone from Life. My wife knew that I longed for the red valley and wanted to go home to familiar sights, and she agreed to move to the village I had recently left behind.

It is likely that our return to the red valley saved our lives, because it was not many years later that the mower destroyed Gozer's village. The news was hard, because all of my wife's relatives were there, and it was some months before we could get word of those who survived.

The next time I saw Nanta was a summer or two after my wife and I returned to the red valley. I had gone home to visit my father and mother, travelling in the company of traders for protection. I found that the village had a few market stalls and the beginnings of a street of shops. There was some argument between a trader and a villager, and Nanta was summoned. He looked impatient and agitated. I wasn't close enough to hear what he said, but the picture is still in my mind. He stood there so tall and supple, able to take on the wilderness, with his hair still long and his feet still bare, and he was wearing the old fur-lined jacket he had won at archery so many years ago. The embroidery was threadbare.

The argument went on, and it was obvious that Nanta couldn't handle traders. He, who could read the minds of animals and direct a hunting party with his eyes, was out of his element. Suddenly he flung up his hands in frustration and stalked away, and his voice came out clearly enough then.

"I am no longer Head Man," he said.

He meant it. Nanta resigned, just like that, and Yoam became Chief Councillor, the man who preceded Mekr. Nanta saw me standing there and he came over to me and looked into my eyes with that clear, long-sighted view that was his glory.

"You, the son of Krand," he said, "You will remember how it was here. You are a philosophical man."

I made him a promise. I returned his gaze and I said, "I will remember, Nanta."

I wanted to ask him so many things. Things about the decisions he had made. Things about his relationship with the elves. But his councillors crowded up to ask the meaning of his resignation. The village was in a hub-bub, and so he left me.

I guess Nanta was about fifty-four that day. He only lived about five years after that. I saw him once more on another visit to my home, and he was a man who had given up. He played with his grandchildren. He sat by his doorway and watched the birds, but his bow hung untouched on the wall.

"It is over, Tokra," he told me. "Liba and I began something that will be a legend among the grass people, but will they understand? Will they remember the responsibility that went with the freedom? Will they remember the love and the truth?"

"It was the most wonderful village anyone could ever grow up in," I told him. "I am sorry it is changed, and so is my mother."

Nanta studied my face. "Sometimes I ask myself if it would have been better if I had never marked the trail," he said. "Then Liba and I and our children could have had it all to ourselves. And then I think of your mother and how she ran in the sunlight, and all the others when they were young and so happy, and I'm glad I marked the trail."

"So am I," I said.

I never saw Nanta after that. I think he died the next year. He was too young to die. He just gave up.

Nineteen years ago, when our daughter was five and our son a baby, we heard that two new villages were established setting sun and neither had a dolenter. One was Dyra's village no sun of Hoyim's Lake, and the other had been settled by Gozer. A trail was being cleared from Yoam's village, leading there. It didn't take us long to decide to go to Gozer's village, because all of my wife's remaining relatives were there.

When we arrived at the village of Yoam, we found that my father was ill. He died after several weeks of illness, and Larsh held rites for him before my family and I moved on to Gozer's village. We wanted my mother to travel with us, but the village had been her home from the day she arrived there in a backpack, aged one year, and she refused to leave.

During my father's last weeks in Life I was able to renew old friendships. Liba spread a meal for us on Nanta's carved table, and Mekr insisted that I accompany him on a hunting party as we did in old times. In spite of my father's illness, I spent blissful days in the village, and found myself wishing Nanta were there to see how unspoiled it was, in spite of the shops and the comforts. Wreda and four of Nanta's sons still lived there, including my good friend Ilva.

Ilva resembled his father more than ever now that he was a man, and like his father spent hours of each day encouraging the children to run and jump and climb. Like his father, he had many children of his own. At that time there were five sons and two daughters in Ilva's family. Later there would be two more sons and another girl.

The elves had generally liked best to vie at archery with the villagers. One morning early I went out to gather the dew for my mother and saw Ilva on a target range, competing with two young villagers and three elves. For an instant I thought he was his father, and through my tears I saw the village as it used to be. Even now I cannot remember without the blending of sadness and joy.

It is difficult for me to believe that almost fifty years have gone by since I was a child in Nanta's village, and yet I know the village is still there, because it is not many years since I last went to visit my mother. My mother is still in Life, and so is Liba, and so are many of the people who once ran and jumped and laughed and danced with them, and washed in the cold dew. They are a healthy people in Mekr's village, but I doubt they are giving the same opportunity to their children, because they live like other grass people now. The village is a place of much wealth and many rafts, and the people talk little and perhaps know less about the days of Nanta, when it was the edge of civilization. It is not called "end of settlement" now, because now the grass trail comes no sun of the tall woods. The village now known as "end of settlement" was simply the fifth village no sun of the green lake when I was a boy.

For twelve years following the time of my father's death, I was dolenter to Gozer's villagers and to Dyra's too. My trips to Dyra's village were brief, and I would spend the night while I was there on a raft belonging to Lenk's adopted widow, who is my sister-in-law. I met Dyra only formally, because he was not anxious to be friendly with a dolenter. He had unhappy memories of a dolenter in the village he left behind, a man who had no true understanding of Life and who believed that all that was required of a dolenter was to see that villagers kept strict obedience to the rule.

The gulf was finally bridged, and when Dyra decided to accept me into his village,

I learned what I had been missing in friendship. He was an educated man who read and thought much, and he had met the elf Radd. He had learned about the old religion, and from the time he and his wife lived in the tall woods with the elf, they had followed some of the ancient rites. My daughter and I were invited to a meal with Dyra and his family, and when we entered I saw that Koalee had laid a flower beside each plate, and beside that a small glass of water. Koalee did not know how close I came to tears. I had not seen a flower by the plate since I was a boy in Nanta's village. My hand felt stiff and strange, but I reached for the flower and said the old blessing and placed it in the water.

Later, when she became my daughter's mother-in-law, Koalee confessed to me that she was afraid to lay the flowers by the plates that evening, and almost did not. It was like asking a dolenter if he knew and accepted the old religion, and Koalee wasn't even certain that I would know what to do.

It opened a new day for me. I had found friends with whom I could discuss the old religion and who encouraged me to go on with my study. It is because Dyra's wife put flowers by the plate that night that I decided to write what I know of the Way of the grass people, followed by *The Book of Nanta*. Without Dyra and Koalee, I might never have believed that there were grass people who wanted to read it.

The last time I visited Mekr's village, the old elf Buko showed me a treasure I had not known existed. Carefully hidden in the shelf beneath Nanta's table was Nanta's own copy of the sacred book, the very book he put into his backpack the night he ran away with Liba to escape the chimney maker's son. The book was old and worn, but still clear to read, and in the margins and on the blank pages at the back Nanta had penned his own notes about the discussions that used to be held in those long-ago evenings before my father's fire. I wept when I saw them and could not see, but Buko urged me to read it all and copy the notes. He could not give me the book, because he said it was to be kept for a son of Ilva, but I copied everything Nanta had written, and as I did so, I remembered the sound of his voice, the very expression in his eyes, when some of those ideas first came to him.

It depresses me that words cannot bring back the memories I cherish and want so badly to record. Buko will remember, long after I have gone from Life, but he is not one of us. An elf's memory is total, but it is devoid of emotion. Soon they will all be gone; Liba and Krand and all the others who came out that summer day to win the prizes in my father's village. And then eventually Mekr will go from Life, and even Ilva, and I will go, and I will no longer be able to keep the promise I made to Nanta, the promise that I would remember. But as long as I am in Life, I will still see in my mind the evening campfires, and hear the laughter, and listen to the fairies singing.

–Tokra

GLOSSARY

Bumbler: A bumble bee.

Burning tunnels: To take a large metal funnel with a wooden handle and a lit candle inside. The heated metal melts the snow and the tunnel gradually forms a layer of ice as the funnel is pushed ahead. It is wet work and there is a risk of cave-ins.

Cuddlies: One-piece pyjamas with feet, worn by young children.

Dokrima, Dolenter, Dokrimalenter and Dokrimalitzla: In order to understand these terms, it is necessary to understand something of the language of the grass people and their social structure.

Do is their word for grass, usually referred to in the plural as the grass woods or *do-lan*. *Krima* means people, hence *Dokrima*, the grass people. A *dolenter,* or guide in the grass, is a spiritual and social leader rather similar to a minister or priest in our culture, but he has low status in comparison to a *dokrimalenter* or guide of grassmen. Once a *dolenter* has been thoroughly educated and has proven himself worthy, he can be made *dokrimalenter* and then his status is roughly equivalent to someone with a doctorate in theology and carries much respect.

The only one who can confer the title of *dokrimalenter* is *dokrimalitzla*, an elfin appointee, and the word *litzla* does not translate into English or, as far as I know, into any of the tall men's tongues. It is not even strictly correct to call him an "appointee", as the elves cannot simply appoint someone to the position. They must be discovered. The grass people sometimes live for years without *dokrimalitzla* because the elves will only make the appointment when all the signs of nature are in harmony. He must be exceptionally intuitive and telepathic, for most of his role will consist in keeping in continuous contact with the elves. When there is *dokrimalitzla*, the grass people become more prosperous and are safer because the elves watch more closely over them.

Once appointed, a *dokrimalitzla* has authority over *dokrimalenters* and *dolenters*, making him, in our eyes, a kind of pope, but he also holds a symbolic function as supreme head of all councils. We would more likely refer to him as a king. As the link between grassmen and elf, he embodies for the grassmen a sign that nature will be in harmony and the world will not depart from the Way. Women can also become *dolenters, dokrimalenters,* or *dokrimalitzla.*

Drot: A small annual tax levied on everyone over fourteen to maintain essential village resources such as medicine and school supplies. From this fund, the lampman, the trail boys and those who take turns on the guard tower are paid. The Councillors receive no pay for their work.

Earth wind: A dust storm.

Feathers: A kite.

Finna: A unit of measure for liquids.

Flood: Rainfall heavy enough that a grass person has to access a raft to avoid drowning.

Four-legged shadow: A horse.

Free-floater: When the water is deep enough to cover the pyles and flood the raft, the grass people unfasten the rafts from the pyles and let their homes float freely. If the water grows too deep, it is necessary to cut the anchor rope.

Float space: The shaded space directly under the raft, used for storage or work and play in summer months. In winter it is wrapped in canvas and used to store necessities like fuel.

Glar: Wrong, mistaken, or unsuitable.

Golden wheels: A dandelion.

Grass tree: Any type of grass, usually referred to in the plural as grass woods.

Grass animal: A general term for animals that live near the grass people but are considered non-threatening such as gophers, rabbits, moles, or squirrels.

Hred: Distance equal to one hundred yards.

Kloros: Mushrooms, of which some varieties are poisonous.

Longbeast: A weasel.

Marriage: It has amused me that tall men, reading about the grass people, have sometimes remarked on their "morality", meaning they think it is quaint that the grass people are little puritans who never marry twice and seem to condone no hanky-panky. It is just about impossible for me to explain that the grass people are not moral at all --- the choice is innate. "Impossible" for me because the grass people can't or won't explain it and the elves are equally reticent. Apparently they experience an instinct that weds them to a chosen mate for life. They don't appear to have any desires outside that bond, a phenomenon so unparalleled in "tall man" experience that it can't be understood. The bond is in effect from the time a mate is recognized and the choice is made, which is what Nanta means when he claims that his promise to Liba is "recorded on the Truth." This love bond is a sacred trust and one of the worst crimes in the grassman's culture is interference with another person's spouse or child. Such a departure from the laws of Life is believed to cut the person off from their conscience, and a grass person would have to be mentally unwell or "off the Truth" to do such a thing. If this situation occurs, no grass person would be forced into marriage with the offender. It is because of the lifelong mating bond that village life is safe from the jealousy and rage that accompanies our human "interferences." And yet Dyra was once tempted by the fairy

Violet. Apparently their innocence has to be consciously guarded at times.

Pyle: a post-like foundation created to support rafts and houses, made with wood and cemented in place with a lime mortar mixture.

Quidda: A stringed musical instrument similar to a mandolin.

Rafts: Houses are built on rafts which are raised on pyles for the simple purpose of keeping the grass people and their abodes out of the water in a heavy rain. Regular visitors sometimes maintain rafts for their use when they are in the village or they may have relatives or friends to take them in. You may ask permission to sleep on a traders raft. Traders seldom visit a village more than four times a year, so the raft is often used by travellers.

Rangebeast: A coyote.

Seccar: A beverage made from chicory, similar to coffee.

Second chimney: This is not used for fire but holds the air pipe. This expandable pipe can extend to about twenty-four inches and, on top of an eight inch float space, this is a considerable height. The top is closed and most pipes have more than one air hole on the sides, so the sheltered side can be kept open and the wind side closed by a damper to keep out the snow. On clear days it will be rotated to catch the wind and admit the maximum of fresh air. If you come upon a grass person's village in winter, you can see the air pipes sticking up out of the snow.

Seed tree: Any weed or flowering plant from approximately four to thirty-six inches in height, which goes to seed annually. These are prized if the seeds are edible and are used to make nut meat and oil, as well as for snacks. Some are ground into meal and used for baking, but they are never confused with the cereal grasses such as wheat, oats, and barley, which are called grain. Woody seed trees are used for building or to climb in a rainstorm, but when a grasswoman speaks about a seed tree she invariably means an edible one. The seed tree Koalee grows by her raft is dill. It is a great favourite of hers and she uses it in loaves, soups, stews, and preserves. Another useful seed is from the sunflower, if the villagers fell one of those giants, they all share and there will be oil and nut meat aplenty.

Snow walkers: Are similar to snowshoes, but they are patterned after the webbed feet of birds.

Spreading tree: Is what we would call bushes, from raspberry right up to willow. We must remember that, relatively speaking, an average stalk of grain is a tree that is sixty feet tall to a grassman. Our perception can hardly cope with that.

Tall tree: What we call trees: poplar, birch, elm etc.

Truth: My concise *Oxford Dictionary* defines truth as the "quality or state of being true or accurate or honest or sincere or loyal or accurately shaped or adjusted." The elfin dictionary of the grassmen's tongue defines Truth as "the voice of Life." After years of study of the grassman's culture, I have had moments when I think I have sensed intuitively what Truth is to a grassman, but it continually slips away. Putting it into words is extremely difficult.

I believe the matter has to be considered from several angles. To begin with, it is almost certainly rooted in the same experience which we "tall men" have come to call "the voice of conscience" and what social scientists have named "truth claims." There is no doubt that a grassman, hearing the *Oxford Dictionary* definition, would nod in agreement. If you're honest, you're honest, and your conscience is clear. Your relationships with others are trustworthy, for we can sense when we are in the presence of insincerity.

A second dimension of Truth, as Nanta would have defined it, is much further removed from our frame of reference, and it gets harder for me to understand. The grassmen live much closer to nature than we do, a direct result of their small size. We hear the insects humming in the tall woods. The grassmen are down there with them. Sensitive grassmen like Nanta can hear the elves thinking, obviously a form of telepathy which links nature's creatures. The elves and grassmen believe that whatever transpires is recorded on the Truth, a belief similar to one held by Christians who tell you that St. Peter will meet you at the pearly gates with the record, and not a line will be erased. The elves believe that the record is stored in a kind of invisible computer made of the collective thoughts of all living things. The elf Radd called it "the timer" because to him it is an absolute. The elves have no god, but the timer is in control of all living things, and as such, it must be respected. Grassmen, being much less telepathic than the elves, may become superstitious about the timer. They feel awed to be part of the great collective of living things and they have a sense of duty toward nature. It is not surprising that, in turn, they tend to pray to nature to make their time among the living safe and productive. Whether a grassman means "God" when he says "Life" I have never determined to my satisfaction, but I have the impression that Truth is seen as only one part of a larger and powerful spiritual force which they call "Life."

Now, in case you are beginning to wonder if I exaggerated when I said it would be hard for us to define what a grassman means by Truth, let me explain another aspect of the concept. I *think* I am right about this, but even if I am, I am not sure I can explain it clearly. I know that the ancient Egyptians placed great emphasis upon the truth. Pharaoh Akhnaton appended "living in truth" to his signature. The Egyptians symbol for truth was the quill --- the written word. But if our interpretation of Egyptian culture is correct, the truth was part and parcel of Maat, and Maat was the social system. In Egypt you had social institutions, the pharaoh as a representative of God on earth, and a well-defined pattern of life in which every individual knew their place. The Egyptians lived by a grand design and the design was Maat.

The grass people speak of "The Way" and their culture is very traditional. Every grassman knows his place in the system, and change is limited. Even their name, the dokrima, or "people of the grass," indicates that they see themselves as having a specific place in the scheme of things. Am I taking too big a risk, then, if I suggest that the grass people live by the Way and the Way is Maat?

Their religious structure seems to substantiate that argument. The dolenter, or "guide in the grass" is accepted as a religious advisor but also as an advisor in all aspects of the culture. His secondary title is "Student of the Way." If he qualifies and becomes a dokrimalenter, or "guide of grassmen" then his secondary title becomes "Master of the Way." Even then, he has no real authority over council, unless, as happened in Dyra's home village, council allows him to take over.

So I have suggested that there are four aspects to the grassman's concept of The Truth: truth as we define it, Truth as a telepathic computer, Truth as instinctual obedience to the laws of Life, and Truth as a stable cultural pattern. I offer this concept without guarantee. Only the elves know The Truth, and the elves will never tell.

Villages: Grass people live in small, tightly knit communities and expect a good deal of conformity from each citizen. A high degree of mutual respect and responsibility is essential to their survival. A grassman's village is governed by a Chief Councillor and other councillors, usually numbering from two to four. The councillors retain office permanently unless incapacity or incompetence forces the villagers to ask for a change. Villages are identified by the name of the Chief Councillor. If a village becomes too large, young trades people decide if they want to leave and form their own village, along with others who choose to move there.

Walking shadow: A tall man.

Water wheeler: A duck or goose.

Wheelers: A predatory bird that will sometimes attack grass people, e.g. nighthawks, ravens (not to be confused with the peaceful seed bird).

Wildbeast: A badger.

🐰 🐰 🐰

ILLUSTRATIONS

THE GRASSMAN'S HOUSE

Flood marker
Pyle
Float space
wind guard
Table cemented in
anchor

THE TRAIL RUNNER

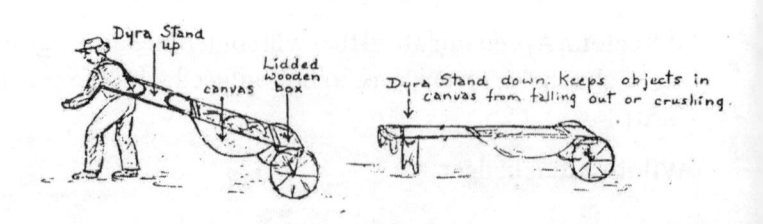

Dyra Stand up
canvas
Lidded Wooden box

Dyra Stand down. Keeps objects in canvas from falling out or crushing.

THE NEW LAND

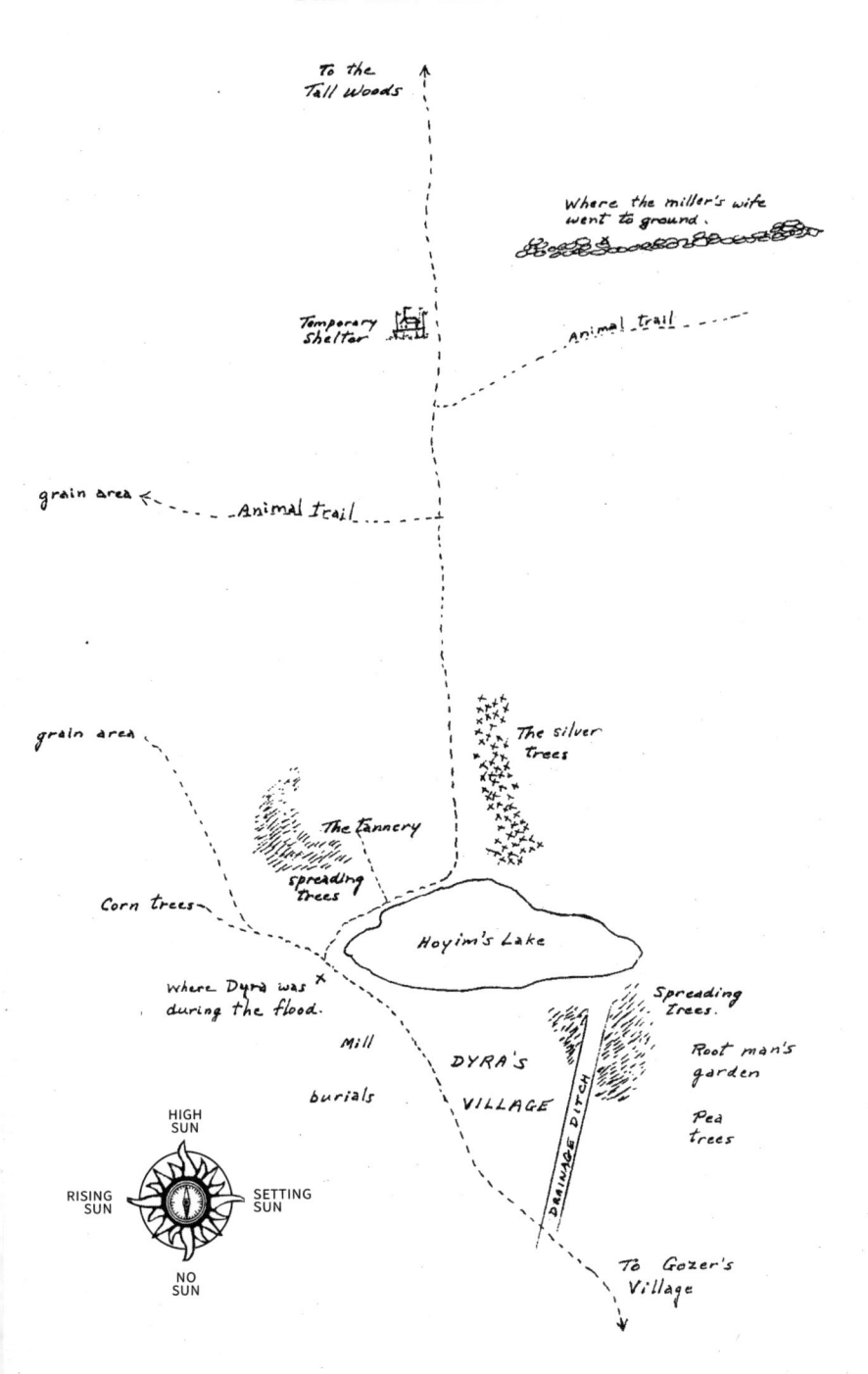

To the Tall Woods

Where the miller's wife went to ground.

Temporary Shelter

Animal trail

grain area ← *Animal trail*

The silver trees

grain area

The tannery

spreading trees

Corn trees

Hoyim's Lake

Spreading trees

Where Dyra was during the flood.

Root man's garden

Mill burials

DYRA'S VILLAGE

Pea trees

DRAINAGE DITCH

HIGH SUN
RISING SUN — SETTING SUN
NO SUN

To Gozer's Village

MAP OF THE VILLAGE – 13TH YEAR

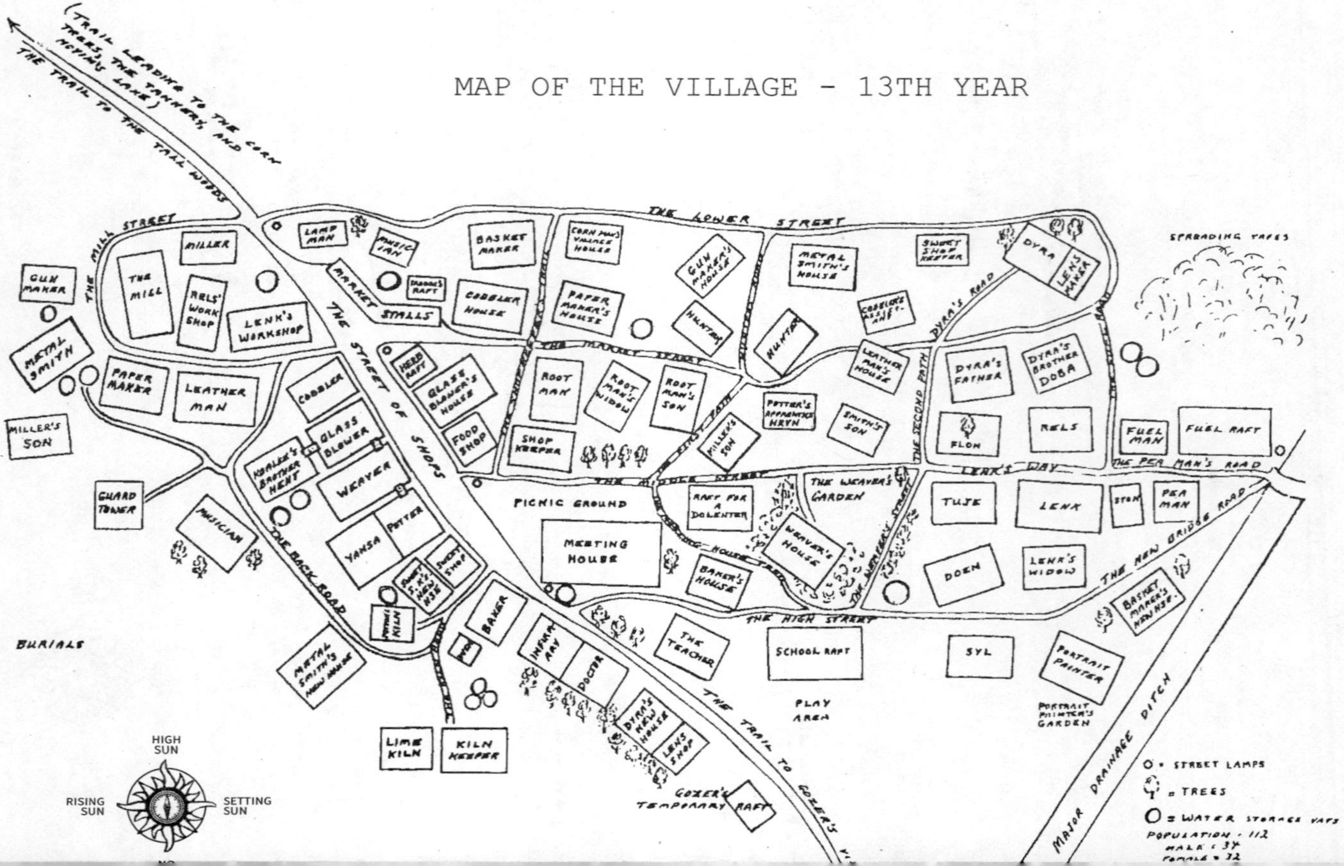

WRAPPING A HOUSE

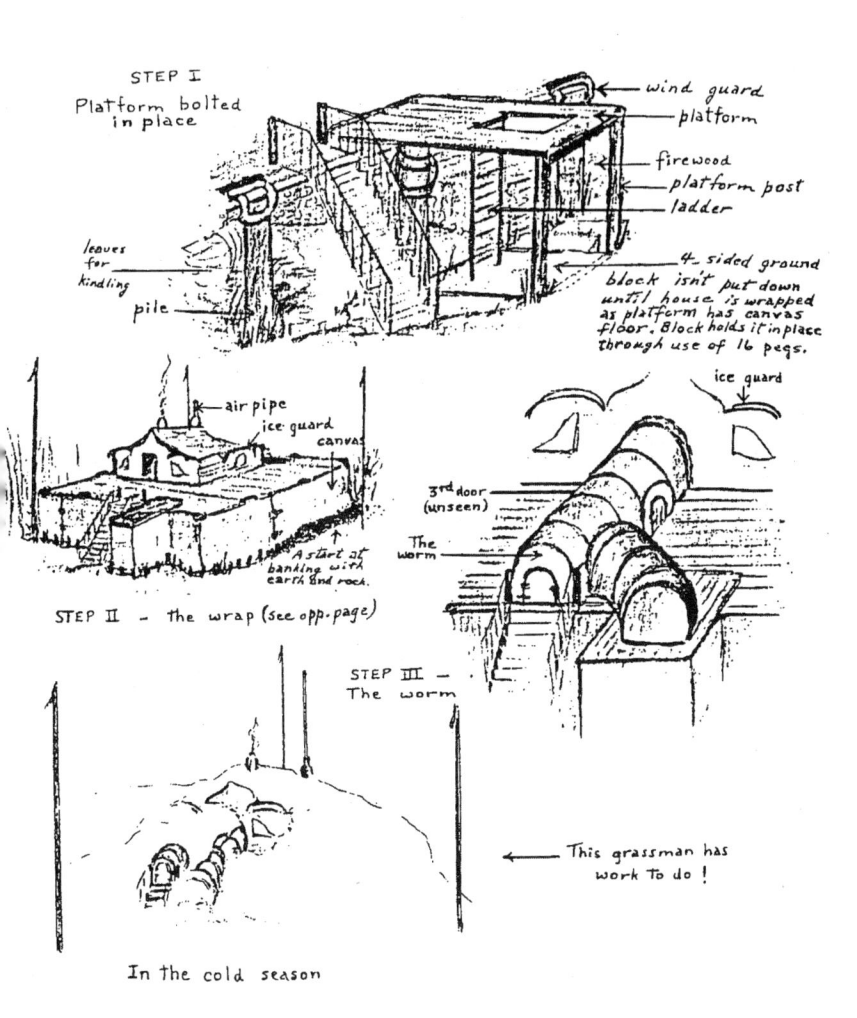

STEP I — Platform bolted in place

- wind guard
- platform
- firewood
- platform post
- ladder
- leaves for kindling
- pile
- 4-sided ground block isn't put down until house is wrapped as platform has canvas floor. Block holds it in place through use of 16 pegs.

STEP II — The wrap (see opp. page)

- air pipe
- ice guard
- canvas
- A start at banking with earth and rock.

STEP III — The worm

- ice guard
- 3rd door (unseen)
- The worm

In the cold season

← This grassman has work to do!

*Infrequently, platform posts are removed in summer. Some grassmen find uses for them. Lenk slings a hammock. Doen has used his for a swing for his small ones.

LINEAGE CHARTS

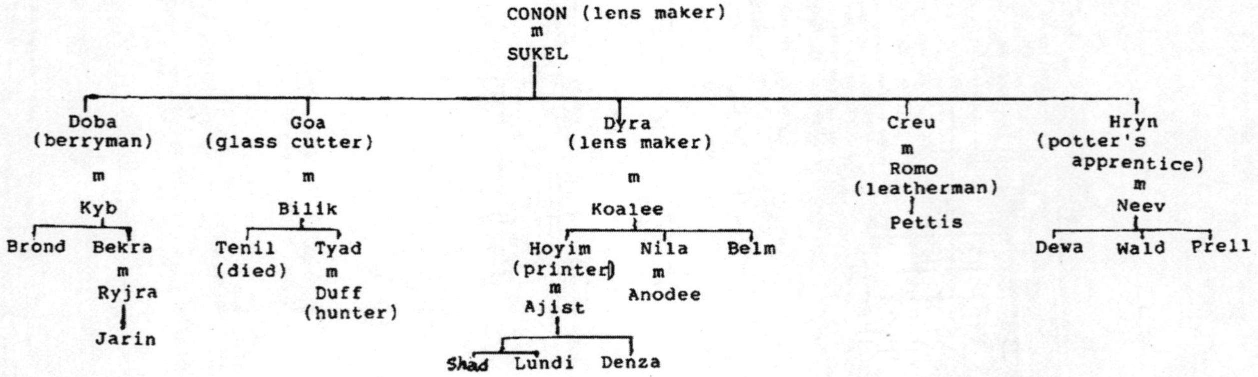

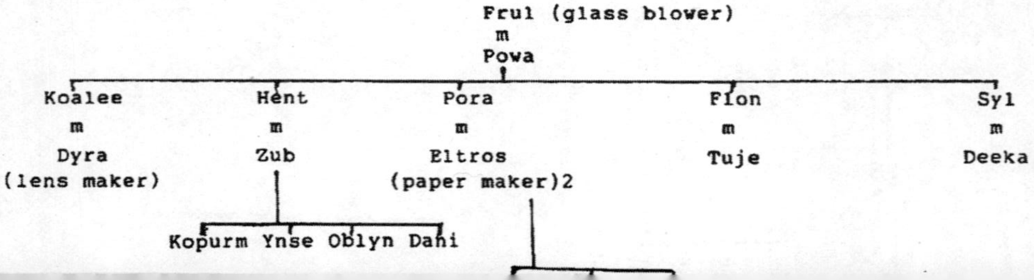

```
                                    CONON (lens maker)
                                         m
                                       SUKEL
    ┌─────────────────────┬─────────────────────┬─────────────────────┐
  Doba                   Goa                   Dyra                 Creu         Hryn
(berryman)         (glass cutter)          (lens maker)              m        (potter's
    m                    m                     m                    Romo      apprentice)
   Kyb                 Bilik                 Koalee              (leatherman)     m
 ┌──┴──┐         ┌──────┼──────┐         ┌─────┼─────┐             Pettis        Neev
Brond Bekra    Tenil   Tyad   Duff    Hoyim    Nila  Belm                  ┌─────┼─────┐
   m          (died)        (hunter) (printer) Anodee                     Dewa  Wald  Piell
 Ryjra                                   m
   │                                   Ajist
 Jarin                              ┌────┼────┐
                                  Shad Lundi Denza
```

```
  Koalee              Hent              Pora               Frul (glass blower)    Flon        Syl
    m                  m                 m                     m                    m          m
  Dyra                Zub              Eltros                Powa                 Tuje       Deeka
(lens maker)    ┌─────┼─────┬─────┐  (paper maker)2
              Kopurm Ynse Oblyn Dahi
```

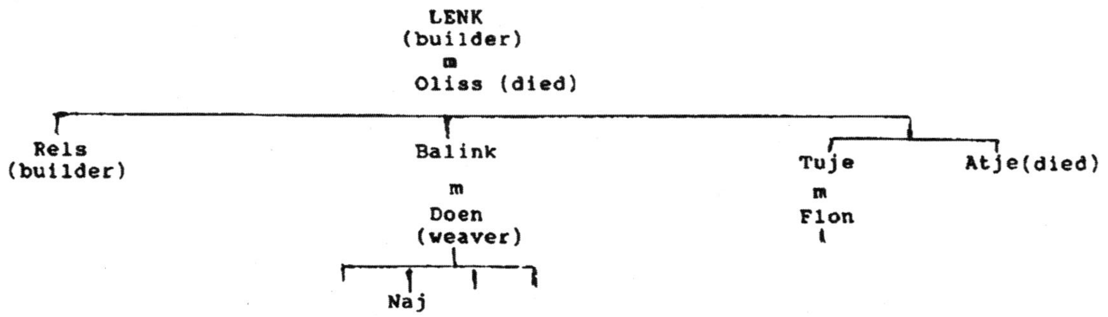

LENK
(builder)
m
Oliss (died)

Balink
m
Doen (weaver)

Naj

Tuje
m
Flon

Atje (died)

Rels
(builder)

AUTHOR'S NOTE

I've been asked what gave me the idea for the story, *The Grass People*, and that's a toughie, because I am now ninety-five years of age. I began the book when I was forty-seven and it took over twenty years to complete. Since a writer's life may feed into any story that comes to mind, I would have to literally dissect many decades of living in search of the bits and pieces that may have inspired this story. In fact, the book had been completed for years before it dawned on me that Koalee bore a strong resemblance to my Grandma Parley. Not only was Grandma short and stout, she was hospitable, loved caring for the sick, loved growing things, was always busy, and had a reputation for being a pretty good shot with the gun if coyotes threatened her chickens, and – this is the clincher – she really had no sense of humour.

Certainly the poem which introduces the book, "Little Folks in the Grass" by Annette Wynne, was the real source of the story. It was in a book of poetry I received as a child and I can still remember how it caused me to visualize the "little folks" as tiny humanoids. I was an only child and I lived on a farm until I was ten, so I walked many miles on country roads, coming and going to school. The prairie was my environment and I knew the familiar fields and bluffs (the "tall woods") so well. Farmers ploughed around the bluffs and sloughs in those days, and there was a small slough surrounded by pussy willows and tall grass. The earth rose slightly on one side of the pond and I can recall choosing that as the site of a village for the little grass people.

Many experiences will have fed into the story through the years, but probably the "magic" elements are mostly from my imagination. I have always been fascinated by the possibility of telepathy, so it seemed only right to me that the elves should be able to communicate mind-to-mind and that the grass people, if wide awake, should be able to tune in.

It's been pointed out to me that it's possible to read a lot of meaning into *The Grass People*. Are they in fact a warning to humans that we too are vulnerable in an uncertain environment? They could be a model, too, if we could learn to take responsibility for each other as the grass people do. But none of this was on my mind when I wrote the story. I was just enjoying getting to know the grass people. I like those little people. I admire them. It really doesn't matter how they came to consciousness. They just are. (So remember to watch where you step!)

– Kay Parley

Kay Parley is an author and journalist, a visual artist, a former teacher, and psychiatric nurse. She has written twenty-seven books, but *The Grass People* is her first fantasy novel. Kay began writing *The Grass People* in 1976 and finished it twenty years later. She is also a weekly syndicated newspaper columnist and volunteers as a public speaker who advocates for mental health. Kay is ninety-five years old and still writes every day on an electric typewriter. She lives in Regina, Saskatchewan.